"Alexa Martin's romances never fail to deliver perfectly paced swoons, charming humor, and profound questions. *Better than Fiction* delights with bookish rom-com joy on every page, with a wonderfully relatable heroine whose connection to the man she's learning to love underlies her moving journey back to herself. This is a romance for the reader and the dreamer in everyone."

—Emily Wibberley and Austin Siegemund-Broka, authors of
The Roughest Draft

"Alexa Martin is a powerhouse! In *Better than Fiction* she delivers another one of her signature stories—clever, relatable, flirty, and warm. Between these pages is a loving tribute to independent bookstores and the people who find home and community among their stacks. Don't miss this unputdownable story about what it means to be truly loved in more ways than one."

—Rosie Danan, author of *The Roommate*

"*Better than Fiction* is a charming, heartfelt rom-com, filled with great characters, laugh-out-loud banter, and some very cheeky seniors. It's also a sensitive portrayal of grief and a timely reminder of the vital role books and bookshops play in bringing people together. I loved it."

—Freya Sampson, author of *The Last Chance Library*

"Even at its most tender and aching moments, *Better than Fiction* is charming and honey-sweet to its core."   —NPR

"Martin is an incredible storyteller and has a unique ability to blend fiction with real-life situations in the sports world."

—*New York Times* bestselling author La La Anthony

"The writing is snappy, the pacing is quick, the romance is sublime, and the humor is off the charts. Alexa Martin delivers a stellar love story, and I can't wait to see what she writes next."

—*USA Today* on *Intercepted*

"Martin scores a touchdown of a debut with *Intercepted*, a witty rom-com set in the world of professional football players and their wives."

—*Entertainment Weekly*

"Alexa Martin's books are the ultimate reading escape, filled with fabulous characters; witty, dazzling prose; and swoon-worthy romances."

—*New York Times* bestselling author Chanel Cleeton on
Mom Jeans and Other Mistakes

"Alexa Martin is so good at this; I'm so impressed by how nuanced and thoughtful this book is, while still being hilarious and sexy!"

—*New York Times* bestselling author Jasmine Guillory on
Fumbled

"Alexa Martin is an auto-buy author for me. *Mom Jeans and Other Mistakes* is a celebration of the strength, joy, and complications of female friendships that span our lifetimes. I will read anything Alexa Martin writes!"

—*USA Today* bestselling author Lyssa Kay Adams

HOW TO
SELL
A
ROMANCE

ALEXA MARTIN

BERKLEY ROMANCE
NEW YORK

BERKLEY ROMANCE
Published by Berkley
An imprint of Penguin Random House LLC
1745 Broadway, New York, NY 10019
penguinrandomhouse.com

Book design by Alison Cnockaert

Library of Congress Cataloging-in-Publication Data

Names: Martin, Alexa, author.
Title: How to sell a romance / Alexa Martin.
Description: First edition. | New York: Berkley Romance, 2025.
Identifiers: LCCN 2024052540 (print) | LCCN 2024052541 (ebook) |
ISBN 9780593816356 (trade paperback) | ISBN 9780593816363 (ebook)
Subjects: LCGFT: Romance fiction. | Novels.
Classification: LCC PS3613.A77776 H69 2025 (print) |
LCC PS3613.A77776 (ebook) | DDC 813/.6—dc23/eng/20241118
LC record available at https://lccn.loc.gov/2024052540
LC ebook record available at https://lccn.loc.gov/2024052541

First Edition: July 2025

Printed in the United States of America
1st Printing

The authorized representative in the EU for product safety and compliance is
Penguin Random House Ireland, Morrison Chambers, 32 Nassau Street,
Dublin D02 YH68, Ireland, https://eu-contact.penguin.ie.

For anyone who has searched high, low, and maybe
even pyramid-shaped places for community

HOW TO
SELL
A
ROMANCE

I THINK I'VE girlbossed a little too close to the sun.

When I signed up to attend a skincare convention, I assumed I'd have a nice quiet weekend filled with soothing colors and spa music wrapping me as tight as the fluffy robe I knew I'd be wearing. It would be the perfect calming experience before the new school year started and my days were filled with finger paint mishaps, recess accidents, and an overabundance of hyper five-year-olds.

Oh, how wrong I was.

Instead, conference room B at the fancy schmancy hotel I could never afford is packed to capacity, and every direction I look, there's another blissed-out woman on the verge of crying over serums, toners, and moisturizers . . . oh my! Neon colors cover every surface of the room and pop music blares so loud from the speakers that the only sounds rising above it are the wails of excitement each time the presenter announces a new product.

It's a chaos I was not prepared for and honestly? I chose kindergartners.

Just as the noise begins to level out, Raquel Alessio, the president of Petunia Lemon, lifts the microphone to her red-painted lips. "And if you thought that was exciting . . ."

She pauses for effect and even though I find it a little gratuitous—I mean, we've already been in this room for five hours, and respectfully, get to the point, ma'am—the crowd around me eats it up and I have to respect her showmanship.

Behind her, the screen showcasing the new nighttime serum bundle begins to fade as the steady roar of high-pitched screams begin to rise until a picture of an island appears.

And that's the exact moment everyone in the room—minus me—loses their ever-loving mind.

The woman to my right jumps out of her seat, and the wide-brim hat that has knocked into me countless times flies off of her head. To my left, the gorgeous blonde turns so red, I think she might pass out. All around me, excitement explodes like an episode of Oprah's Favorite Things . . . but times a million.

"That's right!" Raquel shouts over the screams reverberating in the paneled conference room. "An all-expenses-paid trip to Petunia Island is back! Who's ready to slather their skin with our triple action sunscreen and spend a week basking beneath the Caribbean sun with their sisters in skincare?"

Just like every other aspect of this conference, the video begins to play without a hitch. Images of women wearing their Petunia Lemon branded gear and holding frozen drinks with umbrellas appear on the screen. "We love Petunia Lemon!" they shout to the camera.

My skin begins to tingle as I fall into a trance watching count-less carefree faces saunter across the screen, their heads thrown back in laughter, long hair glistening in the sun. Their stress-free smiles taunt me, laughing at my broke behind while they live their best, wrinkle-free life. Worry lines? About what? Not days spent fretting over rent and student loan payments, that's for sure.

"Before Petunia Lemon, I could've never imagined a vaca-tion like this. I never thought all I'd have to do to get here was talk to my friends about the products I was already obsessed with," Jackee (35, Kentucky) says. "This is my third trip to Petu-nia Island and not only do I get to enjoy it, I get to enjoy it with hundreds of my closest friends!"

Hundreds of her closest friends? I barely have two.

The skeptical part of me I vowed to wear like a knight's ar-mor this weekend, that's slowly been chipped away at, crashes to the ground. I can feel the excitement I've been trying to sup-press in my toes, slowly washing over me like the gentle waves lapping on the shores of Petunia Island. Maybe this really could be my life.

"Will we see you here?" five women say in perfect unison before holding hands and jumping off of a yacht into crystal blue water.

The video transitions from ocean tranquility to what can only be described as a proper rager. But instead of teens taking shots of cheap vodka, this party is full of middle-aged women throwing their arms in the air and dancing their hearts out be-neath flashing lights. The camera zooms in on the performer onstage who, if I'm not mistaken, won last season of *The Voice*. It's like a fever dream from my wildest *Real Housewives* fantasy, and I want nothing more than to whoop it up with my sisters in skincare over watered-down drinks and 2000s pop classics.

I've only been served an assortment of sparkling water since I've been here, but suddenly, I'm chugging the Kool-Aid along with everyone else in conference room B.

"How amazing was that?" Raquel struts back onto the stage, her flushed skin glowing even beneath the harsh lights. "I have to tell you, before Petunia Lemon, I worked for a Fortune 500 beauty company. There were articles in *Forbes* about how well they treated their employees, but nothing they ever did for us compared to Petunia Island. Every time I go there, I have to pinch myself because we have, without a doubt, the best company in the world!"

The room breaks into another round of applause, and I can't help it, I'm on my feet cheering along with the rest of them.

Who even am I?

"And all you have to do for an all-expenses-paid vacation to our private island is to have three consecutive months of two thousand PV"—the mysterious point system everyone except me seems to understand—"and grow your Empowered Skincare team to twenty consultants! So many of you are already there, and with the new products we're introducing this weekend, you're going to beat this number tenfold. I really believe that this year is going to be our biggest year ever!" She moves effortlessly across the stage despite the four-inch heels on her feet and scans the crowd. "Amber Johnson, we were lounging on the beach together a few months ago. How many consultants on your team are coming to Petunia Island with you this year?"

A camera quickly finds Amber, and her poreless face fills the screens around the room.

"We're all going to be there!" Amber yells back, and a group of what has to be at least thirty women start jumping up and down around her.

"Yeah you are!" Raquel pumps her fist in the air before pointing back into the crowd. "If you stop making excuses and commit to telling your friends about these products, you can not only change your skin, but change your life. This is *your* business. There is absolutely no reason I shouldn't see each and every one of you at Petunia Island next spring!"

Raquel slips the microphone back onto the mic stand, waving long, slender arms and blowing kisses to the crowd, who are eating up her every movement. By the time she makes her way off of the stage and the fluorescent lights kick on overhead, I can't tell if I feel like I had ten drinks or I need them. The floor vibrates, the air crackles, and my veins feel like they're pumped full of Pop Rocks.

Eight new products, five speeches, three videos, and one island later, they've sucked me right in. I haven't felt this passionate about anything since that time I decided to pledge a sorority my freshman year of college.

I didn't get in . . . but I was super enthusiastic, and they do say it's the effort that counts.

"Oh my god! Emerson!" Nora dodges blonde after blonde as she rushes toward me. "Wasn't that amazing? I told you it was going to be amazing, but that was extra amazing! Tell me what you think. Are you sold? You're sold, aren't you!"

"I think I might be sold," I admit, and her blue eyes practically triple in size. "But I'm still worried about the cost."

Nora Stone, my principal and professional fairy godmother, is sunshine in human form. To her, everything is either amazing, incredible, fabulous, or divine. If she's having a down day, she *might* say something is in need of zhuzhing or it needs to "take a break." Her optimism can be off-putting for some people, but as someone in a profession where the only thing harder to find than a bright spot are funds, it's what keeps me going most days.

"I totally understand, I felt the same way when I first joined," she says. "We're in education, it's not like we have a ton of extra money to spend."

"I feel like my bills are going up every month. The thought of spending more is kind of overwhelming."

I make the same amount I made last year, but it seems like it doesn't go half as far. The only reason I was able to come to this convention was because Nora's friend, Jacqueline, had something happen with her kid and couldn't make it. They didn't want the ticket to go to waste, so they gave it to me. Although, I'm not sure I would've accepted if I realized how much parking was going to cost me.

"I get that." She takes my hand and pulls me into a now empty row of chairs. "But you really couldn't pick a better time to join. Petunia Lemon just implemented a brand-new buy back policy so there's zero risk in joining now. If you sign up and realize in a few weeks or months that you're not into this, you can send all of your product back and get a full refund."

"Really?" It almost sounds too good to be true, but if there's one person I trust not to lead me down the wrong path, it's Nora.

"Really," she says before leaning in closer. "But I know you're going to love it."

I take a deep breath and look around the room. It's still packed with hundreds, maybe thousands of women just like me who are saying this opportunity changed their lives. If they can do it, then why can't I? Not to be cocky or anything, but I am kind of awesome. And if I can get a classroom full of kindergartners to listen to me, I can definitely sell face wash and moisturizers.

"Fine," I say after waiting a beat. "I'm in."

"I knew it!" Her high-pitched cry blends in effortlessly with the rest of the room. "Say it, say it right now!"

"You're worse than my students." I roll my eyes, but my heart's not in it. I'm still too jazzed from fucking Petunia Island. "You were right."

And she was.

I lost count of how many excuses I came up with over the last three weeks to try to get out of this conference. I hadn't been so creative since my college writing class. But for some reason, Nora didn't buy the story about my nonexistent dog eating my keys.

Shocking, I know.

"I don't know why you doubted me," she says. "You should always listen to your principal."

"Alright now." I bump my shoulder into hers as we catch up with the sea of women exiting the conference room. "Let's not get too cocky."

"I can't help it, I knew you were going to love this." Her pale skin burns so red it almost matches her hair. "Just think about how much fun we're going to have. Can you imagine us on

Petunia Island together? No talk of angry parents or state test-ing. Just you, me, the sun, and an endless supply of frozen mar-garitas? I think that's what some would call paradise!"

I haven't had a vacation outside of Colorado since I was twelve when we drove to Chicago to see my dad's family. It was in the middle of a heat wave and our car broke down on the drive home. I still remember my dad cracking jokes trying to keep me laughing and my mom calm.

The next summer, he was gone.

"It would be amazing, but the extra income would be even better." I tell her something she's well aware of since she's the person who hired me. "You should see how much I've already spent on classroom supplies this year."

I posted my classroom wish list, it's just that with the econ-omy the way it is, people don't have the funds to contribute. And when they do, kindergarten isn't usually the top priority since people think we just take naps and finger paint all day.

Something I know couldn't be further from the truth.

Kindergarten is a child's introduction into the education sys-tem. It's up to me to set the foundation for the rest of their aca-demic careers. When I accepted this job, I vowed to foster an excitement for learning and a curiosity that lasts a lifetime. And it's hard to accomplish that in a room with blank walls and no school supplies.

"I get that." Empathy wells in her eyes. She might not be in the classroom anymore, but she was in my shoes once. She un-derstands my struggle. "I want you to know I wouldn't have in-vited you this weekend if I didn't think you'd absolutely kill it as a consultant. I've seen people make life-changing money after only a few months."

After a weekend of watching testimonial after testimonial of women who were able to retire themselves and their husbands, I know she's not exaggerating. I love my job and I definitely don't have a husband, so retirement isn't my goal, but it would be nice to teach without panicking about how I'm going to pay my student loans or go grocery shopping without obsessing over the price of eggs.

Whoever said growing up was fun lied.

Adulting is a scam.

"Well you've convinced me." I've been riding the teacher struggle bus for years now; maybe it's time I try something new. "Show me where to sign up."

"Oh my god!" She stops the flow of foot traffic to stop and hug me. "We're going to have so much fun! Let's hit up the hotel bar and I'll buy you a drink while we get you all signed up."

If I knew free drinks would be involved, I would've said yes weeks ago.

"Then what are we waiting for?" I loop my arm through hers as we weave through the crowd. "Let's go order some serum!"

I'd be lying if I said the skepticism wasn't still lurking beneath the surface. I'm well aware there's no way it's as easy as they've pushed all weekend long. But it's either this or become an Uber driver . . . and with the way my road rage is set up, nobody wants that.

Anyways, it's just a little skincare.

How bad could it really be?

2

I DON'T WANT to be a downer among the girlbosses of the world, but something feels a little off about buying my own business with five clicks and for the low, low price of two hundred dollars.

Well, two hundred dollars before Nora and three other very persuasive, very tipsy, and slightly scary women convinced me that I just *had to add* the signup bonuses. The "discounted" products were apparently imperative to my success as a Petunia Lemon consultant, and since they're the experts and I'm the people pleaser, how could I say no?

No, really. How do people say no? Much to my dismay, it's a skill I never acquired.

By the time we got to the payment page, my quaint little business came out to a whopping total of over five hundred dollars. I had to use my emergency credit card to pay for it.

I'm going to have to get a side job to pay for my side hustle!

Money-back guarantee. Money-back guarantee. Money-back guarantee.

If it hadn't been for Nora sitting next to me, acting as my personal hype woman and promising that it would pay for itself within the month, I'm not sure I would've gone through with it. But she was and I did. Now I'm a little more in financial debt, but I have a friend surplus.

And you know what that sounds like to me?

Balance.

I'm here for a good time, not a long time.

Plus, what's five hundred more dollars on top of the bone-crushing, soul-sucking amount I have left to pay for my student loans? And with these products I just ordered, at least I won't have to worry about the anxiety causing me to age faster anymore. Goodbye stress lines and pimples!

"Are you sure you don't want to come out with us?" Nora asks again, the words slightly more slurred than when she asked me five minutes ago. "We're going to get nachos and margaritas!"

If there is one thing that can tempt me in life, it's nachos and margaritas. Tequila is my frenemy. I love her so much, but she always leaves me with regrets. And as much as I love Nora, she's still my boss, and I cannot allow Tequila Emmy P to make an appearance around her.

"I really wish I could, but I have to head home." The regret in my voice is authentic, but it doesn't stop the rest of the table from trying to change my mind.

"Please come, Emerson!" Ashley . . . I think her name is Ashley? No. Alice? Amber? Alyssa! Alyssa shouts from across the table. "It's going to be so much fun!"

"It sounds like fun and I wish I could, but I have to—" I try to think of an excuse, but it's been so long since I've been asked out that I'm rusty. "I have to go home and . . . water my plants."

As far as excuses go, plants are pretty terrible ones.

Add this to the growing list of reasons I should get a cat. I've been a volunteer at The Barkery for over three years now. It's a great way to get my cuddle fix in, but one of these days I'm going to have to give in and bring a new kitty friend home.

Or move into the shelter.

I'm down for either.

"Oh boo!" Nora shouts, even though I'm right next to her. "You're no fun!"

"Excuse me?" My hand flies to my chest, and an extremely offended gasp escapes my mouth. "How dare you!"

I may be a lot of things, but no fun isn't one of them! I'm a delightful, hoot and holler, fantastic freaking hang . . . something Nora knows firsthand since I'm the most fun teacher at Nester Fox Elementary.

"You're right. I'm sorry!" She wraps her arms around me and pulls me into a sloppy, Pinot Grigio–scented hug. "You're the most fun! You created Karaoke Wednesdays at school!"

See? Point proven.

But even if she didn't admit her wrongs, I already have a plaque to prove it . . . and by plaque, I mean a custom-painted canvas that my best friend (and art teacher coworker) made for me after I complained that nobody appreciated how much fun I was.

But it still counts.

"Apology accepted." But *only* because her apology was swift and she's so drunk that I know she won't remember this in ten minutes, let alone the morning.

"So now will you come with us?" she asks.

Again.

"Answer's still no." I pull away, trying to remove myself from her drunk clutches as discreetly as possible. If I'm going to make a clean getaway, it's now or never. "I'll call you tomorrow so I can hear all about it."

And coming from me, a person who has a strict text, don't call policy, this is a big deal . . . an honor, if I might say so myself.

She opens her mouth to say something else, but before she does the waitress appears with another round of tequila shots, and all thoughts about me joining the party fly out the window. The second her attention focuses on the packed tray, I dart out of the booth with no hesitations and not a single goodbye.

It's not that I don't understand the appeal of an Irish good-bye, it's just not for me—most of the time. Not only am I a people pleaser to the nth degree, but in general, I'm just a people person. I love talking and I thrive in crowds. When I was a kid, my mom would avoid taking me to the grocery store because I'd strike up conversations with every person who passed.

Stranger danger? I don't even know her.

I love meeting new people and hearing their stories. I can hold full conversations with anyone, anywhere, at any time. And even though I am perpetually and tragically single, I've never been on a date where conversation lulled.

All of that to say that I've never understood when a person tells me they "don't like peopling."

Until now.

And listen, it's not because everyone hasn't been absolutely lovely. They have! It's just been . . . a lot.

A lot of yelling. A lot of enthusiasm. A lot of wooing. A lot of drunkenness.

A lot of everything.

Which, coming from a kindergarten teacher who once cleaned up a domino throw-up situation, an entire canister of glitter, and a bloody nose in a single afternoon and still managed to organize an after-school happy hour? That's saying something.

And not anything good.

By the time I reach the elevator that goes to the parking garage I paid an absurd fifty dollars to park in for the day, I feel like I felt that one week I decided to train for a marathon. I'm beyond exhausted, my body aches, and my head throbs, but at the same time, I'm so amped up that if I go home, I'm not sure I'll ever be able to fall asleep.

I should definitely go home.

I need to go home and go straight to bed.

I absolutely should not go up to the rooftop bar and have a quiet nightcap.

That'd be a terrible decision. Horrible. I absolutely cannot spend another cent tonight.

The elevator doors slide open, and I mean to push the button to the garage, but somehow my finger slips and I accidentally push the button to the rooftop bar instead.

Oops.

I take off the giant Petunia Lemon badge around my neck

and tuck it into my purse as the elevator glides uninterrupted to the roof. Maybe without the neon-sign credentials around my neck, I'll be able to end this weekend with a quiet night of people watching.

The doors open and the cool Denver air lures me out to the patio. Despite the city lights and the string lights zig-zagging overhead, the stars still manage to shine bright above, and the full moon spotlights the growing crowd as they gather around the bar. As a native Denverite, my love of this city is a cornerstone of my entire personality and nights like this only reinforce my loyalty.

I don't know what I was expecting for a Sunday night, but for some reason, I incorrectly assumed there'd be at least one table open. The party from the conference downstairs has leaked to the rooftop, and everyone I pass has a Petunia Lemon lanyard dangling from their neck. I brace, ready for more woo-girl cheers and offers to take shots, but with my lanyard tucked away safely in my purse, I cease to exist to them. They look straight through me as I search the rooftop for a single table or seat. I even bump into the woman who sat next to me during the sunscreen panel yesterday. She brushes me off without a flicker of recognition. It's like I'm Hannah Montana and I just took off my wig.

I take a few laps around the rooftop, not able to find even a single barstool open. I'm about to give up hope and make the sad, lonely trek back to the parking lot when I notice a couple standing up from their tiny table tucked safely away in the corner of the patio. The moment the woman puts her purse on her shoulder, my vision laser-focuses on the dirty, glorious table. An athlete I am not, but in a flash, I'm a goddamn all-star. I'm like an NFL player, dodging Petunia Lemon reps left and right, ready to tackle anyone who gets in my way, until I finally make it to the end zone . . . I mean the table.

I almost break into a celebration dance before I remember that I a) have zero rhythm and b) don't want to make a complete fool of myself. So instead, I pull out the woven chair and sit down like a civilized adult who has at least a modicum of sense. I am, after all, a small business owner now.

It feels like it's only a matter of seconds before a waitress arrives to clear the table and drop off a menu.

"Thank you so much." I take the menu even though my drink order hasn't changed in more than two years. I've been on a mission to find the best old fashioned in the city, and I've heard especially good things about the one they serve here.

I glance at the food as the waitress walks away and decide to add a side of sweet potato fries to my order. It would be irresponsible to have another drink on an empty stomach, and I'm nothing if not responsible . . . just not financially or romantically or—

You know what?

Never mind.

I put the menu down and even though my fingers are itching to reach for my phone, I keep it tucked safely inside of my purse. I may not be able to afford therapy right now, but as a millennial with access to the internet, I've been researching ways to improve my mental health for free. One of the pieces of advice I see most often is to put down the devices and learn to be present in the moment. And since I refuse to implement the other tools—exercise more and cut out sugar? The audacity!!!—it's the one I've decided to work on the most.

I lean back in the surprisingly comfortable chair and take in the view. The glass guardrail, while sparking my slight fear of heights, gives an uninterrupted view of the city. It's too dark to see the mountains, and I wish I'd said bye to Nora a little earlier so I could've been up here for sunset. Little lights rise from the streets, climbing up the mountains I know so well. All around me, groups large and small move about in the sparse open spaces. Conversations fill the air and laughter swells. I watch as the women I met yesterday hug and sway to the music, their smiles wide and skin glowing. It's the final night of the convention and with checkout in the morning, it's clear they're taking advantage of every last second with one another, and it makes me reconsider joining Nora for a night on the town.

Thankfully for my bank account and probably my tequila-averse liver, the thought comes as fast as it goes once the waitress drops off a little bowl of spiced nuts and takes my order.

A night bonding with women who may or may not remember it in the morning might be tempting, but nothing can top an old fashioned made with Madagascan vanilla bean–infused sugar and sweet potato fries served with homemade jalapeño ranch.

Unfortunately for my personal life and my waistline, food and a good craft cocktail will always beat out any and all competition.

I grab the bowl of nuts off of the table, carefully pushing the almonds to the side in favor of the pecans and walnuts, surprised when the waitress returns like the freaking Flash.

Except, when I look up with grateful eyes expecting to see a gorgeous cocktail garnished with a maraschino cherry and orange and lemon peel, I'm stunned to silence when I'm met with something impossibly more gorgeous and welcome than an old fashioned.

Or more accurately, *someone* more gorgeous.

In the words of Carrie Bradshaw—*and just like that*, this night just got a whole lot more interesting.

3

"HI." HIS VOICE is as deep as thunder in a summer storm and I swear I can feel it rumbling in my chest.

I fight to keep my jaw from falling to the table and twist my head up—and up some more—until I finally come eye to eye with the most attractive man I've ever seen.

In my life.

"Hi." My rather extensive vocabulary completely abandons me in his presence.

"Luke Miller." He introduces himself and gestures to the empty chair across from me before asking, "Mind if I sit?"

Mind if I sit on your face?

"Of course not!" I answer too fast, my voice too high. I feel my cheeks heat as I try to fight back the X-rated thoughts I'm almost certain are being broadcast on a neon sign above my head. Something I'm even more convinced of when his eyes darken and his smile widens. "And I'm Emerson. Emerson Pierce."

"Emerson." He says my name slowly. Caressing every letter, rolling every syllable. I've always liked my name, but coming out of his mouth? I fucking love it. "Thank you for letting me join you tonight."

"Of course." I try my hardest to keep my voice steady and my eyes on his face. But it's a useless endeavor when he folds his large body into the much too small chair and the fabric of his pants strains against his thick thighs.

Holy crap.

I'm no better than a man.

"Busy night." He pulls my attention back to his face once he's seated. "I've never seen it so crowded here before."

"Really?" I will my mouth and mind to get out of the gutter and work together again. "It's my first time coming here. I didn't know if this was the norm or not."

There. Two full sentences. Gold star, Emerson.

"I guess it depends on what's going on. It can get pretty crazy if there's something big happening nearby—" He gestures to the rapidly increasing group of Petunia Lemon ladies overtaking the bar, "or in the hotel."

As if just to put the exclamation on his point, a few of the women let out ear-rupturing screams in perfect synchronization. The hottie across from me widens his eyes and I can't help but laugh. I'm just grateful that my Petunia Lemon lanyard is safely hidden in my purse and I can plead ignorance to the scene around us.

The waitress returns with my drink but her steps falter when she gets close enough to take in Luke. She stands frozen beside the table, slack-jawed and awestruck. A hazard I'm sure all service workers must encounter when coming face to face with someone as hot as the man in front of me.

"One old fashioned." She becomes unstuck and places my cocktail on the table before reaching into her pouch for a menu to hand Luke. I bite back my smile at the small tremor in her hand. "For you, sir. Could I get you started with something to drink?"

"Thank you." He turns the full force of his smile to her and takes the menu. "Let me see."

Her face burns scarlet and I want to reach for her hand, let her know she's not the only one affected. But as soon as his eyes begin to scan the menu, my solidarity nosedives off of the roof, and I take this opportunity to scan him.

Simply put, the man is gorgeous. He looks like someone took a Ralph Lauren model and mixed it up with an Avenger. Resembling one of those things is dangerous, but both?

It's lethal.

He has a head full of thick, wavy, dark hair. The lighting is terrible and I can't tell if it's black or brown, but neither do I care. I only care that it's long. And not sloppy long, either. No, bedroom long. The kind of long that causes my fingers to itch to dig into it and hold on for dear life as the nights turn into days. He has sun-kissed skin that hints to a summer full of days spent outside, soaking up the Colorado heat before fall chases it away. His eyes are so bright and so green that looking into them feels like a vacation. Dark scruff covers his cheeks and chin, but even so, I have no doubt that it's hiding a jawline that would cause even Michelangelo's statues to crumble in shame.

"I'll have a whiskey on the rocks." He orders before he looks back to me and catches me staring red-handed. His smile deepens as he holds my gaze. "Are you eating?"

I nod my head, unable to look away and suddenly feeling

famished. It's just unfortunate that what I want isn't anywhere on the menu. "Just sweet potato fries."

"I'll do the sliders," he says to the waitress without looking at her. Something that I could perceive as rude if I didn't think it was so fucking hot. "And a side of sweet potato fries."

The rooftop is growing louder by the second, but I can't hear any of it. Once the waitress leaves, Luke and I sit in silence, studying . . . no, *appreciating* each other. And as we do this, this silent dance that is better than any foreplay I've ever experienced, I come to a terrible, unsettling realization. While everything about this man is basically sex-on-a-stick wrapped in a great pair of slacks, none of that matters.

Because even if he didn't have the hair or the skin or the jaw, I would—with 1,000 percent certainty—still be in a complete and utter choke hold over this man. Yes, he's beautiful, but it's the way he looks at me that makes me want to melt into a freaking puddle. Nobody has ever looked at me like he has. The moment he trained those green eyes on me, I was ready to risk it all.

And risk it all I shall.

"So . . ." I break the silence. "Are you just here for the bar or do you have a room?"

His eyes darken and his tongue darts out to lick his bottom lip. I cross and recross my legs beneath the table to try and temper the growing need between my thighs.

I've never been so forward before, but what's that saying? Fortune favors the bold? Desperate times call for desperate measures? YOLO?

"I have a room." He leans forward and his voice drops to a gruff whisper. "We could get the food to go?"

I have a rule about food, particularly about French fries. I do not order them to go. French fries are only good when they first come out. When I go to a drive-thru, I either pull over or put my safety second and eat them while driving. Fries are only to be eaten hot and crispy, otherwise just throw them in the trash.

But at this moment? With this man? The only thing going in the trash is that rule.

"I like that idea." I don't recognize my own voice. It's so quiet and breathy, it's a miracle he can hear me. "To go sounds great."

I reach for my old fashioned and take a much deeper sip than I intended. It might've been the reason I made the journey to this bar, but I can't tell you what it tastes like. I think it's good? All I know for sure is that whiskey is good for my soul and my racing nerves.

I'm no stranger to a night of fun, but for some reason this feels different.

Bigger.

My body thrums in anticipation while my mind goes blank. As if it's aware of secrets my brain isn't yet privy to.

By the time the waitress arrives with his drink, my heart feels like it's going to leap out of my chest. Despite the cool evening breeze, my face is flushed and beads of sweat form on the back of my neck. Sparks shoot back and forth between us, my nipples hardening beneath the focus of his gaze. Every single nerve ending is so lit up that even my fingertips ache.

"Thank you." He takes the drink from her hand, not patient

enough to even let her put it on the table. "Is there any way you could have our food sent to my room instead?"

"Of course." Her knowing eyes flicker to me, but the embarrassment a girl with a modicum of shame should feel is nowhere to be found. Instead, brazen pride causes my spine to straighten as I meet her look head-on, an unspoken "you go, girl" flying between us. "I'll just need your name and room number."

"Luke Miller." He repeats the name he gave me earlier, and the part of me that listens to way too many true crime podcasts is relieved to know I haven't been lied to. "Room 528."

"Great, I'll be right back so you can sign for it and then you're good to go." She turns to leave, and although I can't be certain, I'm pretty sure she winks at me before she leaves.

Girls supporting girls at its finest. The Spice Girls would be so proud.

Her back is barely turned when Luke lifts his crystal glass into the air. "Salud."

I watch as he brings the whiskey to his lips and, even though he ordered a drink that is meant to be savored, he shoots it back.

I follow suit immediately.

I gulp back the old fashioned, not at all regretful that I'll have to come back another time to see if it lives up to the hype. Warmth trails down my throat and settles in my stomach, finally reining in the butterflies that have been raging from the moment he first sat down. His eyes never leave my lips, a small smirk pulling at the corner of the mouth I already wish was on mine. But since it's not and knowing I have his full attention, I can't deny the feminine urge to bring the cocktail pick with two cherries skewered on it to my mouth. I delight in the way his eyes follow the movement, his smile fleeing as he watches with undisguised desire. I take my time, parting my lips—that I belatedly wish were painted red—and sucking the cherries off one . . . at . . . a . . . time.

"Fuck it. They know my room, they can bill me at checkout," he grinds out between his flexed jaw. I can't even put the stick back into my glass before he's out of his chair and my hand is wrapped in his and he's pulling me out of my seat. "We need to get to my room. Now."

I grab my purse off of the back of my chair and tighten my grip on his hand as he weaves us through the crowded bar. He pushes the elevator button much like my kindergartners would, frantic and impatient. And when it finally arrives, he pulls me inside the empty space the same way, not even waiting for the doors to slide closed before he pushes me against the wall and his mouth lands on mine.

All thoughts leave my mind, but if they didn't, I'm pretty sure I'd be thanking god for the best kiss of my life . . .

And Petunia Lemon for putting my ass in the hotel just in time for it to land in his bed.

4

BY THE TIME we arrive at the fifth floor, it's been 800 hours.

Or eight seconds.

I have no idea how much time has passed because the moment his mouth touched mine, time ceased to exist.

The elevator dings to alert us of our arrival, and even though I know this means I'm one step closer to ripping the shirt off of this virtual stranger, it also means I have to stop kissing him. And now that I've had a taste of his mouth, a single second without it feels like a million years of suffering.

His fingers intertwine with mine, and he leads me out of the elevator. I pull him back, needing a second to gather myself because when he did that one thing with his tongue and his teeth, my legs turned into Jell-O and they're having a hard time getting their act back together.

He stops and turns to me, a small smile playing at the corner of his mouth.

"I know," he says. "But the faster we get to my room, the faster we can resume."

I gasp.

"You're a witch!" I do happen to have a nasty habit of talking to myself, but I know for a fact that I didn't let any of my inside thoughts out just now. "How'd you know what I was thinking?"

His deep chuckle rolls over my skin and down my spine until it hits me square between my thighs. Dear god. Can something about this man not be hot???

"I think you mean a warlock." He winks. "But unfortunately, no. It was less magic, more wishful hoping that you're feeling just as ready as I am."

Oh.

Wow.

I bite my bottom lip, trying—and failing—to prevent my giddy smile from taking over my entire face. I'm too old to be smitten, right? At my age I should be immune to pretty words and great kisses. Right?

Wrong.

I don't know much about Luke Miller, but I do know all that matters, like:

1) He knows how to order a drink.
2) He looks great in a suit.
3) He's an expert with his tongue.

Clearly, number three is what I find most encouraging. And why, even though I usually like to take control in situations like this, I'm ready to hand over the reins and be absolute putty in his strong, capable hands.

I follow behind him as we run down to his room like two

schoolkids who've never been in a hotel before. Our laughter echoes off the eclectically decorated walls. The ornate frames shake as our heavy footsteps make quick work of the much-too-long hallway. By the time we reach his room, my chest is heaving, and while I'm well aware I need to up my cardio routine, I know it's not because of my less-than-stellar fitness level.

He grabs the key out of his back pocket without letting go of my hand, and before I can even blink, we're inside of his room and my back is pressed against the door.

"That was impressive," I gasp against his mouth. "What else can you do?"

"What can I do?" His eyes darken to emeralds as they travel down my body. When his gaze returns to mine, I have to bite my lip to fight back a moan at the determined, sexy-as-hell look on his face. "I think it's better that I show you."

"All action and no talk?" A rare breed, indeed. "What a pleasant surprise."

"I'm full of surprises." He leans in, and the heat of his breath against the shell of my ear causes shivers to explode all over my body. And then, as if he can sense my losing battle to keep hold of my final strands of self-control, he pushes his groin against me, the massive bulge straining so violently against the fabric that I can't help but think it must be painful. "But I'm even more full of action."

I'd like to say that I react to this like a lady. That I pull inspiration from the heroines in the historical romances I love so much. That my lips part delicately and I bat my lashes at him, quiet and reserved in my need for him.

But that'd be a lie.

I go absolutely feral.

"Then what are you waiting for?" I wrap my hands around the back of his neck, pulling his face to mine and nipping at his bottom lip. In normal circumstances, I might be a teeny bit embarrassed by how forward I'm being, but luckily for me, I'm too consumed by the overwhelming lust and desire clawing at my insides. "Prove it already."

His dark eyes sparkle, and before I know what's happening, my shirt is across the room, my bra is on the floor, and I'm on his bed with my hands pinned above my head.

"Jesus." His voice is thick and raspy. I squirm beneath him. "You're like Christmas fucking morning. The best-wrapped present under the tree, and all I want to do is rip off the wrapping and play with you for hours."

Hours?

"I could handle hours." Underneath him? I think I could handle anything. Except waiting another freaking minute. I understand the appeal of suspense, but this is getting ridiculous. "But if you don't hurry up and take off your pants, I think I might self-destruct."

"Oh no." He chuckles and the vibrations from it are almost enough to set me off. "I can't have that."

And thankfully, the seriousness of my horniness sets in and he finally—FINALLY—gets naked.

I lean up onto my elbows to take in the view in front of me. I knew from the way his suit clung to certain parts of his body and the way he felt pressed against me that he wasn't going to be hard to look at, but nothing could've prepared me for this. The man is huge . . .

In all places.

Like most people, I often ponder what it would be like to be Taylor Swift. What her life must be like to be so inspired that you can write bop after bop after bop. But laying topless on this bed, staring at a man with my lipstick smeared across his face, his hair mussed from my hands? With those green eyes focused on me? I feel the sudden urge to pull out a pen and paper to write sonnets about rolling hills of green and eyes of jade. I want to memorialize this moment. I want to wax poetic about the strength of his thighs and the safety found in his arms. Lying beneath his gaze, I finally understand what it really means to be inspired.

"Stop looking at me like that." He kneels on the edge of the bed and his fingertips graze my stomach before unbuttoning the Abercrombie jeans social media convinced me I needed.

"Like what?" My voice quivers and breaks as I watch him slowly slide down my zipper.

"Like you're ready to throw everything else away"—he keeps his eyes locked on mine as he glides my jeans down my legs and tosses them next to his suit—"and stay in here with me forever."

Holy crap.

"This is just one night." I tell him the god's honest truth. I have time for a lot of things in my life . . . like work, volunteering, work, and in my spare time, more work . . . but I don't have the space or time for another person. Definitely not a man who can turn me to jelly and erase the outside world with a single look.

"One night?" he repeats, disbelief clear in his voice. "We'll have to see about that."

I go to challenge him, to let him know in no uncertain terms that this will never go beyond the hotel lobby. But before I get the chance, my underwear is gone and Luke's mouth is between my legs.

"Oh my god!" My mouth falls open and silent moans steal my breath away.

My hands latch on to the back of his head without thought or permission, and my hips arch off of the bed. I can't tell what's up and what's down or if I'm trying to hold him to me or push him away. All I know is that I've never, in my life, felt like this before. As if every single nerve ending in my body has been activated, and they are being lit on fire one . . . by . . . one. Until every inch of my body is burning, ready to explode.

"That's it," he growls against me, and I feel it in my toes. "Let go, baby. Give it to me."

"Luke." His name is a prayer . . . a litany in the small hotel room. One-night stands aren't supposed to feel like this. Exciting? Yes. Maybe even a little dirty. But this feels like my body is an idol and he is living to worship. "Please. More."

I don't know what I'm asking for more of; this already feels like too much. But Luke gives me what I don't even know I need. He adds in a finger, curling it and working me from the inside as his tongue and teeth move at an unrelenting pace. Heat and yearning begin to meld together, pressure building at the base of my stomach. It's too big, like a hurricane preparing to make landfall. Destruction levels unknown.

I try to pull away, but his free hand tightens like a vise on my hip and holds me in place.

"Oh no, Emerson," he says. "You're not running from this."

"It's too much," I gasp, so out of breath it sounds like I might pass out.

"Wrong." His mouth leaves my center just enough to look up at me from between my thighs and says, "It's never enough."

Then without skipping a beat, his mouth lands directly on the mark. He alternates between his tongue and teeth, from fast to slow. He builds me up and takes me down, doing it with brutal accuracy until my body is trembling and my skin is glistening with sweat.

"Please." I'm begging at this point and not even a little bit ashamed. My body has never been this primed for anything in my life, and I honestly think that if I don't come soon, I might die.

"Are you going to give it all to me?" He sounds more alpha than I ever thought the mild-mannered man in the suit could, and I hate how much I like it.

"I'll give you everything." My secondhand couch. My plant collection. My firstborn that I don't even plan on having. "Just please don't stop."

And because he's the best man on the planet, he doesn't.

"As you wish." There's a smile in his voice, and I'm sure if I could pry my eyes open to see it, it'd be the most glorious sight in the world. But I can't because he doesn't hesitate to deliver on his promise.

His fingers twist inside of me in perfect synchronization as his tongue licks and his teeth nip at my clit. The breeze of the air conditioning hits my sweat-slicked skin and raises goose bumps all over. My nipples harden and my breasts feel so heavy, it's nearing on painful. Pressure begins to build deep inside of me, each second pushing me higher and higher until I can take no more. The muscles from my head down to my toes go taut and my fists clench around his unruly hair, holding us in place just as my orgasm rips through me.

A silent scream falls from my lips, and my body trembles beneath his mouth. But even though we've reached the finish line, Luke never eases his relentless assault. Before I even get the chance to comprehend what's happening, one orgasm rolls into two with a sudden ferocity that knocks what little breath I have left right out of me.

Holy shit.

It should be illegal for someone to be this hot and capable in the bedroom.

"Please." The room is spinning and I gulp in air to try to calm my breathing. "I can't take any more."

"Are you sure about that?" he asks, but he's already moving up my body. His hands glide along my sides as he peppers soft kisses over my belly, between my breasts, and up my neck until he arrives at my mouth. "Because I think I could do that all night."

"If you did that all night, I'd be leaving on a stretcher." I have no idea what my exact injury would be, but I do know that my legs would forget how to work and my heart would not be properly functioning any longer.

"We wouldn't want that," he says against my mouth, and I get to see up close the way his eyes gleam and sparkle with thoughts left unspoken.

Maybe one more time wouldn't kill me . . .

"But maybe there's something else we could do—" I let my sentence linger and arch my hips off of the bed so that his cock pushes against my entrance. And after falling apart beneath his masterful touch, I'd be lying if I said I didn't feel at least a tiny bit thrilled at the way he reacts to mine. "If you're up for it."

"Oh yeah," he groans and his cock twitches. "I think I'm up for that."

He's already the most handsome man I've ever seen, but when the boyish, almost giddy smile tugs at the corner of his full lips, my heart stutters in my chest and my stomach flips. This man is going to destroy me in a single night. It'd be rude if I wasn't begging for it.

He rolls off of me and races to his pants crumpled up in the middle of the floor. His excitement gets the better of him, and he drops his wallet twice before finally opening it.

He pulls the condom out with the pageantry of a magician who just executed their best trick. "Voila!"

"Bravo!" I clap and he takes a bow. It's impossible not to get caught up in his excitement, but I'm also not trying very hard.

He's adorable.

And charming.

Nothing I need to see from my one-night stand.

He jumps onto the bed, and before he can take his position back on top, I snatch the condom out of his hand and push him onto his back.

"You had your fun." I rip the wrapper open with my teeth, a move that's been making the boys go wild since my college days. "Now it's time for me to play."

"By all means"—he moves around the pillows and tucks his hands behind his head—"be my guest."

I roll my eyes, but fail spectacularly at hiding my smile. He's really putting a dent in my "hate all men" armor.

I pull the condom out of the wrapper and climb on top of his rock-solid legs. I dated a soccer player once—like a real, played professionally and not just at the rec center soccer player—and his legs had nothing on Luke's. Even though he's lying down and seemingly relaxed, his quads are still flexed and bulging. Quad muscles are definitely my favorite part of the male body. Besides the hot cut near their groin . . . which Luke has. And forearms, but I don't know what that muscle is called . . .

Fuck.

Focus, Emerson!

"You alright there?" he asks.

I think about lying, but realize it's pointless. Luke is hot. He knows it. I know it. Hell, even our waitress knew it! And I will not be embarrassed for having good taste!

"Just enjoying the view." I position the condom at the tip of his almost overwhelmingly large cock and hold it in place. "I don't know if you know this or not, but you are very nice to look at."

"Thank you." His breathing picks up as his gaze roams my naked body. "But I'm far from the star of the show here. I'm the luckiest man in Colorado tonight."

"Just Colorado?" I wink and then before he can answer, my hands make quick work of unrolling the condom.

His eyes turn liquid and his hands fly from behind his head, latching on to my thighs so tight that evidence of this night might linger on my body for longer than I anticipated.

And that thought thrills me.

I move forward, resting my hands on his chest and never losing eye contact as I lower myself onto him. Only the sounds of our moans and heavy breathing fill the room as I take him inch by delicious inch until I can't take any more.

"Oh my god." I still, willing my body to adjust to the massive man inside of me. "You're gigantic."

"Swear to god." His raspy growl cuts through the air like a knife. "Nothing has ever felt as good as you."

I don't know if he means it, and I don't care. Hearing those words come out of his gorgeous, talented mouth causes what little restraint I have left to snap.

My hips move at an unrelenting pace, slamming down as he meets me thrust for thrust. He's so deep inside of me I'm not sure where I end and he begins, and just as I feel that all-too-familiar spark begin to build, he moves his hands to my hips and flips me onto my back.

"My turn." He leans forward and smashes his mouth to mine.

He wraps his long fingers around my ankles and pulls me down the bed in a quick *swoosh*. My peal of laughter abruptly turns into a moan of pleasure when he thrusts inside of me, lifting my ankles to the sky.

Even if I wanted to pull away—which to be very clear, I do not—I couldn't. My legs are locked in place, his strong grip holding me right where he wants as he thrusts into me again and again until neither of us can take it anymore.

His pace picks up and my hands tangle into the comforter, desperate for something to hold onto as electricity builds at my core like lightning ready to strike.

And strike it does.

Stars burst behind my eyes, and I cry out as my third . . . THIRD . . . orgasm of the night tears through me with so much force, it might've ripped me in half. Vaguely, through the pleasure fog, I hear Luke groan as he comes just before he collapses on top of me.

Our sweat-slicked bodies meld together as our breathing slows and we return to earth. My body is limp under the weight of his, and I sink deeper and deeper into the mattress that I belatedly notice is much more comfortable than the old one I have at my house.

His hand moves to my face and his fingers push my sex-mussed hair out of my face.

Sweet.

"That was incredible." He touches his lips to mine before he whispers, "You're incredible."

Yeah.

Super sweet.

"You're not too bad yourself," I whisper back, trying my hardest not to let myself get caught up in the afterglow of fantastic sex and those useless little things called feelings. I know better than that.

"Why don't you go to the bathroom. You can shower or do whatever you want and I'll call down to room service for new drinks and more fries."

"I forgot all about the food." If I'm being honest, I forgot about everything. "But I wouldn't mind fries now that you reminded me."

"Perfect." He rolls off of me and grabs the phone on the table next to the bed. He hits the numbers for room service and looks back at me before I head to the bathroom. "Do you want another old fashioned?"

Oh my god. Who told him this was the way to my heart?

"Yeah." I nod my head. He wasn't even there when I ordered my drink, and he still remembers my order. AI has gone too far, because he can't be real. "Thank you so much."

"Of course," he mouths and shoots me a wink.

He turns his attention to the phone, and I run to the bathroom. Closing the door gently, I twist the lock and listen to his deep voice as he recites our order.

I turn on the shower, looking in the mirror as I wait for the water to heat up. My curly hair is out of control, and my already full lips are swollen from being kissed and nipped for the last hour . . . or two. I roll onto my toes so I can get a view of the fingertip-shaped bruises already forming on my hips. And even though my lipstick is smeared and my mascara is as much beneath my eyes as it is on my eyelashes, my skin is fucking glowing.

I look happy.

Really, genuinely happy.

Something I haven't looked, or felt, in a very long time.

"You don't know better," I whisper to my reflection. "But at least you're going to have fun learning."

As a teacher, I do fancy myself as something of a lifelong learner, but I have a feeling Luke might be my hardest lesson to date.

In every single way.

AFTER I TOOK a quick shower, we spent the night cuddled on his bed watching old episodes of *Chopped* and ordering multiple rounds of room service. Between my old fashioned haze and only having a bar of hotel soap to work with, I didn't have much hope for my curls or my makeup when I eventually drifted off to sleep beside him, but I also didn't have it in me to care. It was honestly one of the best nights I've had in a long time.

Maybe ever.

Which is why the bright Colorado sun peeking through the curtains is such an unwelcome sight.

I crack one eye open and take a quick inventory of how I'm feeling. No headache and I'm not queasy. Excellent! A testament to the power of greasy hotel burgers and top-shelf alcohol. It's not until I scan a little lower that evidence of the night before makes itself very apparent. My thighs are sore and the ache between them is so delicious it makes me yearn for another round. It's a feeling I haven't felt in a while, and now I can't imagine going without it for a day, let alone another year.

"You're up," a deep voice says from the corner of the room, and the butterflies I felt the night before return with a vengeance. "I ordered some breakfast if you're hungry."

Great sex, late night snacks, and breakfast? Maybe the perfect man does exist!

He's sitting in the desk chair, his long legs sprawled out in front of him, his thick, overgrown hair still damp from the shower he must've snuck in while I was sleeping. Even after a late night of drinking and countless orgasms, his green eyes shine bright and clear, with not a bag or circle beneath them.

I don't need a mirror to know I do not look nearly as good.

I pull the sheets up to my chest, now acutely aware of my naked body and bed head in the light of day. "Oh, um . . ."

"It's okay if you don't want to stay." The words come rushing out of his mouth, and if I didn't know better, I might think this god of a man is nervous I might leave. "But at least have some coffee. I ordered too much and I don't have self-control when it comes to caffeine. A professional hazard, really. So if you don't have some, I'll drink it all and then I'll spend the rest of the day talking. It's very dangerous. For me. Not you. My caffeine consumption won't put you in danger."

Oh my god?

He's rambling! Because of me!

"I'd love some coffee!" I don't mean to shout, but I like to even the playing field, and he can't be the only one in the room with zero chill. "And I wouldn't say no to breakfast meat in any form."

"Breakfast meat?" He arches an eyebrow, and I can tell he's biting back a smile.

"Breakfast meat," I repeat. "Bacon, sausage, ham, Canadian

bacon. You know, any meat that you can find on the average Denny's menu."

"Out of all of the great brunch spots in Denver, your go-to reference is Denny's?"

And he knows great brunch spots? That's it. Not even Disney could create a better man.

"It's called longevity." I sit up and take the thin sheet with me, wrapping it around my chest like I so expertly learned during all of the toga parties I attended in college. "When any of these new age, fancy brunch spots last as long as Denny's, then we can talk. Until then, give me a Moons Over My Hammy any day of the week."

"What are you? A lawyer?" he asks, and I realize that during our brief conversation and long night together, we didn't dive much into the details of our lives. "I don't think I've ever heard such a passionate defense for a chain restaurant."

"Don't even get me started on Red Robin," I warn him. I might joke about a lot of things, but bottomless steak fries and Mountain High Mudd Pie are not included. "And no, not a lawyer, but something close."

I walk over to the newest room service tray and lift up the metal lids to inspect the booty. Pancakes, bacon, scrambled eggs, *and* breakfast potatoes. Did I put a spell on him last night? Is he in love with me already? I nab a piece of bacon while I mull over this new possibility.

"Something close, huh?" He pushes away from the desk, and I just now realize his computer is open and he's been working while I've been sleeping soundly—and hopefully not snoring—in his bed. "Don't tell me you're a cop."

A very unladylike snort shoots out of my mouth at the same time I take a bite of the very crisp bacon.

"No!" I choke out the word. The thought of me with a weapon should terrify the masses. "I'm a kindergarten teacher."

His smile changes from the sexy smirk I've gotten used to into something else. Something more open, more joyous. And an expression crosses his face that I see so often in my line of work that I can pinpoint the emotion the moment it appears: pride.

"I have a daughter." He tells me what I already knew he was going to say. "She's actually going to be in kindergarten this year."

I bite my tongue to prevent myself from asking the barrage of slightly inappropriate follow-up questions I have. I just met the man, for goodness' sake! I can't ask where his kid is going to school and how often he works on sight words with her. Creep much? So instead, I decide to go with my normal "kindergarten is the best" spiel—while also checking his left hand to make sure I didn't miss something important before I agreed to spend the night with a stranger.

"She's going to love it." I tell him something I'm sure he already knows. "I really believe that kindergarten is the foundation for a child's educational career. I know some people think it's silly and unnecessary, that we just play games and horse around, but it's where I get to show them firsthand how much fun learning can be. I love it."

I'll never thrive financially, but I think I have the best job in the world, and in the end, it balances the scales.

Well . . . spiritually, definitely not literally.

"She's really excited. It's all she's been talking about all summer long. I promised her we'd go shopping this week so she can pick out her backpack and lunch box." He grabs two coffee mugs and starts pouring from the carafe sitting beside the trays of food. "She's into llamas right now? So we'll see how that goes."

I don't want him to be hotter, but now that I'm picturing this big, strong man shopping for a llama backpack, he's getting hotter! Plus, I'm also really into llamas right now and I'm not sure I'm mentally stable enough to know that I have things in common with the daughter of the man I just had the best sex of my life with. Those lines will get blurry real fast and then I'm the girl scaring away all of her dates in *How to Lose a Guy in 10 Days*. We can't have that.

So I do what any rational, emotionally intelligent human would do.

I change the subject.

"You know what I do . . ." I walk over to his computer and gesture at the now darkened screen. "It's time for you to return the favor."

He hands me a full mug of coffee before gesturing to the cream and sugar packets and takes his seat back in front of his computer.

"My job isn't nearly as fun or idyllic as a kindergarten teacher." He winks, and I fight the urge to tell him about the amount of bodily fluids I deal with on a weekly basis during the school year. "But I love it and I'm pretty proud of the work I do."

"Impressive lead-up." I take a sip of my black coffee, and my body starts to wake up now that it's being fueled by its life source. "Can I try guessing before you tell me?"

I'm actually really good at reading people. It's one of the

perks of being a violently codependent people pleaser. I'll take "reasons to work with five-year-olds" for five hundred, Alex!

He nods in response, and I take a minute to consider everything I already know about him.

He's got a great body, but not from being in the gym all the time. So definitely not a trainer. He knows good brunch spots, but told me in a way where he wasn't trying to prove that he knows all the cool spots. So definitely not a finance bro or lawyer. He woke up early and was doing work on a computer, so he can work remotely and it's probably something he does often since he got straight to it in a hotel room with a strange woman in his bed. And his hands are way too smooth and gentle to do anything outdoorsy or with heavy lifting.

"Okay," I say after I've narrowed down my options. "You travel with your laptop which points to you maybe being a workaholic, but I get the feeling that you're just really passionate about what you do. If I had to guess, you're either an entrepreneur focused on building your own company, you work at a nonprofit with a mission you deeply connect to, or final guess, you're a writer. I can't put my finger on what kind of writer, but I'm keeping my fingers crossed that you're a mystery writer."

"Why mystery?"

"Mainly because I've watched way too many crime documentaries, and I would love to bounce all of my theories off of someone who wouldn't look at me like I grew an extra head. But also, I love mystery books, and it would be cool to know someone who writes them." And doesn't just have a notebook full of ideas that they'll never actually write like me. "Second to mystery would be fantasy, but if you tell me you're the kind of guy who only reads *serious literature*, I will walk out of the door without a second thought."

No offense to *The Odyssey* or anything, it's wonderful, but so are books that are just read for fun. As a kindergarten teacher, I'm very much 'team read whatever makes you happy.' And it's my personal opinion that if you make hating something that other people love your entire personality, you're not actually cool or edgy. You're not even just a massive asshole. You're a massive, *boring* asshole. At least put some effort in and find something niche to hate.

"I do have a bookshelf at home with quite a few memoirs—wait!" he prematurely defends himself when my eyes roll in my head without my permission. What can I say? My facial expressions have a mind of their own, and I cannot be held responsible. "I like fiction too! I like all books."

He likes all books? Too good to be true.

"Horror?"

"We live in Colorado, it's practically a crime not to have read *The Shining*."

"What about romance?" I arch an eyebrow, sure that I've found his first flaw.

"I don't care what it says about me, but I'll read or watch a rom-com over just about anything."

Impressive, but not even he can pass this final test.

"Okay then." I cross my arms and narrow my eyes as I enunciate each word. "Self. Help."

"Alright," he deflates. "You caught me. I avoid that section. I had a college roommate who quite literally almost drove himself insane because he was so afraid of thinking negative thoughts after he went on a self-help book binge. I know there are good ones, but I think a lot of them can be pretty detrimental."

"Well damn." I collapse onto the bed and stare up at the ceiling. "That's the right answer."

I don't shit on people who read self-help books, but I do feel like after reading *The Secret* for the fifth time, you should be obligated to pair it with a mental health expert—and no, a life coach does not count.

"Don't look so disappointed," he says. "Would it make you feel better to know you were right and that I am a writer?"

"Since being right is the most important thing in my life, and I live for an *I told you so* moment, it makes me feel much better." I spring off of the bed, and all signs of despair are long forgotten. "What kind of writer?"

"A journalist." He swivels in the desk chair and grabs his computer. "I did attempt to write a novel in college, but it was not good and I try not to remember."

"Okay, well obviously I have so many questions about that." A few genre questions, but also what kind of college experience led him to spending his free weekends penning a novel instead of camped out in the Taco Bell drive-thru like me. "But first, please tell me you're not the sports guy."

It's not that I don't like sports. I think they're fun and I love going to a game or two. What I don't like is someone explaining sports to me or being forced to spend every Sunday during the fall camped out in front of the TV or worse, someone telling me about their fantasy team. My roommate in college dated a sports management major and he made every game day hell. I can't go back, never again.

"No, not sports." The creases next to his eyes have deepened along with the warmth in my chest. "I'm an investigative journalist."

"Wow, that's actually really cool. It's kind of like crime and mystery combined." I love my job, but it's definitely not *cool*. "How'd you get into it?"

He shrugs, and it doesn't take an investigative journalist to see that he's uncomfortable with receiving compliments.

"I wish I had a cool story, but I was really just a nerd who was obsessed with Watergate. I did a paper on Woodward and Bernstein in high school and that was it. I knew from that moment on it was what I was going to do."

Ambition and determination? Just add it to his never-ending list of green flags.

"You say nerd, I say man with a plan." I nod at the laptop in his hands, more curious now than ever before. "Can you tell me what you're working on, or is it top secret?"

"It's pretty secret, but I can tell you if you promise not to tell."

"Pinky promise." I lift up my pinky, and he wraps his around mine, following my lead as I kiss my thumb and smush it against his. "There. That's basically as official as an NDA."

His grin widens, and I'm nearly blinded by the beauty of it. He moves his finger around on the trackpad, waking up his sleeping computer. Giddy little flutters in my belly have me leaning in closer. I'm just as excited to learn another morsel of information about Luke Miller as I am for the potentially criminal gossip he's going to show me.

"Okay, so, it's not a government takedown, but I'm really excited about it. And since we share similar beliefs about self-help books, I think you'll love it." He turns his computer around to face me, but I can't tear my eyes away from his face. The pure joy, almost childlike giddiness that spreads across his face when he talks about this work is contagious. Who knew that word nerd would be my kink? "These companies are so dangerous, but they hide behind false claims of empowerment. They are filled with predatory monsters, and I'd argue that the majority of them should be labeled as cults."

"I love culty things . . ." I start but lose my train of thought as I begin to comprehend exactly what I'm reading. Words like *gullible* and *desperate* jump off the screen, and declarations of *false feminism* and *mob mentality* make my stomach turn. But it's the repeated usage of two words that has me seeing red. "Is this about Petunia Lemon?"

"Yeah, have you heard of them? I didn't realize how popular they were until I started this project. I knew there was a certain demographic that was more likely to fall into these MLM traps, but I had no idea just how many women this particular company has sunk their claws into." He keeps on going, clearly not sensing the shift in my mood. "It's actually the reason I was here this weekend. They had a big convention, and I wanted to see what it was about. You had to have noticed all the obnoxious people with gigantic lanyards repeating the same five phrases and crying about their 'sisters in skincare.'"

I'm not looking at him, but I swear I can almost hear his eyes roll. Disdain drips from his every syllable, and even though I would cut off my leg for him to shut up, he just *won't stop talking*.

"It was hard to watch," he continues on. "I'm supposed to stay neutral as a reporter, but at what point do you shake these people and tell them to grow up and get a real job? One where they don't prey on their friends. They're all so brainwashed that they actually think they're helping people by introducing them to this money pit. And maybe I could feel bad for them if they just did it to themselves, but these people are sheep and they bring down everyone around them. Dragging their families into financial ruin over sunscreen and for what? An all-expenses-paid vacation? Pathetic."

And it's at being called pathetic by the man who spent all night with his head in between my legs, that I finally decide enough is enough.

My fingers flex around his computer, and I wait for the urge to throw it against the grass-cloth-covered wall to pass. Inhaling through my nose, I use the calming techniques I teach five-year-olds and hand him back his stupid computer with his even stupider article before I slowly stand and walk to my purse in the corner of the room.

"Emerson?" There's hesitation in his voice as he calls after me. "Is everything okay?"

Wow. Look at those A-plus investigator skills.

"Of course." I aim the fakest smile I can muster at him, my voice so sugar sweet it causes the hairs on my arms to rise. "Why wouldn't it be?"

"You seem a little . . . off." For the first time since I met him, his full lips turn down and the lines on his forehead deepen with concern. "Did something I say offend you?"

"Offend me?" I reach into my purse and pull out the Petunia Lemon lanyard I tucked inside last night. His eyes laser focus on the—admittedly obnoxious—neon credentials. "Do pathetic sheep get offended?"

I don't know why, but I assumed that once he realized I was part of this group that he seems to so vehemently abhor, he'd be immediately apologetic. He would grovel at my feet and beg for forgiveness.

I couldn't have been more wrong.

"You've got to be fucking kidding me." He sounds more like a bulldog I helped bathe last weekend than the man I spent the night with. And with the way his lip curls in disgust, he looks more like him too. Just much less snuggly. "This has to be some kind of cruel joke."

"I think the joke's on me," I shoot back, somehow more pissed now than I was moments ago. He was my green flag guy! How did this happen? "To think I thought you were a nice, good guy."

"To think I thought you had a brain."

I gasp. "You did not just say that!"

"I'm pretty sure I did."

Luke may know me intimately, but he doesn't know me well. If he did, he'd know that I'm terrible at saying no (hence my presence and subsequent registration for Petunia Lemon) and that my people-pleasing ways run so deep that I'm still not sure if it's from childhood trauma or just my actual personality. He'd also know that I'm so nonconfrontational, I came home from school with hives almost every single day until my junior year of high school. But most importantly, he'd know that all of that flies out the window the moment I'm presented with a bully. My mom called it the red haze because when I get like this, it's like I see red, smell blood, and nothing and nobody can calm me down.

And unfortunately for Mr. Miller here, I'm feeling pretty fucking hazy.

"You also thought you had talent, so I can see that being wrong is something you're very familiar with." I grab my pants off the floor and slip them on without breaking eye contact. "But what I just read? Your favorites would cringe. It reads like a small, bitter man who is jealous the popular girls didn't invite him over in high school. Even if you had a good point rolled around in there somewhere, it was impossible to find beneath the patronizing, dismissive, and personal tone you set in the very first sentence. That's not journalism. It's a hack job. Just like you." And then, because I like to add a little razzle dazzle to things, I lift my middle finger in the air and deliver my final blow. "Fuck you, Luke. I hope the next time you read your article, you choke on it."

I don't give him a chance to respond before the door is open and I'm running down the hallway. The elevator is right in front of me, but I know I can't chance Luke following me out or worse, having to share an elevator while making my walk of shame. I push open the heavy door to the staircase, and once it slams shut behind me, I lean against the wall and take what feels like my first breath in ten minutes.

I don't know how long I stand there. Could be seconds. Could be hours. I still can't figure out how one of the best nights of my life turned into the worst morning ever.

But I do know one thing for sure: when they said *fuck around and find out*, they definitely didn't mean for me to take it so literally.

6

I KNOW A lot of teachers count down until the end of the school year, but because I have no life, a limited number of friends, and a truly tight budget, I count down until the end of summer.

As soon as the bell rings on the last day of school and I'm shoved into the streets, I start planning the next year. I spend the summer stalking the dollar store and Target's dollar spot (that is no longer a dollar and I do have beef with them), slowly stocking up my classroom decor supplies so that when we're allowed back in the school, I'm ready to set up the cutest, most magical kindergarten classroom in all of the world.

Or at least the Denver metro area.

I decided on a "planting a love of learning" theme and hit the jackpot with the amount of colorful garden supplies I've found. HomeGoods had tons of super discounted flower pillows for our reading corner. I painted rainbows on different size potters that now sit in the middle of the tables, soon to be filled with pencils, crayons, and markers. And because I was avoiding looking at myself in the mirror or thinking about my night with . . . that man . . . I've spent the last two weeks sitting at my kitchen table and crafting an absurd amount of 3D wall art.

"Holy shit." Keisha lets out a long whistle as she walks into my classroom and spins around to take in all the work I've done. "Is this what you've been up every time you say no to coming out with me?"

"It is." Well, this and a healthy dosage of self-loathing. "Do you like it?"

"It looks amazing." She wanders around the room, taking a closer look at the bulletin boards I've covered with all of my laminated signs and affirmations. "What in the world do you need my help with?"

Besides being my best friend, Keisha is also an artist extraordinaire. How she ended up being an elementary school art teacher and not a world-famous artist will forever be one of life's great mysteries. Selfishly, I'm forever grateful for whatever deity above decided to give me a small break in life and put her in my path when I was but a lowly student teacher. The moment we met, it was like I found my other half. We love the same movies, have the same sense of humor, and whenever we go out to eat, we accidentally order the exact same meal. Even our differences align beautifully. She balances me out in a way I never knew possible, and even though I'm not against finding a love match someday, I rest easy knowing I already found my soulmate.

"My reading corner." I point to the corner in the back of the room filled with green pom poms and handmade leaf garland. "I want there to be a big tree that climbs up the wall and onto the ceiling. But I don't want a decal this time, I want it to be papier-mâché so that it has texture and comes out of the wall. The problem is, the flowers are the full extent of my wall art talent, and I have no idea how to do it. I did order all of the supplies the internet told me I needed though."

"Caviar dreams with tuna fish talent?"

"Absolutely."

No point in denying the obvious. I love to craft, but I'm notoriously terrible at it. I can muster together flowers if there is a detailed, step-by-step tutorial, but that's the entirety of my skill. I almost didn't graduate because I was so close to failing my pottery class in high school. My teacher thought I was mocking her until my mom showed up with a chest of the projects she'd kept over the years for proof that it was actually a lack of talent, not malicious mockery.

"I'll do it, but you're going to have to help me." She pulls the hair band off of her wrist and twists her dreadlocks into a bun on the top of her head.

"You're the best!" I pull her tall, slender body into a hug and try not to take it personally when her body locks up beneath me. Physical touch is her least favorite love language. "Your first day of school matcha latte is on me!"

Gift giving is her favorite.

"First two days," she counters. "And a margarita on back-to-school night."

Two days? She's losing her touch. I was prepared to go up to the first week of school. Sucker.

"Deal!" I squeeze her a little tighter before finally letting her go and following her to the corner.

She gets to work immediately, hand-drawing the most majestic tree up the base of the wall toward the ceiling. Because I've "worked" with her before, I know that when she said she needs my help, she really just needs me to fetch supplies, or like now, hold the chair steady so she can sketch the branches onto the ceiling.

"So," she says as she finishes the final branch. "Are you ready to tell me where you've really been these last few weeks or am I going to have to pry it out of you with old fashioneds?"

She knows me so well.

"I told you, I've been—"

"You're so full of shit." She cuts me off. "Do not fucking lie to me. I know you weren't sitting in your house and cutting construction paper this entire time."

"Anyone tell you that you have a foul mouth?"

You'd think an elementary school art teacher would have a cleaner vocabulary, but she uses swear words as liberally as the glitter she encourages the kids to add to every project.

"Only my mom, dad, pastor, and every single teacher my entire life." She steps off the chair and looks down her nose at me, just one more con of being a short girl with a tall best friend. "Now drop the shit and tell me what happened. I let you sulk for long enough."

I plop down on one of the tiny beanbags I bought for the reading corner. "You're so annoying."

"I know you are but what am I?" She sticks her tongue out and sits across from me. "Spill, or I won't finish your tree."

"Fine, but everything I tell you stays between us."

"Duh." She rolls her eyes. "Who else would I tell? You're the only person I like."

See? Soulmates.

"Okay. So . . ." I'm not usually one who struggles to find words, but I'm also not one who has a one-night stand with someone who turns out to be a raging fucking asshole. And there are so many layers to this story that I don't even know how to begin. I guess at the beginning. "Has Nora ever told you about—"

"Shut the fuck up!" She cuts me off before I can get started. "I swear to god, if you tell me this is about you falling for that bullshit she's always going on and on about, I will hurt you."

"What do you mean?" I know exactly what she means.

"You're too smart to play dumb with me. You know what I'm talking about. Gardenia Lemon? Lemon Poppyseed? Blueberry Muffin?"

"Petunia Lemon," I correct her, but only because she'll go on all day, and she has a tree to make.

"Yes!" she shouts before remembering she's supposed to be mad. "She's been trying to pull me in for years. Please tell me you didn't fall for that."

"I didn't want to . . ."

"Emerson! No!" She throws her head back and clutches her chest. A little too dramatic for my taste. "I can't believe she got you too. I'm pretty sure she suckered in Lilah Jenkins from third grade before she quit last year. I know for a fact Anna joined, but I'm not sure if she's still in it or not. She's too nice to gossip, so getting dirt out of her is like pulling teeth."

As if conjured by the devil himself, Anna peeks her head into my classroom and her soft, melodic voice floats through the room. "Did I hear my name?"

"Anna! Come, sit with us." I wave her in. "Are you ready for a new year?"

"I think so." Her trademark ballet flats gently pad across the floor until she sits down ever so gracefully on the beanbag next to me. "I decided to switch up the curriculum this year and try some new songs and instruments with the kids. I'm really excited to see how it goes."

Like Keisha, Anna has way too much talent to be working as the music teacher at an underfunded public school. She knows how to play something like seven instruments and has the voice of an angel. Our music programs are so good that parents arrive up to an hour early to get the good seats and the choir has won multiple competitions under her lead.

She's a star on stage but is quiet as a mouse off of it. I worked with her for a year before I heard her speak outside of the classroom. I was partnered with her for team building one year and practically had to bully her into opening up. I'm so glad she did because she's one of the most interesting people I've ever met. She was in the Colorado Youth Symphony and spent the summer before her junior year performing all across Europe. She still performs over summer break and tutors in her spare time.

"It will be amazing, you're magic in the music department," Keisha reassures her. "But we already know that. What we don't know is if you're magic with Nora's makeup group too."

"It's skincare," I correct her. "Not makeup."

Anna's eyes go wide. "Do you mean Petunia Lemon?"

"Yes! See, Anna knew what I was talking about. They're the same thing." She sticks her tongue out at me before looking back to Anna. "Did Nora recruit you too? How long have you been in it?"

"Um, well." Anna shifts on the tiny beanbag, and her petite body almost tumbles off. "I'm not really doing it anymore. I've been busy with preparing for the school year and you know . . . stuff."

Oh yes, the all-encompassing "stuff." Very specific.

"But you liked it, didn't you?" I know Anna is quiet, so this was probably the perfect group to pull her out of her shell. "Everyone has been so nice and making a little extra money is always a bonus."

"I met a lot of people, and it was very interesting." Anna glances down at her watch before standing up faster than I knew was possible with these beanbags. "Shoot! Sorry, I have to go. I'm supposed to have a meeting about the new instruments we're getting."

"Have fun!" I call to her back as she hurries out of the room. "And remember, no parents like the recorder."

I don't even teach the third grade, and I still hear the parent complaints.

"Really, Em?" Keisha grabs the flower pillow next to her and lobs it at my head. Lucky for me, she's an art teacher and has terrible aim, so I dodge it easily. "She sprints out of the room at the mention of Petunia Lemon, and all you can think about are recorders?"

"First of all, don't throw things at me!" I launch it back at her. I was a softball player until I went to college, so I hit her square in the forehead. Like a goddamn winner. "And second, that's not why she was running. You heard her say she had a meeting!"

"Oh my god." She drops her head into her hands. "I knew you were oblivious sometimes, but this takes the cake. No wonder Nora was able to get her claws into you."

"Rude! I'm not oblivious." I wish I could have the pillow back so I could throw it at her harder this time. "And if you really want to know the truth, it's your fault I joined in the first place!"

"What?" she shouts, and I watch her thoughts cross her face as she makes the very wise decision not to take aim with the pillow again. "How is this my fault?"

"Remember when you went to Georgia for a week to visit your family and left me all by my lonesome?" I jog her memory of the hurt and betrayal she bestowed against me. "Well, Nora must've sensed your abandonment and invited me to the Petunia Lemon convention that weekend. And because I was sad and lonely, I said yes."

"She promised you free drinks, didn't she?"

Dammit.

"And a free facial."

"Emerson." She groans, and I've never heard anyone sound so disappointed in me, and once I put diesel gas in my mom's car. For real . . . not the TikTok prank going around.

"I didn't want to say yes, but there were so many people and everyone was so nice to me." I try to remember everything from the convention as I plead my case. "And the products are so cute! I mean, really. Have you seen them? It's all so bright and whimsical and fun! Plus, you know everything pays for itself. All you have to do is talk about it on social media and then you're making money while you sleep. And there's an island!"

She leans forward and grabs my hand. "You sweet, sweet summer child."

"Whatever." I rip my hand away from her. "This is what happens when you go on vacation without me. Now you have to join and come to a meeting with me next week. Consequences to your actions and all that."

"First of all." She holds a finger in front of my face. "That wasn't a vacation. I was going home to see my great-grandma for her ninety-fifth birthday, and I spent all weekend in the church or the nursing home. My uncle preached that I needed to get married the entire time, and it's in a dry county, so I couldn't even sneak away for a shot of tequila. Two"—she adds a second finger—"I'll attend a meeting with you, but only if you promise to provide me with at least one cocktail the night of the meeting and coffee the morning after. And, now listen closely because this is the most important part, you can't expect me to ever sign up. You know I don't believe in putting all that junk on your face."

She wouldn't believe in putting junk on her face, but that's only because she has the skin of an angel. Even now, sitting beneath the terrible fluorescent lights, her skin is glowing like she's lounging on the beach at golden hour.

"One, you're right, that sounds horrible, and thank you for not inviting me. I'm sorry," I say. "Two, yes to the coffee and cocktail, but once you're there, you're going to want to join me for vacation on Petunia Island."

"Petunia Island?" Her eyes bug out of her head before she

laughs so loud, I'm surprised the ground doesn't shake. "That's a fucking Jordan Peele movie! They'd be out there trying to suck the melanin out of me so they could add it to their next serum."

I don't want to encourage her bad jokes with my laughter, but I can't help it. She's probably not wrong, and it might not hurt for me to keep an eye out just in case. "I hate you so much."

"You love me." She speaks the absolute truth. "And you're laughing, but I'm being serious. I know you trust Nora, and I can't put my finger on it, but something about that woman's spirit doesn't sit right with me. You're too trusting, and I need you to keep your guard up."

"I know, I know." This isn't the first time she's shared this warning, and it's the one thing we don't agree on. I wouldn't have my job or friendship with Keisha without Nora, and as much as I love Keisha, it's the one piece of advice I haven't listened to. "But I promise, if you just give her a chance, you'll see what I see."

"I'm going to have to pass on that offer." She doesn't even pretend to consider it before snapping her fingers in my face. "Now tell me the rest of the story, because I know you didn't avoid me all because of face wash."

After I paid the exorbitant parking fee and navigated the congested Denver streets back to my apartment, I vowed never to utter the name Luke Miller ever again. Once the glow of great sex and top-shelf bourbon had begun to fade, any remnants of joy were promptly chased away by the burning heat of humiliation. I reassured myself that nobody ever needed to know what happened. But that was when I thought I could just avoid it altogether. As much as I'd like to keep that terrible, horrible, amazing night locked in the recesses of my brain, I've never lied to Keisha and I'm not going to start lying to her now.

Especially not over some terrible, trash man.

"After the convention was over, I went up to the bar."

"For your old fashioned?" She knows me so well.

"They use vanilla bean–infused sugar. You know I had to try it!" I throw my hands up in the air. I'm defenseless against a well-crafted cocktail. "But while I was up there, I met someone . . ."

"Oh my god." Keisha's eyes triple in size, and the ever-present glow on her cheeks turns red. "*You* met someone? Have you been ignoring me for a secret boyfriend?"

"A boyfriend?" I almost choke on the word. "Never!"

The last time I had a boyfriend was my sophomore year in college. When we broke up, he made it his mission to spend his every waking hour spreading lovely rumors about me to anyone who would listen. And because he was a starter on the basketball team, everyone listened. So now I do my best to look but not touch when it comes to humans of the male variety. A rule very much reinforced by my time spent with Luke.

"He came up to me while I was waiting for my drink. I let him sit with me and we talked for a little bit. He was staying at the hotel and you know . . . one thing led to another." My hands begin to sweat and my thighs clench as I remember the way he looked at me up on that rooftop. "But that was it. I didn't even get his phone number."

"You had a one-night stand? You dirty little skank!" Her voice ricochets off my freshly constructed paper-covered walls. I dive across the reading rug and slap my hand across her mouth. An impulse I immediately regret when I remember she's wearing bright red lipstick.

"This is a precious, innocent space." My eyes dart to the door, making sure none of the other kindergarten teachers are rushing in to catch a glimpse at what's causing all the commotion. "You can't just go around shouting the word *skank* in here or I'll make you sage it again."

The last time Keisha saged our classrooms, she set off the fire alarms, and we had to have a meeting with the fire chief and Nora about fire safety and being considerate to coworkers with high sensitivities to scents. It was a reasonable request, and in response Keisha saged Nora's office the very next day.

She peels my hand off of her mouth, and much to my relief her lipstick is still perfectly in place and I have not turned her into a Joker cosplayer.

"I have known you for five years and you haven't so much as mentioned a man's name in passing. Now, you want to drop a bomb that you had a one-night stand"—she pauses for dramatic effect, an art she's perfected over the years—"two fucking weeks ago! And you think I'm going to be calm about it? Girl, please be so fucking for real. I can't believe you've been holding out on me."

"I wasn't holding out on you. Trust me, nothing about that night is worth remembering." *Except for the way he looked at me, touched me, and talked to me.* "It's just one more cautionary tale as to why I shouldn't be allowed to leave my house unless it's for work or survival. It was awful."

"Nice try." She purses her lips, obviously not trusting me. "You're full of shit and you know it."

"How so?" She's right, but still very rude for her to call me out like that.

"Because if it was as horrible as you're making it out to be, you would've called me as soon as you got in your car. Bad nights with strangers make the best stories to laugh over."

This, unfortunately, is the truth. Keisha tells the best stories, and I live to impress her with my own tall tales. I would never deprive her of the opportunity to find entertainment in my misfortune.

Dammit.

I fall back against the empty wall and groan. "I hate when you're smart and right."

Life would be so much easier if I didn't choose this gorgeous, creative, critical thinker as my best friend.

"Sucks for you since I'm always smart and right." She tucks her legs beneath her, crisscross applesauce style, her eyes sparkling with mischief and joy as I squirm beneath her watchful gaze. "Now tell me about this mystery man and explain why I'm just now hearing about this."

And as much as I told myself I never wanted to think of Luke Miller ever again, as soon as I start telling Keisha about him, I wish I could relive that night together again . . . and again.

And again.

7

THE FIRST DAY of school is like if someone were to mix together Christmas with my birthday, throw some puppies and old fashioneds on top, and roll it all around in glitter. It's the best day of the year.

The sheer joy and excitement I find in meeting my new students and seeing their eyes light up when they enter my classroom is the highest high in the world. Nothing makes me happier. It's why, even though I make pennies, I know I'll do this until the day I die.

I adore my classes every year, even when I have more students in need of a little extra love and attention, but this year is off to an especially promising start. Not only did the parents I meet in the morning all seem lovely, but the kids have been getting along all day. There was no crying at recess—everyone laughed and giggled as we played our games, and they were all engaged when we started learning our songs. And, the cherry on top, nobody in the class shares a name!

"Okay, friends." I clap my hands together two times to indicate eyes on me. "It's time to clean up our spaces and make sure our backpacks are ready to go home. Who wants to help me hand out lunch boxes?"

We still have thirty minutes before the day ends, but I've found that giving them the time and space to wind down at the end of the day is best for everyone. This way nobody is crying because they can't find a folder or they need to go to the bathroom, and I'm not frantic and frazzled when parents approach asking how their child's day went. Next week I'll have a job chart ready to go, but for the first week, I like to see personalities and who volunteers naturally before assigning positions.

The push and pull to get children to grow and thrive is such a delicate balance. I want to make sure I'm challenging them without ever making them feel ashamed or embarrassed about what they're comfortable giving. I want to spotlight their strengths and teach them how to challenge their fears. So, for that first week, I never call on anyone who isn't raising their hand or volunteering for a position. This room is a safe space for introverts and extroverts.

Thankfully, this group of kids has a lot of hand raisers.

I point to the adorable little girl with curly dark brown hair and a freckle-smattered nose. Her little pigtails she came in with this morning are falling out, and the tights beneath her skirt were ripped to shreds after the first trip to the playground.

"Isla, thank you so much for volunteering. Can you come up here so we can show the rest of our friends how we will get our lunch boxes back for the rest of the school year?"

I've barely finished asking the question before she's out of her seat and sprinting to where I'm standing in the corner of the room. It's like she has too much excitement in her tiny little body to go any speed other than fast.

I point to the lunch box bin, a glorified laundry basket that I glittered and hot glued to death with ribbon and fringe. "At the end of every day, one friend is going to get the lunch boxes out of the bin." I demonstrate by pulling out the first one I see and holding it high over my head. "When you see our friend lift your lunch box in the air, I want you to put a bubble in your mouth," the fun way of saying puff out your cheeks and keep your mouth closed, "and raise your hand high in the air so your friend can bring you your lunch box. Then I want you to tuck it into your backpack so it can go home with you."

Jaxon, a little boy with a faux-hawk and a mischievous glint in his eyes, follows my directions and raises his hand in the air, quickly and quietly putting his lunch box in his backpack before aiming his proud, toothy smile at me.

"Great job, Jaxon," I say, and watch as his smile doubles in size. "After we have our lunch boxes put away and our backpacks ready to go home, I have a special game for us to play. Is everyone ready?"

A loud chorus of little cheers explodes around the room, and Isla gets to work right away, moving as fast as her little legs can go so we have plenty of playtime left before it's time to go home.

ISLA AND I stand together as the last of her classmates walk away holding their parent's hand. The bright smile she wore all day wobbles as her little eyes begin to gloss over with unshed tears.

When Isla's mom dropped her off in the morning, she told me that her ex-husband, Lucas, would be the one picking Isla up from school. She's far from the first divorced parent I've encountered, and even though I could tell she was trying to keep it together, the all too familiar roll of the eyes and deep frown said she was struggling to keep her thoughts about her ex to herself.

"You know what?" I reach for Isla's hand and squeeze it tight in mine. "I have some extra snacks and a new board game in our classroom. Do you want to play Candy Land with me while we wait for your dad?"

Her bright green eyes light up at my words, her excitement chasing the fear straight off of her face.

"I love Candy Land!" she shouts on the now empty sidewalk. "My daddy always says I cheat, but he's just really bad. He always gets the ice cream cone card and has to go back to the beginning."

Her twinkly little giggles are like music to my ears as we make our way back inside. We stop inside of the door to give Lisa, the school secretary, Isla's name so she can call Lucas to make sure he's on his way. Isla keeps chatting as we wind through the hallways, telling me more stories about all the games she plays with her dad and the Candy Land–themed birthday party he threw for her fourth birthday. I listen carefully, asking more questions and laughing at her jokes, and only interrupting so she can pick which color she wants. Red, because it's "the closest to pink." Adorable.

I know teachers aren't supposed to have favorites, but I can't help it, and she's quickly climbing to first place.

"How did you like your first day of school?" I ask her as I move my character to the next purple square on the board.

"I loved it!" She swipes away the stray piece of hair that keeps falling in her face. "Daddy told me I would love it and make lots of new friends and he was right."

The more she talks about her dad, the more it's evident how close they are. My irritation at the man who forgot his daughter lessens, and I just hope it was a simple mix-up and not something more serious.

"He was right." Every time I saw Isla, she was sitting with a new friend, her bright, gap-toothed smile not leaving her face once. "Sounds like your dad is a very smart man."

"Well that's generous of you to say," a deep voice calls out from behind me. "Hi, Bear, I'm so sorry I'm late. Mommy and I got a little confused."

As soon as Isla hears her dad, our competitive game of Candy Land is all but forgotten.

"Daddy!" She springs off of the floor like only a child can do and runs across the small space in record time.

I follow her lead, pushing off of the floor—only much slower— and turning to greet her dad. He's squatting down, his face blocked out by Isla's tiny frame, but I can tell he's got a great head of hair on him and his arms look fantastic in the pinstripe shirt.

"You must be Isla's dad." I make sure my voice is cheerful as I approach. I know the first day of school is overwhelming for everyone, and he already sounds frazzled so I don't want to make it worse by letting any lingering irritation slip through. "It's so nice to meet—"

I start, but the rest of the sentence lodges in my throat when

Isla's dad stands and the world around me crumbles. Familiar green eyes, eyes that took in every single inch of me not even a month ago, meet mine. The air in the room feels like it disappears as my lungs go frozen in my chest. The color drains from his face, and his mouth falls open.

"You've got to be fucking—"

"That's a bad word, Daddy!" Isla cuts him off, her distressed little voice snapping us back into reality. "Say sorry to Miss Pierce!"

Oh sweet, wonderful child. If only she knew how much he had to be sorry about.

"You're right, Bear." Luke . . . I mean, *Lucas* says to Isla, who has now firmly cemented herself as my favorite student of all time. When he moves his gaze from his daughter to me, so many emotions cross his face that I almost forget that I hate him. "I'm so sorry, Miss Pierce."

"Thank you for that apology, Mr. Miller." I couldn't hold back the smug, shit-eating grin on my face even if I tried . . . which I don't.

"You're welcome," he grits out between his stupid, straight, annoyingly perfect teeth.

Someone who is such an asshole should not be allowed to be this attractive. Because even though my brain knows I hate him, my body is struggling to remember. And while I've experienced a lot of things in this classroom, being turned on by a parent is not one of them.

"Miss Pierce." Isla grabs my hand and pulls my attention away from her now glowering dad. "Can I show my dad what we made today?"

Out of the corner of my eye, I can see him shaking his head no, but I'm not a parent and what would I look like saying no to that face. If she's excited about her work, I can and will only stoke those flames. Even if it means prolonged exposure to her asshole of a father.

"Of course you can." I point to the table where the pictures are all spread out. "Why don't you go get it and I'll tell your daddy how great you did on your first day of school."

She nods and skips away, and her pigtails finally lose their hard-fought battle, long curls cascading down her back as she goes. She's so cute that I almost forget her dad is the devil.

"Daddy, huh?"

And just that fast, it all comes back to me.

"You so wish." The smile on my face is as phony as it is wide. "Only in these walls and your dreams."

"Good to see your memory of events is as reliable as your decision-making. Still wrapped up in your cult?" The cutting edge in his voice slices just as deep as it did the last time we were together. "I can't believe you're the person I'm supposed to trust with my daughter's education."

I don't really care what he thinks of me joining Petunia Lemon, but hearing a parent doubt my ability to care for and educate their child hits me so deep, it nearly knocks me over. And because this situation was never covered by any of my professors, I don't know how to handle it.

"Listen, I know we aren't each other's biggest fan. You don't like me and the feeling is very much mutual." I keep my voice low and glance over my shoulder to make sure Isla is still preoccupied with her art-finding mission. "But what we do have in common is a shared desire for Isla to have the absolute best school experience possible."

He opens his big-ass, talented mouth, but I hurry on before he can interrupt.

"Look around this classroom." I gesture to the reading corner tree that turned out better than I could've ever imagined. Twinkly lights dance around the perimeter of the room, and my flowers bloom from the walls. This place is magical, and not even he can deny it. "I've spent countless hours making sure this is the best environment for every child who steps foot in here. I know our time together didn't end well, but I told you how much I love my job and you know how seriously I take it. I'm not going to let what happened between you and I affect Isla, and I can only hope you won't either."

He deflates in front of my eyes. The tension in his jaw eases, his shoulders slump, and the fight leaves his eyes. "How was her day?"

It's not an apology, but I take it for the olive branch I know he means it to be.

"You have one amazing little girl." I tell him something he must be aware of. "She was a social butterfly, making new friends left and right and going out of her way to make sure some of our more quiet friends were included. We practiced sight words, did a review of the alphabet, and numbers. She did a great job and is clearly a very bright child."

Pride radiates out of him with such ferocity, it almost hurts to look at. His love and adoration for his daughter is plastered across his face. And even though I want to think he's a troll, it makes him all the more attractive.

"Was she okay when I wasn't there at pickup? Our parenting plan had it written that her mom would get the first day of school and I would pick her up before bedtime and get day two." The anger in his voice is back, but now that it's not directed at me, it's much easier to handle. "I didn't know she wasn't coming to pick her up until the school called me."

Unlike sleeping with my student's father, I am very capable of handling parental disputes. I hate it every time, but at least this is a problem I can assist with.

"I'm so sorry that happened." I let the sincerity ring from my voice so there is no room for misinterpretation. "Isla's mom told me this morning that you would be picking her up from school. If you'd like, I can send you both an email each morning to make sure we're all on the same page regarding Isla and her schedule."

"That would be great actually, thank you." It looks like he's sucking on a lemon, and even though I shouldn't take any joy in this situation, I do feel a small thrill knowing he's already having to eat his words from moments ago.

"And she was a little sad when she was the last one here." I don't want to twist the knife that's already cutting him deep, but I know it's important to be honest about all of Isla's day. Not just the good parts. "But once I told her I had Candy Land and some snacks in my room, she cheered right up. She was telling me all about her birthday party and how bad you are at the game. She was on her way to beating me for the second time when you got here."

"I didn't know you could be bad at that game, but I somehow manage to lose every single time. Isla—"

"Daddy! Look!" Isla skips between us and cuts him off. She holds up the paper with her bright pink handprints. "Miss Pierce and Miss Allen helped us do our handprints! She said we will do one on the first day of school and one on the last day of school to see how big we get."

Lucas . . . Luke? Lucas? Luke takes the picture from her and raises it to his face. "Whose hands are these?"

"They're my hands!" Her giggles echo in the empty room.

"Your hands?" He looks closer at the picture. "No way. These hands are too big and you're still supposed to be my baby."

"I'm in kindergarten now, I'm not a baby anymore. Right, Miss Pierce?" Isla looks to me for backup that I'm more than happy to provide.

"She's definitely not a baby anymore. She even helped me pass out lunch boxes at the end of the day." I give Lucas another detail from her day. "And she did such a good job that I think her dad should take her for ice cream at Little Man to celebrate."

"Oh wow." Lucas shifts his focus back and forth between me and Isla. "She was that good of a worker? Little Man is a pretty special treat."

"I was that good, Daddy. I gave everyone their lunch boxes so fast that we were able to play a superspecial game before school was over."

As a teacher, it's very important that I support all my students' dreams for ice cream treats and puppy requests. "It's true."

"Well if Miss Pierce says it, then it must be true," he says, and I try not to snort at the irony of it all. "Why don't you put these handprints away so we can go celebrate."

"I can take the picture." I hold out my hand and take the picture from Isla. "You hurry and get your backpack, okay?"

"Okay!" she shouts over her shoulder, her little feet making quick work now that ice cream is involved.

"Little Man Ice Cream?" Lucas whispers as we watch her go. "You couldn't have said McDonald's?"

"Only the best for my students." I grin just before a still running Isla zooms right past her dad and straight into me.

"Bye, Miss Pierce." She wraps her tiny little arms around me and hugs me tight. "I had the best day ever."

"I had the best day too." I hug her back, her little voice melting my heart and solidifying my love for my job even more. "Let's do it again tomorrow, okay?"

She nods, letting me go and taking her dad's hand in hers. They walk to the classroom door, and Lucas pulls it open for Isla before he turns to me. "Thanks for giving my girl the best first day."

He doesn't wait for a response, which is probably a good thing since, for the second time this afternoon, he's rendered me speechless.

Not seconds later, the door swings back open, and I'm embarrassed at the way I nearly fall to my knees with disappointment when Keisha fills my doorway instead of Luke.

"Oh my god." She whistles, leaning her head back into the hallway to no doubt appreciate the view of watching Lucas leave. "Is that one of the parents in your class? He's so fucking hot."

"Oh, Keisha." I collapse into the new-to-me aerodynamic

chair Nora rolled into my room before school started this morning. "Do I have a first-day story for you."

I don't have to say more before Keisha is seated, ready for the piping hot tea my life just won't stop providing.

Every school year is new and exciting, but I can say without hesitation that this is the first time I feel well and truly fucked.

Literally.

EVEN THOUGH I do enjoy the occasional to frequent old fashioned and I was known to dabble with the wacky tobacky a time or two back in college, I'm pretty staunchly anti-drugs these days. A position I waver on one day a year, every year, since I began teaching: back-to-school night.

And for some totally unknown, not at all Lucas-related reason, I'm more nervous this year than ever before.

"Are you sure it looks okay?" I straighten out the piles of the information packets I spent all last night assembling and triple-check to make sure the beginner reader books I bought for each student are placed neatly in front of the name plates on their desks.

"It looks amazing," Keisha says way too fast.

I throw my hands in the air. "You didn't even look!"

"I've looked a hundred times." She grabs a cheese cube off of the tray I ordered from the grocery store. "It looks great and you have a cheese tray and juice. They're going to love it. Do you want to know what my parents are getting?"

"If you say you got the dessert tray I wanted, I'm going to lose my mind." That thing was like a hundred dollars, and as much as I wanted to impress my parents with my snack options, I couldn't swing it.

"Emerson, my love, please be so for real." Her body shakes with laughter, but I don't see what's so funny. Back-to-school night is for anxiety, not fun! "My parents are getting a warning."

"A warning?" My eyebrows scrunch together, and I can feel my forehead wrinkles deepen. Note to self, ask Nora which Petunia Lemon product to use for that.

"A warning. Multiple warnings, actually." She holds up her hand and begins to tick off her fingers. "Don't email me about paint on their clothing. Don't call me because you saw an idea for an art project on Pinterest. Don't reach out because I made your kid read a book about art instead of doing art one day. I don't want to hear it. I'm not spending hours of my time answering unnecessary emails."

It's only the second week of school, and I already have an inbox full of emails from parents. I haven't been able to get through them all, but from what I can tell, they range from sight word concerns and dietary needs to recess updates and carpool line protocol.

"Stop it!" I don't know if I'm horrified or in awe of her. "Do you really tell them that?"

"Of course I do." She sits in one of the kindergarten-sized chairs, and it makes her already long legs look even longer. "I try to be nice about it, but I also remind them that I am the only art teacher for almost five hundred students. It's my goal to teach their children the skills, technique, and history they need to learn while also making them excited about their craft and proud of their work. It's not my job to follow the whims of social media trends or tend to their laundry concerns. If we get this out of the way now, it makes the year much more enjoyable for all of us. You should try it."

And throw away years of pushing my feelings to the side in order to avoid any and all conflict? Who does she think I am? Some kind of quitter?

"Forthright and direct communication? Like a professional adult?" I scoff at the idea. "I think I'll pass."

"You do you, boo." She raises her cup of sparkling grape juice and toasts the air in front of her. "Just don't come crying to me when you're stressed and inundated with parent phone calls about how little Johnny came home singing about dinosaurs which is in direct opposition to their religious beliefs."

Confide in your friend one time about the kid who was almost pulled out of your class because of a dinosaur lesson and she holds it over your head forever.

"That was *one* time! And his name wasn't even Johnny. It was . . ." I close my eyes, searching the furthest corners of my brain to try and remember. "It's on the tip of my tongue."

What was it? He was in my class three years ago, and even though I remember his shaggy brown hair and the red sneakers he wore every day, I can't for the life of me remember his name.

"Jacob? Johnathon? Jasper?" I list out names. This is going to make me crazy. "Elijah?"

"Lucas!" Keisha, the comedian, shouts.

"Oh god no. Could you imagine?" I laugh at the thought.

"What kind of kid is named Lucas anyway? He probably came out of the womb a grumpy, middle-aged man."

"My mom did say I was grumpy, but I'm pretty sure I was still a baby," a deep voice says from right behind me. "And the name is growing rapidly in popularity. You'll probably have quite a few kids named Lucas in a few years. "

My eyes snap open, and I spin around in my chair. My knees crash against my desk, slamming into it with such force that my Stanley cup—which a parent bought for me, no way am I dropping that much money to drink water—tips over and spills all over the packets that were, at one point, stacked nicely.

Of fucking course. I don't know what it is, but whenever Luke enters my orbit, chaos follows. He's like my own personal Mercury retrograde.

I snatch my Stanley off of the table and set it on the floor beneath my desk.

"No, no, no!" I grab the packets that managed to stay dry and toss them onto an empty desk before rushing to save the rest from complete destruction. But when I turn around to rescue them, I stop dead in my tracks when I see that Luke has beaten me to the punch.

"Grab a few more paper towels, please." He glances up from the mess in front of him. "They aren't too wet, I think we'll be able to salvage them."

"We"? Am I part of a we with Luke?

No! This is absolutely not the time to go there. I bought and set up a printer in my apartment to avoid getting yelled at for hogging the school printer. I went through two ink cartridges so parents would have all of the paperwork and resources they need for the school year. I absolutely refuse to let that go to waste.

Keisha runs back into the room waving the blow dryer she uses to dry the water paint art the little kids always get a little too carried away with. "I have a blow dryer!"

I didn't even realize she left the freaking room! I'm grateful for her quick reflexes, but I'm even more annoyed that the moment Luke appears, the rest of the world seems to fall away. I don't even want to notice him, let alone be consumed by his presence.

"You're the best." I plug it into the extension cord beneath my desk and turn it to low; the warm heat makes quick work of the waterlogged papers.

I try to remain calm, but Luke is too close. He holds down the papers on my desk while I aim the blow dryer at them. His cologne invades my personal space, and unbidden memories of our evening together spring to the front of my mind. His large body bumps into mine as we try to avoid this crisis and sends my body into overdrive. My brain remembers the bad, but my body can't seem to forget the good.

The incredible.

"I'm going to go to my room to hang up a few more pictures," Keisha shouts over the blow dryer, her eyes flickering back and forth between me and Luke. "Are you going to be okay?"

NO!

"Of course. Go." I wave her away with my free hand. "I'll bring this back to your room at the end of the night."

I can tell she doesn't believe me—which, good! I'm clearly

lying through my fucking teeth—but after some hesitation, she nods and goes.

Leaving me alone.

With Luke.

Again.

The gentle whirring of the blow dryer masks the awkward silence as we work in tandem, me drying the papers and Luke placing them beneath the kids' encyclopedia to keep them flat, until we're finished. Crisis successfully averted.

I collapse into my desk chair and wipe the beads of sweat from my forehead. I can only imagine what I look like, but I'm sure the slicked-back ponytail I worked on for much longer than I'd like to admit is completely ruined. Luke, on the other hand, has never looked more put together. His thick hair is smoothed back, and he's wearing a suit that fits him so well it has to be custom. He tucks his hands into his pockets and shifts on his brown leather derby shoes. I know I need to thank him, but the words taste like acid rising from the back of my throat.

"Thanks for helping." I'm being sincere, but even I can hear how false the words ring.

"You're welcome." He smirks, a knowing gleam sparkling in his emerald eyes. "How much did you hate saying that?"

I consider lying just to shut him up, but on principle, I try to be as honest as possible. I'm not saying I don't lie on occasion, but I save those for hard and important topics, like why I have to leave an event early or the quarterly "sick" day I take. No way am I staining my soul to protect Lucas "Luke" Miller's feelings.

"A lot." I don't even attempt to soften the blow. "You helped, but it was the least you could do since it was basically your fault to begin with."

"My fault?" His shocked laughter explodes like a gunshot in the empty room. "How? Because I heard you talking shit about me? Very unprofessional, by the way."

"Oh please! Your entire career is basically glorified shit-talking." I lean back in my chair and cross my legs, hoping I look much less bothered than I feel. "And if you would've arrived on time like a normal parent, you would've never heard my tiny little joke at your expense."

He shrugs, completely—and irritatingly—unfazed by me. "Fifteen minutes early is on time and on time is late."

"Yuck. Don't quote Lombardi to me." I stick my tongue out like I'm gagging. "Number one, I'm not your employee, so that doesn't apply to me. Number two, no Pack no. We don't do Packer references in this classroom."

Also, that's a stupid rule. I'm sure this is what the internet would call a hot take, but I think showing up thirty minutes early is light-years ruder than arriving thirty minutes late. I don't need the pressure of trying to guess when someone is going to show up. If I tell you a time, that's the time. But I'm not surprised that the Sir Knows-It-All standing in front of me would go by his own rules.

"I thought you said you didn't do sports," he says, missing—or more likely ignoring—my point.

I don't know what pisses me off more: the willful obtuseness leaving his gorgeous mouth, him forcing me to think about the time we spent in that hotel room, or even worse, knowing that he still remembers everything . . . even the offhand comment I made before things went up in flames.

"I never said I didn't do sports. I love sports. What I said was I hoped you weren't a sportswriter, because sports people annoy me." I should stop there. A mature person would stop there. "Even though it seems like you can accomplish that anyway."

I can't help it. He brings out the worst in me.

"Oh." He nods slowly, and I can see the wheels turning in his mind. Like I'm a puzzle he's determined to put together. "Then what's your problem with the Packers?"

"Dear lord." I throw my head back and groan. I guess persistence and an all-around sense of nosiness is a professional hazard of being a journalist, I just never realized how irritating that could be until now. "I thought you didn't like me. Why do you care?"

"I was just making conversation." He raises his hands in front of his chest like he's warding off a wild animal, which only serves to piss me off that much more. "I didn't realize the Packers would be such a sensitive subject."

"It's not," I snap, using one of my precious lies because it absolutely is a sensitive subject. I'm sure this conversation would already be over if I just told him my dad was a Bears fan, and call me stubborn if you want, but I've already given this man so much. I refuse to give him another piece of me, no matter how small it may seem. "I just don't understand why you think anything personal should be up for discussion. I'm your daughter's teacher, not your friend."

Not to mention the fact that he's made it abundantly clear that he doesn't like, respect, or trust me. Why he would think I'd open up to him is beyond me.

"You're right." He steps away, his voice gentle—maybe even apologetic—and his eyes more puppy dog than infuriating sex god. "Sorry for asking."

Just as fast as the anger came, it goes. An unwelcome rush of guilt hits me like a freight train. He didn't know he was stepping into the dead dad danger zone, and I guess if I'm going to demand a professional relationship from him, I should probably not call him annoying (to his face) and snap at him every time he focuses his stupid, sexy AF eyes on me.

This would be so much easier if he was a monster who was terrible in bed.

I close my eyes and take a deep breath, bracing for the searing pain that comes from apologizing to someone you hate. But before I can even exhale, the classroom door swings open and another two parents arrive.

Oh no.

How disappointing.

"Welcome!" I greet the couple with what some might consider too much enthusiasm. I recognize the woman, but this is my first time seeing the man she's with. "So nice to see you again, Mrs. Anderson. Thank you for coming tonight."

She introduces me to her husband, who happens to be the spitting image of their son, and I show them around the classroom. I walk them through the different stations set up in the room, point out the reading corner and explain the different sections of books based on reading levels, and show them to

Ethan's desk. And I do it all with a smile, ignoring the searing pain as the green eyes I've spent weeks dreaming about burn a hole into the back of my head.

I guess I'll just have to apologize another time . . . or never. Whichever comes last.

THEY SAY FORTUNE favors the bold.

I don't know if it's true, but if it is, I must not be bold.

Because I'm definitely not favored.

"Please." I cross my fingers and close my eyes, praying to the Honda gods that have served me so well over the years to come through just one more time. "If you turn on, I promise I will get you that oil change you've been asking for."

Okay, so, sure. I guess one could possibly say that I should've seen this coming.

I mean, has my oil light been on for about two . . . or five months? Yes. Have I also forgotten to turn off the overhead light a couple dozen times because I lost my phone? Also yes.

But these things happen.

And really, if anything, this speaks to a much larger manufacturing problem. We were supposed to be in flying cars by now! How have they not at least figured out how to make cars that don't need an oil change every three months?

That's absurd.

I'm a woman on the go, I don't have time for this nonsense.

Actually, when I think about it, this is really Elon Musk's fault. I bet if he actually tried to solve problems instead of spending billions to destroy democracy and the social media platform formerly known as Twitter, this wouldn't be an issue.

And don't even get me started on Bezos.

I hold my breath and twist the key in the ignition one more time, hoping for a miracle, but knowing it's not going to come.

Click click click.

I hit my steering wheel, and the little beep of my horn blares in the empty parking lot with every furious punch. I only stop when my knuckles begin to ache.

"Okay, Emerson." When it comes to panicking, on a scale of one to ten, I tend to land at about a 13.5. It never serves me well, but I know it will be exceptionally bad if I let myself spiral now. Freaking out in an elementary school parking lot won't get me home. I have to keep it together. "Calm down. You're alright, you just need to think."

Like any independent adult, all I want to do is call my mom. But she's on a three-week cruise with her boyfriend, and I refuse to put anything on her plate that will cause even the slightest amount of stress. If she finds out I'm stranded in a parking lot, there's a good chance she'll take control of the ship and steer it back stateside.

Instead, I open up my phone and scroll through my contacts, trying to find anyone who could help me get out of this situation of my own making. I know, without a single doubt, that Keisha would definitely come get me. But I also know that she left back-to-school night over an hour ago with plans of taking an edible or two before passing out on her couch while reruns of *The Bachelorette* provide her version of white noise. I could still try to call, but she's the heaviest sleeper I know when she's sober. There's no way she'll hear her phone after an evening of THC sleep therapy.

My phone is full of numbers, but as I pass over contact after contact, I still can't come up with one person to call. It's not that I don't have friends. I do. And if the amount of numbers saved in my phone proves anything, it's that I might have too many. The problem is I don't feel comfortable asking 99 percent of them for a favor. I'm sure they would do it, but in my relationships, I pride myself on being the giver. The thought of anyone seeing me as a taker makes my stomach churn and my neck sweat. But desperate times call for desperate measures, and since Nora is my sister in skincare now, she shouldn't mind doing this.

Right?

Plus, she only lives like ten minutes from the school, so it won't be too out of her way. I'll bring her sushi for lunch tomorrow . . . and maybe a bottle of wine.

My finger hovers over her name lighting up my phone screen. All I need to do is touch it, and all of my problems will be solved.

Just one little tap . . .

"Emerson?" Nora answers after the second ring, concern evident in her voice.

"Yeah, hi." My stomach curls up like a snake, twisting my nerves into knots. "I'm so sorry to bother you. I know you're probably exhausted after back-to-school night."

An easy assumption considering how absolutely knackered I am right now.

"You're never a bother. I'm just catching up on some *Housewives* on the couch," she says. "What's up? Is everything okay?"

"Yeah," I say without thinking. The nasty little habit of never being a nuisance kicks in even when I'm calling for help. "No, wait. I don't know why I said that. Everything isn't okay."

"What's wrong?" There's a sense of urgency in her voice, and the sound of women screeching at each other in the background disappears. For the first time since I put my keys in the ignition, I feel a sense of relief. I knew I could count on her. "Did something happen with your Petunia Lemon order? You're not backing out already, are you?"

"What? Petunia? No. It's . . ." I stumble over my words, almost forgetting why I called in the first place. "It's my car. It won't start."

"Oh, thank god." She lets out a relieved sigh, and the sound of angry housewives fills my phone again. "I already called customer service once today, I would not have been happy if I had to call them again."

"Ummm . . ." I'm rarely knocked speechless, but even I have no idea how to respond to that. "Yeah, that would've sucked."

Almost as much as being a single woman, alone in a parking lot with the sun beginning to set. I've watched my fair share of crime procedurals, and I'm pretty sure this is how almost all of them start.

"Tell me about it. They were about to get one very angry Nora followed up by a strongly worded email." That might not sound like a real threat coming from most people, but Nora does have quite the talent for writing intense emails and Yelp reviews. "Okay, sorry. Now what were you saying about your car?"

This call has gone so far left that I almost forget why I called in the first place, and all the courage I worked up to ask for help is long gone.

"It won't start." I rush the words before I chicken out and hang up and resign myself to hitchhiking home instead. "I'm still at school. I hate to bother you, but I was wondering if there was any way you could swing back to the school and help jump my car?"

There. I asked for help, and the world didn't end or catch on fire.

Not even a tiny bit.

"Oh my goodness, Emerson! I'm so sorry." Concern colors her words again and I feel a little guilty for the emotional rollercoaster I've sent her on tonight.

"No, please. Don't be sorry." I brush off her worry, not wanting to cause her any more stress than I already have. "This is totally my fault, I'm just so grateful you answered."

"You know I'll always answer for you," she says, and I can't wait to tell Keisha about this. One day I'll be able to convince her to give Nora a chance. "But—"

Wait . . .

Did she just say "but"?

My stomach turns to a pile of rocks.

"I just opened my email to respond to the fire department about updated safety procedures, and I had a really strong gin and tonic when I got home," she says. "Any other time I would come right away. Truly. Can I send you an Uber?"

"Oh my god. No." I try to laugh, but it sounds hollow and I'm afraid if I stay on too much longer, it will turn into tears. "I can order my own Uber."

I can, I just didn't want to.

"Are you sure?" she asks. "I'm so sorry."

"I'm sure and please don't be sorry. You're busy. I totally understand."

"You're the best. Please call me the second you get home," she says. "I won't be able to sleep if I don't know you're safe."

After we say our goodbyes, I stare out my front window, trying to figure out what in the actual world just happened and what to do next. I could just do what I told Nora I'd do and order an Uber. I don't live too far from here. It wouldn't be too expensive and at least I'd be home. But all that really means is when I wake up in the morning, not only will I still not have a solution, I won't have a way to work either. And that seems even worse than being stuck in a parking lot at night.

I drop my phone into the empty cup holder, lean back into my seat, and try my hardest not to cry. I think back to the YouTube meditations I did over the summer, inhaling through my nose, holding it for five seconds, and exhaling just as slow. And repeat.

Once I'm calm enough to think clearly, I reach across the center console and open my glove compartment. I grab the leather-bound binder where I keep my registration and car information. At one point in my adult life, I made good decisions, and I'm hoping with every fiber of my being that one of them was signing up for AAA.

I flip open the front binder and almost cry again . . . but tears of joy this time. I yank out my membership card like it's the golden wrapper sending me to the chocolate factory. I unlock my phone and go to the website listed on the card as fast as I can. My fingers dance across my screen, making quick work of entering my member number and login information. I watch the circle twirl while the website takes its sweet time loading, dreaming of being home in my bed and staying there until noon . . . or 6:00 am when my alarm goes off.

The page finally opens and my shoulders sag with relief.

But only for a second.

Because in bold, bright red font, I only see one thing:

Account not active. Click here to restart membership.

"No! Fucking fuck fuck!" I scream into the empty cab of my car and return to using my steering wheel as a punching bag. I usually try to keep my cursing to a minimum so I don't let it become a habit and accidentally drop f-bombs in front of a classroom full of mini mimics. But that's going to have to be a problem for future Emerson, because tonight calls for more than a few bad words. "Stupid, stupid! So fucking stupid."

I knew being an adult would be hard, but honestly? This is too much. I just wanted to eat ice cream for dinner, drink good whiskey, and watch R-rated movies.

The rest of it sucks.

Fresh out of ideas—and fucks—I grab my phone and open my Uber app. I just need to hurry up and get home before this day manages to get any worse.

If that's even possible.

"Hey, Miss Pierce," someone shouts from right outside of my window, nearly sending me through the roof.

I don't scare easily, but my scream is so high-pitched, I hurt my own ears. Unfortunately, when I see who's standing at my window, my groan is even louder.

"You have got to be kidding me."

Because of course, when I found myself in a moment where I didn't think I could sink any lower, Luke Miller is here to witness it.

· 10 ·

"WHAT ARE YOU doing out here?" Luke leans forward and cups his giant hands around his eyes, I guess so he can get a closer look at my despair.

This is my karma. I should've known better.

I thought I had reached the limit of my rock bottom, but just like Lindsay Lohan tried to warn us, the limit does not exist.

Back-to-school night went too well and I got cocky. I forgot just how much the universe loves to humble me. But at least looking at it that way, I can see that as far as cosmic punishment goes, this could be much worse. Luke might be an asshole, but at least he's not a murderer.

Or . . . at least I hope.

The jury's still out on that though.

"Oh, you know"—I open the door since I can't roll down my windows—"just enjoying a quiet night sitting in my car, taking in the view of Nester Fox Elementary."

His eyebrows knit together, and he stares at me much like he did after he found out I joined Petunia Lemon. "Enjoying a quiet night? Taking in the view of Nester Fox?"

"Yes." I stare back at him, hoping he loses interest. The sun might be setting and I might have no way home, but I could be going on day three with no water and even that wouldn't be enough for me to let Luke know I was in trouble.

"Yes?" he repeats after me again.

"Yes!" I throw my hands up in the air. "Are you just going to stand there repeating everything I say?"

"If that's what it takes for you to tell me why you're sitting alone in the parking lot, beating the shit out of your steering wheel and turning the parking lot into a one-man symphony." He straightens to his full height, and tragically, I feel it between my thighs. "Then yes, I am."

I try to keep up my grumpy exterior, but inside I'm not only thrilled that I'm not stranded and alone anymore, but I'm also extremely turned on. "I don't understand how someone as annoying as you can have such a great kid."

"I don't know either." He opens my car door wider and gestures for me to get out. I don't want to follow orders, but my body is still under his spell and reacts without my approval. "My mom is pretty great though. I think it might skip a generation."

"That must be it," I agree, biting back my smile, because even though he's not saying it outright, I can read between the lines. And what he's saying is that if Isla doesn't get it from him, she's definitely not getting it from her mom.

I met his ex-wife, Jacqueline, on the first day of school, but I had the chance to really experience her tonight.

And what an experience it was.

She was so loud, constantly interrupting the presentation with questions that I had either already answered or didn't relate to the topic at hand at all. I don't have any proof, but I'm willing to bet that her rose-gold water bottle was filled with wine. She also called me Miss Pearson all night. I corrected her three times before I gave up altogether. And while all of that was entertaining, the crème de la crème came when she hit on the dad sitting next to her . . . despite her ex-husband being in the room and the man's wife sitting next to him.

When Luke stood up and quietly asked her to join him in the hallway, the other parents erupted into applause.

It was a secondhand embarrassment unlike anything I've ever experienced before, and even though I'm excited to have another story to tell at parties, I hope it's a night that never repeats itself. I can still feel the cringe lingering in my bones.

"So what's going on with your car?" He folds into my driver's seat, sliding it back so he can stretch his long legs. "Do you have issues with it often?"

"Never." I shake my head. "My girl's a Honda. She's been my reliable companion for over a decade."

He twists the key in the ignition, and the *click click click* that's been tormenting me cuts through the air.

A part of me that I will never publicly acknowledge is thrilled. I know firsthand how good he is at turning someone on, but I would've taken it very personally if my car started for him but not me.

"That's what she's been doing for me," I tell him. "She did it yesterday too, but then she started just fine. So I thought maybe it was just like a cold or something. But do you think it's more serious?"

I'm trying my hardest to keep my feelings locked on the inside, but the longer I sit idle in the parking lot, the more they start seeping through my panic-sized cracks. This cannot be serious because there's no world where I can afford a new car right now. I already struggle with my insurance and the ever-rising cost of gas. The thought of adding a car payment to my staggering monthly bill lineup is straight up debilitating.

"It did this yesterday and you thought"—he pauses as if he needs a moment to process my words—"it had a cold?"

"Well yeah." I shrug, not quite understanding what he's not understanding. "You know how sometimes your car will act funny and then they're fine later that day? She has days like that all the time, but she always gets better."

"You're fucking with me, right?" Hope and disbelief color his words. "Please tell me you're joking."

I shake my head, unclear on what the joke would be.

"Why would I be joking?"

"Jesus, Emerson." He closes his eyes and drags a hand across his face. "How are you so smart and so naive at the same time?"

"What can I say?" I smirk, knowing it's as much an insult as it is a compliment, but ignoring it since he's my only chance of getting my car to start. "It's a gift."

"It's something, alright."

He shakes his head once more before he leans over and runs his hand beneath the steering wheel. I'm not sure what he's doing until he finds a lever and pops open the hood of my car.

I move to the side as he climbs out and then try to keep my

jaw from hitting the floor when he pulls off his suit jacket and unbuttons his cuffs, rolling them up to expose his forearms. It's truly the most innocent, nonsexual thing in the entire world, but it feels like something out of my X-rated fantasies. There is something so overtly sexual about a man's bare forearms that just a glimpse causes heat to flood my cheeks.

"What do you think it is?" I don't want to think of all of the worst-case scenarios that could potentially shove me off the cliff and into the ocean of financial ruin, but life-ruining news might be the only thing able to keep my eyes on his face and my mind from drifting to our night together. "My mom needed to get a new engine in her car last year, and it cost more than this car is worth. Brakes too, but I don't think brakes would make it not start. Right?"

I wish I could say rambling was a nervous tendency of mine, but it's not. It's just a tendency. I think it's one of the reasons I work so well with kindergartners. We have the same winding, flowery storytelling techniques.

Instead of answering any of my multiple questions, he ignores me altogether and bends down to take a closer look under the hood. While he's doing that, I take a closer look at his trunk. I can't help myself! He's so hot and the last time I saw that ass, it was naked and covered in scratches from my nails.

He has to be doing this on purpose.

He's pretending to be some great guy, worried about my well-being, but I already know he doesn't like me. What if this is some kind of ploy to catch a woman off guard and lure her to his bed? He could be the person who tampered with my car!

"It looks like your battery is dead and . . . fuck, Emerson." His deep voice pulls me out of my conspiracy spiral. "When's the last time you got an oil change?"

Oh.

That tracks.

Maybe I should lay off of the true crime podcasts a little bit.

"Ummm . . ." I try to think back to the last time my mom visited. She brought her new boyfriend, Stephen, who tried to win my approval by taking my car for a tune-up and then got it detailed. He did win my approval, but it had nothing to do with my car and everything to do with my mom's smile. "I think about eight months ago? No. That's wrong. Probably closer to nine."

"So a year?"

"Most likely." I nod, not ashamed even though I know I should be. "Good to know that you're as skilled in girl math as you are in car maintenance."

"My marriage taught me a lot of things." There's laughter in his voice, but it doesn't hide the sadness lingering behind it. "Math and maintenance were just a couple of them."

"So . . ." As a certified yapper, I'm usually great at filling the silence and making a tense situation lighter. But for some reason, I don't know what to say to my former one-night stand, who happens to be my current student's dad, about his completely whacked ex-wife. Shocking, I know. "What were you doing here anyways?"

Back-to-school night was over an hour before I got to my car.

"Jacqueline wasn't her best self so I drove her home . . . to her home." He leaves a lot of room for me to read between the lines and I do. I knew there wasn't water in her cup. "It was her night with Isla so I stayed a little while and had dinner with her and Jacqueline's mom. I was walking back to my car when I heard your impressive horn work and figured I'd be a Good Samaritan."

"Not the best night for either of us, but I guess I should consider myself lucky." I think we're both surprised by the sincerity in my voice. "Thanks for stopping."

He grunts in response, and I take that as my cue to shut up. He tinkers around for a few more minutes, twisting and lifting things while huffing out a profanity or two. I, on the other hand, study the cracks decorating the parking lot pavement and anything else that will keep my eyes off of his ass . . . and forearms . . . and hair. Anything that will keep them off of Luke, period.

By the time he finishes checking things out, the Colorado sun has long since set. The cool evening breeze is a welcome reprieve from the unforgiving sun in the Mile High City. Crickets chirp in the quiet neighborhood and only stop to let the sound of the occasional engine passing by taunt me.

"I'm not a mechanic, but for at least tonight, I can jump your car and that should get you home," he says, and I can't help it, I damn near knock him over with how hard I hug him.

"Oh my god." I tighten my arms around him, not caring one bit if this is inappropriate or not. I get to go home, and I didn't even have to pay for a mechanic, tow truck, or Uber. "Thank you so much!"

Who needs a knight in shining armor when you can have a DILF in a well-tailored suit with basic car knowledge? Armor and a horse aren't going to do shit for me; from here on out, I'll take a man working under my hood any day of the week.

"You didn't let me finish," he says, and even though this doesn't bode well for me, it's almost impossible to refrain from shouting *that's what she said* in the dark, empty parking lot. "I can jump your car and it will get you home, but it's very likely that you'll have this problem in the morning."

Drat. I knew it was too good to be true.

"Okay, so what do you suggest I do?"

At this point, I'll do whatever he says if it means I get to go home sooner than later, but I can tell that my lack of sarcasm and willingness to listen catches him off guard.

"I think we should jump your car and I'll follow you to Auto-Zone. You can get a new car battery and I'll install it for you, that way you don't have to think about it and only need to focus on getting an oil change."

It's not lost on me how much work this is to do for anyone, let alone a former fling who you're not on great terms with. "You'd do that for me?"

"I'd do it for Isla," he says matter-of-factly. "She was really nervous about school and for some reason I can only partly understand, she really loves you. If I can do something that ensures you're at school tomorrow, I'm going to do it."

Oh . . . duh.

Of course this is about Isla. Why would it be about anything else?

"Well, the kindergartners of Nester Fox Elementary thank you for your service." The familiar burn of humiliation that only Luke seems to provide is making it hard to breathe. My forced smile falters on my face as I throw open my car door. "I'll have to come up with something to repay you."

"I'm sure you'll find a very creative way to pay me back."

The double entendre is unmistakable and my mind goes to a place I try to reserve for late nights and my bedroom. "I am very talented at payback."

"I don't doubt that for a second." His quiet laughter washes over me, and I hate the way it makes my body tingle. "But if you need ideas, I do love Isla's handprint crafts and my new place is severely lacking art. Or . . ." He pauses, and I can almost see his mind working a million miles per minute. "Never mind."

"Oh no you don't." I shouldn't care what he's thinking, but for some absurd reason, I do. And I care a lot. "What were you going to say?"

"Nothing." He kicks an imaginary piece of dirt on the ground. "It was stupid."

"No way. Tell me what you were going to say or else I'll . . ." Or else I'll do what? Let him go home while I fix my own damn car? "I don't know what I'll do, but I promise you won't like it."

As far as threats go, it's not my best work, but it's all I have.

"You're going to say no. We should leave, we don't want the store to close."

Oh. Leverage!

"Then you better hurry up and tell me so we can get going." I lean against the car door and cross my arms across my chest. I am an unmovable force. "Plus, if you already know I'm going to say no, then what's the worst that could happen?"

He mutters something beneath his breath, and it sounds a lot like "this is what I get for doing a good deed." As a teacher, I can confirm, there are rewards for being a good person. But, whenever I look at the internet, it seems the opposite is true and if I wanted anything nice in my life, I should've been a villain.

"Fine, but when I ask, you can only say no," he forewarns. "You can't yell at me."

Omg.

Is he going to ask for sex?!

And if he did, would I yell or take a moment to deeply consider it?

"Fine, no yelling." I agree to his terms . . . kind of hoping it's about sex. "Now tell me."

I expect him to look down, maybe even whisper as he tells me.

What I don't expect is him looking me straight in the eyes, his deep voice not wavering as he asks me the last thing I ever expected.

"I need help with my article," he says. "I know you said you're happy and I'm not asking you to quit or anything. But I'd love to hear about your experiences, good and bad, with Petunia Lemon. What draws you in, any red flags you might see."

Wait . . . What? There's no way I'm hearing this right.

"You want me to be a spy?"

Welp. He was right. This *was* a stupid idea, and I *am* going to say no.

He's lucky I take my promises seriously—and that my safety and well-being is currently resting in his very capable hands—because I might've screamed.

"Not exactly." He's so calm in the face of foolishness, and for some reason I find it as reassuring as I do infuriating. "If I remember correctly, after you read my article, you called it a hack job. And even though that was very harsh, some of your criticism wasn't wrong. My article was unbalanced and too personal. Having your opinion would be helpful."

I don't want to think of Luke as a reasonable, thoughtful, hot person and unfortunately, the more time I spend around him, the less I hate him.

"I can't." I hope I sound more resolute than I feel. "I'm glad you're doing this, but I don't think I should be the person you do it with. Things are already a little complicated with me being Isla's teacher and you know . . . what happened downtown. I'm not sure it'd be a good idea to add something else."

"No, you're right." He takes a giant step away from me, like just being this close to me could cause problems. "I told you, it was a stupid idea."

It's like a switch goes off inside of him and the helpful, easygoing guy vanishes into thin air. His back is ramrod straight, and you don't need to be an expert on body language to know he wants to hurry up and be finished with me.

My feet itch to follow him to the front of my car and offer to help, but I don't. The faster we can get this over with, the better. I sit in my car and adjust the seat so there's no more evidence of his long, strong body in there. And by the time he finally gets my car to start and I follow him to the auto store, I've talked some sense into myself.

Whatever happened tonight was nice, but it was just two adults acting like adults. Nothing more. We've had our problems with each other, but maybe after tonight we can both put our pettiness aside. He can see me as his daughter's teacher, and I can view him as just another parent in my class and not the jack-ass supreme of the universe.

Cordial adults and nothing more.

No matter how hot he is.

And on the plus side, now I don't have to feel guilty when I lie about the oil change that I'm absolutely never going to get.

11

I'M NOT LYING when I say the first week of school is my favorite time of the year.

I'm also not lying when I say the second week turns me into a zombie sloth who needs a month and a half of recovery.

By the time the bell rings on Friday afternoon, I feel like I've been hit by a bus. My feet are killing me, my head feels like it's been slammed with a hammer, and the first signs of the back-to-school sniffles are setting in. Knowing my bank account is two hundred dollars lighter from having to buy a new car battery doesn't help foster a sunny disposition either.

This has been the longest week in the history of weeks. All I want to do is climb into my bed, hide under my covers, and stay there until Monday morning.

And yet, that's exactly what I'm *not* doing.

I guess if there is one perk to tonight, it's that at least I know a Petunia Lemon meeting is the one place I can be sure to be safe from Luke's annoying, gorgeous face since I seem to see him everywhere else. I thought after we went our separate ways after back-to-school night that I'd be able to pretend the incident in the parking lot never happened. Instead, I can't get him out of my head. What if I said yes to working with him? What would spending time with him be like? Could Petunia Lemon be as bad as he says it is?

It's like he cast some kind of spell on me and now everything reminds me of him.

"A week of matcha lattes wasn't enough." Keisha groans from my passenger seat and snaps my attention back to her. "I should've asked for a hundred dollars and your firstborn."

"It's a good thing you're not dramatic or anything." I keep my eyes on the road, but I don't need to look at her to know she's rolling her eyes. "It's not going to be that bad."

"You're right," she says. "It's going to be worse."

Now I'm the one rolling my eyes.

"Oh no." She shoves my shoulder, more worried about revenge than our safety on the road. "You don't get to roll your eyes. You're the reason we're in this mess. I've been saying no to Nora for years, then here you come roping us both into this shit that we don't need and can't afford."

"You know you didn't have to come, right?" It's not like I made her sign a blood oath or anything. "I'd rather you stay home if you're going to go in there tonight talking crazy."

"Me? Talk crazy?" Her attempts to sound innocent fall on unconvinced ears. "I would never."

"You would never?" I don't even try to hide my disbelief. This woman has more audacity in her pinky than most people have in their entire bodies. "So it wasn't you who demanded a full PowerPoint before you let that one woman take you to the mountains? And didn't you break up with a man once because he showed up to your date in flip-flops and a tank top?"

"We were at an art gallery opening, not flying to Cancun!" she shouts much too loudly for my little sedan. "Who wears a ratty tank top and has their toes out at an art gallery opening?"

"Maybe he didn't know the dress code?" I try to play devil's advocate but she's not wrong. I just need to prove a point and I can't give in that easily.

"Hello? 9-1-1?" She fakes a phone call. "Can someone patch me through? The People Pleaser Patrol is on the loose again."

I come to a stop at a red light and turn all of my attention to her. "Oh, I'm sorry. Is this pretend emergency phone call supposed to be you proving that you don't talk crazy?"

"No, the phone call is me being witty and entertaining because I still don't know what you're talking about," she says. "Everything you've said just proves that I have strong standards and stronger boundaries. And you would never imply that a woman enforcing her boundaries makes her bitchy or unlikable, right?"

Dammit.

"I hate you."

And this is why one should never, ever attempt to debate with Keisha Allen. It's also why Nora was so quick to redirect her Petunia Lemon efforts onto me and stopped talking to Keisha about it entirely.

Maybe there is something to boundaries after all . . .

"You love me." She leans forward and turns up the volume knob on the radio. "Which is why you bribed me to join you tonight. We both know you need me or Nora is going to convince you to spend a small fortune that a single kindergarten teacher in her twenties absolutely cannot afford."

"But—"

"But nothing." She cuts me off. "I understand that you see potential in all of this and that's fine. You know I love your enthusiasm. It's really the only reason I haven't given up on the entire world already. But as your friend who loves your soft little heart and respects your empty pockets, someone has to hold you back."

"The products are just so cute though! They gave me a tote bag full of sample products at the convention and I can't even open some of them because I don't want to ruin their boxes."

My mom always says I'm a marketer's dream. It doesn't matter what's inside the packaging as long as I like the branding. I can't help it, I was born a sucker! I will fall for anything bright, colorful, and whimsical, and unfortunately for me and my willpower, Petunia Lemon products check all three.

Plus, even though I might be tired and yearning for my bed, it also gave me plans on a Friday night. Something I haven't had in years. It's so hard to make friends as an adult, and thanks to Petunia Lemon I've gained an entire community.

"All I'm saying is we're going to go and mingle. We'll say hi, eat some free snacks, and swipe a sample or two. But the second"—she leans in so close that I can feel her breath against my face—"and I mean the *second* they try to get you to buy a new product or recruit a new member, we're out of there. Making new friends shouldn't be contingent on how much money you can spend or how many people you know."

"Awwww . . . you love me so much." I turn down a crowded

street not too far away from our school and double-park on the street in front of the address Nora gave me. When the car is finally in park, I unbuckle my seat belt and throw my arms around my best friend. "If you're obsessed with me, just say that."

"Obviously I'm obsessed with you. If I wasn't, my ass would be on my couch, indulging in my Friday night herb, watching reruns of *Living Single* in peace and quiet." She tries to escape my ironclad grip around her shoulders. "Instead I'm spending the night in gentrified-ass West Highland, eating dry cheese and pretending to think that spending fifty dollars on face wash isn't fucking absurd."

Keisha is an enigma.

By day, she's this mild-mannered, matcha-drinking, yoga-loving art teacher. She's got these gorgeous, long dreads that are rarely, if ever, styled the same. She shops exclusively in thrift stores and has the best style of anyone I've ever seen outside of a magazine. She never eats red meat and has toyed around with veganism since I met her five years ago, but is terrified of any and all animals. She's all about her body being a temple while also being a loyal customer to the Flower Pot, her favorite dispensary. I've never heard her Spotify playlist play anything other than nineties gangster rap, and she says *fuck* more than any person I know. Standing at an impressive five feet eleven inches tall, she has the stature of a runway model, but she can still out-drink the manliest of men without batting an eye.

Basically, she's the absolute shit, and I have no idea how I conned her into being my very best friend. I do know that I'm forever grateful and have become approximately 149 percent cooler based on my proximity to her alone.

"Your sacrifices don't go unnoticed." I finally release her, but only because my strength burns out quickly and my arms are tired from squeezing her. "And for this, I shall express my gratitude by providing you with one more drink of your choice, to be given at any time, day or night."

"Night, please," she says like I wasn't already fully aware of her answer. "I know I'm going to need bourbon after a night like this."

"Deal!" This works well for me. I have a feeling I'm going to need spirits to lift my spirits too.

"Also, don't think that just because I've given you time to process, I've somehow forgotten that I left you with Hot Dad Lucas, aka your summer fuck, alone in your classroom on back-to-school night," she throws over her shoulder as she pushes my creaky car door open. "You've been acting weird as fuck, so I know something went down. This is your official warning that you have three days to give me a very detailed account of that night and your every interaction with him since or I will be forced to invoke friendship purgatory."

"I'll tell you whatever you want to know." Friendship purgatory is Keisha's version of the silent treatment, but fancier and more psychologically taxing. She makes plans with you and then pointedly ignores you during said plans. I've never experienced it, but I did witness it with her ex. It was brutal and I never want to be on the receiving end. "But there's really not much to tell. It's not like he's hanging out in the classroom, and Isla goes back and forth between him and her mom, so I don't see him every day."

I have been conducting a morning email with him and Isla's

mom, Jacqueline, to make sure we're all on the same page regarding the pickup schedule. Jacqueline always sends back a paragraph response that normally includes at least two insults pointed at Luke while he's never responded with more than two words and his professional signature of Lucas K. Miller.

If I still cared, I'd be dying to know what the *K* stands for.

"Hopefully that will change." Keisha wishes the absolute worst for me. "Maybe he'll sign up to be the class dad."

I lock my car doors even though I highly doubt that anyone wants the 2009 Honda Civic my mom passed down to me on my sixteenth birthday. I circle around the car, meeting her on the sidewalk in front of the Victorian bungalow sandwiched between the modern monstrosities developers are destroying this neighborhood with.

"Why would you put that evil on me?"

"Because." She shrugs. "Work gets boring and I need something juicy to motivate me. Plus, you said he was great in bed. This would be beneficial for both of us."

"Okay. New rule." I grab her arm, stopping her on the brick-paved walkway. Bees buzz about from the lavender bushes framing us, urging us to continue inside, but this takes precedence. "When we're around other people, especially work people, no talk of Luke slash Lucas and his prowess in the bedroom. The last thing I need is to be the topic of discussion in the group chat between the third-grade teachers. They're mean."

Each grade has their own communication network, but Amber, Jasmine, Brianna, and Rachel—the third-grade teachers—have a group chat that is particularly brutal. It's like they watched *Mean Girls* and thought, "Amateurs. We could be so much meaner," and set about proving it. If they found out I had sex with a parent, they'd run me out of the state. And I love Colorado!

"That would imply I'd want to have a conversation with a co-worker," she says, like I'm an idiot. "I don't like anyone besides you. Why on earth would I ever encourage them to speak to me?"

This is true. One of many perks to befriending a die-hard introvert.

"Sorry." I shake my head. "What was I thinking?"

"Was asking myself the same thing."

A few feet ahead of us, the turquoise front door that turns this house from cute to the most charming house in the entire world swings open and Nora appears in the doorway.

"Oh my goodness, is that Keisha Allen?" she shouts into the quiet evening. "Emmy, you're a miracle worker! I've been trying to get her here for years."

"Emmy?" Keisha repeats beneath her breath. "Gross."

"Be nice," I growl at Keisha through gritted teeth before aiming my frozen smile at Nora. "It's only because she loves me and I promised her there'd be food."

"And wine!" She yells what the slight slur in her voice has already hinted at.

"On second thought"—Keisha's hand latches on to mine and holds me in place—"I'm going to need two bourbons after this."

"You're so dramatic." I brush her off. "Tonight's going to be amazing. Just watch."

One could say optimism is my greatest strength.

No matter how misguided it is.

12

IF I TOLD *you so* were a person, its name would be Keisha Marie Allen.

The moment we walked into the house and Jacqueline Miller stepped around the corner to greet us, Keisha's forced smile transformed almost magically, and her brilliant, smug smile hasn't faded since. It's a look I'm all too familiar with and I know, without a shadow of doubt, she will hold tonight over my head until my final breath.

"Jacqueline, your house is so beautiful," Keisha says to Luke's ex-wife as we stand around the island in her newly remodeled kitchen, snacking on the impressive spread she laid out. "How long have you lived here?"

Without the Stanley full of Pinot, Jacqueline is like another person. She's much quieter and more reserved, almost to the point of being a snob. Not the bad kind of snobby though, the kind where you'd do anything, even join a skincare MLM, in hopes that you might impress her enough that she'll invite you into her inner circle.

"Oh you're so sweet, thank you so much." Jacqueline brings her hand to Keisha's shoulder and it's somehow as charming as it is condescending. "We've been here for about ten years. We were lucky enough to get into this neighborhood early. It's been wonderful to watch this community transform into something so gorgeous."

I bite back my laughter and almost choke on my wine as I watch Keisha battle her inner demons and try to come up with anything nice to say.

"Oh wow." Her words sound strangled . . . and I have a feeling that's what she's trying to avoid doing to Jacqueline right now. "This neighborhood has definitely changed over the years."

Like me, Keisha is also a Denver native. I lived on the southeast side of the city growing up, but Keisha was raised in this neighborhood. Her dad's family is from Georgia, but her mom's family all lived on the same street as her until they were priced out of the houses they called homes for decades. The developers that moved in have not only knocked down the homes that had been standing since the early 1900s, but they've bulldozed the history and community right alongside of it. Besides being a fantastic art teacher and independent artist, Keisha is on multiple boards and attends more city meetings than I knew possible. She does everything she can to preserve even an ounce of the community that raised her.

Poor Jacqueline has no idea that she just made an enemy for life. Because if there is one thing Keisha never tires of, it's holding a grudge. A talent I both respect and fear.

"Right? You should've seen it when we first moved." Jacqueline's already gorgeous smile grows to something that can only be described as straight up dazzling. "I wanted to move to Highland's Ranch, but my ex-husband wouldn't budge on being in the city and closer to his work. I don't like to give him credit for much, but he was able to look through all of the . . . *riffraff* and see the potential of this place."

Keisha's jaw ticks, and her long fingers tighten around the stem of her wine glass. I've watched enough episodes of *Real Housewives* to know it's time for me to intervene.

"So, Jacqueline!" I jump into the conversation before Keisha loses her shit and rips her to shreds. "How long have you been a part of Petunia Lemon?"

"Five years!" She doesn't even have to stop and think about it. "I joined right after Isla was born and never looked back. It's the best thing I've ever done for myself."

"Because she met all of us!" Nora pulls Jacqueline in for a hug and elbows her way into the conversation. She's had three martinis since Keisha and I arrived, and it's really starting to show. "Empowered now—"

"And sisters in skincare forever!" Jacqueline and the rest of the women chant in unison. The knee-jerk, conditioned response is as alarming as it is impressive, and it sends me straight back to the pews of my Catholic-school days.

I look at Keisha, and I have to imagine we're both wearing matching *what the fuck* expressions because actually . . . what the fuck?

"It's our little Petunia Lemon chant." Nora explains what we most certainly didn't ask. "You'll catch on quick."

I think I'm going to have to pass on that one.

"Speaking of sisters, Keisha was telling me Anna is in Petunia

Lemon too." I take a sip of my wine, waiting for the buzz to hit. "Is she coming tonight?"

"Oh god no," Nora scoffs. "She just wasn't cut out for this. You need to have a personality for this business and she was too quiet. It didn't work."

The buzz I'm waiting for must've found Nora instead because wow. That was kind of mean!

"You have to want to be sisters to make this work. Anna was nice, but she kept a distance between us that didn't go over well." Jacqueline tries to soften the knockout punch Nora just laid out. "When I was going through my divorce, these women never left my side. We really are sisters and I honestly don't even know if I would've been strong enough to file without them. They were the ones who convinced me that I deserved better and Isla deserved to grow up watching her mom being the ultimate girlboss who never folded to what a man has to say."

An image of Luke bent over my car, replacing my car battery, flashes into my mind, and I have to work overtime to push it away. I'm familiar with being in awkward situations, but standing in the kitchen of a student's parent and listening to them talk about their ex who not only fixed my car, but gave me the best orgasms of my life is a level of awkward I didn't even know existed.

But besides her ex-husband's ass and my immediate aversion to the term "girlboss," I have to admit that it's really nice to hear someone talk about this side of Petunia Lemon.

I signed up to sell the products, but I'd be lying if I said the bigger draw wasn't seeing how much fun the women at the convention were having. Gathered in the kitchen and knowing how much they support one another only confirms that I made the right decision when I signed up.

I'm so busy with work and trying to stay afloat that I've let my friendships suffer over the years. It's hard to forge meaningful relationships when you aren't sure if you're going to be able to pay your bills. The stress that has been building over these last few years has reached critical levels recently, and I'm not sure how much longer I can do it alone. And I love Keisha too much to lay all of my problems at her feet.

"Cheers to that!" Nora lifts her fourth martini in the air. "Lucas might be hot, but he's such an asshole."

At least that's a sentiment I can agree with.

"I know." Jacqueline rolls her crystal blue eyes to the back of her head. "He thinks he's so much better and smarter than everyone because he went to Yale and wrote for the *New York Times*."

"He worked for the *New York Times*?" I hate that I can't stop myself from asking.

I hate it even more that I'm impressed.

"Barely." Jacqueline plops a cheese cube in her mouth. She's been standing in the kitchen all night, but it's the first thing I've seen her eat. "He was offered a job straight out of college, but we were only there for a year before I told him I couldn't do it anymore and if he wanted kids, we had to leave that awful city."

I never want to stick up for a man, especially Luke, but I can't say I'm on her side here. Getting a job offer at a place like the *New York Times* straight out of college isn't just a big deal, it's huge. But keeping my mouth shut seems like the right choice for a multitude of reasons. Jacqueline's forehead hasn't moved since we arrived, but when it comes to Luke, disdain is written all over her face and there's no way I'm getting involved in whatever went down between the two of them.

"I'll never get over the audacity of that man trying to get you to stop doing Petunia Lemon after seeing how well you did," a woman whose name I already forgot says. "Some men just can't handle having a wife who is more successful than they are."

"Exactly!" Alyssa, one of the women I met at the convention, shouts. "This is why sisters in skincare are forever, even when husbands aren't."

"We even have the tattoos to prove it!" someone else yells from across the island.

Without warning, almost every woman in the room turns their wrist over and reveals an infinity sign tattoo with the letters SIS woven into the symbol. I grab Nora's wrist to take a closer look at the tattoo that I've somehow never noticed before.

"What's sis?" I ask, not sure I even want to know. I've watched enough true crime cult documentaries to be more than a little concerned.

"S-I-S, sisters in skincare," she explains like this is a totally reasonable, and not at all shocking, thing to have permanently etched onto your skin. "Once we make it to the Pink Petunia level, we all get the same tattoo. Then for every level you reach after that, you go back and add a little petunia around it!"

"Wow!" Words have temporarily escaped my brain. "That's . . . That's something."

"I'm just so sorry you have to deal with Lucas, he's so condescending." Jacqueline takes my—tattoo free—hand and turns everyone's attention back to her. "Please know that you can always email me if any issues with Isla arise, even if it's not my day with her. If anyone understands how difficult it can be to communicate with Lucas, it's me. I mean, I still can't believe he forgot my girl on her first day!"

Horrified gasps ring out around me, and my skin itches with how uncomfortable I am.

"Thank you, that's very kind of you to offer," I say, not sure how to navigate this situation. Luke might not be my favorite person in the world, but we've already made some progress, and getting involved in this conversation with Jacqueline—in front of Nora, no less—feels like it would not only be a disservice to me and Luke, but to Isla too. Which is something I refuse to do. "And don't be too hard on him about the first day of school. Mistakes happen, but Isla is a great girl and it's obvious that you're both wonderful parents."

I thought I sounded fair and diplomatic, but if the sourpuss look on her face is anything to go by, it wasn't the response she was looking for. As much as I'd like to backtrack and jump on the "fuck Lucas" train, a train that, not too long ago, I was the conductor of, I stand strong. It's the right decision.

Even if it's the boring one.

Plus, it's not lost on me that while she's throwing Luke under the bus, she's very conveniently leaving out the part where she showed up to back-to-school night drunk and hit on a married parent.

"I think that's enough talk about Lucas for the night." Jacqueline claps her hands together twice, much like I do when I want to garner my students' attention. "If everyone could please follow me, we have a special surprise waiting in the living room."

While all of the sisters in skincare follow her out of the kitchen like worker ants following their queen, I hang back and top off my glass with one of the many open bottles of wine scattered across the island.

"Sooo . . ." Keisha says once we're alone. "Matching tattoos? Exactly how sure are you that you didn't sign up for a cult?"

"You're so dramatic." I evade the question because after tonight, the answer is only about 80 percent. And while that's still a passing grade, if I let Keisha catch so much as a whiff of doubt, she'll never let me live it down. "I'm not getting a tattoo. My mom would kill me if my first one was that unoriginal."

Like my dear friend Keisha, my mom is a big fan of the arts. If I put something on my body because other people did it, and not because it was something personal and special to me, she might disown me.

I love my mom!

She can't disown me over a tattoo!

"Yes, because the lack of originality is the problem here." Keisha rolls her eyes, snatching the glass out of my hand and taking a sip.

"Hey!" I try to grab it back, but she has fast reflexes and longer legs, and easily steps out of my reach.

"You're driving and you have a presentation you need to watch." She looks me dead in my eyes before chugging the rest of the glass with the practiced ease of a fraternity president. She sets the empty glass in the crowded farmhouse sink and snaps in my face. "Chop chop. Don't keep Jacqueline waiting."

I eye another bottle of wine before deciding against it. I already think I'm not Jacqueline's favorite person and keeping her waiting will only make things worse. I don't want to care, but I really, really want her to like me.

Plus, even if I never come to another Petunia Lemon event with her, I'm still her daughter's teacher and pissing a parent off in August would make for a very long year.

"Fine, but since you took my wine, know that I'm down to only owing you one bourbon." I stick out my tongue and run through the doorway the other women went through before she can launch a counterargument and convince me that I owe her four drinks.

It takes me a second to find the group since this house doesn't have the open concept most modern builds come equipped with these days. Still, though it's not small, it's not a mansion and it doesn't take me long to find the living room and Keisha comes sauntering in right after me.

"Now that we've had a little pleasure, it's time to get to business." Jacqueline stands at the front of the room and doesn't even acknowledge our presence. Her blonde hair, Petunia Pink sweater, and distressed jeans are a stark contrast to the traditional, classic look of the room.

While the kitchen has been updated to look much more modern, the living room is chock full of the warmth and character only a house built in the early 1900s can possess. Dark wood molding runs around the base and the top of the walls. The arch doorway mirrors the arched windows at the back of the room, and the original hardwood floors gleam as they peek out from beneath the oversized rugs protecting them.

But even though the architecture is something off of my Pinterest boards, the decor is sad. Not ugly by any means, but when I look around the space, I have no idea who Jacqueline is or what she likes. Besides a picture or two of Isla, this room could belong to anyone in America. Honestly, even the Pottery Barn sales floor has more personality. I'd kill—or get an infinity sign tattoo—for the chance to get in here and fill this space with a little color.

"If you could ask for one thing to help grow your business," Jacqueline asks her enraptured crowd, "what would you ask for?"

"More sample products!" someone shouts.

"Retail space," another person calls out.

"Dedicated spa time." The woman in front of me laughs.

"Yes! Yes to all of that!" Jacqueline yells, and I can see her cheeks turn pink from the back of the room. "What if I told you that Petunia Lemon has been listening to us? What if I told you they figured out a way to give us exactly what we all need to not only take our businesses to the next level, but to outsell and out-provide brick and mortar spas?"

The energy bouncing off of everyone in the room is palpable. I know I can't afford to invest any more money until I start seeing some return on my initial Petunia Lemon investment, but I can't help but be swept up in the excitement happening in front of me. The anticipation is contagious, and Jacqueline is a master at commanding a room. Everyone is practically jumping out of their seats waiting for her to announce the big reveal.

"What do you think?" She looks over her shoulder to a martini-flushed Nora. "Should we tell them?"

"Hmmm . . ." Nora purses her lips and taps a long fingernail against her chin. "I'm not sure they're excited enough. I don't think they really want to know."

I wouldn't be surprised if these two threw it to commercial with the way they're dragging this out. I look over at Keisha, expecting her to roll her eyes at the dramatics happening around us, but even she's gotten sucked in. Ryan Seacrest be damned, Nora and Jacqueline need to host a competition show of their own.

"I was thinking the same thing." Jacqueline arches a perfectly shaped eyebrow, and her shrewd gaze cuts through her living room packed with her sisters in skincare . . . and Keisha. "Who wants to show how much they want it?"

Hands shoot up all around me, but it's Grace, a petite little blonde with a timid smile and kind eyes, who leaps out of her spot on the couch. "I'm going to reach three thousand PV this month and sign three new recruits. I'm ready for Petunia Lemon to help me get there!"

"Yes! I love that!" Nora steps forward. "Who can beat Grace?"

"I'm going to recruit five new empowered skincare representatives and reach five thousand PV for the first time!" Janet ups Grace's goal, and the room loses its ever-loving mind.

I feel like I'm right back at the convention. The energy in the room is electric, and it makes me feel like I can do and achieve anything I set my mind to. Jacqueline and Nora must feel it too.

"Whoa! I think they're ready!" Jacqueline turns to Nora, and a conspiratorial grin spreads across her ageless face. "Can you please go gather the goods?"

"Of course!" Nora attempts a curtsy, but the small motion almost sends her toppling over. I'm pretty sure her bloodstream is 90 percent gin at this point. I'm not sure she's capable of doing anything other than passing out, but she somehow manages to wobble out of the room without face-planting into the thin, original oak floors.

"Holy shit." Keisha's whisper blends seamlessly with the hushed conversations surrounding us. "I didn't know Nora went so hard on the weekends. Are we going to have to bring her home?"

I don't even have time to respond before Nora appears with a box that's bigger than most of my students. I thought the room was loud before, but I seriously underestimated the vocal range of my fellow sisters in skincare. I went to a Harry Styles concert once, and this beats that decibel range by about a million . . . conservatively.

"We all know that Petunia Lemon products are the best in the world. We've seen firsthand not only what they can do for our skin, with their world-class serums and the sunscreen that I'm convinced will keep us young forever, but we've watched them change our lives." Jacqueline begins her speech and doesn't miss a beat. "Thousands of women just like me joined with small dreams. Most of us are hoping to earn a few extra dollars to sign our kids up for dance lessons and maybe meet a friend or two. But we quickly learned that Petunia Lemon doesn't do anything small. Especially not dreams."

She pauses to allow time for light applause, just like I'm sure she practiced in the mirror a hundred times.

"Through this community of strong, passionate women, we've built empires from our kitchen tables with our babies by our sides and created lives we never need to vacation from. And I don't know about you, but I always girlboss, I sometimes gaslight"—she takes a measured pause and places her hands on her hips—"but I never, ever gatekeep."

Just as planned, the joke is a hit. And luckily for me, the laughter is loud enough that only I hear Keisha gag.

"Knock it off," I hiss beneath my breath.

"I'm so sorry." The words ooze with sarcasm. "Next time I'll be sure to laugh at the joke centered around manipulation and mental abuse."

It's settled.

This is the last Petunia Lemon meeting for Keisha.

I'm sure she'll be crushed.

"And now, thanks to our amazing company, we have everything we need to grow our even better community." With the flourish of Vanna White, she opens the box and reveals a gleaming set of equipment that I've only ever seen on TV. "Introducing the Petunia Pro Facial Spa! This professional-quality microdermabrasion and red-light machine will turn every home into a med spa and every friend into a client. Machines similar to this run for thousands of dollars, but thanks to the geniuses at Petunia Lemon, we're able to purchase this for a steal at eight hundred dollars. I know that still might seem like a big investment, but because of Petunia Lemon's money-back guarantee, this is as risk-free as it comes!"

As someone who would classify their luck as questionable, I've never been one to imagine what it would be like if I won the lottery. Hell, I've never even bothered to buy a ticket. But suddenly, in an old Victorian house in North Denver, surrounded by twenty of my closest acquaintances, I feel like I just struck gold. The mass-market art prints framed on the walls rattle, and the glasses on top of the tables shake as everyone leaps out of their seats. Ear-piercing shrieks and peals of laughter cascade throughout the room. The joy and possibility are infectious, and I can't help getting swept up in the excitement. I jump into the group hug in front of me, spinning in circles and screaming along with the rest of the room.

I take out my phone with the rest of my sisters in skincare and follow Jacqueline's directions to log in to our Petunia Lemon accounts. She reads through the product page, and the excitement in the room grows with each benefit listed. By the time she finishes, I can't enter my credit card information fast enough.

Beside me, disappointment and fury roll off of Keisha in equal measures as I pick the payment plan that works best for me. I know she doesn't think I should spend more money on Petunia Lemon than I already have, and I'll love her forever for caring about me, but I just know in my gut that this will be worth it.

They say you have to spend money to make money and with the Petunia Pro Facial Spa, I'm going to prove them right.

13

MY ORDER FOR the Petunia Pro Facial Spa might be delayed, but unfortunately for me, my credit card bill is coming right on time.

"Emerson!" Nora shouts my name over the quiet hum of vendors setting up their booths. "We're over here!"

I pull my sweater tight around me as the chill of the cool Colorado air nips through the Petunia Lemon T-shirt I threw on this morning. I've barely been to a farmers' market as a customer before, let alone to sell something. My shoulders ache under the weight of my backpack I loaded up with products, and I'm worried the bag I'm holding is moments away from breaking, but I'm still afraid I'm not anywhere near prepared.

Finances have been tighter than normal since joining Petunia Lemon with the monthly order we're required to make, but the spur of the moment purchase of professional spa equipment really sent me over the edge. I can't lie, once I got home after the party, I had instant buyer's remorse. I called Nora in a tizzy, hoping it wasn't too late to cancel my order. It was, but she reminded me of the return policy once it arrived and if I still felt like I didn't want it. In the meantime, she encouraged me to get out there and try to sell some products. It doesn't pay as much as recruiting a new member, but it could be enough to ease some of my stress as bills start rolling in.

"Good morning." I take off my backpack and put the bag on an open table when I reach the tent Nora's huddled under with Hayley. "Thank you so much for inviting me today. I can't tell you how much I needed this."

"Oh, please. We're sisters now, whatever I can do to help you, I'll do." Nora waves me off. "I remember how stressful those early days were, but this is the best thing about Petunia Lemon. If you were to start a business on your own, you'd have to figure out everything by yourself. But with us, you have an entire team who's been where you are and are ready to help you out. Right, Hayley?"

"Oh my gosh, yes." Hayley nods her head a little too vigorously for this early in the morning. "This is what being sisters in skincare is all about! I'm so glad Nora asked if you could tag along today. I always have really great turnouts at farmers' markets, and I think it will be the perfect place for you to dip your toe into selling these products."

"I have an appointment across town I have to be at, so I won't be able to stay long," Nora says. "I just wanted to make sure you made it and didn't need anything else. Hayley is the best at in-person sales though; you're in the finest hands."

"I appreciate you both so much and I'm really excited to learn from Hayley today." I unzip my backpack and start unloading all of the stuff I brought. "Just tell me where to go and what to do and I'll do it."

I don't talk about it much (read: ever) but once upon a time, I did work in retail. I got a job at Nordstrom while I was home from college one summer. My friend worked there, and I was hoping to get a job alongside her in Brass Plum, their juniors department, but the only opening was for men's clothing, selling ties, cuff links, belts, and the occasional dress shirt. I went in with dreams of grandeur and left humbled, realizing I didn't even know how to tie a tie, let alone sell one.

It wasn't great. I think I spent more on gas than I made, but looking back, I don't think it was my skills as a salesperson as much as my lack of knowledge of the product. It's going to be different this time. I've spent the weeks since joining Petunia Lemon going to all of the meetings and learning everything I can about these serums and lotions—the "potions of youth," as we call them—and I have a really good feeling about today.

Plus, even if I get nervous, I'll have Hayley by my side to help. What could possibly go wrong?

HAYLEY LEFT.

We had barely finished setting up when her phone rang, and her fiancé was on the other end. By the time she hung up, tears were streaming down her face and she could barely breathe. I thought someone had died! Turns out, the caterer she hired for the wedding reached out to tell them they could no longer provide the vegan and gluten-free option she had chosen, and she was going to have to find a new caterer.

I've never planned a wedding before and I have no idea how much stress she's under, but even though I helped her pack up her bag and told her not to worry, I can't help but think she should maybe worry about me.

At least a little bit.

The sun is high in the sky and it's a perfect Denver day. With fall rapidly approaching, people came out in droves to soak up the warm weather while it lasts. My booth has seen more action than I could've ever dreamt, but as soon as anyone asks me anything, just like when I took the SAT, all the information I've learned vanishes into thin air.

"Sunscreen is really important," I say to the lady who's been picking up and putting down products for the last fifteen minutes. "Nobody wants skin cancer."

"Nobody wants skin cancer"? Out of everything I could've said, that's what I go with?

Idiot!

"Of course not." She puts the sunscreen down and glares at me through the thick-rimmed glasses sitting on her face. "That's how my grandma died."

Oh fucking hell.

And embarrassment is how I die.

"I'm so sorry." I reach beneath the table to grab the rest of the samples I have left and dump them into a branded Petunia Lemon paper bag. "Please, have all of the samples you want. If you like them, we'll be here next week."

Or more to the point, Hayley will be—if there's not another catering emergency. I'll be at home on my couch, still recovering from this interaction.

She snatches the bag out of my hand and whispers something I know I don't want to hear under her breath.

The crowd is starting to thin and while that was, without a doubt, my worst interaction of the day, I'd be lying if I said most of them went much smoother.

I've been here for five hours, and I've only made three sales. And to make matters worse, my booth is sandwiched in between a tamale stand and a gourmet lemonade booth. I've spent more money than I've made and my stomach hurts! Actually, one of the sales I made was to the man selling tamales. He saw me almost break down after another person walked away when I told them how much the serum cost and took pity on me. I'm not against pity sales, but I doubt they're a good foundation for a business.

I look at my watch for the millionth time today and almost weep when I see I still have an hour left. This day has moved like molasses. All I want to do is go home and drink whiskey in the bathtub, but I plaster a smile on my face and try to at least finish the day strong.

Two women start walking my way and that undying flicker of hope inside of me rears back to life. Before Hayley was rushed away, she gave me tips on how to recognize a potential Petunia Lemon customer. Middle-aged women who seemed put together and appearance conscious, designer bags were a plus, and big floppy hats or oversize sunglasses were an absolute yes. And these two women are all of the above.

"Hi! I love your hats." I scoot to the edge of my tent to greet them, and hope I don't sound as desperate as I feel. "Stylish and protecting your skin. Brilliant!"

Brilliant. I definitely sound as desperate as I feel.

"Thank you." One of them picks up a bottle of serum without looking at me. "It's Loewe."

"Oh wow. Nice." I have no idea what that means, but it sounds expensive. "Well, besides your Loewe hat protecting your face from the sun, what else do you use to protect that gorgeous skin of yours?"

I know Hayley said compliments go a long way, but I think that sounded creepy. How do you compliment a stranger's skin without sounding like you want to wear it?

"Besides what my doctor does for me, I wash my face daily, use a vitamin C serum, a retinoid at night, face lotion, and of course sunscreen." She lays out all my talking points for me and for once, I think luck might be on my side.

"What about you?" I ask her friend.

"About the same thing." She puts down the box of our Good Night serum that she's been studying. "Add in an exfoliating mask every now and then."

"No wonder both of you have such beautiful skin." Again, creepy! "You obviously have products you use, but I'd love to introduce you to Petunia Lemon. We are a woman-founded company with some of the top-ranked beauty products in the country. Our products aren't just clinically tested, but proven by thousands and thousands of testimonials. What would you say if I told you our sunscreen is the highest ranked on the market?"

The woman in the Loewe hat looks to her friend, and a smirk that makes my stomach turn pulls at the corner of her mouth.

"I'd say you were full of it," she says. "I sold Petunia Lemon years ago and I can't believe they're still out here doing the same old song and dance. You seem sweet enough, so fair warning, whatever you think you're going to get from this company isn't there. And these 'top of the line' products you're selling? I've found better stuff at Walmart."

My mouth falls open, and I struggle to come up with anything to say. Despite the meetings I've been to, nobody prepared me for this. They take their time walking away, their noses in the air and laughter trailing behind them. And even though I still have quite a bit of time before the market closes, I grab my backpack and start loading up.

The farmers' market was a bust, but I'm going to figure this out.

One day.

Maybe.

14

ONCE SEPTEMBER COMES to an end, the chaos of the new school year is finally beginning to slow down.

Thanks to Petunia Lemon, this year's been more hectic than ever before. I've loved going to the meetings each week, learning about the products and seeing how the other skincare reps go about building their businesses. But it's made it harder than normal to fall back into my previously scheduled program.

I'm a creature of habit, always have been. My mom said I put her and my dad on a schedule when I was a baby, not the other way around. It's one of the things I love most about kindergarten. With a classroom full of kids as young as my students, having a schedule they can rely on is of the utmost importance. Starting our days with the same routine, singing the same songs, and sitting in the same seats allows them the time and space to prepare for the day.

My weekend schedule may not be quite as rigid as a school day, but there's one thing I always make sure I have time for.

I drive into The Barkery's parking lot and slide into the same spot I've used every weekend for the last three years. I started volunteering after I brought my class for a field trip and I will never stop. I usually come on Sundays, but since I'm hosting my first Petunia Lemon party tomorrow, I'm spending my Saturday with them instead. I get to cuddle kitties, walk puppies, and send them away with their forever families. Yes, it can also be sad seeing these poor animals end up in a shelter, but my time here always brings me more joy than anything else. The Barkery does countless acts of good for animals in need in my area, and I'm so grateful to be a part of their community.

I grab my tote bag from my passenger seat, triple-checking that I have my camera and extra memory card, when my phone buzzes with a Facebook notification. I've tagged along with Nora to a few more Petunia Lemon meetings since Jacqueline's house. The sisters in skincare have sat with me, helping me craft "Hey girl" messages to send to old friends and acquaintances in hopes of them wanting to learn more about Petunia Lemon and inviting them to my first party. I've had a few people say yes, but most responses—if they ever respond—have been polite noes.

I swipe open my phone and open the app I didn't even have before Petunia Lemon. There's an unread message from Victoria Lewis.

> Hi Emerson! It's so nice to hear from you after all this time. I'm doing well, just moved to Arizona and am trying to adjust to the heat! 😵 Thank you for inviting me to your Petunia Lemon party, but I think I'm going to have to pass. I joined a company similar to them after Bella was born and although I met a lot of great

women, that business structure just wasn't for me. I
hope you kill it though! Good luck!

Another rejection. Great.

I know they say it's a numbers game, and I just have to keep
reaching out, but there's only so many times a person can hear
no before they want to give up. And I can feel my limit approaching.

Thank god the Petunia Pro Facial Spa is money-back guar-
anteed.

I type out a quick message to Victoria, thanking her for taking the time to respond and requesting a few new pictures of
her adorable daughter before tossing my phone into my purse
and finally heading inside.

"Hi, Emerson!" Shelly shouts as soon as I step foot through
the door. "The talent is so excited to spend the day with you."

"How are the new models doing?" I ask. "Any divas this
time?"

"Always." Her throaty laughter echoes off the tiled floors and
is only drowned out by the barking of the dogs she startled.
"There's one tabby who I'm sure is going to give you problems."

"It's always the cats." I love them, but wow are they sassy.
"Can you tell Tom that I'll be there in a few minutes? I just have
to put my stuff away."

"You got it, hun." Her trademark bright pink–painted lips
curve into an even brighter smile as she picks up the phone.
"Tommy-boy, Emerson will be there soon. Please make sure the
talent is ready for their close-ups."

Once I found out there was a volunteer position to photograph the animals for The Barkery website and help them get adopted, I was instantly interested. And by *interested*, I mean it became my entire personality.

I spent two weeks straight googling pet photography and scanning other shelter websites to see how they got their animals' faces into the world. I texted my mom's phone with so many dog pictures that she ran out of phone storage and limited me to only three dog pictures a day. She also adopted a dog, Bailey the basset hound, and now I spend my days only a little jealous that I'm not the favorite child anymore.

Lucky for me though, she felt so guilty about her maternal betrayal that she bought me a camera and offered to sign me up for photography lessons at the rec center by my house. I obviously took her up on this, and now I get to spend two days a month taking glamour shots of animals.

Besides being a teacher, it's the best job in the world.

I walk down the familiar hallway covered with hundreds of candid pictures of animals who have come through The Barkery over the years. From cats and dogs to turtles and bunnies, all animals are welcome. Even ferrets, which are not my animal of choice, have found their humans here. I push open the door for the volunteer lounge and wave to a few familiar faces as I walk over to the worn-down cubbies to put my stuff there for the day.

Careful not to scratch my lens, I pull the camera my mom gave me two Christmases ago out of its case and drape the long strap around my neck. I tuck the extra memory card in my back pocket and grab the bedazzled collar and puppy bow tie I found in the clearance section of the pet shop last night. Since becoming the unofficial pet photographer for The Barkery Animal Shelter, I have taken it upon myself to provide a plethora of props and accessories for my models. The pet store knows I do this since I'm there every week—and also because I love to talk and happily explained my plan to them—so they always hold the cutest items in the back for me.

I slip the extra hair tie off of my wrist and twist my hair into a bun at the top of my head. It's a lesson I had to learn the hard way, but I now make sure to always keep my hair out of reach of the animals. I step into the hallway and as soon as I do, I hear someone yell my name.

"Miss Pierce!" a tiny voice shouts. "Miss Pierce!"

I turn around just in time to see a fireball with curly brown hair barreling down the hall right before she slams into me. She wraps her little arms around me and looks up with the toothy grin I love so much.

"Isla!" I hug her back. "Hi, sweetie."

"Hi, Miss Pierce!" She loosens her grip and takes a step back. "Guess what?"

"Hmmm . . . let me think." I tap my chin and pretend to think really hard. "You're at an animal shelter. Are you here to ride a tiger?"

"No!" She shakes her head, her giggles music to my ears. "You can't ride tigers!"

"Oh, you're right. I don't think tigers would like that very much," I say. "Did you come to get a snake?"

Her jaw drops and her green eyes go wide.

"Daddy!" she squeals, and that's when I finally notice *him* standing right behind her. "They have snakes here!"

"Oh no." His eyes crease at the corners, his deep chuckle washing over me like sunshine on a stormy day. "No snakes or any other creatures that slither or shed their skin."

I don't ever want to be Team Luke over Isla, but as much as it pains me, I am going to have to agree with him on this one. Isla shrugs, not seeming too bothered by her dad's reptile rejection, and turns back to face me.

"It's almost my birthday and since I'm turning six"—she holds up her hands, showing me six fingers—"Daddy says I'm big enough to get a puppy!"

She bounces up and down, as if she's incapable of standing still with this much excitement racing through her tiny little body.

"Oh my goodness, Isla! That's so exciting!" I hold up my hand for a high five. "Do you know what kind of dog you want to bring home?"

I want an animal so bad, but my one-bedroom apartment is far too small for a pet. And with the amount of time I spend at work, they'd have to be crated up for so much of their day that it wouldn't feel fair to them. Oh . . . also, my landlord doesn't allow them. But I think I could work around that.

"No." She shakes her head and her little curlicues fall into her face. "Daddy says we don't pick our dog, our dog will pick us."

Dammit.

As if Luke saving me in the parking lot and changing my battery wasn't enough, now he has to be a kind, sweet single dad who adopts animals on the weekends?

This is the worst thing that could happen to me.

Why can't he go back to being the condescending jerk from the hotel room so I can remember all the reasons I never want to sleep with him ever again? The audacity of this man!

"Your daddy is very smart." The words taste like sour milk, and I have to fight back my gag reflex. "Before you go look at all the dogs, do you want to see something special?"

She turns back around to Luke and levels him with her best puppy dog plea, "Please, Daddy! Can we?"

I can tell he wants to say no, to keep as much distance between the two of us as humanly possible, but who can say no to that face? Not Luke, that's for sure.

"Fine," he says. "But not for too long. Okay?"

What a sucker.

"Thank you!" Isla gives him a quick hug before running back to my side and taking my hand in hers.

We walk through the shelter, and I show her where all of the different animals are while she tells me about everything from her gymnastics class yesterday to what she ate for dinner last night—cheese pizza for her, olive, onion, and sausage for Luke—and the new night-light she got for her room. It's a llama and she named it Lola because "all llamas need a name."

"This room," I say, pointing to the door leading to the photo studio, "is where I come two times a month and get to do something superspecial with all of the new animal friends who come to stay here. Do you want to see what I do?"

She bounces from foot to foot on her velcro, glitter tennis shoes. "Yes, please!"

"Took you long enough." Tom, a seventy-two-year-old curmudgeon, harrumphs from the recliner in the corner of the room. "Thought they were going to have to euthanize me if you took any longer."

"What's eufanize mean, Miss Pierce?" Isla asks.

I shoot Tom my dirtiest look before turning my attention back to sweet, innocent, doesn't-need-to-know-about-animal-death Isla.

"It's something that can happen when animals get old and sick so they don't feel sick anymore." I brace for a follow-up question, but for once, luck is on my side.

The back door opens and Sadie, another weekend volunteer, walks through the door with a very excited, very wiggly puppy.

"Oh good, you're here!" Sadie says. "This is Bruno and he's your first model for the day. He just got here on Wednesday and he's the very best boy."

Next to me, Isla can't contain her squeal of delight, and proving Sadie right, Bruno sits like the very best boy he is and lets Isla approach to give him ear scratches.

"He's so cute!" Isla says between laughs when Bruno covers her hand with doggie kisses.

"He is so cute and it's our job to help him find a new home," I tell her. "Can you help me do that?"

She nods her head up and down so hard that she jostles her curls out of her ponytail. "How do we do that?"

"Do you see that?" I point to the cabinet in the back of the room. "I need you to go there and pick out a collar that will make Bruno look super fancy and then"—I lift up the camera around my neck—"we're going to take pictures of him to put on our website. That way families looking for a new pet can see his picture and come here to take him home."

Isla jumps at the opportunity, running across the room and throwing the cabinet doors open.

"Oh my gosh!" she screeches, pulling out the basket filled with the bedazzled collars. "They're so sparkly!"

"You've got to be kidding me." Luke's strangled voice pulls everyone's attention to him sulking in the corner. "You take dog portraits?"

"She's the best damn animal photographer we have." Only Tom can compliment me and still make it sound like an insult. I'm pretty sure his vocal cords are physically incapable of producing sounds of joy. It's one of my favorite things about him. "She takes pictures of all the animals, not just dogs. She's so good that adoptions have gone up fifteen percent since she took over."

"You teach children during the week and during your free time, you volunteer to take animal pictures?" He stares at me, his mouth agape as he tries to process this new information. "So they can get adopted?"

"I hate to break it to you, Luke," I say, closing the space between the two of us so that the little ears in the room won't hear me. "But I'm a better person than I am good in bed. And you already know that I'm really, *really* great in bed."

His sharp intake of breath is all I hear before Isla, the cute little distraction, runs back waving a checkered bow tie over her head.

"This one, Miss Pierce!" She gives me the bow tie with one

hand and pulls me away from her dad with the other. "Come on, let's get him a family."

I follow behind her, because it's clear who the boss is here, but I glance over my shoulder at Luke one more time as I go.

And what a mistake it is.

His tongue darts out, licking his bottom lip at the exact moment his green eyes lock with mine. My legs almost give out beneath me, and my heart rate spikes to lethal levels. Because the look on his face doesn't just tell me that he remembers how good I was in bed; it says he wants to do it again.

And fuck me twice—or a hundred times—because so do I.

15

ISLA WAS A fantastic photographer's assistant and took her job very seriously.

Each pet had a carefully picked out accessory and she gave the world's best puppy cuddles to the camera-shy dogs. She was so impressive at her jobs that even Tom told her she did great, something he didn't say to me until I'd been working with him for at least six months.

If it weren't for Mister Bubbles, the gray British shorthair who was recently dropped off when his owner developed an unfortunate, but very serious, cat allergy, I think Isla would've spent the entire day in the photo studio. But much to Luke's dismay, as soon as Sadie walked into the room with Mister Bubbles, Isla fell in love.

I was glad she found her furry soulmate, but the rest of the afternoon wasn't nearly as much fun without Isla's help or Luke's brooding presence in the corner of the room. By the time we finish up with our final model, a white rabbit with big floppy ears, I'm ready for a quiet night on my couch with a glass of wine and Andy Cohen.

I step into the hallway and have déjà vu when Isla yells my name just like she did a few hours ago.

"Miss Pierce!" She runs to me again, but this time I know to brace before she slams into me. "We got Mister Bubbles! He gets to come home with us!"

"Are you so happy?"

"Yes!" She jumps up and down, her voice so high I worry she might set off a riot with the dogs. "Daddy said he can sleep in my room. I'm going to make him a special spot and everything."

"Wow! Mister Bubbles is a very lucky kitty to get to live with you."

Isla slips her little hand in mine, and we walk down the hallway toward a waiting Luke, who somehow looks even taller and hotter holding a cat carrier.

Very inconsiderate of him.

"We're going to the store to buy him a bed and toys." She looks up at Luke with pouty eyes that would break even the most hardened of criminals. "Right, Daddy?"

"Right, Bear." He's putty in her little hands.

I hold open the door for Isla and Luke as we leave The Barkery. It's later in the day, but the sun is still high in the sky. The dry Colorado heat that's been lingering later into the fall is a rude awakening after spending the afternoon in the cool, air-conditioned building. Mister Bubbles meows as we cross the small parking lot and sounds just as unimpressed with the heat as I feel.

"I'll see you on Monday, Isla." I give her a hug when I reach my car. "If you want, your dad can email me a picture of Mister Bubbles and you can tell the class all about him. Does that sound good?"

"Yes!" Her little fist punches the sky. "Vivian loves cats. She's going to be so excited for me."

Vivian sits at the same table as Isla. She has a cat backpack, cat lunch box, wears the same cat-ear headband every single day, and at recess, she recruits girls to play kitten with her.

Simply stated, Isla is not wrong. Vivian is obsessed with cats and will be very happy—if not slightly jealous—of Isla.

Now we just need to get Luke on the same cat-loving page. The poor guy must've asked Isla about a million times if she wanted to go look at all of the dogs before she made her final decision. There was a bulldog I think he had his heart set on. I have to give him credit, though; once she made it clear Mister Bubbles was the pet for her, he never tried to change her mind. That's something that can't be said for most parents I see come through here.

He can be a grade-A asshole when he wants to be, but he's a really good dad.

I wave goodbye to them and watch for a moment as Isla skips next to Luke. He stares down at her with a look that can only be described as adoration, like the moon and stars only hang because of her. My stomach clenches, and the dad tears I long thought had disappeared make a very sudden, very unwelcome reappearance and blur my vision. I hurry to my car, needing privacy in case the worst happens and the tears begin to fall. I put my key in the ignition, desperate for the air-conditioning to blast through my vents, but when I turn it, nothing happens.

Not even a *click click click*. Only silence.

And the sound of my final straw snapping in half.

I try again . . . and again . . . and again. All ending with the exact same result. Nothing.

I close my eyes and lean forward, resting my head on the steering wheel so that the heat of the leather burning my forehead can distract me from the searing, bone-deep despair and self-loathing I feel.

I'm so lost in my wallowing that I don't even notice someone knocking on my window until the door is pulled open and Mister Bubbles is meowing in my ear.

"Let me guess." The disappointment in Luke's voice is as clear as the Rocky Mountains rising from the skyline. "You didn't go get your oil changed, did you?"

"No." I twist my head to the side, looking up at a hulking Luke. "No, I did not."

"Come on then." He pulls my door open wider and offers me his hand. "Isla and I can give you a ride home."

I grab my tote bag from the floor and without thinking, put my hand in his. It's the smallest touch, practically meaningless, yet somehow, it steals my breath away and sets my body afire. Every feeling, every sensation I've been trying to ignore, trying to pretend never happened, comes racing back, filling my body with longing. Making my limbs fall heavy with need.

And because the universe is my biggest hater, instead of being able to spiral in private, I get to sort through these feelings in the front seat of his car. If that wasn't punishment enough, I get the added bonus of doing all this in front of his daughter and the judgy cat, Mister Bubbles.

The worst part of all? The only person I have to blame is myself.

Well, me and Elon Musk.

THANKS TO ISLA, the drive to my apartment on the north side might have been uncomfortable, but it was anything but silent. I thought I knew everything that happened in my classroom, but it turns out, I knew nothing. Isla spent the entire drive filling the car with the constant chatter only a five-year-old can accomplish, telling me the playground gossip and spilling all the kindergarten tea. Let's just say there might be a new seating chart come Monday.

Luke remains blissfully quiet, only chiming in when Isla directs a question to him. I have the distinct feeling he wants me out of the car almost as much as I do. As soon as he turns onto my street, his shoulders sag with what I can only assume is relief.

"Ummm, Daddy . . ." Isla trails off, and Luke's back goes ramrod straight at the all too familiar tone in her voice.

He slows to a stop in front of my apartment and looks back at her through his rearview mirror.

"Yes, Isla?" he asks even though I think we both know exactly what's coming next.

"I kinda need to go potty," she says, confirming my suspicions.

"Didn't I ask if you needed to go before we left?" He does a pretty good job at hiding the irritation in his voice. "We're almost home, can you wait a little longer?"

"I didn't need to go then, I have to go now," she whines. "I can't wait! I have to go really bad!"

"It's okay," I say before I even realize what I'm doing. The regret is swift, but there's no going back now. I can feel the heat of Luke's glare burning a hole in the side of my head as I keep talking. "You can come inside and use my bathroom."

"It's not too much longer until we're home, Bear." Luke tries to undo my blunder, but Isla is already unbuckled and pushing open the car door. "Miss Pierce is probably tired from work and doesn't want company."

"She already said yes, Daddy." She hops out of the car and onto the sidewalk, leaning back inside the car to point at the carrier nestled behind the driver's seat. "Don't forget Mister Bubbles. We don't want him to be scared in the car alone."

She shuts the back door before immediately opening mine, pulling the tote bag off of my lap, and grabbing my hand.

"I love your house, Miss Pierce." She struggles to get my bag over her shoulder. It's almost as big as her, and I'm afraid she's going to tip over, but ever the trooper, she perseveres. "It's so big and colorful!"

"Thank you, but this whole house isn't mine," I warn her in hopes of avoiding future disappointment when she sees my minuscule unit. "You can't tell from the outside, but there are five apartments in this building."

I live in a small, one-bedroom, one-bathroom apartment in what was a single-family home at some point in history. The kitchen is the size of a postage stamp, and the bathroom has an embarrassing lack of outlets with no storage in sight. But it also has exposed brick, a gorgeous community garden, and free laundry in the spacious—albeit creepy—basement. I love all of my neighbors, and my landlord, Frederick, a kooky man who's never met a fedora he didn't love, is the kindest person roaming this earth. He was an old friend of my dad who my mom introduced me to when I was looking for a place of my own after college. He lets me paint the walls (and doors) and gave me a steal of a deal that he still honors despite the skyrocketing rent prices in Denver. I love living here and I doubt I'll ever leave.

"Daddy . . ." Isla stops walking in the middle of the pathway to the front door. Her eyebrows furrow together as she looks up and down my street. "Is this close to your new house?"

Luke's gaze meets mine for just a second before avoiding eye contact as he grunts in affirmation.

Time stops. Oceans freeze. The earth opens up and swallows me whole, spitting me out into the depths of hell.

I mean, sure, Denver's small, but it's not this small! There's no reason that this man, out of all men, should be living so close to me that even a five-year-old notices. I don't know who I need to apologize to for the sins of my past life, but this is getting ridiculous.

"How close are we talking?" I don't know why I ask. I don't want the answer.

"Two blocks down." He points west and then jerks his thumb to the left. "One block over."

"Wow." Of course he's basically my neighbor. Why wouldn't he be? "That's fun and interesting information that I will absolutely think about processing later."

I absolutely will not.

Just like my poor little car, I will ignore this until it causes me to backfire, malfunction, and possibly die.

Luke laughs and startles poor Mister Bubbles who was just

starting to doze off in his carrier. "There seems to be a lot to process."

So many unspoken words linger behind that small sentence and now that he knows where I live, I wonder if I'll ever be able to hear them. Part of me wants them more than my next breath, but the bigger, wiser part of me hopes he stays away and we never have to discuss what happened—what's happening—between us ever again.

I use my key to open the door to my building, and Isla, Luke, and Mister Bubbles file in after me. I'm on the second floor, one of the only requirements my mom had when I was looking for a place of my own. It's annoying when I need to carry in groceries, but the added layer of security helps put my mind at ease at night. Isla takes her time, showing us her number skills by counting all of the stairs.

"Thirteen!" Isla shouts when we make it to the top. "Thirteen stairs!"

"Amazing!" I high-five her before I push open the door to my apartment. "That was such good counting. You're going to get a lot of practice counting how many treats you give Mister Bubbles. He's such a good boy, how many do you think he'll get?"

"Ummm . . ." Her little lips purse and she narrows her eyes, taking her time to answer such a serious question. "Maybe ten?"

"Only ten?" I make my eyes go wide. "I was thinking like a hundred!"

"A hundred?" She giggles. "A thousand!"

"Now you're thinking." I wink, sharing a conspiratorial grin with her just as Luke steps through my door.

"Whoa now." Panic rises in his normally even-keeled voice.

"Let's just give him one to begin with. We have to get the litter box set up and we don't want him to have an upset tummy before his bathroom is ready."

"A cat bathroom?" Like all kindergartners tend to do, Isla erupts into peals of laughter when she hears Luke say the word *bathroom*. Potty humor is king in kindergarten. I have an entire note on my phone filled with bathroom jokes I know kids will love.

And because I am an honorary kindergartner by trade, I laugh right alongside her.

"You two are ridiculous." Luke rolls his eyes and sets down the cat carrier, but he can't hide the smile I see him trying—and failing—to fight.

"Ummm . . ." Isla's laughter begins to fade at the same time her eyes go wide and she starts to bounce up and down. "Miss Pierce?"

"Do you see the door with all the flowers on it?" I take my bag from her shoulder and point down the hallway. "The bathroom is right there."

She nods her head once before she takes off running and leaves me with her dad.

Alone.

In my living room.

The awkwardness Isla so gallantly disguised with her constant chatter rears its ugly head. Silence falls over us like a heavy fog. The only sounds in the room are Mister Bubbles's cat snores and the gentle whirring of the ceiling fan I never turn off. The touch of his hand still burns in my palm, my body fighting so hard to remember what my mind desperately wants to forget.

"So . . ." Luke puts Mister Bubbles's crate down and looks around my acid trip of a living room. "You're a big fan of color?"

I almost laugh at the absurdity of his question. "You could say that."

You know how some people live by the saying less is more?

Well . . . fuck those people—respectfully, of course. In my not-so-humble opinion, more is more, and my maximalist wonderland of an apartment is proof. The only wall I haven't painted is the exposed brick wall behind my TV. It's the perfect background for the TV stand I found at a yard sale a few years ago and painted teal. It was the first piece of furniture I refinished, but not close to the last. When I told Frederick what I wanted to do, he cleared out a spot of the yard and designated it my official DIY corner. I spend more time out there than just about anywhere else.

Hand-painted pots I worked on with my previous kindergartners house my thriving plant collection. My back wall is painted pink, but you can barely see it between the masses of picture frames I've collected over the years. Artwork my students have drawn for me is proudly displayed between prints and paintings from local artists. The olive-green velvet couch my mom found at a thrift store is covered with throw pillows—some that I've bought and a few that I've made—and the shag rug protecting my hardwood floors is the only decor purchase I've ever made in white. And I only ordered white so it wouldn't distract from the floral peel-and-stick wallpaper I applied to my ceiling.

Keisha calls my place a fun house, and even though I know she's referencing a carnival, I still take it as a compliment. My house is fun! It might seem like I have a lot of stuff, but I'm still a firm follower of the KonMari Method. Everything in my apartment has a space and it all brings me joy. The moment something doesn't belong anymore, I donate it in hopes it will make another person happy.

"I don't know what I was expecting," he says, pausing and picking up one of my throw pillows, "but it definitely wasn't this."

"Were you expecting me to be a boring, beige person?" It's almost comical how little this person who I can't seem to get out of my mind or my life knows about me.

He looks me up and down, the heat in his eyes searing a path down my body. I'm wearing my standard uniform for my days at The Barkery: denim shorts, my floral embroidered Converses, and one of my many graphic tees. This shirt is pink and has pictures of Dolly Parton all over it and—just like Dolly herself—it's a freaking delight.

In my six-hundred-and-fifty-square-foot apartment, there's never much distance between me and my guests, so when Luke takes a step closer, he's practically on top of me.

My lungs turn to ice, my body frozen solid as I watch his hand move to my face. He grabs a stray curl and twists it around his finger before bending down and caging me between the wall and his body.

"I think you forget." The heat of his breath grazes the shell of my ear and sends shivers down my spine. "I've felt every inch of you. I watched you fall apart beneath me over and over again. I've seen you wild, baby. Nothing about you, not one thing, is boring."

"You said I didn't have a brain." I'm trying to cling on to any reason to push him away, but the closer he gets, the harder it gets to care about anything but his mouth on mine. "You didn't want me teaching Isla."

"I was pissed. Petunia Lemon . . . fuck." He rests his forehead on mine, his jagged breathing the only sign he's as affected by this as I am. "It ruined my marriage. Jacqueline blew through our entire savings and then filed for divorce when I told her she needed to choose between me or that company."

"I—" I don't want to know any of this. "I don't know what to do with this."

"That's okay and I'm not asking you to." His mouth is almost touching mine. I don't know if I want to pull him closer or push him away. "You're smart, Emerson. You'll see. Just be careful, okay?"

It's like he's almost begging me to hear him, to listen to his warning. He sounds so sincere, and something inside of me, something loud and unfamiliar, is screaming for me to trust him.

"I'll be careful."

I just don't know what I need to be more careful of: the man in front of me or the company I've already invested so much of my time, money, and energy in.

The sound of the toilet flushing snaps us back into reality. Luke falls back, and my body cries out at the loss of his touch. By the time Isla's little footsteps race into my living room, Luke is already holding the cat crate by the door and ready to go.

"All better, Bear?" The huskiness in his voice as he whispered in my ear has been replaced by the voice of a devoted dad who would never be caught with his daughter's teacher against the wall. "We still have to go get Mister Bubbles his bed and I bet Miss Pierce is tired after her long day with the animals."

"Okay." If Isla is sad to go, she doesn't let it show. She smiles her toothy grin and gives me a big hug. "Bye, Miss Pierce."

"I'll see you at school." I hug her back. "Don't forget to send me a picture of Mister Bubbles."

"I won't!"

I stand in my doorway, watching and waving goodbye once they reach the bottom of the stairs. I twist my dead bolt and decide that the million and one things on my to-do list are going to have to wait.

I head straight into my bathroom and crank on the cold water before stepping out of my clothes and into the shower. Even though I'm expecting it, the spray of the freezing water is a shock to my system. My skin turns to fire as it hits me like shards of ice. My fists clench at my sides as I try to resist the desperate urge to add hot water. My eyes screwed shut, my breath coming in rapid bursts, I take the pain, not moving until my body has gone numb to the cold . . .

Until it's gone numb to Luke.

If only the cold could work on my heart, it would make my life so much simpler.

16

I LOVE COLORADO.

I've lived here my entire life, and unless someone offers to fund a move to Ireland or Italy, I'm staying put. I really think it's the best state in America, and I completely understand why the highways are flooded with new residents. The scenery is beautiful, the people are nice, the food is excellent, and the weed is legal. Everything about this state is fantastic.

Except for one teeny-tiny little thing: the weather.

And I'm not talking about the cold here either. Yes, it obviously snows, but it's not that bad. It's usually just a few inches, and the city is really good about treating the streets so they don't get too icy. Plus, I really like the occasional blizzard, and I live in an apartment so I don't have to worry about shoveling. The storms rarely knock out the power, and I'll never be mad about a few days of sitting on my couch and binge-watching television shows.

What I do hate is how fast the weather turns and how hard it hits you. It could be beautiful and sunny one minute and dark and stormy the next. There's no time to prepare. Colorado's flash floods are legendary, and when I was learning to drive, they were one of the first things my mom taught me how to navigate. Thankfully though, I've never been caught in one . . .

Until now.

When I don't have a car.

Because of course.

I stare out of the 7-Eleven window, trying to see if I can spot the bike I pulled out of my storage closet last week. Rain slams against the window; the strong winds whipping it all around are so unrelenting that I can barely see outside. I know I dropped my bike on the sidewalk when I ran inside, but I can't remember where, and I'm not 100 percent sure that it didn't get swept away in the flood waters.

My clothes are sopping wet, and my hair I spent more than an hour straightening for my party today is absolutely destroyed. It feels like I'm standing in a bucket of water—my shoes are so saturated that I fear they'll never be dry again.

Hell, I don't know if *I'll* ever be dry again.

The small store is packed with stranded travelers who needed shelter or a snack to wait out the rain. It should be hot in here from all of the bodies, but instead the air-conditioning blowing from the vents feels like it's going straight to my bones. My teeth won't stop chattering, and my hands are shivering as I take another sip of my Slurpee.

"Are you sure I can't give you a cup of coffee?" the very sweet, very concerned checkout clerk asks me for the fifth time. "I think something hot might be good for you."

"Thank you, but no," I politely decline. "I don't deserve warmth."

Only responsible adults who handle regular car maintenance deserve warmth. I deserve all the suffering the universe is handing to me. It just would've been nice if it handed this to me before I spent a hundred dollars at the grocery store.

I look at the pile of grocery bags sitting on the counter next to the register. The gourmet cheeses and crackers I bought for the Petunia Lemon party I'm hosting are hanging on by a thread. The loaf of French bread I got to go with my spinach artichoke dip is already in the trash. For the death of fresh-baked bread alone, I deserve the sweet suffering only an ice-cold Slurpee can provide.

"Okay," he agrees, but I can tell he doesn't want to. "If you change your mind, please go help yourself."

I'm pretty sure he thinks I'm going to die in his store. And honestly? He might not be wrong. Dying of hypothermia in a 7-Eleven feels very on brand for me.

Luckily for everyone waiting out the storm inside of the store and in their cars hidden beneath the gas bay, the rain begins to slow to a drizzle, and the extreme weather disappears as fast as it came. Soon the sun peeks out and shoos those pesky clouds away. The gray sky turns so blue that if I didn't have the water in my shoes to prove it, I'd think I'd just made the entire storm up.

Customers ring up their final purchases, stockpiling sodas and candy they didn't need before heading back to the mundane day Mother Nature so rudely interrupted. I, on the other hand, stay rooted to my spot in front of the window and wait for Keisha to come save the day. I try not to take offense at the large berth everyone seems to offer as they walk past me. Even I can admit the vibes I'm exuding are rancid. I don't need a mirror to tell me I'm looking more angry, wet poodle than human at the moment. If I wasn't stuck inside my freezing body, I'd avoid myself too!

By the time Keisha finally pulls into the parking lot, I'm seconds away from taking Chris (the 7-Eleven clerk I'm now on a first-name basis with) up on the coffee offer. I lost the feeling in my feet about ten minutes ago, but now my hands are starting to go numb and I'm afraid I'll face-plant if I try to navigate the crowded aisles. I don't have a ton of pride, but even I have my limits.

"That's my ride!" I grab all of my grocery bags and slip them onto my wrist. "Don't forget to listen to more Little Mix songs! You won't regret it."

We bonded over the truly unhinged playlist coming from the speakers. He started talking about his favorite British bands—post-punk bands—and I told him mine—pop girl groups. He'd never heard of Little Mix before, and as an unofficial member of their United States street team, I made him listen to it right then and there.

"I already have them downloaded," he says, "Don't you forget to listen to Joy Division!"

"Aye, captain." I attempt to salute, but my arms are weighed down by the bags. "Thanks again for the taquito."

I might not have said yes to coffee, but it goes against my fundamental beliefs as a junk food aficionado to decline anything crispy and delicious.

I push open the heavy glass door, and relief washes over me just like the crisp, rain-scented air. My bike, though no better for wear, hasn't been washed away by the rain and I won't have to walk to school tomorrow.

"Well, well, well." Keisha cranks down her window and doesn't even pretend to attempt to help me with my bags or my bike. "Who knew all it would take was a little rain before you came begging for Big Ben's help."

Big Ben is Keisha's 1990-something Ford Bronco. It's massive and ugly and if it has too much junk in the trunk (literally) she makes me rock back and forth in the passenger seat to give it momentum up hills. Simply stated, I hate Big Ben and it's the reason I always drive when we have plans.

"Don't get too cocky. A broken-down car, soggy shoes, and pure desperation forced my hand." I pull open the trunk door and toss whatever's left of my grocery haul next to the pile of blankets, two umbrellas, and four ice scrapers strewn across the back. "And I'm still not sure it was worth it."

I round the car and pick my old bike up off of the ground and walk it to the back. I attempt to lift it into the trunk, but my fingers are still trying to regain full feeling and I fail three times. Each failure is more spectacular than the last, but it isn't until I almost fall to the ground with it that I finally fold and give Keisha the words I know she's looking for.

"Fine!" I throw my hands in the air and stomp one foot into a puddle. "Big Ben is the best and I can only dream of driving a car like him. You have the superior vehicle and I only disparage him because I'm jealous you get to drive him."

"Oh my god! I had no idea you felt that way!" She opens her creaky-ass door that I swear could be heard from the moon and meets me at the back of her truck. "Thank you for opening up. I know how hard it is to admit jealousy."

"Oh please," I scoff as we shove my bike up and into Big Ben.

She makes me recite the same speech anytime I need her to drive anywhere. I'm sure I have it in our text thread somewhere, but I've said it enough times that it's ingrained in my brain.

"I don't know why you make it so hard." She tosses her long dreads over her shoulder and lifts up the circle lens sunglasses that only she can pull off so she can level me with her knowing stare. "You don't have to pretend you don't like something when you know you do. It's okay to open yourself up, to put yourself out there."

I have a feeling we're not talking about Big Ben anymore, and I know where she's trying to go with this. It's a conversation I avoid on a good day, let alone while I'm soaking wet and standing outside of a 7-Eleven. So I do what I do best—play dumb.

"I don't know what you're talking about." I slam Big Ben shut and march to the passenger's side door. "I talk about my feelings all the time, you're the one that likes to keep to yourself."

"Bullshit and you know it," she shouts over the car before she climbs into her driver's seat and leans across to open my door. "You talk to your students about how it's okay to be happy, mad, and sad, but you don't give yourself that same permission. You're so afraid of feeling anything that's deemed bad that you bottle everything up."

"That's not true at all!" I lie through my fucking teeth, because it's so true that I almost shatter with the weight of it.

"It is true." She doesn't even attempt to soften the blow. "Have you even talked to your mom about your car yet? Your student loan stress?"

"Why would I do that? I'm an adult. I don't need to run to my mom with all of my problems."

"Or . . ." She drags out the word, and I brace for whatever she's going to say next. "Is it because you're so afraid of being a burden that you hold everything inside and now you're about to explode from the pressure of it all?"

Well fuck me. Is she an art teacher or a psychologist?

It's not that I think I'm a burden, per se, but I saw my mom go through a lot. If she never has to worry about anything ever again, that's what I want for her. Plus, even if there were some truth to me not showing every single emotion—which is not a bad thing, by the way, not everything needs to be made into a big production—I'm not anywhere near exploding.

Things might not be the best they've ever been, but I've been through so much worse.

"I love you for caring, but I'm okay." I reach across the console and grab her hand, grateful to have a friend who cares about me. "I promise."

"And I love you for thinking you're okay." She squeezes my hand. "But you're wet and stranded at a gas station because your car is broken down. You're stressed about bills, but you've already spent what? Two thousand dollars on Petunia Lemon crap even though you've only been a member for two, maybe three months? And last, but certainly not least, you fucked one of your student's parents and now not only does he know where you work, volunteer, and live . . . he's basically your neighbor."

"Fucking hell, Keisha! When you say it like that, of course it's going to sound bad!" Any gratitude I was feeling toward her seconds ago flies out of the stupid, crank-down window. "I mean, attack much?"

"How am I attacking you?" On the surface, this seems like an innocent enough question, but the tone she uses has me regretting every single life choice that led me to this moment. "Are those not the things happening in your life right now?"

"You know they are." I don't even know why I answer; we both know damn well that was a rhetorical question.

"Exactly, babe. The cracks aren't just starting to show, they're shattering. And if you don't stop trying to make everyone else happy instead of focusing on yourself for once, I'm worried you'll never be able to put yourself back together again." She turns her key and Big Ben rumbles to life. "Just think about what I'm saying, okay?"

"Fine." I roll my eyes and lean my wet hair against the headrest even though I know it's going to cause it to tangle. "But I'm not doing it because I agree with you, I just liked the Humpty Dumpty reference."

"I knew you'd appreciate that one." She smiles and keeps her eyes on her rearview mirror as she reverses out of the parking spot. "Now let's go set up for this stupid party."

· 17 ·

AFTER RETURNING FROM the shopping trip from hell, I take the hottest shower of my life and then Keisha and I get straight to work setting up for the Petunia Lemon party I've spent the last month planning.

Keisha works in the kitchen, pulling out my best glasses and arranging what's left of the snacks I bought on the ceramic trays I borrowed from my downstairs neighbor while I attack the rest of my apartment. Sweat falls from my forehead as I rearrange my living room furniture to make space for the folding chairs Frederick told me I could use. I toss my most beloved knick-knacks in a box and replace them with the plethora of products I ordered just for today.

In my bedroom, a white noise machine and essential oil diffuser sit on the nightstand where a pile of books, two water glasses, and bottle of melatonin have lived for the last year. I change out the polka dot sheets and floral quilt my mom made me in high school for a sad, boring white linen set I found on sale at Target last week. And all of the frames and vases normally crowding my dresser are shoved into the bottom of the closet so the Petunia Pro Facial Spa can sit atop it in all of its fancy, eight-hundred-dollar glory.

I do everything Nora told me to do for a successful party.

And it's still not enough.

"Wow." Hayley clutches her wineglass to her chest and the giant diamond adorning her ring finger winks beneath the sunlight filtering in through the lone window in my living room. "Your place is so colorful . . . and quaint."

I know Hayley was trying to be sweet, but it doesn't take a genius to glean the true meaning behind her "compliment." I might be wrong, but I have a feeling she's never stepped foot in a home under two thousand square feet and that no matter how hard I tried to get my tiny, six-hundred-and-fifty-square-foot apartment ready for tonight, it would never be Petunia Lemon certified in her eyes.

"Thank you!" I pretend not to notice the horrified smile frozen on her face. "Please feel free to have a seat wherever you want and help yourself to all of the wine and snacks your heart desires."

"You're the sweetest. Thank you again for inviting me tonight." She gives my hand a light squeeze and scurries off to the small group that's been huddled in the corner for the last fifteen minutes.

I make my way back to my kitchen, avoiding Keisha's eyes as I open up another bottle of wine. I promised myself I'd only have one glass, but that was before guest after guest started filing into my apartment, and not a single one of them was a new recruit.

After my failed attempt to sell products at the farmers' market,

I figured maybe a party was the way to go. I might not be the top saleswoman, but according to my college roommate, I'm cream of the crop when it comes to partying. I curated the perfect guest list and then Nora helped me craft the perfect "Hey Hun" message. My DMs on Facebook and Instagram were in shambles, but people seemed really excited to swing by for drinks, samples, and a free spa session on the brand-new Petunia Pro.

"Guess who's here!" The front door swings open, and Nora saunters through the front door like she doesn't have a care in the world. "And I brought friends!"

I hold my breath, expecting to see Jacqueline in all of her beautiful, not-a-hair-out-of-place glory. I know nothing's happened with Luke in my apartment, but knowing he was here and now his ex-wife will be here too turns my stomach into a rock. I didn't mean for this to get so messy, but drama just seems to be drawn to me.

I paint on the smile I practiced in the mirror this morning, hoping it looks authentic and not terrified and full of guilt. Except when Nora holds the door open and I see who follows her inside, I don't need to be worried at all.

"Oh my god!" I slam my wineglass on the millimeter of open counter space and run the short distance to the door so I can wrap my new guests—who happen to be old friends—in hugs. "What are you doing here? I had no idea you'd be coming."

"Nora asked me yesterday and you know I love a party," Chloe says. "I can't believe you didn't invite me!"

"I know!" Odette cosigns. "I thought you were my girl! See if I sneak you those ice creams anymore."

Chloe is the school nurse, and Odette is my favorite lunch

lady. They both started at Nester Fox this year, and they are perfect additions to our faculty. Last Karaoke Wednesday, they performed a rousing duet of Nelly and Kelly Rowland's 2002 hit, "Dilemma," and it will go down in time as one of the top performances Nester Fox has ever seen . . . outside of the masterpieces Anna creates with the children, of course.

"You're both always welcome at anything I do." I guide them the three steps it takes to get into the kitchen so I can get them a drink. "But if it makes you feel any better, I didn't invite anyone from school. Keisha is only here because I forced her to help me set up and Nora is my upline, so she helped me plan the party."

Since I'm just getting started, Nora and I decided it might be best to get a little more acclimated with Petunia Lemon before I started reaching out to the other faculty members. Plus, even though I've watched all of the training videos on the Petunia Pro and went to a live demonstration, I'm still afraid to use it on somebody who isn't me. I mean really, I'm a kindergarten teacher, not an aesthetician, for goodness' sake! And I'm pretty sure they have to go to school for years, so even though I experiment with the different attachments every day and wear the red-light mask before bed, the margin for error still feels a little too large for comfort. If I messed up my coworkers' faces, I'm not sure I'd ever be able to show mine again.

Now that they're here and I actually have an opportunity to sell some products tonight and recruit a member or two, I'm going to have to pony up and put my fears behind me . . .

And thank Nora for coming through as my professional fairy godmother, take two.

"Did you set your Petunia Pro up in your room like we talked about?" Nora opens my cabinet door and finds the whiskey I wasn't planning on taking out tonight and pours herself a glass. "I want to show our favorite new coworkers how it works."

Nora has been coming into my classroom every Monday since she received her Petunia Pro to rave about the parties she threw for her clients over the weekends. The amount of product she's sold and the new members she's recruited is unbelievable. It's the main reason I finally gave in to throwing one myself.

"Yes, it's all set up on my dresser, and I have some serums and sunscreen samples there too." I've been so afraid to use this machine on others that having Nora step up for me would be a godsend. "Are you sure you don't mind doing it? I watched the videos again this morning and I can try if you don't want to do it."

"I can totally do it." She squeezes my hand, and I know she can sense my nerves. "But why don't you come watch while I do the facials, just so you can feel more comfortable, of course."

"I would love that. Thank you so much."

I know this party hasn't gone exactly as expected, but thank god Nora came to save the day. For the first time since joining Petunia Lemon, things are finally getting going for me. All I needed was a good wine, good cheese, and good friends.

And lucky for me, I have a surplus of all three.

GOOD NEWS: CHLOE and Odette both signed up to be Petunia Lemon reps.

"So . . ." Keisha finishes off one of the many open wine bottles scattered around my apartment. "That was interesting."

Bad news: they signed up with Nora.

"Yeah." I lean back into my couch, staring unseeing at my disaster of a living room, trying to come up with anything at all to say. "Interesting is right."

"It was a really nice party," Keisha says. "Everyone had a great time and your spread was phenomenal."

"It was good, wasn't it?" Even after my bread and some other key ingredients met an early death, everything turned out amazing.

Well, everything except the actual turnout, that is.

"The cheeseballs you made were a hit, but there's still a little bit left if you want me to start putting it away." Keisha dances around what she really wants to say. "Or we could wait a little longer."

I check the time on my watch . . . again. The last guests left about an hour ago, but a stupid, annoying part of me is hoping that someone still might show up. Maybe they got stuck in the storm like me, something happened to their car, and they're still on their way. I know it's unlikely, but a girl can wish.

I'm what the kids would call "delulu" right now, but I don't care. After everything I did to prepare for this party, how much money I spent, I can't throw in the towel just yet.

"Let's give it like thirty more minutes and then we'll clean up."

"Sounds good to me," she says. "But while we wait, should we discuss the giant, Nora-shaped elephant in the room?"

And air my grievances in real time instead of letting them grow and fester overnight? I don't think so.

"I'd rather not."

"Of course you'd rather not." The kid gloves Keisha's been

handling me with start to come off, and I do not appreciate it. "But you're going to have to talk about it eventually."

"*Eventually* being the key word." I stand up and start grabbing the cups and plates that are all over the place. I hate cleaning, but it sounds better than having this conversation with Keisha right now. "I don't even know if there's anything to talk about. She said Chloe and Odette both wanted to sign up beneath her and that's not her fault."

"Bullshit," Keisha spits out. "And you know it."

"No, I—" I start when my phone buzzes on my coffee table. A number I don't recognize pops up on the screen, and the Petunia Lemon boxes stacked on top of each other wobble nearby.

Saved by the bell, literally.

I don't usually answer the phone unless I know who's calling, but since I'm avoiding talking to Keisha and feeling my feelings, having a potentially frustrating conversation with a stranger is a much better option.

"Hello?" I hold the phone against my ear and try to listen through all of the noise coming from the other end of the line. "Hello?"

"Oh yes," a deep, gruff voice I don't recognize says. "Is this Emerson . . . Emerson Pierce?"

"This is she," I respond, my grandma's strict phone etiquette instantly reappearing. "May I ask who's speaking?"

"This is Greg down at Highland Auto Repair, you had your car towed here last night."

My stomach falls to my toes. I knew this was coming, but I'm not ready to know the cost of my procrastination.

"Oh, yes. Hi." I try to hide the dread in my voice. It's not his fault he's probably going to accomplish the nearly impossible task of making this terrible day even worse. "Thank you so much for getting back to me so fast."

"We have your 2008 Honda Civic that came in to us after it wasn't starting." He tells me what I already know and I hold my breath, waiting for the other shoe to drop. "The good news is you don't need a new engine."

The air leaves my lungs in a quick whoosh, and I almost fall to the ground from pure relief.

"Oh thank god!" I wish I could reach through the phone and kiss him! This isn't just good news, it's the best news! I'd been mentally preparing for what a new engine would mean, and no matter how I tried to look at it, it never ended well. "So what is wrong with it?"

Now that I know it's not an engine and I won't have to replace my beloved Honda that I've mistreated so horribly over the years, I can handle anything.

"You have a blown head gasket," he says like that means anything to me. "A lot of times when this happens, you need an engine too, so you're really lucky."

I'm pretty sure he's the only person who's ever told me I'm lucky. After today, the assertion is even more laughable than normal, but it's nice to hear nonetheless.

"Okay . . ." I drag out the word, so unfamiliar with the world of auto repair that I don't even know what to ask. "Can you please explain this to me like I'm five? What does that mean? And more importantly, what is this going to cost?"

I'm sure he doesn't get paid enough to deal with a customer like me, but thankfully, he does anyway.

"The head gasket is an important part of the engine that stops the oil and the coolant from mixing. It's important to keep the engine running smooth and efficiently. With proper care and regular oil changes, they can last a pretty long time." There's some judgment in his tone, but since it's well deserved, I ignore it. "This isn't an engine repair, but it's not a little fix either. I'd say the cost can range anywhere from fifteen hundred to three thousand dollars."

The surge of relief I was feeling retreats into the wild, and my old friends, Anxiety and Fear, are quick to settle back into place.

"That's a pretty big price range." I don't have three thousand dollars to throw at my car, but if the sopping-wet shoes in my closet are anything to go by, I can't afford to not fix it either. "How much is it going to cost me?"

Because I know how my luck works, I'm fully prepared for him to come back on the higher end of the spectrum. I sit back down on the couch, ignoring Keisha's concerned gaze and chewing on my nails. My stomach churns; I'm pretty sure I'm going to be sick.

"I know when you called in, you said Tom sent you over, right?"

"Um, yeah." I struggle to follow the change of subject. When I called The Barkery to tell them my car was sitting in the parking lot, Tom snatched the phone away from Shelly and barked out orders to call this mechanic. And since Tom isn't one to normally share advice, I didn't hesitate before listening. "Tom Cywinski, he told me to call you and let you know he sent me."

"Yup," he confirms. "Tom is a good friend of ours. He helped me find Rita, my pit bull, and helped to keep her safe when the city was coming down hard on the breed. I owe a lot to Tom and he tells me you're good people, always at the shelter, helping the dogs."

I'm not a crier, but for some reason, my sinuses feel like they've been set on fire and my living room gets a little blurry. I don't know if Greg's waiting for a response, but my throat is clogged and I couldn't say anything even if I wanted to.

"The price to replace your Honda Civic gasket would normally come out to around eighteen hundred dollars. But . . ." He lets that hang and the hope I try so hard not to feel seeps right back in again. "Because of Tom and all the good he tells us you do, we're going to knock off most of our labor costs and do it for you for eight hundred dollars."

Eight hundred dollars is still a lot of money, but it's nowhere near as bad as the almost two-thousand-dollar bill. I guess sometimes luck is subjective after all.

"Oh my god," I gasp into the phone, trying my hardest to keep my stupid tears from falling. "Thank you so much."

"So can I take that as permission to get the repairs started?" he asks, and I swear I can hear his smile through the phone.

"Yes." I nod my head knowing damn well he can't see me. "Please get the repairs started."

"Alright then," he says, and I hear the faint clicking of computer buttons in the background. "Looks like we can start those repairs on Tuesday and should have it finished for you by Thursday or Friday. You can pay for the repairs when you pick it up."

I thank him once more before pressing end. I toss the phone onto the couch and take in the deepest breath I can manage before I slowly let it out, realizing what has to be done.

I look at the Petunia Lemon boxes displayed all around my living room, and if there's one more bright side to this whole mess, at least I didn't open most of my inventory. "Well fuck."

"Well fuck, what?" Keisha repeats after me, her patience clearly running dry. "What's happening?"

"Good news first?" I ask and she nods her head. "I can afford to get my car fixed. Bad news? I'm going to have to quit Petunia Lemon and take them up on their money-back guarantee."

"I know you said there was bad news, but I have to be honest, I'm not hearing any. You're not going to be stuck on your bike through the winter. You're escaping a cult without a permanent reminder etched onto your wrist, and . . ." She grabs the old fashioned I made for her and gestures to the rest of the snacks sitting in front of us. "Now we can go back to keeping our snacks to ourselves."

She's not exactly wrong. I might be a little irritated at Nora right now, but I'm still going to hate having to tell her that I'm quitting. She might be disappointed, but at least she can't say I didn't try my hardest. I've spent almost three thousand dollars that I don't have and haven't made a single cent back.

I love people, I just don't love selling to them and evidence would suggest people don't like me selling to them either. Petunia Lemon has been fun, but it's time for me to call it quits.

18

SO FAR, THIS school year has been one of my best years yet. I love all of my students, and I feel like I've finally hit my stride as a teacher. Now that October is in full swing and we've been together for a few months, I'm beginning to see progress in everything from sight words and numbers to our classroom routines. They're all gaining so much confidence, and it's an honor to see them grow each day.

But even though it's been brilliant, nothing is perfect.

The kids are amazing, but there are a few parents who I'm convinced spend their days sitting by their computers and drafting emails to send me about any and everything. I'm doing my best to support them, but I kind of wish I took a page out of Keisha's book and warned them off at the start of the year.

There's also the small fact that I haven't gotten my car back yet. Thankfully it hasn't rained again, but it's getting colder by the day and I'm bracing myself for when I wake up one morning and the sidewalks are covered with snow. Plus, my body still hasn't adjusted to the bike seat, and every time I climb on my bike, I'm more and more convinced that whoever came up with the design was a sadist. It's already bad enough that I look like some kind of delinquent who lost their driver's license or worse, a person who cares about the environment, but my vagina shouldn't hurt this much on top of it.

Just one more reason I need Petunia Lemon to give me my freaking money back.

I rest my pounding head on top of the pile of papers I've been meaning to grade, the sound of classical music about a minute away from putting me to sleep. I've lost count of how long I've been on hold with Petunia Lemon since Monday. Every time I call about returning my inventory and getting my refund processed, they start bouncing me around from one person to the next. I got really close last night, but right when the customer service representative started to ask for my credit card information, the call was magically disconnected. When I called back, I was greeted with an autoresponder telling me it was after hours and to call back tomorrow. I don't want to assume the worst, but the longer this takes, the more upset I'm starting to get.

The soft melody of the current song ends, and I hold my breath before the gentle notes of the next song begin to play. My fingers flex around the phone, and the urge to throw it against the whiteboard is almost too strong to fight. Part of me is so delusional that I'm convinced if I wait five more minutes, a representative will be on the phone to wrap this whole mess up. The realistic part of me, however, knows this is a fool's errand, and there's no way anyone will be able to help before my students return from lunch. Biting back a scream, I hang up the phone.

A light knock sounds on my door, and I glance at my clock. I wasted a good portion of my lunch period, but it's way too early for my class to be back. The only person who ever comes into my room during the school day is Keisha, but she's supposed to be in class right now and she never knocks.

"Come in!" I try to yell, but my hoarse voice doesn't carry as far as it normally does.

I'm expecting one of the other kindergarten teachers to come in, probably to nab some of the extra supplies I always have, so color me shocked when Jacqueline waltzes inside instead.

"Sorry to bother you," she says. "Is now an okay time to come in?"

"Of course." I stand up and walk around my desk to greet her. "Isla is at lunch now, do you need me to go and grab her?"

Other than her disastrous showing at back-to-school night and waving to her in the car pool lines occasionally, she's not a common face at Nester Fox yet. Nothing has happened between me and Luke—well, not again—but I can't help feeling like a very specific brand of dirtbag standing across from her.

"That's not necessary." Her striking blue eyes twinkle beneath the fluorescent lights, and there's not a single hair out of place on her head. She's so perfect that it hurts my eyes. I feel like I need permission to look at her. "I know Lucas is bringing Isla cupcakes for her birthday today, but I wanted to bring a little something special too."

She lifts up the two bags I somehow didn't even see her holding and stares at me expectantly until I take the hint, along with both bags from her hands.

"Oh wow!" Both bags are filled with much smaller bags, and while one of them was nice and light, the other one is so heavy that I'm surprised it didn't break. "Isla is going to be thrilled."

Isla, like most children on their birthdays, has been floating on cloud nine from the moment she walked into the classroom this morning and saw her birthday surprise. It's my little tradition to decorate my students' desks for their birthdays with balloons and a birthday crown or hat. We always have the treasure chest in the room, but I have a special box with bigger toys that I pull out for birthdays. They get to pick one toy, and then I buy them a treat from the lunch room—Isla chose a "Barbie" and an ice-cream sandwich. Odette even snuck in an extra juice box for her.

It's not much, but they love it.

And even though I know I shouldn't have done it because it comes very close to crossing lines, I may have gotten her a cat toy for Mister Bubbles. It's a llama plushie and it was on sale for three dollars! It would've been a crime *not* to get it.

"Those are bags for the kids." She points to the smaller, lighter bags before moving to the larger, heavier bags that, now I'm looking, I can see are filled with Petunia Lemon products. "And those are for the moms. I know it's a little unconventional, but I figured, why not? Moms deserve nice things too."

"They sure do," I agree, although something about this makes me really uncomfortable. "This was very thoughtful of you."

"Right? There's samples of everything in there. The face wash, night cream, antiaging serum, a couple of different sheet masks, and a face roller. I also added a discount card in case they want to schedule a Petunia Pro treatment with me."

I'm attempting to listen, but I'm too distracted trying to figure out how much she must have spent putting the mom bags together. My class has sixteen students and the face rollers alone are fifteen dollars a pop. Add in the sheet masks and the samples that you still have to pay for and that's so much freaking money!

Unwelcome and uninvited, Luke's stupid, gravelly, sexy-assin voice telling me how financially irresponsible Jacqueline is when it comes to Petunia Lemon pops into my head. I don't even know if he was telling the truth, but now I can't help but wonder if she's doing as well as an empowered skincare consultant as she seems or if it's just a front while she digs herself an even deeper hole. I don't know how much she's invested in her business, but considering I sunk over two thousand dollars on product in just a few months, I can only imagine how much she's spent.

But luckily for me, I don't need to know the number to know it's none of my damn business.

"I'm sure they will love this." I grab my keys out of my desk drawer and carry the bags to the closet I always keep locked at the back of the room. Goodie bags are best when distributed right before school ends; if they see them before that exact moment, all hell will break loose. Another lesson I learned the hard way. "I'll be sure to pass them out when we're packing up to leave."

"Oh my god! I almost forgot!" The sound of her heels against the tile floors echoes in the room as she runs after me. "I bought these for the classroom."

She reaches into the massive Louis Vuitton bag tucked on her shoulder and pulls out three brand-new bottles of Petunia

Lemon's triple-action sunscreen. One bottle of that stuff retails for a whopping eighty-five dollars *with* the discount. It's one of their most popular products, but I'm pretty sure it's meant to firm skin and help fight wrinkles . . . not to lather small children in before they run around the playground.

But hey. I'm quitting. What do I know?

"Oh wow!" I say again, beginning to feel like a broken record. "It's so kind of you to think of the classroom, but unfortunately, I can't accept these."

"What?" Her arms fall to her sides and confusion mars her beautiful face. It's the most I've ever seen her forehead move, and like the aurora borealis or a solar eclipse, it's a rare and fascinating sight to behold. "What do you mean? Why not?"

"We aren't allowed to apply sunscreen at school." It's one of those things that feels so absurd, it's almost laughable. Gun laws to ensure student safety? Nope. Laws to prohibit teachers from applying sunscreen? Sure, why not? "If a student is in need of sunscreen, it must be applied at home before they come to school."

"But we live in Colorado!" Jacqueline sounds just as shocked as I was when I found out about this rule. "And it's just sunscreen for Christ's sake!"

The happy glow has long since left Jacqueline's face, and even though I completely understand her outrage, I feel a bit of whiplash at her sudden mood change . . .

And at being her unfortunate target.

"I know, I think it's ridiculous too." I try to placate her. "But because sunscreen is regulated by the FDA, it's considered an over-the-counter drug. I've seen parents bring in their own sunscreen to the nurse along with a doctor's note, but other than that, there's nothing we can do about it."

Her mouth opens and closes, but no words come out. It's the first time I've seen someone look truly flabbergasted. Her pale skin is fire-engine red, and just when I think her head is about to explode, Luke walks in with a giant tray of rainbow cupcakes and hammers the final nail into the coffin.

"Good after—" He cuts himself off when he catches sight of Jacqueline standing next to me with one hand on her hip and the other full of sunscreen. "What are you doing here?"

"Why do you think I'm here, Lucas?" Jacqueline snarls with so much venom in her voice, I have no idea how Luke doesn't pass away on the spot. "I don't know if you forgot, but just because we're divorced doesn't mean I stopped being Isla's mom. It's her birthday. I brought goodies."

She gestures to the bags I'm holding, but it's useless. Luke is focused on one thing and one thing only.

"You've got to be kidding me." He zeroes in on the Petunia Lemon products like a bull to a red flag. His knuckles turn white around the cupcake tray and his entire body goes on high alert. "Please tell me you aren't using my daughter to hawk that shit."

"Our daughter," Jacqueline spits back, meeting his glare with one of her own, and it's the weirdest thing. She seems almost . . . I don't know, excited about it? "And as far as I know, it's not illegal to give out gifts on our daughter's birthday."

"Actually—" I start and shut up just as fast when her poisonous glare cuts to me. Holy shit. How can somebody so pretty be so scary? "You know what? You don't need me. I'll just leave you both to this."

As a Bravo superfan, I'd be lying if I said I didn't like watching drama—it's one of my favorite pastimes—but there's a huge difference between watching drama and being in the middle of it. Like literally, smack-dab in the middle. I stick the bags in the closet as fast as I can manage, trying my hardest to shield the bag filled with more Petunia Lemon from Luke and get the hell out of Dodge.

"Come on, Jac." The familiar nickname is directly at odds with his tone dripping with disdain. "A lot of shit is legal, but that doesn't mean you should do it at your kid's fucking school."

"Oh? Like using filthy language in her classroom?" She doesn't hesitate before she claps back. "You're such a hypocrite."

I wouldn't pick a side if there was a gun to my head, but even so, I can't help but acknowledge she scored a point with that one. And much to his dismay, neither can Luke.

"You're right. I shouldn't have said that." He turns to look at me, ignoring the memo that states I'm trying to make myself invisible over here. "I apologize, Miss Pierce."

I wave them off and busy myself with straightening the books I already organized today. "That's alright, the kids aren't here."

"Did you see that? Do you see how I can own up to my mistakes?" He throws his apology in her face, and if Jacqueline didn't scare the absolute crap out of me, it might've made me laugh. "That's something you've never been able to do."

"Oh please tell me, great and wonderful Lucas, what mistake

have you ever owned up to?" She closes the space between them, and I take this as a threat. "The way you dismissed my feelings about New York? The way you prioritized your work over me? How you tried to give me an ultimatum and give up the one thing that made me happy and feel like myself after having a baby?"

Her voice rises steadily with every question, and by the time she finishes, she's flat-out screaming. I double-check to make sure the classroom door is closed, but I still wouldn't be surprised if someone sends the school resource officer to come check on things.

"I dismissed your feelings about New York?" He stares at her in disbelief. "I quit the job I dreamt of having my entire life because I took your feelings so seriously. We moved to Colorado! And don't you dare throw that company in my face. You know how supportive I was. You're the one who almost ran through our entire savings account to impress a bunch of people who didn't care if we couldn't afford our mortgage as long as they made a buck off of you."

The headache I've been nursing all day makes a sudden, bordering on violent reappearance. I came to school prepared for kid screaming, but I don't deal well with adults behaving poorly and as entertaining—and by that, I mean horrifying—as this has been, I think I've reached my limit. I really don't want to intervene, but I'm not sure I can let this go on any longer. They're like a black hole and the nasty back-and-forth between them feels like it might swallow this entire school whole.

"I'm so sorry to interrupt," I say in the same voice I use when my students are throwing a tantrum. "I obviously don't know what's going on between you both, but it doesn't seem like you're going to reach a resolution today. My students, including Isla, will be back soon, and the last thing I'd want her to see or hear on her birthday are the two people she loves the most arguing. I think it'd be in everyone's best interest for you both to take a break and continue this conversation another time."

I read somewhere that domestic disputes are the most dangerous situations, and I feel like I just threw myself to a pack of angry wolves . . . even though wolves might be preferable. Jacqueline's back goes ramrod straight, and her eyes turn to ice when they cut to me. The hairs on my arms stand as the air in the room goes static and I brace for impact.

"Excuse me?" Her whisper sends shivers down my spine. "What did you just say?"

I don't want to repeat myself. Hell, I don't even think she wants me to repeat myself! If this were up to me, I'd be sitting at my desk, scrolling on my phone until the kids come back. Which—according to the clock that was probably mounted on the wall sometime during the seventies—will be any minute now.

"I respect that you and Mr. Miller have things you need to discuss, but it's a discussion that needs to be held outside of this classroom." My voice is filled with the confidence I don't at all feel, and I'm praying that the old adage of *fake it til you make it* holds true for me. "My students will be back soon and it will be best for everyone if you're not in here when they return."

I think it sounded good, but there's so much blood rushing through my ears that I can't be sure.

"How dare—" she starts, but then, to my immense gratitude and relief, Luke cuts her off.

"Come on, Jac." Where there was anger in Jacqueline's tone, there's shame in his. "She's right, you know this isn't the place to have this conversation. Neither one of us wants Isla to see us like this and if you want, I'll promise to bring her to your house after school."

"You'd do that?" Jacqueline's eyes glisten, and I watch the hardened mask she wears so well crumble to the ground. "It's your night."

"It is." He nods, looking hotter than he's ever looked before. "But it's our girl's birthday and she's going to want to see her mom. I'd never get in the way of that."

Jacqueline wraps her arms around Luke, burying her face into his chest once her tears begin to fall. "Thank you."

I know I just wanted them to stop arguing, but somehow, this moment is so intimate that it's even harder to watch than the fighting.

As a person who's struggled for a long time to show any emotion other than happiness, I get how vulnerable they must feel right now. Thankfully, before this can go on too much longer, the lunch bell rings.

"The kids are on their way back."

This time I don't have to say it twice.

Jacqueline keeps her eyes down, careful to avoid me as she hurries out of the room. Luke follows after her, his steps much slower as he goes.

"I'm sorry," he mouths.

"Please." I wave off his apology like this is something that happens all the time and not the most intense argument I've ever witnessed in my entire life. "It's not a big deal. And don't worry, I'll make sure Isla gets the cupcakes. She's going to love them."

He nods once before pausing at the door. I wait for him, desperate to hear what he has to say, but when the front door to my room swings open, his sad smile is the last thing I see before a class of rowdy kindergartners led by a very special girl wearing a very special birthday crown come flooding into the classroom. And despite the crazy lunch with her wild parents, we still manage to have the best day ever.

I'M WIPING RAINBOW frosting off the desks after all of the kiddos have been picked up when I get paged to the front office.

I never get called to the office.

I avoided it when I was a student because I was Goody Two-shoes would've rather died than get in trouble. I don't get called now because I'm not cool enough to have friends visit me at school and I'm too poor to ever order Uber Eats. When teachers get in trouble, they're summoned by email, not speaker, but even though Jacqueline didn't seem upset with me when she left, that doesn't mean she wasn't. Knowing how close she is with Nora, I can't help the way my brain spins through every worst-case scenario during my walk down the long hallway.

"Hey, Lisa." I wave from the other side of the sliding plexiglass window. I try to sound normal and not like I've just convinced myself that I'm going to be blacklisted from every single Denver public school. "Is everything okay?"

"Everything's great," she says, but something about her tone sounds off. "Why would you ask such a thing? Is there something going on with you? Anything you've forgotten to tell me about? Anything at all?"

Oh yeah, *that's* not suspicious.

I narrow my eyes and look at her out of the corner of my eyes. "Why are you being weird?"

"I'm not being weird," she says . . . sounding weird.

"Lisa . . ." I use the sternest teacher voice in my arsenal, knowing it won't faze her. She's been the receptionist at this school since her kids went here over twenty years ago, and she's completely immune to any and all bullshit. "You are being so weird."

"I just wanted to see how you were doing today. I didn't realize that was a crime." She's using that tone my grandma used whenever she was trying to make my mom feel guilty about something, and Lisa might be good at it, but she's not Irish Catholic immigrant good.

"Tell me what's happening or I swear to god, I'm going to run out that door and bicycle my butt home."

I actually do need to leave soon. I don't know when the sun officially begins to set, but I refuse to ride my bike in the dark.

She must hear the truth in my threat, because she finally gives in.

"Fine! Here." She reaches to the side and, as if by magic, pulls out a white paper bag spotted with grease stains. "This was delivered by a very handsome gentleman who I could've sworn I've seen a time or two before."

From anyone else in the school, I would take this as a threat, but not Lisa. She might love to hear the gossip, but she never spreads it. The woman is a vault. I think it's because she knows she'll get all the good stuff if people trust her not to spread it around the school.

She's a genius.

"Is that"—I look closer at the yellow logo on the bag to make sure my eyes aren't tricking me—"from Denny's?"

My favorite breakfast spot in the world?

Lisa nods and I swear her smile triples in size. "There's a card too."

She hands me a blue envelope.

Logically, I know I should take my food and my card back to my classroom and open them up alone. But who has time for logic in a situation like this? Not me, that's for damn sure.

I rip open the envelope and pull out a card with the cutest picture of a little bulldog puppy. He's all wrinkly and adorable and he's wearing sunglasses! I love it and it will definitely be framed on my hallway wall before the night is over.

Or so I thought . . .

I open the card and all of my hammer and nail plans melt away because *I* melt away. Inside, written in scrappy handwriting, only two words appear.

I'm sorry.

There's no name, but I don't need it. I know exactly who this is from, something that's confirmed when I open the takeout box and find my Moons Over My Hammy sandwich.

The one I told Luke was my favorite meal ever. The one I told him about almost two months ago and he still remembers.

I knew he was obsessed with me!

It would just be so much more fun to hold over his head if I wasn't starting to feel the same way about him.

19

COMPARED TO SOME other states, the allergies in Colorado aren't too bad. The cold weather freezes everything and keeps allergy season short and sweet, but that doesn't mean they never affect me. There's always a week in the fall that kicks my ass. As soon as my headache and scratchy throat come on, I take a Zyrtec and continue on my merry way.

So color me surprised when I was pedaling my ass home from school, a Moons Over My Hammy in my backpack and a smirk on my face, and I started shivering and sweating at the same time. By the time I finally made it home, I ripped off my clothes in my hallway, grabbed the thermometer, and collapsed into my bed.

Other than going to the bathroom and filling up my water bottle, I haven't moved in two days.

I spend five days a week teaching adorable little germ magnets, so I'm used to catching a bug or two. But usually, I see kids going down around me and I can prepare. This one totally caught me by surprise. I guess there is a slight possibility that this could also be the result of getting caught on my bike in a rainstorm and then standing beneath an AC vent in a room full of strangers for thirty minutes.

Not my finest moment, although it should be said, also not my worst. There was one time in college that I took so many shots at a football game that I fell asleep in the stadium bathroom. The janitor found me curled up next to a toilet and called the campus police to remove me. And that, my friends, is what you call a rock-bottom moment.

But honestly, who cares where or how I got this stupid bug? The only thing that matters now is that I feel like I'm going to die and all I want is to call my mom. Which of course, I won't do . . . and *not* because I think I'm a burden like Keisha said, but because my sweet, perfect mother is a worrier. If she finds out I'm sick, she'll nag until she finds out about my car, and then she'll find out about Petunia Lemon and my school loans and everything will be an avalanche of awful!

It's better for everyone if I suffer in silence, like the good Catholic girl my grandma encouraged me to be. And no, I do not go to church anymore, but that's just semantics. Catholic suffering, much like Catholic guilt, can and should be practiced anywhere in the world.

My stomach starts to growl, and I roll out of bed to make the quick journey to my kitchen. My body aches from the top of my head to the tips of my toes—even my earlobes hurt. Sweat has plastered the T-shirt I threw on when I got out of the shower to my back, and I hope it's a sign my fever is finally breaking. I called the doctor when it spiked yesterday, and they told me I'll need to come in if it doesn't go away by tomorrow. Considering

I'm still without a car, I'd really love to avoid pulling up to my appointment on a bike. I'm pretty sure they'd frown upon that kind of thing.

I open my fridge and almost weep when I see how empty it is. I was planning to go to the grocery store later in the week, but feeling like death warmed over kind of screwed those plans up.

"A real adult would've at least had some fruit in the fridge, Emerson," I lecture myself before turning to the tiny cabinet I use as my pantry. It's not much better than my refrigerator, but there's an old bag of Goldfish and a few cans of soup and I can work with that.

I'm digging around, trying to find the right size pot for my soup, when the buzzer for my apartment goes off.

"Shit!" I drop the pan I'm holding onto another pot, and the loud clatter of metals colliding brings my throbbing headache back with a vengeance. That's what I get for trying to nourish myself. I'm better off rotting in bed.

Buzzzzz, it sounds again.

What in the world?

Keisha brought me Gatorade and a bowl of soup from Panera yesterday, but she left this morning for an art gallery opening in New Mexico that will be displaying her work. I know I'm not doing great, but unless I had a fever-induced hallucination and invited someone over while I was out of it, nobody should be at my door.

I wait for the buzzer again, but it doesn't come. Whoever it was probably got the wrong apartment. It happens much more often than a person would think in a building this small. I rummage around in the cabinet for the soup pan, but I don't get any closer than I did the first time before someone pounds on my door.

"What the fuck?"

I never have unexpected guests. I know the smart thing to do would be to ignore it, but I'm tired, hungry, and sick, and I don't have any energy left for self-preservation. I don't even bother asking who it is before twisting my locks and opening the door.

Big mistake.

"Can I—" My raspy voice trails off when I come face-to-face with Luke Miller . . . and he does *not* look happy. "What are you doing here?"

"Isla told me you haven't been in class," he says, and I can't tell if it's a question or an accusation.

"No . . . I mean yeah." This is the first time a parent has shown up unannounced at my house, and I think my brain is misfiring. "I've been sick."

"Figured as much."

I consider being offended, but quickly decide against it. I haven't looked in the mirror today, but it's not hard to assume that I look like I've been hit by the Hot Mess Express . . . just without the hot part. I haven't washed my face or brushed my hair in two days, and when I go to run my hand over my head, my shirt lifts up and the cool breeze against my thighs reminds me that I don't have pants on.

Cool, cool.

Absolutely nothing to see here, folks.

"So now that you know where I've been, do you feel like telling me what you're doing here?" I should tell him showing up at my door is a massive violation of a teacher/parent relationship, that it's time for us to establish boundaries and stick to them. And I almost do! But before I can lay down the law, he bends over and distracts me with the pile of grocery bags sitting on the floor. "What are all of those?"

I clutch at the hem of my shirt and cross my ankles, trying to save myself from the embarrassment of flashing Luke something he's already seen before.

"I didn't think you'd miss school unless you had to," he says, like it answers any part of my question. "I also figured that since I live down the street, the neighborly thing to do would be to check in on you and bring some groceries to tide you over until you're back on your feet."

"I . . ." I step to the side and gesture for him to come in. I'm so taken aback by this unexpected act of kindness that I temporarily forget how to use my words. "I, um . . . thanks."

He walks into my kitchen, and the pots and pans I was fighting with when he showed up look like they've won. They're spread out all over the floor, and the lids are crowding the limited counter space next to my unopened can of soup. I'm not the tidiest person in the world, but this is embarrassing even by my standards.

"What happened here?"

"Oh that?" I squeeze past him and squat down to start shoving everything back inside the cabinet. "I was just trying to find a pot to heat up some soup."

Every time I put a pan back, another one comes sliding out from somewhere else. This isn't new, but usually nobody's standing behind me, watching this unfortunate comedy of errors. I reach for the other pan, but before I can grab it, Luke grabs me. His strong hands make easy work of lifting me off of the floor and setting me on my feet.

"You're hungry?" he asks, but once again, I'm not sure if it's really a question or not.

"I guess so?" I say and hurry to explain when his brows knit together in confusion. "I haven't really had a huge appetite these last couple of days, but I need to eat."

"Alright." He nods once and rolls up his sleeves. "You go lie down. I'm going to put the groceries away and then I'll bring you something to eat."

Ummmm . . . What?

"I'm sorry." I must've misheard, because it sounded like he said he was going to cook for me and then serve me? And that can't be right. "You're going to do what now?"

His green eyes sparkle with humor, and a smile cracks his serious exterior for the first time since I opened the door. "I'm going to make you food while you rest."

He says each word slowly, enunciating every syllable, and it's nice to know he can still manage to be a sarcastic ass while making such a kind gesture.

I don't think this is what they mean when they say *get you a man who can do both*, but I'm into it.

"But why?" It's not that I don't appreciate it, because I do. It's just unnecessary. "It's just soup. I'm pretty sure I can manage that."

"I'm sure you think you can, and no offense, but—" He starts and I brace for what will, undoubtedly, be offensive. "If getting the pot out was hard, then it might be best for you and everyone in this building if you avoid the gas stove until you're feeling better."

"I've lived on my own since I was eighteen! I know how to heat up a can of soup." The thing with being around Luke is that I'm not sure if I'm offended or I just like arguing with him. "I don't need you to do it for me."

"I know you don't need me to do it for you." He braves my germs and closes the space between us. His fingers find the hem of my shirt and the feel of his hands grazing across my thighs is almost enough to make me forget I'm sick. "You take care of everyone around you. This time, I want you to let me take care of you."

I was prepared to argue with him until he left my apartment, but with just three sentences, he has managed to effectively drain the fight out of me for the rest of forever.

Between his sweet words and gentle touch, I have to remind myself that I'm sick so I don't launch myself at him. I want to tell him that when he's standing in front of me like this, he makes me want to throw caution out the window. I don't care that he's a parent or Jacqueline's ex. Nothing matters.

I want to tell him that all I want to do is turn back time and go back to our first night together. To go back to the moment when he first put his mouth on mine and made the world disappear and crack wide open at the same damn time.

But I don't.

Instead, I just say, "Okay."

I leave him in my kitchen and stumble to my room on trembling legs, with my stomach in knots and my heart exploding. I fall into my bed, and as I begin to doze off, I allow myself to wonder what we'd be like together if things were different.

It's so good, the promise of a man like Luke, that in my sick, foggy haze, just before sleep pulls me under, I realize he might be the kind of man you risk it all for.

20

I'VE ALWAYS LOVED my couch. It's pretty and soft and so comfortable that I sleep out here almost as often as I sleep in my bed. I love it so much that I thought it was impossible to ever love it more.

But then I sat on it with Luke.

His large, lean body takes up half of the space on the green velvet cushions, and every time my leg accidentally brushes against his, goose bumps explode over my skin. He draped his arm across the back of the couch at the beginning of the episode and somewhere along the way, his fingers started to play mindlessly with my messy curls.

"I really appreciate your help tonight." I hit "play next" with my remote and take a long sip of the best smoothie I've ever had. "But you don't have to stay if you don't want to."

His fingers stop moving, and I instantly regret diverting his attention away from the TV.

"And not find out what happens between Phaedra and her

castle daddy?" He sounds appalled at even the idea of it. "Not a chance."

I'd like to think I'm the reason he's staying, but I would understand if it was really the appeal of *The Traitors* that pulled him in. It's what perfect television does to you. The next episode starts to play when Luke's hand wraps around mine. He pulls the remote out of my grip and pauses Alan Cumming's Emmy-worthy recap.

"Excuse me, sir!" I try to grab the remote, but he pulls it out of reach. "What are you doing? You just said you wanted to watch it."

"I do." He sets it on the side table next to him. "But I want to talk to you about a few things and I'm not good at multitasking."

It's such a small piece of information about him that I shouldn't even notice it. But like every single little thing I learn about this man, I file it deep into my brain—desperate for any morsel that could help me understand him better.

"Oh, okay." I grab the throw blanket and pull it up to my chin. "What do you want to talk about?"

Before he came over, I barely had the energy to get out of bed. But now that he's fed me and I have some nutrients floating around inside of my body, I can handle a conversation. I assume it's something about Isla or maybe even Mister Bubbles and relax back into my couch.

"Well, first, I really wanted to apologize for the scene Jacqueline and I made in your classroom the other day." His eyes shift from me to the frozen TV screen. "I'm sure you were already not feeling well and I hate that we brought that to you."

"It was definitely a little crazy when it was happening, but I saw where you were coming from. I know how fast things can get out of control when you're passionate about something." I wish I could reassure him that I see fights like that all the time, but I can't. I'm a kindergarten teacher, not a marriage counselor. "Plus, you sent me Denny's, so all has been forgiven."

He laughs and the quiet sound does more to warm me up than this fleece throw ever will.

"I still can't believe you love Denny's."

"What can I say?" I shrug. "I'm a simple girl who loves life's simple pleasures."

"Simple?" His quiet laughter turns loud, and he makes a big show of looking around my living room. "I don't know who you're trying to convince, but nothing about you is simple. You're the most complex, fascinating person I've ever met."

"Excuse me." I untuck my legs from a crisscross position and nudge his thigh with my foot. "I can't tell if that's an insult or not."

"Not." His laughter dies on his lips, and the way he looks at me makes my toes curl. "Definitely not an insult."

The sincerity of his words hits me in the center of my chest and twists my stomach like it's a balloon animal. Whether he's pissing me off or turning me on, nobody has ever been able to affect me with their words like Luke. One way or another, he is trouble. The smart thing to do here is to run as far away as humanly possible, but time with him is a trap and every second he's near ensnares me even deeper.

I know if I'm not careful, I'll never be able to pull away.

"Oh," I whisper. "Thanks then, I guess."

A small smile tugs at the corner of his mouth, and it takes every ounce of strength I have within me not to jump across this couch and kiss it off of his face.

"You're welcome then . . ." He twists the stray curl that's always falling in my face around his finger and tugs it ever so slightly in his direction. "I guess."

The need that's lingered since that first night on a rooftop downtown—familiar and all-consuming—hangs over us so heavy, it's hard to breathe. The air shifts and the room turns static. The steady thrum of electricity constantly flowing between us begins to spark, and we get closer to crossing the barrier that's been trying to keep us apart. I know what consequences lie for us on the other side, but watching his chest rise as his eyes darken, I'm having a hard time caring.

I just can't cross that line with tangled hair and a scratchy throat.

"So . . ." I break the silence and hate myself for doing it. "What else did you want to ask me?"

"Oh, yeah." He blinks a few times and I bite back my smile knowing he was just as far gone as I was. "Any news on your car? I had to go to The Barkery the other day for Mister Bubbles and saw it wasn't there anymore."

Oh god. My car. I bite back my groan.

"It's been the bane of my existence." And not in the fun, sexy Bridgerton type of way, either. "It's in the shop and it should be ready for me. I just need to go and pick it up once I'm feeling better."

And after I get my refund from Petunia Lemon . . . although I'm starting to think that's never going to happen.

"That was fast," he says, with the perspective of someone who hasn't been biking to their workplace for the last eight hundred years. "It wasn't the engine, then?"

"No, that was one small mercy granted to me in this mess. They said it was the . . ." The answer's on the tip of my tongue, but it's hard to focus when he's so close, looking at me like he wants me for breakfast, lunch, and dinner. "A blown head gasket."

"Damn." He lets out a long whistle. "That's better than an engine, but that still sucks."

"It does, but I don't know if you remember Tom, the grumpy old man from The Barkery?" Luke nods and I continue. "He's friends with the mechanic who towed my car in. Apparently, Tom can be extra nice when he wants to and he put in a good word for me. They knocked a thousand dollars off of the price, so it's bad, but not nearly as bad as I deserved."

I've already set oil change reminders in my phone for the next two years. I've learned my lesson and will not be making this mistake again.

"I'm glad to hear that. I had to get a gasket replaced on my old car and I ended up turning that car over and getting a new one. And don't tell Tom . . ." He leans forward and drops his voice to a whisper even though we're the only ones here. "But I wasn't buying his grumpy act in the first place. He snuck Isla two bow ties and a cat toy for Mister Bubbles. He didn't think I saw him adding them to the bag, but I did."

"I mean, he's at the shelter more than I am." Which says a lot considering I'm one of their top volunteers, but animals are much easier to be around than people. I didn't think Tom hated me, more that he tolerated me for the sake of The Barkery. "I knew he had a squishy soft center, but I never thought he'd go out of his way for anyone who doesn't have four legs. Especially not for me."

Luke lets go of my hair, dropping his hand to mine and pulling me closer. "Why do you do that?"

"Do what?" I want to look away, but his emerald gaze holds me hostage.

"Why do you go out of your way to help others and then have such a hard time accepting that people would want to go out of their way for you too?"

"Why do people keep saying that?" Did Keisha get to him somehow? This feels like a setup. "I don't have a hard time accepting help. I just much prefer to be the giver when possible."

His full lips pull into a straight line and his thick eyebrows furrow together. I don't need to know him well to know exactly what that look means. He's calling bullshit and he's not wrong . . .

I'll just never admit it.

"Don't look at me like that." I grab the pillow next to me and lob it at him across the couch, but he dodges it easily. "I do accept help. You literally helped me in the parking lot . . . twice!"

And I was very grateful and only mildly resentful.

I mean really, what do these people want from me? I'm just a girl!

"Not two whole times." He holds up his hands in surrender. "I was wrong, you're great at accepting help *and* taking criticism."

I almost throw another pillow at him, but it's tucked between my back and the couch and I don't want to readjust. So I stick to using my words instead.

"Whatever, smart-ass." I stick my tongue out at him, not at all sorry for resulting to the fighting tactics of my kindergartners. "I am great at those things. Actually, I'm great at all things. So there."

"I'm so sure," he says and just that fast I rethink my no-violence stance. "If you're so great at asking for help, then I expect a phone call when you're ready to pick up your car from the shop. I am your neighbor after all."

"I would do that, but I don't have your number." It sounds crazy considering how often we've been around each other, but it's true. The first night we met, I was set on keeping it a one-night fling and then we got into a fight the next day. I guess I have his number somewhere at school, but using student information for personal use is a boundary I'd never cross. Not even for Luke.

"That can't be right." He grabs his phone on the coffee table and swipes through it until he sees that I'm right. Like always. "Damn. I feel like we should've done this months ago."

He hands me his phone and I enter all of my information before giving it back to him. He texts me as soon as he gets it back and my heart flutters when I see his number light up my screen.

"Is that the . . ." I look at the single emoji he sent me. "Cat with heart eyes emoji?"

"Yeah." He shrugs and his face turns crimson. "Isla said I need to start using it more because of Mister Bubbles. She wants it to be in my top emojis when she gets back from her mom's on Sunday. I'm not a big texter, so I have to get it in when I can."

I mean . . . could this man be any cuter? He's so pure that I can't even tell him he can cheat the system by opening his notes app and tapping on the emoji repeatedly over there.

"It's the perfect emoji, and I for one feel honored to have received it." I almost ask him to tell Isla that I enjoyed it before I remember that would be a very bad, terrible idea.

"Glad you like it." His shy smile pulls on my heartstrings as he tucks his phone away. "Now that you have it, I hope you use it. And I know you're getting your car back soon, but in case you've skipped out on some other basic car maintenance that sends it back to the shop, you can always hitch a ride to Nester Fox with me and Isla."

"Thank you." I hope I'll never have to take him up on that offer, but if I can't get in touch with Petunia Lemon, he might be hearing from me sooner than later. "That's really nice of you."

"Welcome," he says. "I promise I'm only an asshole when I talk about Petunia Lemon, but I know how you feel and we don't have to bring them up."

He's shown up with groceries, cooked for me, and has practically nursed me back to health, but this feels like the biggest olive branch he could offer, and I almost laugh at the timing of it. If he offered this a week ago, I'd grab on and never let go. But now that Petunia Lemon is making it so difficult to get the refund they promised and I can't go to Nora, Luke might be the only person who can help me. Someone alert Alanis Morrisette, I think this is what they call irony.

"Umm, actually . . ." I don't even know how to bring it up. We still have a full episode of *The Traitors* cued up, and I don't want to ruin it. "I kind of need to talk to you about that."

"About Petunia Lemon?" He goes on high alert. The goofy

guy who's been sitting across from me all evening has been re-placed by a man who is all business.

"Yeah." I fidget with my hands, already worried I made a mistake. "Off the record, of course."

"Of course." He grabs my hands and interlocks his fingers with mine. The small touch instantly sets my nerves at ease. "Are you okay?"

"I'm okay, I just think—" I take a deep breath and try to fig-ure out how I want to organize my thoughts. "When Nora in-vited me to the Petunia Lemon convention, I really didn't have any intention of joining, but once I was there, they did such a great job at selling the dream. I do what keeps my bills on the lower side, but a teacher salary can only go so far and it's expen-sive to be alive."

I stare down at the frayed edges on my blanket. I can't look at him right now. I know I sound like such a whiny baby com-plaining about this stuff.

"Nora told me how much money she makes doing Petunia Lemon on the side and promised she'd help me do the same. And she's been great! This isn't on her." I rush to defend her be-fore he can say anything insinuating otherwise. "She takes me to the meetings with her and sent me scripts for emails and texts. She's the one who helped me plan my first party." *That was a massive flop and ended up costing me even more money.* "Maybe I'm not following the directions close enough and I'm sure I could try harder, but I'm not good at asking people for help for free! I'm terrible at selling and I haven't made any money yet. Not a dime."

If I were seeing a return on investment, anything at all, I

could stick it out a little bit longer. But I'm hemorrhaging money I barely had in the first place. Sure, the products are fine, but I was happy with the face wash and lotion I got from the grocery store. Spending almost two hundred dollars a month on skincare when the thirty dollars I was spending was just as effective feels absurd.

"I got a good deal on my car, but it's still going to cost me eight hundred dollars. I could've paid it a couple of months ago, but I got so swept up in Petunia Lemon that I maxed out my emergency credit card to buy this stupid machine they swore up and down would make us rich in weeks." My stomach churns with shame. I knew it was stupid, but it sounds even worse when I say it out loud. "I knew it sounded risky, but they promised over and over again that everything was covered by a money-back guarantee. If it didn't work out for some reason, you could send everything back, no questions asked, and be reimbursed. Zero risk.

"It sounds unbelievable, but it wasn't until you told me about Jacqueline's spending that I started to think back on mine. I hadn't even realized how much I'd 'invested' in this business. The registration fee, the starter kit, products to hand sell, a monthly order here, the new spa system there. I'm up to almost three thousand dollars and I just joined. That's insane. Even if I wanted to stay, I can't afford it. So, I called them to act on the exit plan they assured me of time and time again, but—"

"Let me guess," he finally cuts in. "That's not what's happening and they're making you run in circles to get the answers they promised you."

Sherlock Holmes, this guy.

"I lost track of how long I've been on the phone with them

and how many times I've been put on hold and shuffled around from agent to agent. I swear, each time I call, they have fewer answers than before." Yesterday was my breaking point. My throat was killing me, and the sound of their automated voice telling me to stay on hold almost made my head explode. "I'm sure Nora would help me navigate this if I asked, but she's already spent so much time helping me, and I feel terrible that I'm quitting on her. I know this is a touchy topic for you and I'll totally understand if you say no, but I get the feeling that you might know more about how to get me out of this than anyone else."

"First of all, you don't even need to ask. Of course I'll help you," he says, and I thank god that I'm already seated because sigh, swoon, knock me over with a feather. "But second, and most important, I need you to understand that this isn't your fault."

"That's debatable." I cringe thinking about how easy it was for them to suck all of the money out of me. "Nora did ply me with booze, but nobody held a gun to my head. I did all of this on my own accord."

"No, not true. Companies like Petunia Lemon are predatory by nature and you taking the blame is exactly what they count on. They adapt a structure that keeps certain people on top, and then they spin a Cinderella story that zones in on an already vulnerable demographic. They lure 'consultants' in under false pretenses and make them believe that if they sign up and do exactly what they say, success is easily duplicated. All you have to do is throw more parties, send more messages, and definitely buy more products. The payday is always around the corner and it's always the consultant's fault for not making it. I watched it happen with Jac.

"What they conveniently leave out of their sales pitch is that the people who do manage to reach this level of success are the ones who got in the earliest. They focus heavily on recruiting over selling product, giving the largest payouts to 'consultants' who have brought in the most people. This is shady at best because it often ostracizes the people from their communities once they adopt the mindset that every relationship is transactional. At worst, it's completely fucking illegal. By the time the majority of the people jump on board, the company is oversaturated and there are no more people to recruit or customers to sell to. At that point, it doesn't matter how hard someone hustles, you can't get water from a stone."

For obvious reasons, I've never talked to Luke about joining Petunia Lemon. Yet, here he is, sitting right in front of me and describing my experience to a fucking T! I was flattered that Nora wanted me to join. I thought I was special. I've never considered myself to be gullible but now . . .

"Oh my god! Did I join a cult?" I groan and pull the blanket over my face. "They have matching tattoos and call each other sisters in skincare. Of course I joined a cult!"

I feel the couch start shaking beneath me and yank the cover down.

"Are you laughing?" I level him with what I hope is my most lethal glare.

"I'm sorry." He pulls me across the couch like I weigh nothing at all. "I don't mean to laugh and if it makes you feel better, they haven't been officially designated as a cult . . . yet. I call them cult light, but I didn't know about the tattoos. I'm considering changing my ranking now."

"You didn't know about the tattoos?" I try to focus on the conversation at hand and not how comfortable I am on his lap and in his arms. "Jacqueline has one. It's that little infinity symbol on her wrist. They put 'SIS' in the loop. The acronym for 'sisters in skincare.'"

He watches me for a second before a smile splits his face open and he throws his head back. And I get an up-close look at it all. The way his green eyes go wide with shock. The way his laugh lines deepen. The way his Adam's apple moves up and down while his body vibrates with laughter. Display this man in the Louvre because nothing could be more beautiful than this.

"I shouldn't laugh. I'm sorry, it's so fucked up." He swipes beneath his eyes as his laughter dies down. "This is part of what makes these groups so sinister. They figured out how to create a tight-knit community even with hundreds of thousands of members. So many of their consultants are at home all day with their kids, and they just want to feel like they belong to something again. They find friends and get matching tattoos and that shit keeps them tied to Petunia for longer than any paycheck could."

I could see that.

Hell, I felt that.

I'm still so worried about what Nora is going to say when she finds out I'm leaving. I've met so many wonderful women at the events I've been to, and I know our ties will be severed when I leave.

"It sucks." I tell him something he knows more than I do. "Two more of my coworkers signed up over the weekend. Maybe it will work for them, but if it doesn't, I can't even figure out how to get myself out. How can I help them?"

"You just have to be there for them if they come to you." His voice grows raspy, thick with regret. "Probably want to avoid calling them pathetic sheep and letting them read an article bashing them for joining too."

Nothing about this is funny, but I can't help but laugh.

"Good advice. I think I can manage that." Plus, I'm a terrible writer, so an article from me would have to be . . . "Oh my god."

An idea hits me so hard and fast, it propels me out of my seat. My toes curl with excitement in my fuzzy socks as pieces to the puzzle I didn't even know I was solving begin to fall into place.

"What's wrong?" Luke sits up, his careful eyes watching as I pace back and forth in front of him. "Are you okay?"

"I'm not okay, I'm better than okay!" Forget flu medicine! Coming up with a brilliant idea can do more for your health than anything. "Do you remember how you asked me to be your spy?"

"Not a spy, I just wanted the perspective of someone who was actively inside the group."

"Well now your insider's perspective is that Petunia Lemon makes promises to people and then goes back on them." I'm no lawyer, but there's no way this is legal. "You said your article isn't going well—this could be your smoking gun."

"But aren't you trying to leave? How will it work if you're not a member anymore?"

"I was holding off telling Nora I was quitting until I talked with corporate and everything was in motion." I thought it would take two, three days tops. Now I'm thinking it will never happen. "I'll spend one more day trying to get my money back, but if it doesn't work, I'll just pretend it's business as usual. I'll go to all of the events, talk to all of the members, and then I can report back to you what's happening."

I can tell he's trying to come up with a reason to talk me out of it. I can practically see the wheels spinning in his head, but it's a great idea and he knows it.

"Okay," he acquiesces. "But under one condition."

Conditions?

This might be my first rodeo moving from boss babe to an undercover boss bitch, but I still know I can't let him—a *man?*—take charge. No way. No how.

"This is my idea, you don't get to set the conditions."

"Your idea, but my article," he shoots back with pinpoint precision. "I get a condition."

"Fine," I begrudgingly agree, but only because teamwork does make the dream work. And right now, bringing down Petunia Lemon and saving my friends from ending up broke like me is a very, very big dream. "But only one."

"If you stay in and can't get your money back, you have to let me cover your repair bill."

Out of everything I thought he was going to say, this wasn't even on the list. It's too nice.

Too much.

"I can't let you do that." My hands feel clammy and my head begins to pound. "I have my bike and I can Uber occasionally."

"No, I will cover your repair bill." He doesn't budge and his tone brokers no arguments, which, of course, makes me want to argue more. "And if you're thinking it's a favor, don't. It will be a write-off with work and then you can pay me back when you finally get your money."

Wow. It's almost scary how this man who I both barely know, yet know all too well, seems to understand everything about me.

"Okay, but you have to promise to let me pay you back."

He lifts up his hand and loops his pinky with mine. "Pinky swear."

I kiss my thumb and mash it into his, thinking for only a second how much better it would be kissing his lips.

Instead of climbing on his lap and making out with him like I really want to, I sit beside him on the couch like a nice, responsible adult. For the rest of the night, he fills me in on everything he's learned about the company and I tell him what I know and the red flags I've seen. And as we go over our plans to expose and destroy Petunia Lemon, laughing and strategizing, sitting much too close, I come to two very important realizations . . .

1) Being Luke's inside man is going to be so much fun;
2) it's absolutely going to end with him inside of me.
   Again.

And I'm not even the littlest bit upset about it.

NOT ONLY DO I hate lying, I'm pretty terrible at it.

It's a great trait when it comes to being a decent human, but it's not very helpful when it comes to playing a double agent infiltrating a multi-level marketing company. I was so worried about deceiving the women I've spent so much time around for the last few months that I almost called Luke and told him I couldn't do it anymore. Not only did I think they wouldn't buy a word coming out of my mouth, but even though I wouldn't exactly call any of them friends, I do like them and my stomach has been in shambles thinking about lying to them.

Most of the parties I've been to are at one of the consultants' houses, so when Nora told me she was hosting one, I assumed it would be at her place. I've known her for years, but it's the first time she's invited me to her home, and I've been dying to set my eyes on the "house that Petunia purchased"—her words, not mine.

So color me surprised when I arrive at the address she sent me and am greeted with a medical spa instead of the residential stunner I was hoping to see. I had to triple-check the address on the invite she sent me to make sure I wasn't at the wrong address.

"Champagne?" a gorgeous woman with full lips and a crisp forehead offers, and because my mom taught me manners—and absolutely not because I'm anxious—I accept. "And here's a stress ball for you to hold on to during whatever treatment you have."

It shouldn't have taken me this long to finally realize what's happening, but as I look around the room full of familiar faces that are slightly swollen and makeup free, everything finally clicks into place.

Nora is hosting a Botox party. Super interesting considering that when she raves about how much better her skin has been since using Petunia Lemon products, injectables seem to be conveniently left out. I wonder why that could be?

I just got here and I already can't wait to call Luke.

I take my first sip of champagne for the night, and the last embers of guilt are finally extinguished as I make my rounds in the reception area. I stop and say hi to a few people, asking how their kids are doing and getting an update from Hayley about her upcoming wedding. Small talk feels harder than normal. Now that the glossy facade is gone, I can't help but wonder if all the smiles are real or if they're as fake as the Petunia Lemon results we're being fed. If some of them are draining their checking accounts, maybe they are too worried about losing friends to do what's best for them.

But hey, at least there's good snacks.

I grab a paper plate that's shaped like a set of very full, very red lips and start filling it up with cheese, fruit, and crackers. I get a second plate for desserts. I wonder if I eat enough of these cookies, would my face get full without filler? I should probably test that out. It sounds enjoyable.

"Emerson! You came!" Grace runs up to me waving a syringe filled with something red in my face. "Come do jello shots with us!"

"I can't." I pretend to sound upset, but you couldn't pay me to do jello shots. The last time I did them was in college, and I got so drunk that I was throwing up blue for an entire day. "I drove, so I'm going to stick with my one glass of champagne."

Also—and not that I would ever drink and drive—but I haven't even had my car back for an entire week. There's no way I'm doing anything that would put me—and my nether regions—in danger of being back on my bike. In fact, I'm calling Bikes Together as soon as I get home. I want my bike to have a good home, just not with me.

"Boo. Party pooper." Grace pouts for a millisecond before she's distracted by somebody else and runs off. "Janet!" she shouts across the room. "Do a jello shot with me!"

She's not gone for more than a minute before someone else is shouting my name behind me. I turn around just in time to see Nora and Jacqueline walking toward me arm in arm.

"Emerson!" Nora says. "You came!"

Loose strands of her red hair fall out of the bun at the top of her head, and she's holding an ice pack in her hand. Her already full lips look more swollen than normal, and little bumps are scattered across her forehead like she's been stung by a bee. Jacqueline, of course, looks like her normal, not-a-hair-out-of-place perfect self. There's not a drop of makeup on her face, but I don't think she's had anything done yet. Not that it would matter either way. Botox or no Botox, it's unfair how beautiful she is.

"Of course I came." I hold myself back from going in for a hug like I usually do. I don't want to hurt her face. "Thanks for inviting me."

"Oh please, you're my girl. You're always invited." She unwinds her arm from Jacqueline's, and the little zap of guilt I thought was gone makes a sudden reappearance. "Have you looked at the menu for the night?"

"There's more food?" I look at the spread in front of me and my loaded-up plates. I didn't realize there was a menu too. "This is already so much."

"No, not a food menu." Her melodic laughter floats through the room. She walks to the end of the table to grab a framed card and hands it to me. "A service menu. Your first treatment is on me, but anything after that is up to you. Chloe is in the back already, I think she's doing her lips and the fine lines on her forehead."

My stomach turns. Chloe is barely out of college; there's no way she should be back there, and if it weren't for my party, she wouldn't be.

"Did Odette come?"

Like Keisha, there's not one wrinkle on her flawless, brown skin, and her lips have the natural plump no doctor could immolate.

"No," Nora says. "She couldn't find a sitter."

"Oh, that's too bad." I have to fight to keep the look of pure relief off of my face—maybe Botox would be good for me while

I'm undercover. They can't read the lies on my face if my face doesn't move, right? "Hopefully she'll make it to the next one."

I put down my dessert plate and look at the framed menu she handed me. It's like reading a foreign language. The lines that are frozen on her face deepen on mine as I try to figure out what I'm looking at. I've never been to a medical spa before, and the long list of services offered, the resolutions to problems I didn't even know existed, is overwhelming to say the least.

"You probably want to start with the crow's-feet." Jacqueline offers her unasked-for and unwanted opinion. "Or maybe a little filler for your lips."

I almost laugh in her face because if there's one thing I know I don't need, it's lip filler. I can thank my dad for that. The instant loss of credibility takes away the sting of her words.

"Or whatever you think will make you feel your best." Nora tries to talk over Jacqueline. "I just thought you'd have fun trying things out. Dr. Hubbard is the best, you're going to love her."

I'm not sure why in the world she'd think I'd have fun trying things. I've never expressed any interest in Botox or fillers, and if anything, I've told her how much I hate anything having to do with needles. No shame to anyone who does partake in everything on this menu, but I'm only twenty-eight. I'd like to give myself the opportunity to age before I decide to do something about it.

Maybe it's because I lost a parent at such a young age, but the only thing I see to aging is beauty. Reaching an age where your joy can be read on your face, where your story can be seen by all, is a privilege. I'm not in a rush to erase that.

"I'm sure she's amazing, but I'm not sure I'm ready to try anything right now." I never thought I'd have to try and gently reject getting Botox with my boss, but here we are.

"Are you positive?" She lifts her ice pack to her mouth, and disappointment is written all over her swollen face. "Dr. Hubbard offers Petunia Lemon products to all of her clients, so you know she only believes in using the top of the line."

Do I know that? I thought I knew that the stupid serums and spa system they're refusing to refund me for were all women needed to stay looking youthful and wrinkle-free. Nobody told me that it only worked in tandem with cosmetic procedures.

"I'm sure, I'm just going to be a spectator tonight," I tell her again, hoping she can hear the finality in my voice.

I already feel bad enough for spying on her party, and no is my least favorite word. If she keeps pushing it, I know I'll cave. And I like my face the way it is!

"Alright," she gives in. "But if you decide you want to try, it's okay to change your mind."

"Speaking of changing your mind," Jacqueline cuts in, "I know I signed up to chaperone the field trip to the pumpkin patch next week, but I was invited to Petunia Lemon headquarters as one of their top representatives so I'll actually be out of town now."

"That's huge! Congratulations." I can't tell if she's offering me this information to let me know she can't attend anymore or if she's just bragging about her trip. "Thanks for letting me know. I'll send out an email and I'm sure I'll be able to find another parent to join us."

"No need." She waves me off with the dismissive flick of her wrist I've become so accustomed to when I'm around her. "Lucas said he'd take my spot since he'll have her while I'm gone."

"Oh perfect." My nerves feel like they're choking me, and I pray she can't hear it in my voice. "I'll reach out to him this week so we can get him approved."

For some totally unknown reason, the excited flutters I've been feeling whenever I think of Luke are nowhere to be found when it's his ex-wife who's bringing him up. When I'm alone, it's easy to tell myself that I haven't done anything wrong, that I could've never anticipated who he was the night we met. Yet, as I stand across from Jacqueline, it does nothing to assuage the shame I feel.

I might not have known who Luke was that night in July, but I know who he is now and as hard as I've tried, it hasn't stopped me from wanting him any less. It sure as hell didn't stop me from spending Friday with him, formulating our plan to bring Petunia Lemon down, or curling into his lap while we finished *The Traitors* once we were done.

It didn't stop me from falling asleep that night, wishing he'd fall asleep beside me.

The shame of it all is suffocating, but it's still not enough to stop me from wanting him more than I've ever wanted anyone before.

It's a wicked cycle, and I have no idea how to escape.

"Great, I'll tell Lucas to check his email." Jacqueline grabs my hand and I nearly recoil at the touch. "And you really should consider the Botox. Preventative is the way to go."

Holy shit.

Why is she such a bitch, and why am I obsessed with her?

My mouth flaps around like a fish on dry land as I try to form a response . . . any response at all. But it's no use. She's long gone by the time my brain reconnects to my mouth.

"Just ignore her." Janet appears next to me, her speech and her stance a little wobbly from the jello shots Grace talked her into doing. "She's a bitch to everyone at first."

"Really?" This shouldn't make me feel better. She's going to hate me forever if she ever finds out the truth about me and Luke.

"Yup." She takes a cookie off of my plate and bites into it. "She made Grace cry for the first two months. I think she's taking it easy on you because of Isla."

If this is her nice, I'm not sure I could handle her going hard. It's good to know there are some benefits to the teaching degree I'll be paying off until I die.

"Thank goodness for Isla then."

"True that." She nods her head in agreement and finishes off the cookie I was very excited to eat. "And don't listen to her about the Botox either, you don't need it. That's just her being an asshole again."

"Thank you." I rub at the frown lines between my eyes that feel like they're growing deeper with every minute I stay at this party. "That's nice of you to say."

"Not nice." She smiles and takes my hand in hers. "Just truth."

Ugh.

The guilt I keep telling myself not to feel rears its ugly head again. I really, genuinely like Janet—maybe even more so when she's drunk—and I feel awful lying to her face. She's one of the few people I think I could become real friends with outside of Petunia Lemon.

I just have to hope that eventually she'll see the light and join me on the outside. But after talking to Luke and discussing everything he's found on Petunia Lemon and companies like it, I'm not sure it will happen.

When Luke was telling me about how insular these groups are, part of me hoped he was exaggerating. I thought maybe because he's a journalist he couldn't help but sensationalize everything for the sake of his story. But when I had lunch with Nora on Tuesday and asked her more about Anna, I knew he was telling the truth. As soon as I mentioned her name, Nora's entire demeanor changed. I've never seen her act so cold before, and I once watched her laugh with a parent who threatened to bash her car windows in and follow her home!

"Hi, everyone." Nora claps her hands together at the front of the room. "I just wanted to take a moment to thank you all for coming out tonight. I know this is a little different than our normal get-togethers, but I'm grateful you all took the time out of your busy schedules to join me for a little self-care."

Nora gestures for someone to come join her, and a woman who I have to assume is Dr. Hubbard takes her place beside Nora. Jet-black hair falls down her back in thick waves, and it's a stark contrast to skin so pale I'm not sure it has ever been exposed to sunlight. If someone told me she was a Cullen and she secretly shimmered like diamonds, I would believe it. She simultaneously looks twenty-five and forty-five and I love everything about her.

Maybe I will try some of her services after all.

"If you're new here," Nora says, almost to remind everyone that she's still standing there too, "this is Dr. Hubbard. Not only is she an amazing dermatologist who I come to see every four to six months, but she's one of the top Petunia Lemon consultants in the country. She's so graciously offered to share some of her expertise with us tonight. Be sure to take notes, ladies, we can all learn a few things from her."

Polite applause fills the crowded space, and Nora finds the open seat next to Jacqueline. A door at the corner of the room opens, and Chloe walks out with an ice pack to her mouth. She's looking around for a place to sit, and I wave her over to come sit by me.

While she's weaving through the room and everyone is focused on Dr. Hubbard, I reach into my purse, pull out my phone, and start recording. I have no idea what the good doctor is going to say, but based on my previous experience with Petunia Lemon, I can almost guarantee that she'll say at least one thing that's so out of pocket, I'll need video proof.

Chloe reaches over to me after what feels like forever and arches her brow at my raised phone . . . or at least I think she arches? It's hard to tell with the little bee sting marks crossing her forehead.

"For Odette," I whisper, nodding to my phone. "So she's not all the way left out."

"You're so sweet," she says, and the seed of guilt I've been trying to avoid takes root. "She'll love that you thought of her."

God, I'm such a liar. I really hope this pays off in the end, and I don't just spend months deceiving my friends.

"Thank you so much, Nora." Dr. Hubbard pulls my attention

back to her. Her smooth, cultured voice is so calming, it's no wonder so many people trust her to put needles in their faces. "I'm so honored to host my fellow sisters in skincare here tonight. I always love my job, but on nights like tonight, I just have to thank Jesus for putting me on this path and placing Petunia Lemon in my life. I truly believe that I'm doing what I was placed on earth to do and I know I'm not alone!"

A crescendo of "amens" and "yes girls" are shouted around the room, and I struggle to keep a straight face. I can't imagine doing anything other than teaching. It may not be glamorous and I might be poor, but I'm happier and more fulfilled than I could be doing anything else. So while I understand feeling like your job is a calling, there's just something in her zealous declaration that makes my culty spidey senses start to tingle.

I just can't put my finger on it . . .

Yet.

"As Petunia Lemon consultants, we have the distinct honor of not only getting to experience the best skincare products on the market, but we get to share the joy and love that can only be found through fellowshipping with your sisters. And because we carry the responsibility to share this company with as many people as we can, I want to talk to you tonight about why it's so important that we present ourselves in the best way possible and give you a few tricks to accomplish that."

What seemed so warm about her moments ago begins to take on a sinister tilt. My skin starts to crawl as I listen to her, but as I search the room to see if anyone else is feeling like me, I only see wide smiles and enthralled faces. Everyone is on the edge of their seats, waiting to hear what else Dr. Hubbard has to say.

"We can all confirm that the products Petunia Lemon sells are top-of-the-line, right?" She pauses so we all have the chance to answer her rhetorical question. "But even with the best skin-care products, sometimes it's important to take a few extra steps beyond what a serum can do. As business owners, it's crucial to not only identify our market, but to discover their pain points. It's the only way we'll learn how to help them.

"As one of the earliest Petunia Lemon representatives, I've been doing this for a long time. I've gone on every company vacation since they've started offering them and I've spent countless hours talking to our fearless founder, Raquel, learning how to be the best Petunia Lemon representative there is. Raquel has spent countless hours in my chair, and she will be the first to tell you that our faces are the best advertisement we can have. You ladies here tonight are doing the best thing you could possibly do for your business. By going the extra mile to keep your faces looking young and line free, you'll be showing future customers that with Petunia Lemon, aging is optional!"

Anyone who was seated jumps to their feet and applause erupts around me. Nora rushes to hug Dr. Hubbard before telling her to take a bow. The room is so loud, I can barely hear myself think . . . which is probably a good thing because I think I might be going crazy. I don't understand how I can be the only person in the room thinking this is not okay.

I stop recording and tuck my phone back into my purse, hoping that nobody noticed. The clapping and cheering finally begin to die down but the energy in the room is more wired than ever. Women who had already gotten a treatment or two grab the framed menus spread all across the room, scanning them for what to do to their faces next.

And when their attention turns toward me, I take that as my cue to get the fuck out of Dodge.

"I actually have to head out," I tell Grace, who, by the way, seems way too intoxicated to do something like this. "I have to be up early and I want to get home at a decent hour."

"Boooo!" She hands the menu over to Chloe and grabs another jello shot syringe. "You're no fun."

That's usually a challenge because I love being fun, but for once, I'm okay with it. Because while my plans might not include a sore face and nasty hangover, they do include Luke.

And that wins every single time.

22

SATURDAY DIDN'T WORK out with Luke because he had Isla.

I love Isla, but kids have zero discretion. Jacqueline already knows they saw me at the pet shelter and I helped them find Mister Bubbles. I'm sure she was able to write that off as a coincidence, but I doubt she'd feel the same if it happened a second time.

Since I'm basically an FBI informant now, I have to be more discreet.

"Isla's much better at this than you," Tom complains from his chair in the corner of the room. "I don't even think you're trying."

"I'm sorry." Luke sounds flustered as he hands me the pearl and rhinestone collar to put on Sophie the corgi. "I've never had to pick out this many pet accessories before."

"Oh, for Christ's sake!" Tom's bark is louder than any of the dogs we've met today. "Corgis aren't pearl dogs. This is ridiculous."

"Look at that face, she loves feeling fancy." I fasten the collar around her neck and give her some belly scratches. "I, for one, think she looks adorable."

"Of course she looks adorable. She's a goddamn corgi." Tom throws his hands in the air like *he* can't deal with *us*. "You think the Queen of England would pick a dog that's not adorable?"

"Well, I—"

"Oh no you don't." Tom cuts me off. "Don't you even get started with that Queen Meghan and Queen Beyoncé stuff again."

"Again?" Luke asks.

"Yes, again," I defend myself. "If we are going to post these pictures on Beyoncé's internet, it's only fair that we address her correctly. And Meghan—"

"Didn't I say not to get started?" Tom cuts me off—again— and pushes out of his chair to go to the accessory wall himself. "This sounds like you're getting started."

Luke's body shakes with laughter and mischief dances in his eyes. "It does sound like you're getting started."

"You haven't even seen me get started." I get Sophie to sit in front of the white backdrop and grab my camera off of my stool. "But you will."

His eyes drop down the V of my sweater. "Promise?"

"Dammit, Luke." My cheeks feel like they're on fire, but thankfully when I glance over at Tom, he's not paying attention at all. "Why are you even here? You're not an official volunteer."

We had plans to meet up later today to exchange information and go over our next steps, but he showed up at The Barkery not long after I started taking pictures of this week's animals.

"Joke's on you because Isla and I came back last week. We filled out a lot of paperwork and guess what?" He holds out his arm in front of him and opens his fist. "You're looking at the newest Barkery volunteer."

"Did you . . ." I want to focus on that last part, but my brain is hyper-fixated on one small detail and I know I won't be able to move on until we address it. "Did you just drop the proverbial mic?"

"Mic." He holds out his arm in front of him again and repeats the motion. "Drop."

"Oh wow! Doubling down, I see." I don't want to laugh, but I can't help it. "That was very millennial dad of you."

"Tsk tsk," he clicks his tongue. "What's that saying? Oh, that's right. Haters gonna hate, hate, hate, hate, hate."

Everything in the room, even sweet Sophie and grumpy Tom, fades away as I place Luke's words in my head.

"Did you just quote Taylor Swift?" I have to be wrong. There's no way I heard him right.

"Damn straight," he says proudly. "I have a six-year-old little girl. If you don't think we have frequent dance parties to Taylor, you're very mistaken."

He's a Swiftie?

I did not need to know this.

"She's another one of my queens," I whisper, and the urge to fall in love with him right here and right now is almost too strong to overcome. "It's a long list."

"No more queens!" Tom throws a plain bow tie at my head, and it's a very effective way of snapping me back into the present moment. "Now get on with it, me and Sophie don't have all day to sit here and listen to you two flirt. Take the damn pictures so he can take you out."

I feel my eyes bulge out of my head, and the blush that just began to fade makes a reappearance so fast and furious even Vin Diesel would be impressed.

"Yeah, Emerson. Listen to Tom and hurry up," he says. "I'd really like to take you out."

I'm usually very firm in my decision to ignore all men and their requests, but I guess I'll go along with this one.

But just this once . . .

And any other time he asks me out.

IN A WORLD filled with fashion influencers, I'd call myself stylish adjacent.

I know what I like and I buy it whether it's in style or not. I'm a kindergarten teacher and my wardrobe shows it. I tend to gravitate toward the more whimsical side of life and because of that, most of my clothes are items that will impress kindergartners, not adult men who might want to take me out on a date . . . if this even is a date.

After we finish up with pictures and take a couple of high-energy huskies on a walk, Luke follows me back to my apartment so I can change out of my fur-covered sweater into something a little nicer. The last time my mom was in town, she made me buy a simple black dress, and I toy with the idea of pulling it out tonight. Luke didn't tell me where we're going, and it'd be the safe choice. But then I see my favorite fall sweater and grab it instead. Nothing about my time with Luke has been safe, and I don't know why I'd start now.

The sweater's green like Luke's eyes, with mushrooms and

flowers embroidered along the hem and up the sleeves. The V-neck cuts so low that I always wear a camisole beneath it, but tonight I opt for my ivory lace bra—and the matching, extra lacy panties—instead. I'm sure it's not everyone's brand of sexy, but it works for me. I pair it with my wide-leg jeans and the green Nike dunks I found for a steal on eBay. My curls got a little frizzy working with the pups, so I run to the bathroom to refresh them and swipe on some mascara, Fenty blush, and lipstick when I finish. It's not much, but I think I look great.

And judging by the way Luke looks at me when I walk into my living room, he agrees.

"Ready to go?" I drape my crossbody bag over my shoulder and adjust my sweater. "Are you finally going to tell me where we're going?"

"Maybe," he says. "But before we go, do you mind if we talk?"

Dread clogs my throat and my stomach crashes through the floor. *Do I mind if we talk?* I mean really, could there be a more ominous question?

"Um, yeah. Sure." I smile through clenched teeth. "About what?"

He scoots over and I accept the unspoken invitation to join him on the couch. He turns to face me, and even though he's the person who initiated this conversation, he seems just as nervous as I am. It does not bode well for my confidence.

"I feel like so much has happened between us. You're Isla's teacher and now you're helping me with my article. I just really wanted to sit down and make sure we're on the same page about everything."

"Of course, good idea."

I knew it. I knew it was too good to be true. I let myself drift into the fantasy of Luke when I needed to stay in reality. Everything is so complicated with us, I should've known he wouldn't want to cross boundaries.

"I know the smart thing to do would be to keep things between us professional, and Lord knows I've been trying, but,"— he takes a deep breath and my heart stops beating—"I don't want that. It might not be the best idea, but I want to see where things go between us."

I don't know what comes over me more, relief or excitement. All at once, I somehow feel like I could explode and am the most settled I've ever been. It's like my body is finally catching up to what it has been trying to tell me all along: this thing between Luke and I can't be denied . . . no matter how hard we tried to fight it.

"I want that too." The smile I've been biting back takes over, and my face feels like it might break in two. "A lot."

Just thinking about being able to kiss him whenever I want is enough to make me kick off my shoes and pull him back into my room for the rest of the night. Why would I need food when Luke is an entire snack?

"Good," he says. "Now that we've gotten that cleared up, I'm just going to do one more thing before we leave."

"What—" I begin to ask, but his mouth is on mine before I can finish.

I've spent the last few months since we kissed trying to remember the way his mouth felt on mine. The sparks that shot off like fireworks when our mouths touched. It was always somewhere in my mind, even when I didn't want it to be. I convinced myself I was building it up in my imagination. That there was no way it was as good as I remembered.

But now, sitting on my couch with his lips on mine, I know I was wrong. Because somehow, this kiss is even better. It's different than what we shared over the summer—less frantic, more gentle. His hand glides across my back, pulling me closer to him, as his tongue twists with mine. His touch is familiar now, yet no less exciting. Just like the first night we met, my body turns liquid beneath him and my mind goes blank. Nothing else in the entire world matters more than figuring out how to do this for the rest of forever . . . or at least tonight.

"Are you sure you want dinner?" I ask when we pull apart. "I think I have a frozen something in my freezer."

His quiet laughter is just like a glass of whiskey: smooth, rich, and a balm to my nerves. One taste and I could never be sober.

"As delicious as something frozen sounds and as much as I love your apartment," he says, leaning forward and touching his lips to mine once more, "I'd really like to take you out on a proper date for once."

That's sweet.

Really sweet.

"Okay," I give in. "If you insist. But first we should go to the bathroom. I need more lipstick, because I left most of what I just applied on your face."

WE ONLY KISS three more times before we finally manage to make it out of my door and into his car. Pretty successful if you ask me.

"So . . ." I lean across the armrest, unable to stop myself from being as close to him as possible. "Where are you taking me, Mr. Miller?"

"Oh, Miss Pierce"—he puts his car in drive, his glance lingering before he focuses on the road—"wouldn't you like to know?"

I don't usually like surprises. I love being in charge and putting together a good itinerary. I love the safe and secure options. But when it comes to Luke, none of that seems to matter. All of my self-preservation and self-control goes out the window the second he steps into my orbit.

"Nope." I lean back against the leather seat of his Acura SUV and turn my head to take in his profile against the Denver scenery blurring behind him. "I'm just happy to be along for the ride."

His fingers flex around the steering wheel, and his jaw ticks beneath his trimmed beard. His mouth stays shut, but I can practically read his mind as his thoughts cross his face.

"I'm glad you're happy," his raspy voice whispers in the quiet of the car, and his hand finds its place on my upper thigh. "Because there's nobody else I'd want to take with me."

The light turns green, and my heart rate accelerates along with the car. Luke keeps his hand on my thigh, and I stay as still as possible so that he'll keep it there forever. His thumb moves up and down near the inside seam of my jeans and every time we hit a bump, it inches closer and closer toward my center, making it so I forget to breathe.

By the time he pulls into the parking lot, my head is spinning and I've lost track of time. He turns off the car, and the interior lights flash on beneath the dimming Colorado sky. Thankfully, I don't think they're bright enough to showcase just how flustered his touch made me.

"I hope you're hungry," he says.

I unbuckle my seat belt and by the time I'm out of the car, he's right next to me, folding my hand in his as we walk up to the front of a restaurant that I've driven past a million times but have never been to.

Campus Lounge has existed for a while, and even if I didn't know that as fact I could guess as soon as we step inside. The retro signs and interior make it seem like it's been around for so long, it's come back in style. It screams comfort and fun over romance and class. Thank god I went with my sweater and sneakers over the black dress still hanging in my closet. It's a cool place, but I'd be lying if I don't start to question whether or not I jumped to conclusions about what's happening between us.

It's a Sunday night and die-hard Broncos fans, all sporting their Sunday best jerseys, scream at the TVs and high-five one another around the packed bar. Luke grabs my hand, wrapping his fingers tight around mine as he navigates us through the orange and blue crowd to a booth tucked into the back corner.

"Fuck. I'm so sorry," he yells over the crowd. "I can't believe I forgot there was a Broncos game tonight."

"This would've never happened if you were the sports guy," I joke. Being taken to a sports bar on game day by accident is still a million times better than being taken to a sports bar on game day on purpose.

"The pitfalls of going out with a curious nerd are never ending. Hopefully my memory for the little things will make up for some of them though." He hands me a menu across the table. "I almost took you to Red Robin, but Campus Lounge does a great burger too, and they have something else I thought you'd like."

He points to the cocktail section of the menu, and it only takes me a millisecond before I see it.

"Oh my god!" My eyes move back and forth between him and the menu as something warm and fuzzy comes over me. "They have an old fashioned flight?"

"That is your drink?" Nerves look so out of place as they flash across his usually confident face. "Right?"

I haven't forgotten a single detail of our night together, but I haven't allowed myself to imagine that Luke hasn't either. Even when he sent me Denny's, I spent more time talking myself out of what it could've meant than I did actually enjoying it. But now, with Luke sitting in front of me, the gentle pride evident on his handsome face, I can't deny it anymore. That night meant just as much to Luke as it did to me, and he's doing everything he can to prove it to me.

"It is." I don't even attempt to hold back my smile anymore. We might be in a sports bar, but I was wrong, it does scream romance. "I've been on a mission to find the best one in the city and I didn't even know this place existed."

His smile triples in size and just like the Grinch, so does my heart.

"Oh, thank god." He leans back against the vinyl booth cushion and lets out a relieved sigh. "Let's hope they're good then."

Even if they are the worst old fashioneds I've ever tasted, they'll still be the best because I'll be drinking them with him. No matter what they taste like, the only thing I'll remember about this night is the amount of thought this gorgeous man, who could probably get anyone he wants, put into bringing me here.

Of course I can't tell him that though. I'm so glad he opened up, and I know that we both want to explore this thing between us, but I'm still not ready to show all of my cards just yet.

"They have a bananas Foster one," I point out instead. "There's no way that could be bad."

Despite the rowdy crowd, the service is still quick and wonderful. The waiter comes over and takes our order—two whiskey flights, one campus burger with sweet potato fries for me, and a brisket French dip with tots for Luke.

"Tater tots are the only acceptable choice if you're not going with sweet potato fries." Or onion rings. Never plain fries and never, and I mean *never,* a side salad. That's an offense I think should be punishable by jail.

"I'm glad you approve." He smirks over the rim of his water glass, which they brought us while we wait. "I'll give you a tot if you give me a fry."

"Deal." I extend my hand over the table and he shakes it. Unfortunately for me, this zaps my body awake, and I remember that the thing I'm most hungry for is the man sitting across from me.

Another thing that should be punishable by jail? Turning someone on by shaking their hand.

It's just bad manners.

"So"—I tuck my hands beneath my legs to keep them from fidgeting—"should we discuss my findings from the last meeting?"

The other perk about a place like this is it's the last place I could ever picture Jacqueline spending her Sunday—or any—night. Campus Lounge has whiskey flights and beer on tap. Jacqueline gives off more cosmopolitan and champagne vibes. And I say that with zero judgment because I also love champagne and cosmos. They're delicious and I'd challenge anyone to attest otherwise.

"Oh, yeah." He rubs his hands together, and a sly smile tugs on the corner of his luscious mouth. "I've been dying to see this video you've been teasing me with."

"It's worth the wait." I grab my phone out of my purse, and as I'm pulling up the video, the booth dips and Luke slides in beside me. "I've watched it so many times and I swear, it seems more absurd every time I watch it."

"Where was the party again?" His thigh rubs against mine, and he drops his arm across the booth like it's the most natural thing in the world. "Nora's house?"

"Oh no, no, no, Mr. Miller. Nora hosted it, but it wasn't at her house." I hand him the phone, almost giddy knowing what he's about to see. "Just watch and see."

He hits play, but instead of watching along with him, I stare at his face so I don't miss a single reaction.

"Is that . . . wait." His eyes narrow as he starts to process what's going on. "Are you at a doctor's office? Is she a . . . oh my god. Holy shit. What the fuck?"

I choke back my laughter as he drops f-bomb after f-bomb, and by the time the video comes to an end, his eyebrows have nearly touched his hairline.

"That was . . ."

"Freaking insanity!" I finish his sentence for him. "I couldn't believe what was happening when I was there. I was the only one who seemed shocked by it. I seriously felt like I was in another dimension."

He finally turns his face away from the phone, but I can't read his expression. "Do you know what this means?"

"What?" I thought it meant they were a bunch of no-good liars, but the look on his face makes me think it's even more.

"The Raquel she mentions?" He gestures to the video playing again. "She's talking about Raquel Alessio, the president of Petunia Lemon. She's saying this isn't just something a few representatives in Denver are doing; this is a directive coming down from the very top to encourage lying and fraud to lure customers in."

"Holy shit." I repeat his earlier sentiment as the seriousness of what I caught registers. "I knew that name sounded familiar, but I couldn't place it until right now. I can't believe they let me record this."

Not that I asked, but you'd think they'd announce a no cellphone policy or something.

"They're so convinced that nobody would ever leave that they aren't careful when they're in a room full of members," he says. "A few people have told me they realized the products aren't what they advertise, but they never explained what they meant."

"I've always used drugstore products, and I thought it was just me, but I haven't noticed a difference in my skin at all." I take my phone from him and email him the video so he can have a copy to do with as he pleases. "If they're encouraging their members to get medical procedures, I wouldn't be a little bit shocked if the ingredients they're pushing aren't what they claim either. Is there a way you could get their products tested to see if they're really what they say?"

"Damn. That's such a good idea! Why didn't I already think of that?" The arm draped across the booth falls to my shoulder, and he pulls me in for a hug. "You might be the best inside man who's ever lived. How the hell am I ever going to pay you back?"

"I'm not sure, but I trust you to figure something out."

A million and one dirty thoughts cloud my mind, and by the way his eyes go dark and he pulls his lip between his teeth, I think he can read every single one of them.

Or at least I hope he can.

I might be playing with fire, but for once, I'm not afraid of getting burned.

I'm just excited to feel the heat.

23

NOT THAT I'M surprised, but I was right. The bananas Foster old fashioned was a ten out of ten, top marks, best old fashioned I've ever had. And if it weren't for the feel of Luke's body pressed next to mine and the way he listened to me so intently, hanging on my every word, it would've been the high point of the night.

Well, that and when the Broncos won and a very enthusiastic man came over and pulled me out of the booth and threw me into the air. I mean, that wasn't fun. It was actually kind of scary. What was fun—and still a little scary—was how fast Luke was out of the booth and standing between me and the football guy.

Luke can call himself a nerd all he wants, but he's also at least six feet tall and has a body like a superhero, and as that guy learned tonight, he's more than capable of defending himself and whoever he's with.

"Oh wow." I stand behind him while he unlocks his front door. "You and Isla weren't lying, this *is* close to my house."

After dinner was over, I wasn't anywhere close to ready for the night to end. I was trying to think of any reason to keep our time together going when Luke asked if I wanted to see how Mister Bubbles was doing. Of course I jumped at the opportunity. As a Barkery volunteer, I'm obligated to always say yes when it comes to seeing one of our animals. Also, since he already knows where I live, it only seemed fair that I see his place.

"It's a great area, but it's been an adjustment moving from my old house." He pushes open the door and flips on the hallway lights. "I knew that neighborhood like the back of my hand. I miss walking to the bakery down the street and grocery shopping at the little mom-and-pop shop that'd been around forever. And it had a huge backyard where Isla and I used to garden together every spring and summer. There's a small space in the back where we added some planters, but it's not the same."

The thought of him gardening shouldn't be so freaking hot, but I'm learning that anything and everything this man does turns me on.

Most especially, the way he looks at me.

"It's not the same, and I'm sorry you had to go through that." I'm even more sorry that the thing Jacqueline signed up for, thinking it would be good for her and her family, ended up being what tore it apart. "But it looks like you've done a lot with this place. I'm sure Isla and Mister Bubbles love it here."

When I think of what a divorced man's home would look like, I think of cold, almost clinical spaces filled with a lot of leather, white walls, and a TV that's so big, it's a miracle it fit through the door. But even though I'm just at the entrance of

Luke's home, I know that's not the case here. Three framed black-and-white photos of Isla at different ages line the walls and little tchotchkes sit atop the entryway table.

To be honest, there's more personality than I saw in Jacqueline's entire house in just this small space alone. Her home is beautiful. His is lived in. Both are wonderful, but lucky for me, I much prefer Luke's route.

"Thank you." He kicks off his shoes and tosses his keys into the little homemade clay tray on the table. "The transition wasn't easy, but I wanted this place to feel like home for Isla, not just some place she visited to see her dad. Mister Bubbles was the final piece to the puzzle and now she loves it here."

Freaking hell. This man is going to kill me. Could he be any sweeter?

"I'm sure she does." I follow his lead and take off my shoes too. "And I'm sure you hear this all the time and it won't mean much coming from me, but you're an amazing dad. Isla's so lucky to have you in her corner."

"Why wouldn't it mean much coming from you?" He cocks his head to the side and his brows furrow together. "You're her teacher, it honestly means more coming from you than just about anybody else. Thank you for saying that."

"You're welcome," I whisper back, not knowing what else to say.

"Alright then." He leans down and touches his lips to mine before taking my hand and pulling me behind him. "Now let me show you around before I try to pull your sweater off in the entryway."

Oh. Nice.

I don't think I'd mind the entryway now that he mentions it . . .

"If I remember right, we didn't make it much past your hotel room door either." My hand tightens around his as I think back to our last night together. "I'm not sure we should break away from tradition so easily."

Seeing him almost every week, knowing what his mouth feels like against mine, what his beard feels like rubbing against my thighs, has been damn near torture. It didn't matter how much I told myself I hated him, my body refused to forget how much it loved him. Dinner was great, but I spent almost all of it waiting for it to be over so we could be alone together. It's been months of me closing my eyes and seeing his body on top of mine. Now that we're here again, I don't want to wait a minute more.

"Tradition, huh?" He slows and turns to me, his eyes dropping to my cleavage and the lace edge of my bra that's peeking from beneath my sweater. "I wouldn't want to be the one to break that."

My breasts fall heavy under his intense gaze and goose bumps rise across my skin in anticipation of feeling his hands on me again. I take a step toward him, needing his touch more than I've ever needed anything in this world, but before I can reach him, I'm up in the air and thrown over his shoulder.

"Luke!" I scream his name through my breathless giggles and wrap my arms tight around his waist as he runs through his condo and reaches the stairs, taking them two at a time. "What are you doing?"

"Hush," he says, but I barely register it over the sting of his hand splayed across my ass before I'm off of his shoulder and flat on my back. "I needed to see you on my bed and fuck, Em, what a sight it is."

The fight dies on the tip of my tongue when I see the way Luke is watching me. He's looking down at me like I'm a work of art, something precious and beautiful to be treasured. Like he can't believe his fucking luck that I'm lying in front of him, sprawled across his bed, ready and waiting.

"Luke," I whisper into the quiet of his room, fighting the urge to squirm beneath his intense gaze. I'm fully clothed, but I've never felt so exposed in my entire life.

"Hold on, baby," he whispers back. "I didn't take you in last time. I didn't appreciate what was right in front of me and I'm not making that mistake again. I'm not going to forget a single detail about tonight. Not the way your cheeks flush the same color red as your chest when I tell you how beautiful you are. Not the way your curls look fanned across my pillows. And never, not ever, will I forget the way you're looking at me right now."

I know people are into athletes and financiers or whatever, and while everyone is allowed to have their own interests and opinions, they're all wrong. The only man anyone should ever date is a writer. Because . . . oh my god? Did he really just say that to me?

"I really hope you're not planning on going anywhere now." It's hard to talk with the need building between my thighs. "Because after that, I'm not sure I'll be able to let you go."

"Good." He climbs on top of me, his body boxing me in underneath him. "I let you walk out my door once, Em, but I'm going to do everything in my power to make sure that never happens again."

"That sounds good to me." Flutters of excitement build in my belly as I let the promise of Lucas Miller sink in . . . a promise, I realize, that will still never measure up to the man above me.

He drops his head into the crook of my neck and his tongue traces a path until his teeth nip at my ear.

"I'm glad you like the way it sounds, but now," he whispers, and the heat of his breath against the shell of my ear sends shivers down my spine, "I'm going to make sure you like the way it feels."

He says no more. His mouth at my ear disappears and suddenly, so does my sweater.

"My god, Em." His breathing deepens as his fingertips dance along the scalloped edges of my bra. "I knew when I saw this sticking out of your sweater it was going to be good, but it's better than I imagined. *You're* better than I imagined. Everything about you is a dream come to life."

I don't know what to say or even how to begin to respond to that, so instead, I do the only thing I can do. I wrap my arms around his neck and bring his mouth down to mine.

The kiss starts out gentle. His warm hands roam down my arms and across my bare stomach. His soft lips move against mine until he coaxes my mouth open and his tongue tangles with mine. I pull him closer, moaning into his mouth as I feel the weight of his body, his hard press against my soft causing something in both of us to snap.

Our hands turn frantic.

My fingernails claw at his back while his hands twist into my hair. He pulls my head back, exposing the delicate skin of my throat, nipping and biting his way to my chest. The quiet sting of his teeth only intensifies the pleasure pooling deep in my belly.

He lets go of my hair, his hands not hesitating before they find the cups of my bra and he yanks them down. He palms my breasts with his hands, rolling and tugging my nipples between his thumb and forefinger until I'm writhing beneath him, begging for more.

"Please, Luke." I'm desperate for more. Desperate for him. "I need you."

"You have me," he murmurs against my breast before sucking one of my nipples into his mouth hard and fast. "I knew it from the first night we met, that you'd be the one to unravel me."

Nobody has ever touched or spoken to me the way he does, reverent and impassioned, as if he couldn't breathe without me. As if I'm the one thing he's always been missing. I wrap my legs around his hips and try to pull him closer to me, convinced that the barest amount of pressure will set me off.

"Pants. I need you to take off my pants." My voice is unrecognizable, breathy and full of need as the pressure steadily building between my thighs becomes unbearable. "I need you inside of me."

"You're going to have to be patient, Em," he says even as his fingers make quick work of unbuttoning my jeans. "I've gone to bed every night since finding out you lived around the corner, picturing you in my bed. I fall asleep imagining all the ways I could make you come. Now that you're here? I'm going to take my time. I want to spend all night watching you fall apart time and time again and I need to know that you want that too."

His words set off shock waves in my body that I feel all the way down to my toes. The promise of the man hovering above me is unlike anything I've ever experienced before, and I know, without a shadow of a doubt, that I'll never experience it again.

"Yes. I want that." My limbs fall heavy in surrender as the control I usually feel melts into the sheets beneath me. "I need that."

The words have barely left my mouth before my pants are off, and he's standing at the foot of the bed, his eyes slowly traveling the length of my body wearing nothing but lace.

"Fucking hell," he growls, the final tendrils of control slipping through his fingers. "You have no idea how beautiful you are. Inside and out, the most beautiful woman I've ever seen."

"You're not so bad yourself." My heart spasms alongside my core, feelings and passion colliding in ways I never knew possible. "Though maybe we could even things out a little bit and you could take off your shirt too?"

His shirt hits the floor, and he's back on top of me in a flash. It's like he's stepped straight from a magazine cover into bed with me. I run my hands across the hard ridges of his abs, reveling in the feel of his smooth, tan skin soft beneath my fingers until he grabs my arms and pulls them high above my head.

"You can play later," he assures me. "But now it's my turn."

He pushes up on his knees and pulls off the belt I didn't even know he was wearing. The thrill of realizing his pants are going to join mine on the floor quickly turns to confusion as the leather winds around my wrists.

"Is this okay?" he asks gently, the heavy rise and fall of his chest the only indication that he's just as worked up as I am. "I don't want to do anything you're uncomfortable with."

I've never done anything like this before, and I take a minute to think about it. The leather is still loose around my wrists and I know he'd stop the second I asked him to.

"Yes," I say, before repeating the sentiment from earlier in the night, a new meaning behind my words. "I said I trusted you and I meant it."

His mouth drops to mine, fast and hard before tightening the belt and securing it to the slatted headboard behind me. I pull at the restraints, testing to see if they'll hold and moaning when the belt bites into my sensitive skin. I push my legs together, almost ashamed by how turned on I am . . . embarrassed by the wetness growing between my legs.

"Oh no." His rough hands glide down the insides of my legs and force them apart before he drops his head between the apex of my thighs. "No more hiding from me, Emerson. I'm going to explore every single inch of you."

He pulls the thin lace separating us between his teeth and slips a finger inside of me without ever breaking eye contact.

"Don't look away." He bites the inside of my thigh when I throw my head back. He removes his finger and I miss it instantly. "You're going to watch me as I eat you from the front"— his tongue swirls around my clit before his hands palm my ass and he lifts me in the air—"to back." I stare, dumbstruck, as he drags his mouth across my opening and down to my ass.

I never thought I would like anything that feels so wrong, so forbidden, but my body doesn't agree. I begin to tremble under his touch, nearly coming apart at the seams.

"Oh yeah. You like that, don't you?" He rips off my panties, flinging them across the room before his fingers are back inside of me, curling at just the right spot. "Fuck, Em. You're so wet."

I open my mouth, but no words come out. Only moans as his mouth latches on to my clit, biting and sucking until my body is slicked with sweat. And right when I think I can take no more, he pulls his fingers away and slips one into the place that has never been explored.

The sudden jolt of pleasure pushes me over the edge, and it's like a bomb detonates inside of me. Shocks of electricity shoot from my skin, and my back arches so high off of the bed, I feel like I'm levitating. I scream out, the sound bouncing off the bare walls of his bedroom, ensconcing us in an echo chamber of pleasure.

"Luke." I gasp out his name as I try to catch my breath. "I can't."

"You can," he murmurs against my core, and the vibrations only add to the rapidly building crescendo. "And you will."

He lowers his mouth back down, licking my arousal while that forbidden finger works me from behind. Without warning, a second, impossibly more intense orgasm tears through me. I dissolve into a puddle of nothingness as stars explode behind my eyes and my head swims. The world falls out of focus, and I try to remember who and where I am.

"Holy shit," I whisper as I come to. "That was . . ." I try to think of anything that could encompass what that was, but my words trail off when I realize there's no word in the English language that could even come close to describing it.

"Yeah." Luke's weight rests on top of my body before his mouth takes mine, my taste still on his tongue. "That was."

"I need you inside of me." My hands are still tied above my head, so I pull him closer with my legs. The feel of his zipper pushed against me nearly makes me come for a third time. "Please."

I'll whine, plead, or beg. I've waited months, and I'm ready to do whatever's necessary to feel him inside of me again. Luckily for me though, he's just as ready as I am.

He rolls to the side of the bed and opens the bedside table to grab a condom. He stands up and unbuttons his pants, allowing them to fall to the ground and his erection to spring free. My memory didn't do it justice. It's bigger than I remember, thicker too. A bead of pre-cum drips from the head, and I lick my lips, wanting to taste him as much as I want him between my legs.

"Next time." He reads my mind as he rolls the condom down his thick shaft. "When I come this time, it's not going to be in your mouth. We'll save that for later."

My nipples harden and my mouth waters. The control this man has over my body should be concerning, but it's not. It's fucking exhilarating.

"I wish I could take this slow." He crawls back over to me, and my insides clench as he lines up his cock with my opening. "But I don't think I can."

"I don't want you to. I need you to lose control." I tell him the god's honest truth. "I want you to get lost in me the same way I'm lost in you."

"Then you haven't been paying attention." He leans down and whispers in my ear, "I've been lost in you since the second I watched you step off of that elevator all those months ago."

But I don't have the time to let those monumental words sink into my brain, because instead, Luke sinks into me.

All of my air leaves me in a single whoosh as he thrusts inside of me. His pace is relentless. He drives into me time and time again until my toes start to curl and the all too familiar pressure begins to build again. My insides clench around him and I close my eyes, ready to fall apart all over again when all of a sudden, he's gone.

He grabs me by the hips and flips me over, slamming back into me from behind before I can comprehend what's going on. One strong arm wraps around me, holding my back to his front while his other hand makes quick work of finding the sensitive button between my legs. He doesn't slow down, his mouth at my ear whispering words I can't hear over my moans and the sound of our skin slapping together.

Then, just when I think I can't take anymore, he thrusts in as hard as he can, filling me to the hilt and simultaneously pinching my swollen clit. He groans his release and at the same time my body convulses as electricity explodes from every last nerve ending in my body. Blood rushes through my ears, drowning out the sounds of my cries until my body goes limp.

Gently, he turns me around, laying me on my back while he unwraps the belt from my wrists. He pulls my arms down, massaging my shoulders and peppering kisses across the marks the belt left behind.

"Wow." My breathing finally calms, and the room comes back into focus. "How was it better than the first time?"

I didn't think anything could ever top the first time.

"Because." He wraps his arms around my waist and pulls me closer to him. "When it comes to you and me, Em, things are only going to get better. You just have to give me a chance."

I shouldn't believe him; it sounds much too good to be true.

But even if this is another lesson I have to learn the hard way, I won't mind. Because I have a feeling that letting him ruin me might be the best thing that ever happens to me.

"Okay." I touch my lips to his. It's quick and sweet, the opposite of everything we just did. "I'll give you a chance under one condition."

"Anything." His eyes go soft, and the lines beside them deepen. "What is it?"

"You have to promise—" I let my words linger, and my hand makes its way between his legs. "That next time I get to tie *you* up."

"Oh yeah." His raspy laughter fills the room, and he pulls me on top of him. "That's a promise I can most definitely fulfill."

And then, because he's a man of his word, he does exactly that.

24

I DON'T HAVE many regrets in life.

I mean, sure, should I have avoided dying my hair blond in my junior year? Yes. Do I wish that I didn't wear that acid-washed jean jacket on picture day two years in a row? Of course. Were the three martini shots, two glasses of wine, and five tequila shots necessary on my twenty-first birthday? Absolutely not.

But in the grand scheme of life, those are no big deal.

Small fries, really.

The only thing I should regret is allowing the man I'm seeing, the man I'm sleeping with, the man I'm reluctantly—and uncontrollably—falling head over heels for, to come along on a field trip with my class.

"Miss Pierce's class!" I clap two times and yell out to the busy bus filled with tiny feet, happy chatter, and carefree giggles. "I know we are excited, but can we please get some bubbles in our mouths?"

Like magic, all my little ones puff up their cheeks and the noise dies down.

"Great job, friends," I compliment them before I go over the field trip instructions for the thousandth time. "Now, remember in class that everyone was assigned a buddy and a number? If you look up"—I point to the numbers above the seats—"you'll see a number. When you see your number, that's where you and your buddy will be sitting on our way to the pumpkin patch and on the ride back to school. Show me one finger if you understand."

Little arms shoot into the air, all showing me the number one.

Perfect.

"Okay then." I clap once this time around. "Let's get to our seats so we can hit the road."

The noise picks up again, but when I see everyone getting to their correct seats, following directions, and keeping their hands to themselves, I let it go. It's a field trip, after all; they're supposed to be talking with their friends. It's part of the fun.

Once my students are all settled, I turn my focus to the five parent volunteers tagging along with us today.

"Alright, now parents." I smile at them all . . . well, almost them all. "First I want to thank you again for tagging along with us today. I know this can be overwhelming, but I can't tell you how much it means to the kids to have you here today.

"As you just heard, all of the students have been assigned a buddy, so your child will not be sitting with you. It's easier for everyone if they are paired with a classmate, then once we're at the pumpkin patch, you will each have your own group of buddies. For the bus ride, I'd appreciate it if you could help me with my zone defense." I point to the strategic rows I left open when assigning the kiddos their numbers. "I'll be sitting up front so I can talk to our bus driver, Mr. Johnson, but if two could sit in the back, two could sit in the middle, and one could join me at the front, that'd be wonderful."

"I get carsick on buses, so I'll take the front." Luke beats the other parents to the punch and slides into the seat where my backpack is sitting. "If that's okay with Miss Pierce, of course."

"Of course." My smile is painful, and I wonder if any of the other parents can see straight through me. "That'd be great, Mr. Miller."

"Oh, please. Mr. Miller is my dad." He waves me off, and the devilish smirk I'm becoming too accustomed to tugs on the corner of his mouth. "Please, call me Luke."

"Luke, got it." It's too bad I have to be a good example because I really want to kick him right now. "Thank you."

I don't think we could be more obvious, but the other parents seem to be completely unfazed by us as they walk down the aisle and settle into the seats on the bus.

"You know"—I sit down beside him, careful to leave extra space between us—"there's an open seat over there if you think that'd help with your motion sickness."

"Motion sickness." He chuckles to himself. "I've never had motion sickness in my life. Suckers."

"You're going to be a bigger problem than the kids, aren't you?"

I don't know why I'm shocked. I knew this was going to be the case when I woke up to a text from him this morning saying he couldn't wait to "roll around in the hay" with me. If I hadn't already used so many of my sick days, I would've called out right then and there. I don't know how I'm going to manage spending an entire day next to this man, pretending my legs don't quiver and my stomach doesn't do flips anytime I'm near him.

"Maybe . . ." He glances over his shoulder to make sure nobody is around before he rests his hand on my knee, and his voice drops to a whisper. "I missed you this morning."

"I missed you too."

Since Jacqueline had to leave town this week, she kept Isla until yesterday when she dropped her off at school. This meant that I've had full custody of Luke and boy oh boy, did we take advantage of it.

We woke up early on Monday morning and grabbed a coffee before we had to be at work. He sat in my living room, inspecting my wall art and asking questions while I got ready for school. Then I had to reapply my makeup and fix my hair after I walked out of my room and he got a good look at me.

He'd meet me at my place when he got off of work, bringing dinner with him until I insisted I'd cook. We'd sit on my couch, eating and going over our days until we'd eventually make our way over to his house for the night so I could snuggle Mister Bubbles.

And maybe so we could take advantage of his king-size bed.

It was only a few days, but when I had to climb into my bed last night, I didn't find the joy it usually brings. The quilt I've always loved so much pales in comparison to being held tight in Luke's arms, his face nestled into my hair. I may not believe in finding a person to complete me, but that doesn't mean he hasn't felt like the perfect fit.

"Jacqueline doesn't get back until Monday night, but Isla was asking to go to The Barkery this weekend." His hand bounces with the bumpy road, but it never leaves my leg. "Would you want to meet us there? Maybe we could take some of the dogs for a walk and sneak in a picnic."

"You want to walk dogs and have a picnic with me and your daughter?" I keep my voice low even though the noise on the bus is growing louder with every mile we travel. "That sounds a lot like boyfriend-girlfriend territory."

"Well yeah." He tilts his head and his eyebrows knit together. "Is that not what's happening here?"

I know we talked about our intentions after the Campus Lounge, but this still feels like it comes out of left field. I haven't had a real relationship in a long time. Part of it was self-imposed because people are trash and the other part is because every time I thought things were going to get serious, they told me they wanted to keep it casual. I didn't even know people had boyfriends anymore. It's like you go from being friends with benefits to getting married. There is no in-between.

Unless, I suppose, you find someone like Luke.

"So what I'm hearing is that you're asking me to go steady while we're riding a school bus." The butterflies in my stomach flap so hard that I think I might fly. "This is very high school of you."

And I'm into it.

High school Emerson who was never asked to homecoming or prom is screaming right now! Keeping my hands—and my mouth—to myself is a testament to my self-control because all I want to do is lean across this seat and kiss him. As much as it sucks that we're in public right now, it's very fitting that we're on a bus when I feel like a giddy little schoolgirl.

"I mean . . ." His voice drops so low that I can barely hear him over the squeals of excitement filling the bus. "I thought I made it clear when I gave you five orgasms in one night."

"Six," I correct him. "But who's counting?"

Pride shines in his face the way I'm sure need shines from mine.

"I'm not sure, but I'm hoping my girlfriend's counting." His fingers tighten around my knee. "But if you need more time, that's okay too. I'll take you however I can get you."

I've never felt this happy before, and it physically hurts trying to keep it all inside. If I could throw up hearts and rainbows, I would. I want to run around screaming that I not only have a boyfriend, I have the best boyfriend.

But I can't run or scream or throw up, so instead, I pull his hand off of my knee and twist our fingers together, hoping it can convey even a modicum of what I'm feeling inside and say, "I'm definitely your girlfriend."

And then, just like in all the romance movies, I hear a slight commotion behind me followed by the unmistakable high-pitched screams of horrified kindergartners.

"Miss Pierce!" So many kids scream at once that I can't decipher who's talking. "Ben threw up!"

Back to reality.

But at least in this reality, at the end of the day, I have a man to call mine and a very effective way of relieving my stress.

25

"**LET ME MAKE** sure I have this right." Keisha puts a hand on my arm to stop me from opening my car door. "The man you claimed to hate brought you soup, which led to you being his inside man, which somehow turned into him volunteering at The Barkery, going out, and now he's your secret boyfriend because he's still the parent of one of your students? Do I have that right?"

Soooooo . . .

I might have left out a few key details when I asked her to help me with my Petunia Lemon sabotage. And by a few details, I mean everything about Luke.

Oops.

"Yeah." I nod my head. "That about covers it."

"Well fuck me." She leans back and takes a deep breath. If either of us smoked, I'd offer her a cigarette. "I really can't leave you alone, can I?"

"I told you, I make impulsive decisions without you." When she's gone, I don't have anyone to run my ideas by, and this is what happens. "Next time, could you please think about me be-fore you have an art exhibit and a family emergency back-to-back?"

"I'll be sure to tell my grandma she needs to run her heart problems by you in the future."

"Thank you." I pull my keys out of the ignition. "That's all I ask."

"But really, thank you for sending those cookies to my mom's house," she says. "I didn't even know you had her address."

I didn't have her address. I spent an entire afternoon putting all my internet sleuthing to work to figure it out, but she doesn't need to know that.

"When you're stressed, I'm stressed." What can I say? I'm a very codependent person. "And when I'm stressed, I need cook-ies. So I thought it might help you as well."

"You didn't need to do it." Her voice thickens with a show of emotion that is so unlike Keisha, I almost panic. "But I can't tell you how grateful I am that you did. It meant a lot to me."

"Of course I didn't need to do it, but you know gift giving is my love language." I wave her thanks off. I'm not prepared to feel feelings right now, not when I'm prepped and ready for bat-tle. "Plus, what I really wanted to send you was wine. But you were stuck in a dry town and cookies were the best I could do."

"Well . . ." She shakes her head and clears her throat. Looks like I'm not the only person who hides my emotions anymore! "Will there at least be wine at this thing tonight?"

"Duh." I ask a few questions before going to Petunia Lemon events now, like where it is, will there be medical procedures, things like that. But alcohol is a given. "I think they put more thought into the alcohol selection than into the products we're supposed to be talking about."

Just one of the thousands of red flags I've found since I realized Petunia Lemon is not what it seems to be.

"Oh good!" She unclasps her seatbelt and pushes open her door. "That makes things easier for me then."

I climb out and lock my car. I doubt anyone would be interested in my car, but it's been through too much lately to tempt fate. Car theft would absolutely push me over the edge. I drop my keys, attached to the new, special key chain Luke gave me, into my purse and meet Keisha on the sidewalk.

"Do you need me to go over the plan again?"

Since Keisha was at my failed Petunia Lemon party when I decided to quit, she was shocked to find out I was still a sister in skincare when she got back to town. And because she knows me better than almost anyone on the planet, she didn't buy my BS story about still loving the products and wanting to honor my commitment to the brand. I lasted maybe thirty minutes before I confessed my entire plan to her, and she eagerly volunteered to help bring them down.

"I think I got it," she says. "We're just going to pretend like you've finally convinced me to join, right?"

"Mainly, yes. I just need you to seem excited about the opportunities and the products. If you get the chance, maybe ask point blank if the only thing they use for their skin is Petunia Lemon products." Since I already have them on camera admitting to Botox, this will cement the lies even further. "I'm going to talk to Nora about the refund policy and see if I can catch them lying about that too."

"I know you still have hope that Nora isn't covering up for them," she says, the look on her face making it clear she doesn't share my faith. "But no matter what happens, I have your back."

"I appreciate that." I squeeze her hand, so grateful that if I can't have a sister in skincare, I'll always have a sister in life. "Also, if I didn't tell you already, I'm obsessed with your hair tonight."

"Thank you!" She touches the Bantu knots all over her head. "Last time I tagged along, two women touched my hair and a third attempted. This is my protective style for my protective style."

"Brilliant." And infuriating that people still think it's okay to touch another person without permission. "I hope it works."

"They should be the ones hoping," she says. "I was only nice last time for you. I'm not playing by the same set of rules tonight and I will hurt someone's feelings."

"It'd be well deserved." We turn in at the walkway up to Jacqueline's house. "Just make sure you record it if you do."

Each step we take to the front door feels like someone is winding my muscles up tighter and tighter. Tension runs down my spine and I'm afraid one small word will snap me like a rubber band. The worst part is I'm not sure if I feel so anxious because of the information I'm trying to get on Petunia Lemon or because I'm going to spend the evening laughing and smiling in Jacqueline's face, only to leave and call her ex-husband.

"Oh no." Keisha grabs my hands and turns me to face her. "I don't know if you're spiraling over Petunia Lemon, Jacqueline, or both, but you need to snap out of it."

"I can't help it!" I whisper-shout, my nerves getting the best of me. "This is my first time around her since . . . you know, things happened with Luke. I'm freaking out a little bit."

"Well stop it," she demands, like her words will make it happen. "You're always so worried about everyone else's happiness and you can't do that tonight. This company is horrible, and not to be a bitch, but so is Jacqueline. You met Luke before you knew her, and there's nothing for you to feel bad about. So let's go drink some free wine, dig up some dirt, and get the fuck out of there so you never have to see her again . . . except for teacher conferences and school events until the end of May."

At least she started out strong? I have no idea how this got so messy, but she's right about one thing—the faster we do this, the faster we can leave.

"You're right." I take a deep breath and square my shoulders. I reach into my purse and turn on the key chain that happens to be a recorder. I was going to wait until later to start recording but I'm worried if I don't do it now, I'll forget when it's time. Luke reassured me there's enough storage to last all night and he better be right, because if I have to be an inside man after tonight, I'm convinced it'll give me an ulcer. "Let's get this over with."

We march up to the door and I don't even get a chance to ring the bell before it's thrown open.

"Emerson!" Jacqueline pulls me in for a hug, and my hackles immediately shoot into place. "I'm so glad you made it!"

Considering the last time I saw her she was pointing out all of the problem areas on my face, a warm reception from her was the last thing I expected.

"Umm . . . hi." I hug her back even though this feels like a trap. "Thanks for inviting me."

"Oh please, you know I love to see you. Sisters in skincare, remember?" She pulls away from me and turns her attention to Keisha. "And you must be the new consultant I heard all about? I'm Jacqueline, it's so nice to meet you!"

There it is!

It all makes sense now. She's putting on a show to add another person to this crazy-ass company. It's just too bad she not only already met Keisha, but has had multiple conversations with her.

She holds out her arm to shake Keisha's hand and the second-hand embarrassment coursing through my body almost makes it hard to stand. But even so, I can't help but notice the way not a single line appears on her face when she aims her ultrawhite, megawatt smile at Keisha. Dr. Hubbard really is a master at her craft.

I can see the thoughts running across Keisha's face as she decides whether or not she's going to choose violence.

Thankfully for the rest of our night, she takes the peaceful route.

"Keisha." She shakes her hand. "So nice to meet you, Jasmine."

Okay.

She chose the semiviolent path. I approve.

"It's Jacqueline actually." She puts an emphasis on the c sound, and I have to pull my lips between my teeth to stop myself from laughing. "Like the former First Lady, Jacqueline Kennedy."

"I'm so sorry!" Keisha's smile matches Jacqueline's in both size and authenticity. "I'll be sure to remember that next time."

"Oh don't worry, it's not a big deal." The muscles on her face may be frozen, but not even that's enough to mask that it absolutely is a big deal and Keisha should 100 percent be worried. "Come inside, grab a drink."

We follow her into the kitchen, and there's already a crowd swarming the island housing three charcuterie boards and more wine bottles than I can count at first glance. Nora is chatting with Chloe and Odette is pouring a glass of wine that gets so close to the rim, it's a wonder it doesn't spill onto the floor.

"Impressive pour, Odes," Keisha says. "I've never seen that skill at school."

"Girl, school is the reason I've acquired such a skill." Odette laughs. "I love my job, but that cafeteria gets loud and by the end of the day, a heavy pour is the only thing that keeps my brain from exploding."

"Well, please feel free to help yourself to as much wine as you want too," Jacqueline cuts back into the conversation, clearly not liking being left out. "We're just waiting for a few more people and then we'll move to the living room. I have samples you can try and we'll fill you in on all of the latest Petunia Lemon news."

Jacqueline is back to ignoring me and keeps all of her attention focused on Keisha. And honestly? Thank god. I already feel bad enough, so I'm not sure I could handle her finally being nice to me as I'm plotting against her in her own house.

"This looks amazing," Keisha says, and it might be the only real thing she says all night.

Jacqueline might not be great with names and faces, but she sure knows how to throw a party. These boards aren't something she threw together on a whim. She had to have spent close to five hundred dollars on the food alone. As a person who frequents the wine aisle in the grocery store, I know the wine isn't anything to sneeze at either.

It's like the best girls night you've ever been invited to, and it's exactly how they suck you in.

Fool me once . . .

"Nora!" I push down my nerves and determination takes their place. "Do you mind if I steal you away for a second? I just have a couple of questions before I finish registering Keisha."

Enough is enough.

I'm ready for this entire charade to be over.

"Oh my goodness. Absolutely!" She grabs her wineglass off of the table and loops her arm through mine. "Your first recruit! I'm so proud of you for sticking with this. I knew you could do it."

"Thank you!" I bite down on my tongue. After knowing what I know now, I'm so grateful I'm not the person who signed Odette and Chloe up, but I still can't believe she brought them to my party, gave them my samples and food, and then signed them up underneath her. The shady bitch.

"Of course, you know us sisters in skincare always believe in one another." She pulls me into a hallway and I have to keep my eyes focused on the spotless hardwood floors to avoid the family pictures still hanging on the walls. When she pushes the door open and I see where she's taken me, I almost pass the fuck out.

"Is this—" I hope my wide-eyed horror reads slightly less horror-y—and even less whore-y, which is what I'm really feeling like now—as I take in the pink walls and llama decorations. "Is this Isla's room?"

"I know, it's so weird being in your student's room." She flops down on Isla's twin bed and sends her stuffed animals scattering. "But isn't it so cute?"

"Adorable," I choke out.

It feels like my throat is sealing shut. I have to get the fuck out of here.

"So . . ." She tucks her legs beneath her, and I get the feeling I'm not the first person she's brought into this room. "What do we need to do to get Keisha signed up tonight?"

Focus, Emerson. Ask and escape.

"She's just a little worried about the cost of everything." I sit next to her on Isla's bed and position my purse between us, hoping my recorder is picking everything up. "Obviously, you know she's an art teacher and with the monthly orders, she's afraid it will add up and she won't be able to make the money back fast enough."

Nora knows Keisha is an elementary school art teacher, but what she doesn't know is that she's been quietly selling her own art and has been added to small galleries across the country for the last year. It's been a long time coming, and she's finally making enough that if she didn't love her job so much, she wouldn't miss her measly salary.

"I think we can both understand that fear. Finances are always such a double-edged sword, especially for teachers like us," she says. "But you have to spend money to make money and this isn't like buying a sweater. She's investing in her future. Where else can you buy your own business for a few hundred dollars?"

These were the exact same things she said to me. But back

in July, I believed what she was saying. I didn't realize she was just reciting a list of talking points she memorized years ago. A fury unlike anything I've ever experienced starts to bubble up from somewhere deep inside of me.

"That's what I told her." I struggle to keep a straight face. I'm not sure I'm a good enough actress to pull this off. "But she wanted to know about the refund policy and I didn't know what to tell her. I'm not super familiar with it, so I didn't want to tell her the wrong thing."

I hold my breath. There's still a chance I wasn't wrong putting my trust in her. It won't be great for Luke's article, but I really hope whatever she says next will restore my faith in her.

"You just tell her that Petunia Lemon has a company-wide return policy." She shrugs, not answering my question at all. "She can look it up on the website."

I already looked it up on the website. It says a bunch of nothing and tells you to call them for more information. And when you call, the only thing you get is dizzy from the circles they talk in.

"I know that, but she was asking if I knew anyone who's received the refund." The lie slips effortlessly off my tongue. Maybe I'm not terrible at this after all. "I told her I didn't because I'm so new, but I'd ask you. I think she just wants to know she has options."

"Tell her she won't need options when she signs up because the products are so great." Her happy-go-lucky attitude starts to shift into something I've never experienced with Nora. It's as off-putting as it is unnerving, and I don't like it one bit. "Not knowing someone who's gotten a refund means we have happy customers. That should be enough for her."

"Okay . . ." I can't drop it now. She's so defensive, and now I know she's hiding something. "But what if it's not?"

"Then make it enough," she snaps, her fair skin reddening to the color of her hair before she pauses and takes a long breath. "Listen, the policy is in effect, but it's an unspoken rule that nobody uses it. There are certain loopholes that are in place that protect us as their uplines from having to pay back commissions. From my experience, if anyone tries to get a refund, corporate moves so slow that they realize it's better for everyone if they don't try to take the quitters' way out and work harder. Or if they aren't cut out for it, they take their losses and leave the company with some dignity."

And there it is.

I know I shouldn't be surprised but I am, and the disappointment I feel is bone-deep. I trusted Nora. She knew everything about my situation, but she only cared that I was a name she could check off of her list. Another person she could profit off.

But now, I'm going to be the person who makes sure she never does this to anyone ever again.

"That makes sense." The muscles around my mouth quiver as I try to keep the smile on my face. "So the return policy is just to ease nerves and get people into Petunia Lemon who might not otherwise. Then once they're in, they won't leave."

"Exactly!" She lets out a sigh of relief, and all signs of anger flee her face. "It's basically just something to help their consultants reach those customers who are standing in their own way. When you make it to headquarters, they'll explain it so much better."

"That's so clever, but can't we get in trouble for that?" I

should wrap this up while I'm ahead, but I can't stop myself. I need to know her answer.

"I don't think so." She shrugs like scamming thousands of people out of their hard-earned money is no big deal. "Because they don't ever actually deny a refund, there's nothing that can be done."

"No wonder this company does so well."

The bunch of evil fucking villains.

"Right?" She stands up, and I guess she is as done with this conversation as I am. "Now let's go sign up Keisha."

I don't notice any of the pictures on the wall as we make our way back down the hallway. All I see is red.

When we walk into the kitchen, Jacqueline is still doing her best to court Keisha.

"You said they're called Bantu knots? They're so beautiful," Jacqueline says before reaching up to touch Keisha's hair, but Keisha steps out of her reach at the last second. "Oh my god! Has anyone told you about our charity measure? I think you'll really love it."

I stop behind Keisha, curious to hear what Jacqueline's going to say. I've been to more meetings than I can count at this point, and this is the first time I've heard anything about charity. Maybe they have at least one redeeming characteristic.

"Really?" Keisha says through clenched teeth. "What is it?"

"We partnered up with an organization in Africa so we can send women our serums and creams," Jacqueline says, her voice full of pride. "Once a year, a group of Petunia Lemon consultants fly to Africa and teach them about the products and what it means to have a business of their own. This way they can go back to their villages and spread the knowledge."

My jaw almost hits the floor.

I've heard some wild things at these meetings, but this might be the most unhinged of them all. I look around the room, expecting to see a room full of faces reflecting what I'm feeling, but instead, they're all wearing huge smiles and nodding along with Jacqueline.

I'm in the fucking twilight zone. There's no way this is real.

"That's amazing." Keisha somehow manages to keep a straight face, and I don't know if it sparks my respect or fear. "Where in Africa do you go?"

Oh god.

I grab onto the edge of the counter, knowing there's only one way this is going to end.

"Where?" I see the confusion fighting against the Botox between Jacqueline's eyebrows. "I'm not sure I follow?"

"Where do you fly into to do this charitable work?" Keisha asks again, and I see the vein in her forehead starting to throb.

"Did I not say?" Jacqueline looks around the room for validation. "It's in Africa."

"But where in Africa?" Keisha doesn't back down.

"Just, you know"—Jacqueline waves her hand in front of her—"Africa."

Holy fucking hell.

I knew the conversation was going to end this way, but it doesn't make knowing that a grown-ass adult has no idea Africa is a continent, not a country, any less shocking. The only bright side to this entire conversation is that while most of the sisters in skincare who are watching this conversation go down don't seem to think there's an issue, Chloe and Odette are both wearing matching horrified expressions.

"I know that." Keisha's hands enter the equation, and if I don't intervene soon, she's going to hurt Jacqueline's feelings so bad that she might never recover. "But where—"

"Oh my god! I forgot that I actually have to be somewhere tonight." I grab Keisha's hand and pull her behind me. "Thank you so much for having us. See you all soon!"

I don't wait for a response before we're out the door and running back to my car.

"Oh my god!" I say to Keisha when we're back inside my car. "That was . . ."

I don't finish my sentence because I don't think I'll ever know what that was.

"Emerson, I'm going to tell you something and I really need you to hear me, okay?" She puts her hands on my shoulders and stares deep into my eyes. "Any guilt you felt about anything around that woman? I need you to release it."

"But—" I try to interrupt, but she doesn't let me get far.

"No." She shakes her head. "The second Isla is back with her horrific fucking mother, I need you to show up at that man's house in nothing but a jacket and a pair of heels and I need you to fuck the shit out of that man. And while you're doing it, I need you to know he upgraded by a million percent and that the second you walked into his life was the moment his life changed for the better."

"Oh." I nod, my face heating thinking about all the things I might do to him. "I can do that."

"Damn right you can," she says. "Now take me home so you and Luke can get to work destroying those bitches."

She doesn't say please, but I listen to her anyway.

Because I am going to bring them down, and I'm going to laugh in every single one of their smug, lying faces when I do.

26

LUKE HITS STOP on the recording I brought him over and just stares at me dumbstruck for so long that I think I might have broken him.

"Luke?" I ask. "You still there?"

"Yeah. Sorry." He shakes his head and snaps out of whatever trance he was stuck in. "I'm just trying to comprehend how the hell these people are real."

"You married one." I don't want to kick a man when he's already down, but there is one pretty major detail he's leaving out. "And procreated with her too."

"Fuck." He groans and throws his head back. "Thank god Isla takes after my side of the family."

"Jacqueline's never been particularly kind to me"—in fact, she's been downright rude—"but even I can't ignore how charismatic and charming she can be. I think Petunia Lemon brought out the worst in her, but I have no doubt you saw the best in her. Considering how wonderful Isla is, I know there's a lot of good in her."

If *Mean Girls* took place with a bunch of women in their thir-ties who were involved in a cult-adjacent company, Jacqueline would 1,000 percent be the Regina George. Even when you hate her, you can't help but like and maybe even admire her. I can't imagine what she was like before she attached that giant chip to her shoulder.

"That's nice of you to say," he acquiesces, with a timidness I'm not used to in his strong voice. "I think I've just had a hard time allowing myself to remember the times before our mar-riage went up in flames. It makes publishing this piece harder."

"Are you having second thoughts?" I don't know how his job works, but I have to imagine pulling the piece would cost him way more than money. "Is walking away from this an option?"

I can't lie, I'd be disappointed if he did. And not just because of my stellar work as a double agent, either. Now that I know how terrible Petunia Lemon is, I want to do whatever I can to make sure anybody who joins from here on out does so with their eyes wide open. But my feelings aren't his obligation, and if he feels this would harm the mother of his child, and therefore his child, I couldn't fault him for changing his mind.

"Absolutely not," he says with zero hesitation. "I'm going to add in what you gave me tomorrow and then I'll send this draft over to my boss. I'm hoping it will be out by the end of the month, early next month at the latest."

"Oh wow." I do the math in my head. "That's soon. Are you prepared for what the fallout might be?"

Since I was recruited by Nora and she's my boss, Luke prom-ised to keep my name out of the article. My supersleuthing ways will stay in the dark as long as I want them to. But even knowing

I won't be facing direct impact when this article hits, my stomach still twists into knots thinking about how everyone will react.

"I don't know if I'm ever ready, but it comes with the territory. In this line of work, if you aren't making people mad, you aren't doing your job." He tries to play it cool, but doesn't do a very good job. "Obviously it's more personal this time, but I still believe in what I'm doing. I hate knowing it will hurt Jacqueline, but in the long run, I hope this will be the wake-up call she needs. And even if she never gets over it or forgives me, I know this will prevent other people from falling victim to the way these companies scheme and manipulate people. How are you feeling?"

"I'm excited for this to come out but part of me feels guilty for turning on them." I might not see anyone outside of the Petunia Lemon get-togethers, but I always enjoyed talking to Janet and Grace. They haven't been with the company for too long, and I think out of everyone, I feel the most guilty for keeping this from them. Mister Bubbles must feel my stress. He snuggles deeper into my side, purring as I scratch the spot behind his ear he likes so much. "I'm so angry that I allowed myself to fall prey to them, but I know compared to most people, I got out fast and relatively unscathed. They put you through so much, I don't know how you're doing it."

I don't want to excuse his behavior from the first morning we met, because he was an asshole, and I didn't deserve any of that shit. But knowing what I know now, I can see where he was coming from. He viewed Petunia Lemon—rightfully so—as his enemy, and I might not have known it at the time, but I sided with the wrong team.

"It's actually really helped me process a lot of what happened. It showed me that my divorce wasn't because I was an unsupportive partner, and it wasn't Jacqueline caring more about a corporation than me and Isla." He grabs his laptop off of the coffee table and makes quick work of entering his password. He opens up the article before handing it to me. "I spoke to a lot of families while putting this together. We weren't the only one destroyed by Petunia Lemon, but thanks to this piece, thanks to your information, hopefully we'll be the last."

I sit in silence, reading the article I last saw what feels like a lifetime ago. The sting I felt reading it the first time is no longer there, but not only because I've changed and have a new perspective. Luke's tone is completely different as well. The resentment that laced every word before is nowhere to be seen. The anger has been replaced with empathy and understanding. The only time I sense judgment is when he's discussing the ways this corporation exploits women who are hoping to find community and money for dance recitals.

The article has evolved and so, I realize, has the author.

"This is . . ." I struggle to find the words. It's a piece exposing greed and corruption, it shouldn't almost move me to tears. "It's amazing, Luke."

"I didn't see the big picture before. I couldn't see it . . . not until I walked into your classroom." He takes the computer out of my hands and pulls me closer. "It's so cliché and corny, but I was able to turn my pain into purpose. And then, without even seeing it coming, I was able to open myself up to finding happiness again. To finding you."

How is this man real?

"I put on mascara and brought you a gift tonight." I try to blink away the stubborn tears trying to fall. "It's going to be very rude of you if you make me cry."

"I'm sorry." He pulls me onto his lap and drops his head to the crook of my neck. "I'd never want you to think I'm rude."

His tongue traces the line of my collarbone, and the cool air in the room follows suit. Goose bumps explode across my skin as anticipation blooms deep in my belly.

Nobody should be able to use their words and their tongue so effectively. Every time I'm around this man, he brings me to my knees.

Literally and metaphorically.

He wraps me in a giant bear hug. His hold is tight and secure as he pulls me flush against his hard chest. The bulge between his legs rises by the second beneath me, and I squirm in his lap trying to get closer. I twist my fingers in his hair and pull his face up to mine as my breathing deepens.

"Don't be a tease." I wanted it to be a demand, but it comes out as a plea instead. I have no self-control when it comes to him.

One touch is all it takes and then desperation takes over.

"Tease you?" He touches his mouth to mine as he finds the hem of my maxi skirt. "I would never."

My breathing speeds up as his fingers travel up the outside of my legs. "You would and you do."

"It's not teasing. I just love the way that when I kiss you here"—he sucks at the sensitive skin below my ear and kisses all the way down to my cleavage—"you blush down here."

Considering the way my entire body lights on fire the moment he touches me, I'd be surprised if all of me didn't burn bright red.

"Does it?" I tighten my hands in his hair and anchor him to me. "What happens when you touch me somewhere else?"

He's like tequila and I get drunk off his touch. I lose all my inhibitions; he emboldens me to say things I never, in a million years, thought would leave my lips.

"Hmmmm . . ." His fingertips flex into my thighs. The slight bite of pain is a delicious contrast to the gentle feel of his mouth on my breasts. "Should we find out?"

"Oh yes." I nod vigorously. Science was never my favorite subject, but this is one experiment I can definitely get behind. "We should."

He doesn't answer . . . at least not with words. He pulls my legs apart. It's so forceful and unexpected that I lose my balance. Luke's hands grab me by my hips and hold me in place.

"Hold on, Em," he whispers, his voice thick with longing. "This is going to be fast."

The anticipation of what's to come is almost as heady as his touch. Heat pools between my spread thighs, and my breathing turns into moans as I link my hands behind his neck, holding on tight as instructed.

"Good girl." He leans in and crushes his mouth to mine. His teeth nip at my bottom lip, and his tongue licks away the sting as he swallows my moans. "Now don't let go."

I don't usually love to be told what to do, but the faith I have in Luke and his magical hands inspires an obedience I've never felt before.

He moves his hands back to the inside of my thighs and

spreads them slowly this time. His eyes drop to my mouth, watching me as I struggle to breathe as his hands move closer and closer until they're where I want—no—where I *need* them the most.

Beneath his touch, time ceases to exist. I don't know how long he toys with me, his hand inching closer only for him to yank it away. But by the time his fingers graze across the underwear I wish I would've left at home, I'm so wound up that I almost come on the spot.

"Fuck." His groan comes from somewhere deep inside of him as he pulls the fabric covering me to the side and slips a finger inside of me. "You're so wet for me. You love it when I touch you, you love feeling me inside of you, don't you?"

Before Luke, the idea of dirty talk made me cringe.

"Yes." Now it makes me whimper. "I love it so much."

"I can tell. I fucking love it too." He adds another finger inside of me, filling me and stroking until I begin to writhe on his lap. "I want to feel you come on my hand."

He starts moving his hand faster, his fingers curling inside until he hits that sensitive spot, and when he pushes his thumb against my clit, it's like he presses a button that sends me to the fucking moon. I touch the stars as blood rushes through my ears and I cry out my release.

"Give it to me, Em." He pumps his fingers into me harder and harder, not letting up until my first orgasm rolls into my second. "That's it, baby. I want it all, every last drop."

I arch into him, moans pouring from my mouth as I rest my head against his chest. Soft and gentle, he removes his fingers and runs his hands up and down my back while my trembling body comes back down to earth. My body buzzes and my skin feels numb as sparks of electricity jump from each and every nerve ending.

"Holy shit," I whisper when I can finally breathe again. "How are you so good at that?"

"Trust me, Emerson, this is all you." He puts his hand beneath my chin and tilts my face up so I'm looking directly at him. "You do things to me, you make me feel things that I've never felt before. When I'm with you, all I want to do is make you feel as good as you make me feel."

That was sweet. Really, really sweet.

"Well then"—I touch my lips to his—"I must make you feel really freaking good."

"That you do." He smiles against my mouth and thrusts his hips up so that I feel his erection. "And if you're up for it, I could show you all over again."

Instead of answering, I push off of his lap and stand in front of him, stripping down until I'm wearing nothing at all and his emerald eyes are jet black.

And when he pulls me down onto his couch and lifts my legs over his shoulders, he shows me exactly how good I make him feel.

Three times over.

27

I LOVE HYPERBOLE.

Everything makes me literally want to die. If I exercise at all, I've run a thousand miles. The last time I wore a pair of high heels, I crushed all the bones in my feet. Basically, I'm very dramatic about any and all things in my life and that will never change.

But, when I say that the last month has been, hands down, the absolute best month of my life? I'm not exaggerating.

Not even a little bit.

I spend my days in the classroom, working with a group of kids I absolutely adore, my weekends with adorable animals, and most evenings with Luke. My life has never felt so full. Being with Luke feels like someone yanked me out of my life and threw me into a rom-com that turns X-rated when the sun goes down—and sometimes when it's still up.

Things with Nora have been a little tense since Keisha didn't sign up for Petunia Lemon, but I've still been going to the meetings and pretending to be happy to be there. I figured it might look pretty suspicious if I left right before an article written by a parent in my classroom came out. Once the article finally goes live, I'll exit out of the company. And hopefully, I won't be the only one leaving. Until then though, I keep showing up with a smile on my face and a recorder in my purse, enjoying the spectacular spreads and chatting with the women I've come to really enjoy.

Priorities, you know?

Despite the sun shining high in the cloudless, bright blue sky, the cool November air is here to stay. When I checked the forecast this morning, it predicted snow later this week, so I'm soaking up these final days where the kids will get to run some of their energy off outside instead of having to sit through indoor recess.

I finish off the iced coffee I brought in from home and toss the protein bar wrapper in the trash. My kids are with Keisha for art, and I have a little over thirty more minutes to get my room set up for the science project we're working on together. I unlock the cabinet stuffed to the brim with supplies I've collected over the years and pull out the plastic bin labeled "slime." I know I'll get at least one angry parent email at the end of this, but the kids love it so much that I don't even care.

I'm filling up ziplock bags with leaf confetti and glitter when my classroom door slams open and Nora barges in. She startles the crap out of me, and the copper glitter I'm holding flies out of my hands, raining down on me like remnants of the saddest parade ever.

"Emerson!" Her normally pale skin is downright translucent, and panic drips off of her like sweat on a summer day. "Have you checked your email?"

My stomach makes like the *Titanic* and sinks. I've been waiting for this moment for what's felt like forever so it doesn't take
long to realize what's going on. The article is live.

And I have to pretend to have no idea.

"No." I gesture to the glitter piled around my feet. "I was setting up for our science experiment. What's going on?"

"The *Post* just published an article about Petunia Lemon."

"And that's a bad thing? Isn't more exposure good for us?"

"It's not . . ." She stops and draws in a deep breath. "It's not
a complimentary piece, Emerson. It's bullshit and completely
full of lies. It doesn't say it straight out, but it practically accuses
Petunia Lemon of being a cult!"

"A cult? Why would they say that?" I try to sound shocked,
but I'm nowhere near a good enough actress for this. They have
matching tattoos, for goodness' sake! This can't be the first time
she's heard the accusation.

Thankfully she's too in her head to notice my empty words
and fake surprise. She paces back and forth in front of my desk,
mumbling nonsense as different emotions pass over her face by
the second. In the few minutes she's been in my room, she's
gone from ghost white, to fire-engine red, and back again. But
even watching her and trying to keep up with her bordering-on-
manic ramblings, I still can't tell if she's more scared or angry.

"It's such bullshit, I can't believe anyone would be dumb
enough to fall for it, but Odette already told me she's thinking of
backing out and you know if she goes, Chloe will follow her.
This is all because of Jacqueline's vindictive, piece of shit ex-
husband!" she snarls, her hands balling into fists at her sides.
Guess I'm going with angry, not scared. "I told her she couldn't

trust him. He's still pissed about her leaving him and has been desperate to get her back this entire time. I don't blame him for not being able to move on, but not even I thought he'd stoop this low."

I've been preparing for this article to drop since the first conversation I had with Luke about helping him. But somehow, in all my preparation, I didn't even consider what would be said about him. And, even on the off chance that I had thought about it, being still in love with Jacqueline would've never crossed my mind. I start to cough and I don't know if I'm choking on air, delusion, or audacity, but either way, I can't catch my breath.

"Are you okay?" Nora eyes me with concern and hopefully not suspicion.

"Yeah." I nod and hold up a single finger as my coughing fit dies down. "Sorry, I swallowed down the wrong tube. You think Jacqueline's ex did this to win her back?"

Just referring to Luke as Jacqueline's ex makes my stomach turn.

"Isn't it so demented? Out of all the ways he could go about winning her back, he chooses the most spiteful tactic." She sits down on one of the kid chairs, but unlike my very plentiful behind, her cute, tiny one isn't exploding over the sides. "Why men? Am I right?"

"You're right," I agree, hoping with everything in me that she's wrong, and I haven't just been played by a gorgeous, nerdy, sex genius. "Thank goodness for sisters in skincare."

"Oh my god! Yes!" She claps and hops out of the chair so fast I almost get whiplash. "I got so distracted, I almost forgot the main reason I came in here. I'm hosting an emergency meeting at my house tonight."

"Tonight?"

Luke was going to cook dinner and we were going to binge a to-be-determined Bravo show.

"At six." She nods expectantly, and I realize it doesn't even cross her mind that I could have other plans. "I've already been in touch with headquarters and they've been on the phone with legal. But I figured it'd be best to get everyone together and make sure we're on the same page as all of this misinformation starts coming out."

Yeah, *misinformation*.

I'm so sure.

It's hard to look at her without my lip curling up in disgust. I don't understand how she can stand in front of me and lie with a straight face. At least I have the decency to feel some shame when I lie to her.

It's on the tip of my tongue to tell her I can't go. Now that the article is out, it'd be easy to say no and tell her I need to think about things on my own. That'd be the smart thing to do.

But when have I ever done the smart thing?

"I'll be there."

THE GIRLS ARE panicking.

When I walk in, I've never seen anything like it in my life. It's like they've set their hair on fire and nobody knows where the extinguisher is. Everyone is talking over one another. Some people—Jacqueline and Nora—are yelling while others are literally crying in the corner. It's chaos, and if it weren't for Janet spotting me across the room, I would've turned around and left.

"Can you believe this?" Janet's always perfect nails have been bitten to the quick. "I don't even know what to think."

"I know." I look around the room, half expecting somebody to jump out and confront me. "Did you read it?"

One of the tactics I decided to go with tonight is to ask more questions than I answer. The last thing I need is to get caught in a lie with tensions this high. I've never been part of a witch hunt before, but I have a feeling that's about to change.

She nods almost imperceptibly. "I had to see what they were saying but now I don't know what to think."

"What do you mean?" Another question.

Way to stick with the plan, Emerson!

"It's just . . ." She glances over her shoulder, and her voice drops so low that I can barely hear her over the noise in the room. "Nora is telling me it's all lies, but I've seen some of the stuff the article mentions firsthand and if it's not wrong, then why would they say it's not true? I feel like they might be covering their tracks."

The seeds of doubt have been planted, and I can't wait to tell Luke that they're already sprouting.

"That is weird." I echo her sentiment but avoid adding my own. My heart feels like it's going to explode in my chest. I'm more nervous now than when I was getting the dirt to Luke. "I wonder why they're doing that?"

"Alright, ladies!" Nora shouts from the front of the room, and poor Janet damn near comes out of her skin. "Can everyone please take a seat so we can clear this all up and get back to business as usual?"

I follow the herd deeper into her living room, and the sour taste in my mouth causes my stomach to curdle as I get my first real look at Nora's place. From the outside, her house looks cute and unassuming. It's not small, but it's nothing extraordinary. On the inside, however, it's a different story.

Unlike Jacqueline's adorable house, Nora's lacks the Victorian charm, but not because it was never here. No, it's because Nora has gutted and remodeled it from—what I can only assume is—top to bottom. Built-in shelves frame the electric fireplace glowing with the light of a fire she turns on with the click of a remote. The recessed lighting is only upstaged by the ultra-modern chandelier I doubt she ordered from Wayfair. The rug covering her hardwood floor is bigger than my entire living room and the couch that people are piling onto looks remarkably similar to the Restoration Hardware couch that costs more than six months of my rent.

It shouldn't be a shock considering what I know she's already lied about, but seeing with my own eyes that her "struggling teacher act" was just that, an act, takes the knife already lodged in my back and twists it.

"I know everyone has a lot of questions after the garbage the *Post* published today, and I promise we'll get to them, but I wanted to start by reminding you about the company you already know and love." She turns on the giant flat-screen mounted above the fireplace, and a video much like what they showed at the conference begins to play.

I watch closely, trying to remember what drew me to them back in July. The luxe shine I thought it had is so clearly plastic. The video is cheap and flimsy, and everything that seemed so great rings false. Watching now, it's obvious that it's a company built on lies, thriving on the insecurities of women who want something to believe in and a place to belong. If I wasn't so pissed at Nora for luring me in, I'd hate myself for falling for it.

The video comes to an end by zooming in on an image of a group of women with their arms draped around one another, the Petunia Lemon logo plastered across all of their chests. Call me a cynic, but I wouldn't be even a little bit shocked to find out it's an AI-generated image. After everything I learned, I'd be a fool to think anything they present is real.

"No matter what that horrible article claims, we know the truth," Nora says. "We are sisters in skincare and that will never change. It's easier for the mainstream media to push lies and discredit us as silly little women than it is for them to admit that we've cracked the code. This is a classic case of the patriarchy trying to put us in our place all because one scorned man couldn't handle that he was left and his wife is thriving without him."

Jacqueline stands up and joins Nora at the front of the room. Her blonde hair falls in glossy waves down her back and her perfect, full lips turn down at the corner of her mouth. Her waist looks impossibly small in the skintight turtleneck and jeans she's wearing, and even though you can tell she's been crying, her eyes seem even bluer than ever. Not only is she stunning, she's the mother of Luke's child, so I can't fault people for assuming Luke is doing this as some twisted way to get her back. If I didn't know what I know, I'd think the same thing.

But for the first time in my entire life, I'm in a relationship with someone who is so honest and open, that despite listening to people telling me how desperate he is to get back together with his ex, the possibility has never even crossed my mind. In fact, the nasty insecurities I've felt in every relationship I've ever been in are nowhere to found. Because, and not to toot my own horn or anything, that man is completely obsessed with me.

And the feeling is very, very mutual.

"What we really need to focus on is who was giving him this information." Nora pulls my attention back to the conversation at hand. "Because even though Lucas's article is full of lies and exaggerations, it's clear that somebody who's been claiming to be one of us is really working with the devil."

Fear spreads through my body as nervous glances shift around the room. This must be what criminals who return to the scene of the crime feel like. Paranoia makes it hard for me to sit still, and my hands shake with the urge to confess.

"I'm sure you've noticed that the group gathered here is much smaller than normal. Jacqueline and I spent a lot of time this morning compiling our most trusted circle and we narrowed it down to you all." She gestures to the women huddled in her living room. Guilt and relief battle for dominance as I realize so many of the people I know love this company are missing. "You've dedicated your time, money, and energy to Petunia Lemon, and we know that everyone here tonight are our sisters in *and* out of skincare. It's up to us now to weed out the person or persons spreading these malicious lies about the company that's given us so much."

Nora's battle cry works as intended, and a scary calm falls

over the room. The fires that were running wild when I walked in have lit the torches of women ready to grab pitchforks. I look over at Janet and the broken expression she had at the beginning of the night has transformed into a look of determination. She's not alone either.

It'd be impressive if it weren't so fucking terrifying.

Nora's eyes gleam beneath the perfect lighting and her cheeks flush with the excitement of a challenge she's ready to meet. "Who's going to help us defend the sisterhood?"

The room bursts into applause, and my false cheers fall flat in the sea of enthusiasm. If I wasn't already convinced this was a cult before, I would be now. These women have been provided with an article full of facts pointing out how problematic and predatory Petunia Lemon is, and all it took was one person calling it fake news for them to jump back in line.

"Now most importantly," Jacqueline finally jumps in, wiping away a stray tear, "who's ready for wine?"

Laughter lightens the mood as everyone moves into Nora's fully renovated kitchen. After a day like today, a glass of wine feels more necessary than ever before, but I know I can't stay. And when my phone vibrates in my purse, and I see Luke's name flash on the screen, I know exactly where I need to be.

28

BETWEEN NORA BEING plastered to my side at school and my phone dying after the emergency meeting, I haven't been able to talk to Luke all day. Last time I checked before my phone went black, I had eight missed calls from him and three voice mails. I normally abide by the speed limit, but I drove over to his house as fast as I could, only to find that there was not a single parking spot on his entire street . . . or the next.

Luke's front light flickers on as soon as I hit the walkway to his house. He swings the door open and his large body fills his doorway. I was already moving fast, but I speed up the moment I see him.

"Are you okay?" He meets me on the porch, and as soon as his arms wrap around me, all of the stress that's built up over the course of the day melts away. "I've been trying to get in touch with you all day."

"I know, I'm so sorry." I loosen my hold on him just long enough for us to walk inside, latching back on to him the minute the door closes behind us. "I'm not sure if you heard or not, but a certain article came out today and things were a little nuts. Today was wild."

"They told me it was going to publish on Friday. If I knew it was coming out today, I would've warned you before you went in." The stress is evident in his voice, and I hate that he's been so worried. "I was beginning to panic when your phone started going to voice mail."

"I figured it had to be something like that happened." He's been filling me in on every update, and I knew he wouldn't not tell me something like this on purpose. "I wanted to call you, but Nora was on me like white on rice all day long and then my stupid phone died."

I used to have a phone charger in my car like a responsible adult, but I brought it into work one day and it's lived in my desk ever since. Something I'll be sure to remedy tomorrow.

"Nora was on you?" The worry that had started to die down picks back up again. "I went through all of the documents again, your name isn't listed anywhere."

"Oh no, it wasn't anything like that." I kick off my shoes inside of his door before plopping myself in the spot I claimed on his very comfy couch. "She was just freaking out about the article, and I think she needed someone to vent to. But . . . never mind."

I stop myself mid-sentence. This man just published an article that he's spent months working on. Today is for celebrating and drinking champagne, not listening to me moan about Nora.

"Oh no," he says. "What were you going to say?"

"I wasn't going to say anything." The lie slips effortlessly out of my mouth thanks to all the undercover work I've done with Petunia Lemon. "I just want to hear about your day. Have you heard from the Pulitzer people yet?"

"Yeah, okay." A humorless laugh falls from his lips. "You know you're a terrible liar, right? It's one of the best things about you."

Okay . . . so I guess it wasn't so effortless after all.

"Excuse me, sir. You weren't saying I was a bad liar when I was getting dirt on Petunia Lemon." I feign offense. "And also, you're wrong. Obviously my top traits are my ass, hair, and fantastic sense of humor."

I mean really. My honesty? How dare he!

"I can't argue with that." His hands find my ass, and he pulls me off of the couch and onto his lap. "Why don't we call it a four-way tie?"

I touch my mouth to his, physically unable to be this close to him without kissing him. "I guess I can agree to that."

"Good." He leans back just enough so he can look into my eyes without having to break contact. It's the perfect position, and I'd be the happiest girl in the world if we could have every conversation exactly like this. "Now tell me what you were going to say."

Okay. I take it back.

Maybe not *every* conversation.

"Nothing. I was just—" I start to come up with another excuse when a timer goes off in his kitchen. "Is that dinner? Did you cook for me?"

"Depends." He shrugs, not giving away a thing. "Are you going to actually tell me what happened with Nora and the rest of the Petunia Lemon women today or am I going to have to pull it out of you somehow?"

My insides quiver thinking of all the ways he could go about getting the information out of me, and I consider going that route until my other insides, aka my stomach, begins to growl. It's a hard decision, sex or food, but I left Nora's before taking advantage of the pizza and cannoli she ordered from Lechugas and I'm starving.

"Fine, I'll tell you." I give in to the infuriating, gorgeous, wonderful man beneath me. "But first, I want you to know you're very frustrating and stubborn."

"I can live with that."

Annoying.

Cute, but annoying.

"There wasn't much that was unexpected. I don't know exactly what time the article came out, but Nora came into my room while the kids were in art. I could tell the second she walked in what happened. Even when Nora is stressed, she still has this innate poise to her. But not today. She was losing it, Luke." I know it's not funny, but I almost laugh thinking of the way she looked when we walked to our cars after school. Her shirt was untucked, her hair was falling out of her bun, and her perfect makeup was smeared to oblivion. It was like she went to war, only the war was with herself. "She told me she was on the phone with legal all day and then after school, she hosted an emergency meeting. She only invited the consultants she trusts the most and I would've felt guilty if the meeting didn't take place in the million-dollar house she absolutely did not purchase with her principal's salary."

"She invited Jacqueline and I over for dinner a long time ago," he says, and I instantly want to know every detail about this story he's held out on me. "You know I'm not her biggest fan, but even I can't lie about that house. It's really nice."

"Eh. It's alright." I sound bitter, but it's less because of how much I know she spent and more because of the design choices. Houses like that are supposed to have charm. Why buy an old house if you're just going to tear down what makes it special? "But anyways, she was really just working overtime to defend Petunia Lemon. She said the accusations you lodged against them were baseless, just another example of the patriarchy trying to bring women down. And then, you know," I say, dropping my voice to a whisper, "she said you wrote it out of revenge because you're still in love with Jacqueline."

"Can you please speak up a little bit?" His eyes narrow on my mouth, and his body tightens under me. "Because it sounded like you said I was still in love with Jacqueline and there's no way I heard that right."

"To be fair, I'm not actually the one who said it, Nora did, and also, if you think back to a few minutes ago, I didn't want to tell you in the first place. I wanted to eat." I remind him of the reason we're still sitting on his couch. "I knew it would make you mad and I didn't want any of their crap getting in the way of you having an amazing day."

It's not that I think I'm always right, but I am correct approximately 98 percent of the time (Petunia Lemon excluded), and it will probably be best for all of us if he just accepts that now.

"You know that's bullshit, right?" His voice rumbles through my body like a bass through an amp, and there's a sense of urgency in his words that wasn't there only moments ago. "Of course I loved Jacqueline once upon a time, but that's been over for a long time. I would not be here with you if I still had feelings for her."

Even when I didn't like Luke, I trusted him. No part of me ever thought he was just dragging me along for this story.

"I know, I never thought you would," I try to reassure him. "Plus, once you found out I was Isla's teacher, you had to at least pretend to love me."

"You're wrong." He tilts my chin so I'm looking directly at him and can't miss the sincerity pouring out of his emerald eyes. "There's no pretending to it. The moment I sat across from you and you smiled across that table, you made the entire goddamn world fall away. Everything Jacqueline ever did to me disappeared right then and there and I saw the promise of a life sweeter than anything I could've imagined. A love bigger than I ever knew possible."

"It hasn't been long enough. You're a parent in my classroom." My hands shake and my body trembles as I try to think of all the reasons he shouldn't be saying this. "You can't love me."

Not yet. Not like this.

Too bad Luke doesn't agree.

"I can and I do," he says. "And you can try to deny it, but I know you love me too."

I know I should argue with him. He doesn't know what he's talking about. We've been in this bubble, sneaking around and seeing each other in secret. Everything is so exciting, but we can't know if this is real, not until we wait. I need to convince him that he's wrong.

He doesn't love me, and I don't love him either.

Except when I try to tell him, nothing comes out.

Because as much as I want to tell him otherwise, I know he's absolutely right.

"You love me?"

"Even when I didn't want to."

"Well then." I twist in his lap, straddling his hips as I stare into the green eyes that captivated me from the moment he first looked my way. His words flow through my veins, and the rightness fills my body with so much warmth that not even the snowiest Colorado day could ever make me cold again. "I'm glad you want to now."

"Not just now." He touches his lips to mine. "I want to forever."

When I walked in his door tonight, I didn't know what to expect. In all of the scenarios I had run through my head, not a single one ended up with me in his lap and his lips on mine after he told me he loved me. Never in a million years did I ever think reality could far surpass anything I could dream up.

His mouth is pressed against mine, his strong hands splayed across my back as his fingers make easy work of my bra clasp. We're so focused on each other that we don't notice Mister Bubbles hopping off of the couch or the sound of his front door opening.

We don't notice anything until it's too late.

"I can't believe you would stoop so low, Lucas." Jacqueline's voice cuts through our silent moans. "If you wanted to get back at me so bad, you could've called me instead of—oh fuck! Lucas!"

She shouts when she sees the scene playing out in front of her. I jump off of Luke, and my hands frantically try to reclasp my bra as Luke springs off of the couch and tries to shield me from her view.

"What the fuck, Jacqueline?" I've heard Luke mad before, but never like this. "How did you even get in here?"

She stares down at his hardwood floors and holds up a key. "You still keep it above the door."

He grabs the throw blanket folded over the back of the couch and even though he's so pissed that he's practically shaking, he opens the blanket and gently drapes it over my shoulders to cover me up before marching across the room.

"This doesn't belong to you." He snatches the key out of her long, manicured fingers. "You have no right to barge in here like this."

"I needed to talk to you about the article. I didn't know . . ." She finally looks up, and when her eyes land on me, I watch in abject horror as the confusion on her face quickly transforms to hurt before finally landing on anger. "You? Oh you have got to be fucking kidding me."

"I'm not doing this with you tonight. You need to leave." Luke tries to move her toward the door, but she's finished listening to him. Now that she's focused on me, it's like he's ceased to exist.

"I can't believe this! You're my daughter's teacher." Icy daggers shoot from her blue eyes, and the cold I thought vanished seeps deep into my bones. The expression on her face is chilling, and if looks could kill, I'd already be six feet under. "You're my daughter's teacher and you're fucking my husband!"

"Ex-husband," Luke interjects. "Remember? You filed for divorce? I haven't been your husband for more than a year."

"Oh my god." She doesn't even acknowledge that he spoke. Her eyes go wide, and I see the exact moment the final puzzle piece falls into place and she realizes I was the person who has been working with Luke. "This was all you, wasn't it?"

"Jacqueline, it's not what—" I don't know what I'm going to say, but she cuts me off before I can figure it out.

"Don't you even fucking try. I told Nora there was something about you, I told her!" She waves her hands around like they're knives and poison-laced laughter spills out of her over-plumped lips. "But sleeping with my husband and trying to bring down Petunia Lemon? This is beyond. Wait until I tell her."

"You have no idea what you're talking about, Jacqueline." Anger rolls off of Luke like waves crashing onto an obliterated shoreline. "I swear to god, if you don't get out of my house, I'll report you for breaking and entering."

"Don't worry, I'm leaving." She spits the words at Luke, but they sound more like a threat than a regretful farewell. And when she looks back at me it's not the hatred, but the unveiled glee, that turns my blood to ice. "When Nora and I are finished with you, not only will you not see my daughter anymore but you'll be lucky if you step foot inside of Nester Fox ever again."

I watch her back as she storms out of the front door and try to cling on to the dwindling hope that her threats are empty. But when Luke turns to me after he locks the door behind her, I know without a shadow of a doubt that Hurricane Jacqueline has just started and when it comes to the devastation she's going to leave in her wake, my battered body will be the first thing found in the wreckage.

"So . . ." I look at Luke, fighting back the stupid tears that really want to fall. "I think that went pretty well, don't you?"

29

I WAS IN sixth grade when my dad died.

Some may say there's never a great time to lose a parent, and while they'd be right, I'd still like to state for the record that middle school is an extra shitty time to experience it.

I remember walking in to school for the first time after he died and being so nervous, I almost threw up in the trash can outside of the main entrance. If I think about it too long, I can feel my clammy palms and the way my knees damn near knocked together as I stood outside of Mrs. Cabriano's first period science class.

Before my dad died, it was my favorite class of the day. It had all of my friends, and Marcus, the boy I'd had a crush on for two years, sat directly behind me. The week before my dad died, we had progressed from quiet smiles to written notes. If you know anything about middle-school flirting, then you know that notes are a pretty big freaking deal.

But that was before I sat at home for two weeks, the first of which was spent pretending to be okay for my grandparents until they flew back to Chicago. The second was spent pretending I believed my mom was okay when in reality I could hear her crying through the walls every time she closed a door. I wasn't sure if the person I was at that point could be the carefree girl who laughed at his jokes.

I remember looking over my shoulder to make sure the hallway was empty before I closed my eyes and whispered a quick plea to my dad or whoever was listening that when I entered the room, things would be like they were before I was called down to the office and told my life would never be the same. I just wanted to be Emerson again, not this poor, sad girl with a dead dad and heartbroken mom. For a few hours a day, I wanted to forget what had happened to me and be a regular twelve-year-old who talked about music with her friends and had a crush on a boy.

When I walked inside that day, Mrs. Cabriano gave me the same bright smile she gave everyone else and when I sat at my desk, there was a note waiting from Marcus.

Looking back, I think that was the day I fell in love with the classroom. I might not have known I wanted to be a teacher, but I knew I would do whatever I could to give a kid the same safe space Mrs. Cabriano gave me. And after that day, I never felt nervous stepping into a classroom ever again.

Or at least I didn't.

Not until today.

Never in my life has a weekend moved slower. I couldn't even make myself go to The Barkery. When I called to let them know I wouldn't make it in, Shelly sounded so concerned, I thought she might alert the police.

Dread stretched every second into a lifetime as I watched my phone and waited for it to light up with Nora's name. I refreshed my email every second, wondering if she'd fire me that way, and my lungs froze every time I heard footsteps in my hallway. Without Luke staying by my side, his calm, steady presence trying to convince me that everything would be okay, I'm not sure I would've gotten out of bed this morning.

I hover outside of my classroom door, my heart beating a million miles a minute. I feel like I'm about to come out of my skin just picturing what could be waiting on the other side. Nightmares kept me up all night, and I'm convinced the boogeyman is hiding inside my room or that—even worse—all of my stuff has been put into boxes and there's a new teacher sitting behind my desk.

But when I finally gather the courage to crack the door open and peek inside, specks of glitter wink across the floor as the morning sunlight pours through the windows, and the only monsters in sight are the clay sculptures my students made for a Halloween craft. Everything is exactly how I left it, down to the flowers some of the girls drew on the whiteboard and the empty water bottle I forgot on my desk thanks to all the Petunia Lemon madness. My pictures still hang on the wall, my books are tucked neatly where they're supposed to be placed on the shelves, and against all odds, it's still my name on the top of my desk.

I set about my morning routine, taking all of the chairs off of the desks and setting out the morning work before I sit at my desk and turn on my computer. I open my email and triple-check one more time to make sure I didn't miss anything from Nora, but there's nothing. I had thought about talking to her before school today. But her car wasn't in the parking lot when I pulled in and that pep talk I gave myself while getting out of the car has already worn off.

I guess there's always tomorrow.

And there's still a chance—albeit a very slim chance—that Jacqueline left Luke's house and thought better of telling Nora. I could be freaking out over nothing at all.

"Emerson Pierce." Lisa's voice booms though the PA system, sounding just as boisterous at seven in the morning as she does at three in the afternoon. "Please report to Nora Stone's office."

Well fuck. I guess I wasn't freaking out over nothing.

Nora's well aware of the phone extension to my room, and I know this because she calls me damn near every day. She's sending me a message by summoning me to her office in such a public way, and I hear it loud and clear.

I understand that she's probably pissed and feeling more than a little betrayed, but she's not exactly innocent either. She might not want to admit it, but she took advantage of me and our friendship. She used me so she could make money even knowing that it put me in a tough financial situation. As a friend, that's shitty. As my employer? It's downright despicable.

I grab my keys and stick them in the oversize pockets on my rainbow cardigan. I lock my classroom door behind me, trying to keep a straight face despite the absolute riot taking place in my stomach. I wave to the other kindergarten teachers and say hello to Blaire, a fourth-grade teacher, as she passes me in the hall. When the front office is in sight, I see Lisa at her desk, sipping on her coffee while she buzzes the front door open for Anna.

Anna is struggling to open the door with two giant bags in

each hand, so even though I know Nora hates to be kept waiting, I run past the office and help her instead.

"Thank you so much, Emerson." She drops the bags on the ground and takes a second to regroup. She's a little out of breath and definitely frazzled. "I probably should've made two trips, but it's cold outside and I'm too lazy to make this walk more than once."

Ever since Anna found out about me joining Petunia Lemon, she's been super distant. This is honestly the most she's talked to me since. I've wanted to tell her what I'm doing with Luke, but I didn't want to put her in an awkward position at school or make her feel like she had to lie to Nora.

"I'd rather break an arm than take two trips to carry my groceries, so I completely understand." I peek into one of the bags and see . . . "Are those Easter eggs?"

It's November. Where's she getting these from?

"They are for now, but soon they'll be maracas." She puffs a stray piece of hair out of her eye. "Or at least maraca adjacent."

"I'm sure the kids will love this, and bless you for having the patience of a saint." I can handle noise to a certain level, and even though it hasn't been tested yet, I'm almost positive home-made maracas are way beyond my noise tolerance limit. Thank goodness my class's special is library today. "Can I help you carry some of these?"

"Thank you, but I think I got it." She starts to gather the bags off of the ground, strategically loading them onto her wrists until they're damn near at her elbow.

Is this how people feel watching me when I refuse to accept help?

"Anna, please. Your arms look like they're about to snap off."
I hold my hand out to take some of the bags. She clearly needs
help, and it will only take a few minutes. Plus, it will put off my
meeting with Nora for a little longer and maybe my nerves will
be able to settle down. "Let me help."

"Actually, Anna, I'm going to need to steal Emerson for a
moment." Nora appears behind me like freaking Beetlejuice.
"But you look like you've got this under control."

She looks like she has this under control? She looks like she's
about to topple over!

"Of course." Anna's smile tightens and something about her
seems off when her attention turns back to me. "See you later,
Emerson. And thanks again for all of your help."

She hurries off before I have the chance to respond and
leaves me alone with Nora.

"Nora!" I close my eyes and paste on my brightest smile before turning to face her. "Good morning."

She doesn't so much as attempt to return the effort or at least
pretend to be cordial. The smiling eyes I'm so used to seeing are
hard as stone, and her mouth is set in a straight line. There's no
warmth in her face at all. She says nothing in greeting and turns
on a high-heeled foot toward her office.

As bad as I thought this was going to be, I'm pretty sure it's
going to be worse.

I steel my spine and follow behind her, waving to Lisa as she
watches us pass by with a look of concern shining bright upon
her face. Nora pushes into her office and walks straight to her
file cabinet in the back of the room, pulling open the drawer
with way more force than necessary.

"Close the door and take a seat," she orders over her shoulder, never once looking back to make sure I was following her.

I do as I'm told and sit in the same chair I sat in when Nora offered me my job. Now, I worry it's where I'll be sitting when she takes it away.

The chair seems harder this time around, less comfortable. I attempt to sit still, but Nora is a master at professional torture, and no matter how hard I try, I can't get my leg to stop bouncing up and down. My nails that have just begun to grow revert into nubs while I wait. I rub my sweaty palms across my sweater and jump when I accidentally brush them against my keys in my pocket. All the while Nora stays focused on the contents of a folder and diligently ignores me.

She still avoids eye contact when she turns to face me. I don't know if it's supposed to intimidate me or not, but it doesn't . . . or at least not really. Thanks to my history as a devoted people pleaser and rule follower, there's nothing in my file that she could hold over me. She might think she did me a favor by hiring me, but she didn't. I earned it. I'm damn good at my job, and it's the only semblance of relief I have going into this meeting.

"So, Emerson." She drops the folder on the table and finally looks at me. She lowers herself onto her leather chair, glowering at me over the rim of the nonprescription glasses she loves to wear. "I'm assuming you know why we're here?"

"I don't, actually." I'm so proud of how strong and steady my voice sounds. "Although I'm pretty sure there are a few possibilities."

Nora's eyes widen just slightly, but it's enough to tell me she expected me to be a quivering mess. She knows how much I hate confrontation, and while that's true, I've never been a pushover. I stand up for myself and what I believe is right, even when it makes me feel like I need to throw up. That will never change . . . especially not today.

"Okay then . . ." She steeples her hands in front of her chest and leans forward. "Why don't we start with the undisclosed relationship you're having with a parent in your classroom?"

I figured that's where she'd start.

"Sure, what would you like to know?"

"When the relationship began would probably be a great place to start."

"Of course." This is the one question I was hoping she would ask. "I first met Mr. Miller at a rooftop bar in downtown Denver after spending the day at the Petunia Lemon conference you invited me to. Which, if you remember, was weeks before the first day of school where I would eventually find out that he was Isla's father."

The realization that she's responsible for me and Luke meeting washes over her face. Her eyes widen and her mouth falls open before she can catch it. Even if the rest of this meeting goes downhill, at least I'll have that reaction to look back fondly on.

"And when you found out he was a parent in the class?" She pushes her hair over her shoulder and adjusts the glasses she has no reason to wear. "What did you decide to do then?"

"Nothing." I resist the urge to squirm beneath her shrewd gaze. "When the school year started, we weren't speaking and as we rekindled our relationship, I didn't think I was obligated to bring it to the school, seeing as we weren't exclusive yet. It hasn't affected my students, not even Isla, nor has it caused my behavior in the classroom to change."

"So you're saying that you'll only do what's required of you and nothing more." She deliberately misconstrues my words. "Is that what I'm hearing?"

"I don't know what you're hearing, but I know that's not what I said." Heat rises up my neck, and I try to ignore it. I knew she'd want to get me worked up so I'll say something she can use against me, but knowing doesn't make it any less frustrating. "I think my track record at school for going above and beyond what's required is well documented."

"So is that what sleeping with a parent was to you? Going above and beyond?"

She aims those words at me with pinpoint precision, and as hard as I'm trying not to react, I can't help but flinch.

"No, not at all." Shame washes over me, leaving me feeling dirty and embarrassed. "It wasn't like that. He helped me—"

"Oh, I'm sure he did," she snarls, the mask of indifference falling from her face. "I vouched for you, you know. Said what a great person you were and how hard you'd work to grow Petunia Lemon. And then you turned around and not only spread malicious lies about us, but you came to Jacqueline's house and pretended to be her friend while the entire time you were off screwing her husband! What kind of woman does that?"

"He's not her husband, for starters. When it comes to Jacqueline, you know as well as I do that we were never friends." Sleeping with a parent already crossed enough boundaries, there's no reason to try to make it worse with lies. "And as much as you're trying to convince yourself otherwise, I never spread a single lie about you or Petunia Lemon."

"Are you trying to say that you had nothing to do with Lucas's article?"

"Not at all." I lean forward and look straight into her eyes, taking the time to enunciate each word so she can hear just how serious I am. "I'm trying to convince you that the only person who lied about Petunia Lemon is you."

Her head jerks back like I slapped her.

"How dare you!" Her face burns bright red. "I gave you the opportunity to be great and *you* didn't take it. That's not a result of me lying, that's a result of you being a failure."

I've had too many conversations with Luke and read his article too many times. I've seen the numbers and statistics that prove it's not about an individual not putting in enough effort, but a system that is set up to watch people fail. But still, even knowing that, Nora's words penetrate the armor I hoped would protect me.

Nora scents out the blood in the water like the absolute shark she is.

"Is that why you went after Lucas once you found out he was with Jacqueline?" She leans back, a smirk that hints at anything other than humor pulling at the corners of her mouth. "You couldn't beat her in Petunia Lemon, so you thought sleeping with her husband would make you feel better about yourself?"

"He's not her husband," I repeat, knowing it's no use. "I don't know what you want from me. I didn't report our relationship? Okay, fine. There's no rule against dating parents, but I can still see how you'd have a problem with that. You want to give me a warning or write me up? That's fine, do it. But Petunia Lemon? That has nothing to do with what we're doing here."

"Is that what you think? That you get to decide what we're doing here?" She laughs—out-and-out laughs—and that sinking feeling in my stomach from earlier returns with a vengeance. "I hate to tell you this, but you aren't in charge here."

"I never said I—"

"And what I think you're failing to grasp right now is how serious this could be for you." Nora talks right over me like I didn't say anything at all. She grabs the folder that's been sitting on her desk and flips it open again, slowly scanning it over before spinning it to face me. "What do you see when you look at that?"

I pick up the folder and try to find whatever Nora is seeing that could be so horrible. My resume is in there, along with a few letters of recommendation. My school picture from last year is there, and while it is bad, I don't think it could be used against me for anything other than proof as to why bangs are not for me. There are a couple of nice letters from previous parents, but the only thing I find shocking is that she still has paper files.

Unlike teachers in other grades, there's no state testing to determine how well or not well a teacher is doing in their classroom. Kindergarten doesn't abide by the same markers older grades have, but even without them, I know I'm doing right by my students. Every year, the first-grade teachers seek me out to tell me how my students are thriving in their classes, how prepared and confident they all seem. That might not be in my file, but it doesn't mean it's not true.

"I don't know." I close the file and push it back across her desk. "I see a teacher who worked hard to get here and had good recommendations. I'm still getting acclimated with my new role, but parents have been happy and my students are doing well."

"You know what I see?" she asks, and since I know she's about to answer, I keep my mouth closed. "I see someone who has old recommendations from college professors saying how much you loved working with students but how easily it could veer into disrespecting boundaries that might make you dangerous to keep in the classroom. I see a young woman who endured a serious trauma when she lost her father when she was young and now, as an adult, she's forming inappropriate bonds with the fathers in her classroom to try to make up for it."

I don't talk about what happened to my dad to anyone. For obvious reasons, it's a time I don't like to revisit, and it always comes with those sneaky emotions I can't control. When I opened up to Nora about his death and how it affected me, I did so in confidence. I was telling her why it was so important for me to make my classroom a safe space for my students. For her to weaponize that is lower than low, and any inkling of respect I might have had left for her evaporates into thin air.

"How could you?" A feeling of hurt and betrayal I never thought possible slices me open, and I have to look down to make sure she didn't actually stab me in the chest. "You know that's not true. You'd never be able to prove it."

"This isn't a criminal case, Emerson. I don't have to prove it." She rolls her eyes as if she's put out by having to explain her evil plan. "All I have to do is allude to it, and thanks to Jacqueline walking in on you two together, it shouldn't be too hard. I've honestly had teachers terminated for much less, and Colorado doesn't have tenure, so it's easy. Unfortunately for you, your teaching record is so short, I'm not sure you'll ever be able to find a position again. Unless . . ."

Panic hits me like a wave, pulling me down to the ocean floor. Darkness shrouds me as the surface moves further and further away, until I'm certain I'll never be able to breathe again. Out of everything in my life, teaching is the one thing I know, without a doubt, I need. It isn't just my passion, it's my purpose, and without it . . . I'd be nothing.

"Fine." I give in on a breathless shout. "Whatever you want me to do, I'll do it. Just please don't take this to the school board."

"Oh good." A grinch-like smile pulls on her lips. "I knew you'd come to your senses eventually."

I search for any trace of the friend I once had but the person in front of me is nothing more than a stranger. "What do you want me to do?"

Tears spring to my eyes as thoughts of breaking up with Luke cross my mind. I know he'll fight me on it, but he knows how much I love teaching and we won't have to be apart forever. It will suck, but we can wait to be a couple until Isla's not in my class anymore. Or at least I can wait and hope he can too.

"You need to get Luke to retract the article." Her calm voice pulls me out of my head. "How he procured the information in that article was unethical and it is riddled with lies."

It takes me a moment before what she's asking begins to settle in. Unethical? Miss Blackmail wants to talk about what's ethical now? What a fucking joke.

"He won't do that." I know how hard he worked on it, and

I'm not even sure he could retract it at this point. "It's been picked up by so many other outlets. What will a retraction even do at this point?"

While I was busy trying not to fall into an anxiety-ridden depression over the weekend, Luke was fielding calls and emails from news outlets across the country. The article spread like wildfire and went viral overnight. Petunia Lemon reps worldwide were reaching out to tell him their horror stories. He's even been in touch with a general attorney who's looking into launching a lawsuit against the company. I don't want her to take me to the school board, but this is a bell that can't be unrung.

"His claims aren't credible. He needs to admit that the article is exaggerated and biased because of his lingering feelings for his ex-wife who, by the way, is thriving with Petunia Lemon. If he retracts his article, the others will fall away." She must be brand-new to the internet and the way it works. "If he doesn't put out a full apology by the end of the week, I'll have no choice but to bring you in front of the school board and begin the process of termination."

"Nora, please." I'm ready to beg at this point. I know Luke says he loves me, and there's a chance he would retract it. The problem is, I would never ask. "Please don't do this."

"I'm not the person who did this, Emerson, you are." She stands with my file and looks down her nose at me. If it weren't so concerning, this level of delusion would be admirable. "You have until the end of the week. I hope you make the right choice."

She walks to the door and pulls it open. Quiet chatter fills the front office as people catch up after the weekend. I don't know how long we were inside, but the bustle of teachers moving around has picked up.

I walk back to my room, staring unseeing at the artwork hanging on the walls, trying to figure out how in the fuck I'm going to make this right. Especially when the right Nora wants is wrong and the real right thing will get me fired.

And to think, I joined Petunia Lemon for a second job, and now it's going to be the reason I have no job. I don't know what kind of math problem that is, but I do know that either way, I'm 100 percent fucked.

· **30** ·

I ONLY LASTED until lunchtime before I called down to Lisa and requested a sub to cover my classroom for the rest of the day. I love to show up as my best self for my students, but that became more and more impossible as the day went on. Between the possibility of losing my job, the reminder of my dad, and the terrible ultimatum Nora has given me, I almost burst into tears during story time. I was worried I was liable to snap at the first fight or accident, and I never want my bad mood to touch my students.

That was two days ago.

It's only November and I've used more sick leave this year than I have in all of my other years combined.

It's actually kind of funny when you think about it. My relationship with Luke was never a problem until Nora made it so. Looks like she's proved her point after all.

I turned my phone on do not disturb when I got home, but it's long since died and I have no plans to charge it. I didn't want my mom to worry, so I sent her a text before letting her know I was turning off my phone for a week for some downtime. If there's an emergency, she knows to call Frederick and he'll come get me.

Luke, on the other hand, didn't get the warning. He's had Isla since Monday afternoon, so thankfully he hasn't been able to drop by for a surprise visit. I miss him, but it's for the best. If he comes over, I know I'll crack and tell him everything. It's already Wednesday and I'm halfway to the deadline I'm never going to meet. Once it passes—along with my career—I'll fill him in on everything that happened.

I hate the way time moves. It's so slow when you need it to go fast, and it speeds by when you want it to slow down. I know they say time's a thief, but I think that's bullshit. Time can't be a thief: all it does is give. It's the reflection of our lives, the marker of our wins and reminder of our losses. Time allows us to see life for what it is, a series of fleeting, precious moments that we will never have again.

I just really wish this particular series of moments would hurry up and go by.

I've been googling employment law since I got home on Monday. There has to be a way I get through this with my job, boyfriend, and integrity still intact. There's no way I can let Nora win this easily.

Episode I-have-no-idea-what of *Grey's Anatomy* is playing in the background, with Meredith and Christina acting as my devoted support system while I try to find a solution I'm beginning to think will never come, when the knocking at my door begins. I stop typing and I hold my breath, praying to Shonda Rhimes that it's not Frederick behind my door. I'm holding on by a string right now, and a mom-related emergency would be the frosting on a shit cake that I couldn't handle. The knocking stops, and I let out the breath I've been holding. It doesn't happen often, but solicitors do manage to make it into the building sometimes. This must have been one of them.

I let out a long exhale and relax back into my poor couch that's gotten way too much use lately and close my computer. My eyes hurt from staring at it all night and day so I decide to take a break and look at a bigger screen a little farther away. I restart the episode and turn up the volume, hoping this is one of the sad episodes that rips my heart out so I can cry about something other than my own life for forty minutes.

Then the knocking starts again.

"Open the door, Em. I know you're in there," Luke's voice booms from the other side of my door. "I saw your car outside and I just heard you turn up the TV."

Dammit. Thwarted again!

"Go away," I groan. "Let me wallow in peace!"

"You've been wallowing peacefully for two days. Let me in."

Meredith's in the middle of a very intense conversation with Christina when I hit pause, and I hope Luke knows how much I'm willing to sacrifice for him. I climb off of the couch, double-checking to make sure there's no evidence of my conversation with Nora in sight before going to the door.

"You know you're very annoying, right?" I pull open the door, quickly reminded that while he is in fact very annoying, he's also very, very handsome. So handsome in his button-down shirt and navy blue slacks that it reminds me I haven't brushed my hair or teeth since Monday morning. "I'll be right back!"

I sprint into my bathroom and turn on the shower before he can stop me. It's quick, but I still manage to scrub all of the important parts and, on the off chance he wants to take off my pants later to cheer me up, shave my legs. My teeth brushed and curls refastened into a bun, I glance in the mirror one last time. It's not perfect, and I'm not going to win a modeling competition or anything, but it'll do.

"Sorry about that." I join him back in my living room and sit down on the couch beside him. "You didn't hit play?"

I don't know if that's because he didn't want to lose my spot (good) or because he doesn't like *Grey's Anatomy* and wasn't interested (bad). I know I don't have a lot of ground to stand on in my current predicament, but being down bad has never stopped me from casting judgment on others, and it won't stop me now.

"I didn't want you to lose your spot." He hands me the remote. "I don't know if you've seen this episode yet, but it's a good one and you don't want to miss it."

"You know"—I snatch the remote from his hands, annoyed by his perfectness, and hit play—"if you could stop being wonderful for a single second, that'd be super helpful."

I'm about to be unemployed, possibly publicly shamed for sleeping with a parent, and banned from teaching for all time. He's probably going to win a freaking Pulitzer. There's no way he's going to stick around. It will be much easier for my heart if he does some terrible things for me to latch on to before he leaves me.

"You know I can't help it." He tucks me into his side. "But if it helps, I can hold you hostage on this couch until you tell me what the fuck happened at school on Monday. Then you can explain why you've been ignoring me ever since."

I try to pull away from him, noticing belatedly that him pulling me close had less to do with wanting to cuddle and more to do with preventing me from running away.

He's good.

I thought I hadn't wanted to call him because I knew he'd want to help, and I didn't want to lay my burdens on his shoulders. I told myself he had enough on his plate dealing with Jacqueline, and he didn't need to deal with my problems on top of that. And none of that was a lie, but now that he's sitting in front of me, asking to know, I know it wasn't the truth either.

I love giving to others. From my time at school to volunteering at The Barkery, my life feels more complete when I'm able to be of help to those around me. But, if I'm honest with myself, there's something more to it. Part of me fears that if I have nothing to give, I'm worth nothing. That if I ever ask for more than I can give, I'll be a dead weight people can't wait to unload, and this situation with Nora inadvertently confirmed it. She loved me when she had something to gain from me, but the second it ended, she was ready to throw me in the trash.

Luke has done everything to prove how much he cares, but the nasty voice deep inside my brain is worried that since I'm no longer helping him with his article—and could possibly do harm to it—I won't be worth sticking around to him either.

I could keep everything happening to myself. I've done it my entire life and I'm good at it. It's safe. But as I burrow deeper into his side, taking comfort in the feel of his strong arm wrapped around me, maybe for once the safe option isn't the right one.

I don't know what things are going to look like between us a year from now. Hell, I don't even know what this weekend is going to bring. What I do know is I want this thing with Luke. I want to see what a future with him by my side could bring and for that to happen, I have to be honest with him. Even when— no, *especially* when—it makes me want to claw out of my skin.

"If I tell you, I need you to promise that you will just listen. Nothing else."

"I promise I'll listen." He tightens his grip around me and runs his lips along the top of my head. "I promise we will talk and I promise that I won't do anything we don't discuss first."

It's not the answer I wanted to hear, but I like it all the same.

I dive headfirst into everything, starting with getting called down to the office via the PA system. I tell him about how Nora pulled me away from Anna and how she made a giant show out of grabbing my file. I thank him for sitting with me last weekend, that I was able to stand my ground for much longer than expected thanks to our talks. I fall down a side tangent about how I thought she was going to demand we break up and the lies I'd already come up with so we could still date in secret. His body tightens and his jaw clenches a few times, but he never interrupts, and by the time I get to the part where she's issuing the ultimatum, my guards have completely lowered. I'm so lost in the story, I'm completely oblivious to the way his laughter has stopped and how danger lingers in the air.

"She used your dad against you?" His voice is barely a whisper, but the anger comes through loud and clear. "And threatened to present you as some kind of predator if I don't retract my article? Am I getting this right?"

"Um . . . yeah." I go on high alert. I know he said he wouldn't do anything without talking to me first, but I've never heard him sound like this before—not the morning after we met, not on the first day of school, not even when Jacqueline waltzed into his living room. "But I don't even know if she'll really act on it. She could've just been trying to scare me so I won't do it again."

"She wasn't." He lets me go and reaches for his phone on my coffee table. "There's no way I'm letting you lose your job over this."

I lunge for his phone but he dodges me with ease. Terror swirls around in my gut as I imagine him retracting the article. Not only did he work tirelessly on it, but it has given so many victims of Petunia Lemon a voice and I won't let Nora take that away from them.

"I'd rather lose my job than let that disgusting company keep getting away with this." I try to grab the phone again, but I'm no match for his long arms. "If you retract this, Nora will use it as ammunition to keep abusing her power and recruiting more people. I know there are other teachers who have joined under her too."

Just thinking about how many people she's probably taken advantage of over the years brings my blood to a boil. I trusted her implicitly, and not only did she use me, now she's leveraging things I told her in confidence against me. It was so easy for her; there wasn't an ounce of guilt on her smug face when she thought she won. It was like she already knew the result.

"Wait . . ." I sit down on the couch and play the conversation between us over and over in my head. "She said she's had people fired for less."

"Nora did?" Luke stops typing on his phone, all of his attention focused on me. "What do you think that means?"

"I'm not sure, but she was way too calm in our meeting." Everything felt so calculated . . . rehearsed. As if she'd acted out the performance more than once before. "When I walked into her office, even Lisa was looking at me weird. Like maybe she already knew what was about to happen."

Come to think of it, when I called Lisa about a substitute taking over, one showed up within twenty minutes. I didn't think anything of it then, but the only way a substitute could've gotten there that fast is if they had been called way before.

"Holy shit." I leap off of the couch and run to my room to grab my charger and plug in my phone.

"What's happening?"

"I don't know yet." Adrenaline pumps through my veins as some of the pieces start to fall into place. "But I'm going to find out."

I'm still trying to sort through everything in my head. I knew something happened between Nora and Anna, but Nora had no hesitation before sinking her claws in me, Chloe, and Odette. There's no way this behavior just started. Really, the only question I have now is how long has this been going on and how many victims has she left in her wake.

My phone screen is still painfully black, and the suspense is starting to feel like it might kill me. The walls seem like they're closing in on me as I pace back and forth in my tiny room. When I see my phone light up, I leap across the table to grab it and accidentally knock my purse over in the process. The spare change and Dum-Dums that have been living at the bottom of my purse for months spill across my floor. The lip gloss I've been trying to find for weeks rolls under my TV stand, but none of it matters.

Because as soon as it turns on, my phone lights up like a Christmas tree with message after message from Anna, Odette, Chloe, and countless numbers I don't even recognize.

I put my phone on speaker so Luke can listen with me, and as I go to hit play, my nerves turn to static while my stomach flips around like Simone Biles.

And by the time Anna's quiet voice blares through my speakers, a fire lacing her words like I've never heard from her, I know that when I'm done with Nora, Luke's article is going to be the least of her worries.

31

THE PART OF me that hated conflict died alongside my trust in Nora.

Friday passed by without Luke retracting his article on Petunia Lemon, and the nerves I thought I'd feel were nowhere to be found. In fact, as the seconds ticked by, the anticipation of seeing how Nora would react made me downright giddy. And when she called me down to her office the following Wednesday with the union rep sitting beside her, I couldn't even pretend to be upset by the news.

Nora might've gone low, but unfortunately for her, I was prepared to go to hell.

"Are you sure you want to do this?" Luke tightens his hand around mine as we stand outside of the doors to the school board hearing I requested. "We can still figure out another way to make this happen."

I touch my lips to his, and my red lipstick stains his mouth just so. "I'm positive. This is the way it has to be done."

Nora didn't realize it, but when she moved to get me terminated from my job, she put the final nail in her own coffin. I was
on paid leave. I had nothing to do other than spend my days
preparing for this meeting, and in doing so, I dug up so much
dirt on Nora that you could call me an archaeologist.

"You've got this." Luke repeats the words he's told me hundreds, if not thousands, of times. "Now go kick her ass."

I let go of his hand and pull open the door to the conference
room. The school board sits at the front, the innocuous group
all sitting behind a long desk with their nameplates in front of
them. This is the last meeting before winter vacation, and it's not
hard to see they're ready for a break. Most are wearing respect-
able suits in an array of neutral hues, but one member, Flora, is
decked out in a bedazzled sweater, big dangly earrings that look
like presents with a matching necklace, and a rhinestone-
encrusted headband. I know there's a chance she might vote to
end my career tonight, but I appreciate her festive accessories
anyways.

An aisle with a podium in the middle separates two sections
filled with folding chairs. It's larger than I expected and pretty
empty . . . for now. Thoughts of people crowding the room make
me want to turn and run.

"What am I doing?" I'm used to talking in front of tiny humans who think fart jokes are the pinnacle of humor; I don't
know what I was thinking when I decided to do this. "How can
I call this off?"

"Relax," Luke whispers into my ear. "You have statements
and witnesses. You're prepared and she has nothing on you. She

won't be able to prove a thing because none of the allegations she's bringing against you are true."

I pull my shoulders back, still not feeling totally confident, but with Luke by my side, I know I can at least fake it until I make it. "Thank you."

We take our seats in the second row, and even though the meeting isn't supposed to start for another twenty minutes, a steady stream of people is already arriving.

I try not to watch the door, my breath catching every time it opens and I brace to see Nora, but I can't help it. I haven't seen or heard from her since I walked out of the school, and I think I would've been happy to never be in the same room as her ever again.

Once the article came out and I didn't have anything to hide anymore, I made sure Keisha and Anna knew that I wanted them to give my number to anyone who needed it. I've spent hours reaching out to teachers who left Nester Fox before I even arrived, and all of us have similar stories. Nora befriended us, making us feel safe and close to her, before swooping in and introducing Petunia Lemon. The teachers like me, who went for it, got to stay on her good side while the teachers who said no were met with instant retaliation. Even when she wasn't the principal yet, she would figure out how to weaponize the power she did have, like uninviting them from lunch or organizing teacher get-togethers and excluding them from the group.

Every time the door opens and a familiar face steps inside, my nerves settle a little more. I know my name is the one up for discussion tonight, but I'm not alone. Even some of the teachers

I talked to that I haven't met show up, coming to give me a hug before finding their seats in the back of the room. By the time Keisha and Anna come in and join Luke and I, I'm feeling more confident than I have since this entire ordeal began.

"Can I just say one more time that I'm so fucking proud of you." Keisha takes the hand Luke's not holding in hers. "I've had the hardest time biting my tongue at school and I can't wait to watch Nora's sorry ass go down."

"Me either." Anna's cheeks flush under the harsh fluorescent lights. "I can't believe how many people she's done this to."

A door slams and familiar, carefree laughter turns every-one's attention to the back of the room. Nora struts into the room, her head thrown back, laughing at something Jacqueline or one of the other Petunia Lemon girls surrounding her said.

It's strange. I thought when I laid eyes on her that I would feel a rush of anger, that the resentment I've been harboring would run to the surface and I'd have to hold myself back so I didn't scratch her eyes out. But instead, I feel nothing.

Her red hair falls down her back in loose waves and her eye-liner is drawn on so sharp, she must've gone to a makeup artist. She's never looked better. From her pale skin that glows in these winter months to the smart suit and power heels she's donning, she looks like she's ready to take over the world.

But it's all fake. Nothing about her is real and what's not real can't hurt me.

The small group walks down the aisle, scanning each row for a place to sit. When they finally reach mine, I watch as Nora's eyes go blank and the smile falls off of her face. She turns around and whispers something to the group, and when they break apart, five matching sets of glares turn toward me. But when Jacqueline catches a glance at who's sitting beside me, she flinches, and her delicate features twist in pain. She's not my favorite person in the world, and even I can't help but feel for her.

If I threw the man next to me away for a night cream and an average, overpriced serum, I'd cry myself to sleep every night for the rest of my life.

"Do you think Jacqueline is going to speak against me?"

"Probably." Apologies linger in Luke's solemn voice. "But it doesn't matter. Not only did we meet before the school year, even if we didn't, your union rep said there are no rules against it. You have more than enough evidence to prove Nora is only acting out of revenge."

"What he said," Keisha says. "Nora's such a bitch and it's about time someone brings her down. And I know Jacqueline's the mother of your child and all, but she's awful and it won't hurt her to be knocked down a peg or two."

"You're not wrong." Luke drapes his arm over the back of my chair, and Jacqueline's face goes white before she looks away. "She's been even more terrible lately. I swear she didn't used to be like this."

"I'm not sure I believe you." Keisha speaks for all of us. "But considering you've shown great taste in your current girlfriend, I'll give you a pass. But only on this. Don't think I'll ease up on you in spades just because you're with my girl."

"You better not, because when I beat you, I want to be sure I got you at full strength."

Keisha and Luke both came over the night I was put on

leave. They tried to cheer me up with games, junk TV, and junkier food. Over the course of the night, they started talking about the neighborhood, and Luke told Keisha he's been working on a series to help with preservation and prevent new businesses from taking over the legacy shops. They've been best friends ever since.

Before Keisha can take the trash talk any further, the side door at the back of the room opens. The final board member comes in and takes her seat in the middle of the table and gets the meeting started.

It's my first time at a school board meeting and I don't know what to expect. They start by calling the meeting to order and reciting the mission and vision of the board. They recognize students and teachers and then go into the community portion of the night. They call speakers to the podium one by one, each person taking their time to express themselves and their needs. I thought it was going to be boring, but the more people that speak, the more invested I'm becoming. It's inspiring to see community members care so deeply about the schools and our children's education. I'm so distracted by it that I forget why I'm here.

Until they call my name from the front of the room.

"Next is the matter of Emerson Pierce." Levi Roberts's deep voice echoes off of the bare walls. "Principal Stone has cited allegations of inappropriate behavior and forming disruptive and disturbing connections with the fathers in Miss Pierce's classroom. She claims that Miss Pierce's personal relationship with one father in particular has caused disruption inside of the classroom by showing favoritism to one student over others, creating an unsafe and unstable environment for the kinder-gartners in Miss Pierce's class."

I've read her complaints and allegations against me too many times to count. I can see the words when I close my eyes. Nothing he said is new, but hearing it coming from this man's mouth in front of a crowd is more devastating than I prepared myself for.

"First we will hear from Principal Stone, then we will move to Miss Pierce, before ending with witness statements. Principal Stone"—he gestures to the podium in between the aisles—"we've read your statement, is there anything you'd like to add?"

Not a hair is out of place as Nora steps up to the microphone. Sharp pains shoot through my chest, and I grab onto Luke's hand, holding my breath as she starts to talk.

"Hello, board members, thank you so much for giving me the opportunity to speak with you tonight." Her smooth, cultured voice booms from the speaker system, and she sounds just as put together as she looks. "It is with great sadness that we are here tonight in the matter of Emerson Pierce. I first met Miss Pierce when she was a student teacher at Nester Fox and she worked with me in my classroom. She was a great student who showed a lot of promise and was very enthusiastic about her job. However, even back then, she had problems with boundar-ies and forming relationships with students and their families that crossed the line we as educators must value."

Keisha pulls out her phone and starts tapping away as she hisses something that sounds a lot like "dumb lying bitch" be-neath her breath. My grip on Luke tightens as I listen to her spew lie after lie. I came in tonight thinking she was just an asshole, but watching her say all of this crap with a straight face, I'm thinking it might be something much more sinister.

"We offered her a permanent position at Nester Fox when she received her teaching license. Learning how to create healthy boundaries with students is something we all have to learn and I was hopeful Miss Pierce would learn hers once she was in the classroom." She takes a shaky breath and wipes an imaginary tear from the corner of her eye. "Unfortunately, this year she's shown us that not only has she not learned how to respect her students' families, she's actively causing harm by having an affair with the father of one of her current students. This has resulted not only in gross favoritism inside of the classroom, but she even wormed her way into this student's birthday celebration, picking out her pet even though this student's mother desperately wanted to be involved."

Now Luke's the one hissing something under his breath.

"Instead of focusing my time and attention on important school matters, I've been fielding calls from angry parents. The mother of this particular student no longer feels comfortable with her daughter in Miss Pierce's class. This is all very upsetting, but I'm sure you can see how this has been a distraction and violation worthy of dismissal. I hope that in her future teaching positions, Miss Pierce will learn from these mistakes and be the teacher I know she's capable of being. Thank you."

Nora returns to her seat and the quiet whispers grow into a rowdy rumble.

"Thank you, Principal Stone," Levi says. "Miss Pierce, if you'd like to speak, now's the time."

I stand from my place between Luke and Keisha, my knees

weak with fear and regret as humiliation burns hot across my skin. I keep my head down as I approach the microphone, but I can feel the searing gazes of those casting their judgment on me.

"Thank you, board members, for providing me with a space to defend myself from the dishonest claims brought against me by Principal Stone." I grab onto the podium with shaky hands and try to steady my voice. "I hate that it has come to this. I'm embarrassed to be standing in front of you today, wasting your valuable time so Principal Stone can seek revenge and spread her lies."

I hear a sharp intake of breath from my right and without looking, I know it's Nora. I don't know if she's putting on an act for the room or if she's genuinely shocked that I'm not letting her get away with this, but either way, it incenses me so much that I forget to be nervous.

"The truth of the matter is that Miss Stone has been abusing her power as principal and has been doing so for years. Outside of being the principal at Nester Fox, Miss Stone is one of the top consultants for Petunia Lemon, a multi-level marketing company that sells skincare products. She uses her influence as principal and knowledge of how much her teachers make to convince them to sign up under her for this company. She goes on to profit immensely while the teachers lose money each month. And when a teacher voices concern about Petunia Lemon, or worse, decides to leave, Miss Stone punishes them at school as well."

"That's a very serious claim, Miss Pierce," says Isabel, the board member sitting in the far-right seat.

"I'm aware." I reach into my purse, pulling out witness

statements from all of the teachers I managed to track down while I was on leave. "These are all statements from teachers who have worked for Miss Stone and have either quit because the work environment became so unbearable or were forced to resign when Miss Stone threatened to blackmail them. I am here today not because I started a relationship with a man over the summer, who I discovered later happened to be a parent of my student, but because I worked with this parent to expose the lies and fraud happening at the hands of Miss Stone. When she found out that I was a source behind an article about Petunia Lemon, she told me she would fire me if I didn't get the article retracted. Obviously"—I gesture to the conference room—"I didn't do that and here we are."

Chairs rustle behind me as whispers turn into yells.

Nora pushes her way back to the podium and snatches the microphone away from me. "She's lying!"

"Miss Stone!" Levi calls her name, wearing the same shocked expression as the rest of the board members. "Please take your seat!"

Nora always has an air of superiority about her. It's in the way she holds herself, how she looks down her nose at everyone around her. She never gets flustered because she always thinks she's the smartest person in the room. But right now, that person is nowhere to be seen.

"No!" Her face is red and her movements are erratic. The hair that was so flawless when she walked in is disheveled as she runs her hands through it again. "She can't be trusted! I brought the father's wife today, she can tell you how much damage Emerson has done to her family. She can prove that Emerson is a liar!"

Any respect I had for Nora flitted away long before I stepped into this room, but it's still hard to witness her come apart at the seams like this. The group of women who walked in like human shields avoid looking at her, and Jacqueline ignores her request, instead sinking into her seat and hiding behind a curtain of blond hair.

Desperation permeates the air as understanding begins to sink in for Nora.

"All you had to do was get the article removed." Rage turns her silky voice unrecognizable as she aims her furious glare toward me. "Why couldn't you do that? This never had to happen!"

I've thought about coming face-to-face with Nora more than I've thought about anything else this week. I've run through exactly what I wanted to say to her, how I would scream and yell, proving to the world what a terrible person she is.

"You did this to yourself, Nora." But now, looking at her standing in front of me, the anger is gone and all I feel is pity. "I hope one day you'll be able to get the help you so obviously need."

I gather the papers I brought as proof and tuck them back into my purse before I walk away, leaving a hysterical Nora behind me—literally and metaphorically. The room buzzes around me, and urgent whispers turn to shocked yells as curious eyes follow me back to my seat, but amid the chaos, I only see one person.

Luke watches as I walk to him, a gentle smile pulling at the corner of his mouth and green eyes radiating pride. I'm barely back to our row when his arms pull me into his chest and he's whispering in my ear, "Would I be wrong if I said that was the sexiest thing I've ever seen?"

The stress of the last few weeks melts away, and I laugh, actually outright laugh, at the hearing where I thought I might lose my job. "I would never fault you for your feelings."

"Alright then," Levi says into the microphone. The poor guy looks like he's been run over by a bus. "In light of everything that has been presented to us tonight, it is clear to the board that Miss Stone has been abusing her power and prioritizing her own well-being over that of her students and faculty. The board has come to the unanimous decision to remove Miss Stone from her position as principal at Nester Fox Elementary."

The room goes wild again, and Nora's angry screams rise above the rest before her entourage circles around her and escorts her out of the room. It's very dramatic, and I have to wonder if this is a common occurrence at school board meetings. If so, I might need to come more often. If it wasn't my job on the line, this could've been fun.

Once Nora has been removed, and the room has settled down, Levi gets on the mic for what I'm hoping will be the final time of the night.

"We usually end these hearings with witness statements, but since a decision has already been made, they aren't necessary. However, if there is anyone who has something they'd like to say, the floor is now open."

I'm sure I'm not the only person ready to call it a night and forget this entire thing ever happened, so color me surprised when Luke stands and moves to the podium.

"Good evening, my name is Lucas Miller. I'm the father of Miss Pierce's student, the author behind the Petunia Lemon article, and the very proud boyfriend of the wonderful woman who stood before you tonight." His deep voice calls the attention of the entire room, and my heart explodes in my chest. "When I met Miss Pierce, I had no idea she would be my daughter's teacher. I had no idea how much she would change my life by simply walking into it. To know this woman is to know love. She dedicates her days and her money to making sure her kinder-gartners begin their educational careers in a way that will foster a love of learning for the rest of their lives. She puts her entire being into her students and making sure they know the class-room is a safe space for them. She encourages the kind of curi-osity, kindness, and authenticity that has made my daughter and all of her classmates excel in and out of the classroom.

"When I found out about these outrageous claims, I knew I couldn't be the only parent appalled by such vicious lies. Miss Pierce is too humble and would never want to impose on the parents in her class, so I took it upon myself to reach out to them." He nods at Keisha and she runs to the back of the room. She pushes open the doors and all of a sudden, parent after par-ent enters the conference room. "Every parent in my daughter's class is here tonight, along with parents from previous years as well. I talked to over fifty parents, guardians, and loved ones and not a single person declined coming tonight to attest to what an amazing teacher, advocate, and human Miss Pierce is."

"Mr. Miller," Levi says as he takes in the never-ending parade of parents still making their way inside of the room, "you do know these meetings have a two-and-a-half-hour limit, don't you?"

"Sorry about that, sir," Luke says. "But when it comes to this woman, I'll spend forever making sure the entire world knows how amazing she is."

Luke goes blurry and the room disappears around me as the tears I've been fighting since I walked out of Nester Fox, uncertain if I'd ever return, finally begin to fall. Only now, they're not from sorrow.

They're falling because I not only found the love of this gorgeous man who will stop at nothing to make sure I know how loved I am, but because I know I'll get to love him for the rest of my life.

EPILOGUE

IF I THOUGHT I loved my job before, I had no idea how good it could be without Nora's toxic energy lingering behind every corner.

To put it lightly, the hearing didn't go the way Nora thought it would. Not only did it end in her losing her job as principal at Nester Fox, somebody caught her meltdown on camera and it may have gone viral.

Like, really, really viral.

And just about every person who watched the video sought out Luke's article on Petunia Lemon. So thanks to her meltdown, more think pieces and follow-up articles than I could've ever imagined began to spring up. So many victims of Petunia Lemon's lies came forward that after a few months, they put the company on pause so they could restructure . . .

And file for bankruptcy.

"Emmy." Isla uses the name she calls me outside of school and wraps her little hand in mine as we close my classroom door and head to the parking lot. "Do you think we can go visit

Mr. Tom tomorrow? He said he had something superspecial for Mister Bubbles and my body is too excited to wait until Sunday."

My body also gets very excited over surprises.

"I don't see why not," I say. "But let's ask your daddy first, okay?"

As if I willed him there, which is what I'm always trying to do, Luke pushes through the front door.

"Daddy!" Isla drops my hand like a hot potato and runs right into her dad's arms. Lucky. "Can we go see Mr. Tom tomorrow? Emmy said we could."

"No," I correct her when I catch up to them. "Emmy said to ask Daddy first."

"I don't see why not." He sets Isla on the ground, and she skips away to say goodbye to Lisa.

"Emmy said to ask Daddy, huh?" He wraps his arms around my waist and pulls me into him. "What do you want to ask for?"

"From you?" I roll onto the tips of my toes and touch my mouth to his, and the butterflies I still feel whenever I'm near him take flight. "Absolutely everything."

"For you? I can do that."

ACKNOWLEDGMENTS

First, thank you to Kimberly Whalen. The amount of work you've done for me, the way you've advocated for me and my books, is the reason I'm still writing. You stepped in and not only validated my feelings but showed up for me in a way I didn't know was possible. I'm forever grateful to have you on my side.

Kristine Swartz, my editing fairy godmother (who is younger, cooler, and smarter than me), thank you for your patience, encouragement, and expertise. Thank you for not only believing in all of my wild ideas but encouraging them. I love the magic we create in the pages of these books, and I can't wait to see what we cook up next!

To the amazing team at Berkley, thank you for everything you did to make this book happen. Your support means everything, and I'm so thankful my books have found a home with you.

To booksellers and librarians everywhere, thank you for what you give to authors and readers alike. Your joy and enthusiasm are the backbone of this community, and this world would be a much darker place without you.

I should be embarrassed to have not only the amount but the quality of friends in my life: Abby, Tav, Maxym, Lindsay, Taylor, Brittany, Lin, Suzanne, Ali, Melissa, Sarah, Natalie, Meredith, Andie, and Rosie. You all inspire me, keep me sane, and motivate me every day. I'm so lucky to know and love all of you.

Denise, Frannie, Grandma Frankie, and GPJ, moving closer to you has been such a blessing. We love you so much.

Mom, Grandma, and Grandpa, I miss and love you endlessly.

Derrick, who would've thought student council class would've brought us here? Thank you for always supporting me and standing by my side. I can't wait to see what else we create together. I love you.

DJ, Harlow, Dash, and Ellis, I know I tell you every day, multiple times a day, but I love you so much. Being your mom is the best thing that has ever happened to me. I'm forever proud of the amazing, smart, kind, wonderful humans you are. You are my absolute world.

And of course, to the readers. Thank you for picking up this book and going on this journey with me. This would not be possible without you, and I am forever grateful.

Keep reading for a preview of Alexa Martin's

NEXT-DOOR NEMESIS

Available now!

IF I HEAR *live, laugh, love* one more time, I'm going to die, scream, rage.

I know my mom means well, but my phone's almost out of storage thanks to the abundance of uplifting memes and Bible verses she won't stop sending me. Maybe I'd appreciate her unrelenting positivity if I was still in LA, enjoying my oat milk latte from the adorable café I wrote in almost every day. But for some reason, the never-ending text stream hits a little different when I'm fifteen feet away, sitting in my childhood room, and notifications keep interrupting the shame spiral I've been living in for the last two months.

I swipe away her latest text message and nestle deeper into the frilly comforter of my childhood past. I make sure the volume is all the way down—after all, who needs sound when every single word is ingrained in my brain?—and hit play on the video that has quite literally ruined my life.

To say the camerawork is shoddy would be a massive understatement. The video bounces and bobbles around as the image blurs in and out until a woman standing in an empty parking lot wearing nothing but spike high heels and a silk robe comes into focus.

A woman, of course, who happens to be me.

Jazz hands!

Honestly, it's borderline offensive that after all the time I spent in Los Angeles, all the scripts I wrote, all the internet content I produced hoping to hit my break à la Issa Rae, *this* is what has millions of views. You flip out and threaten to bury your lying, thieving ex *one time* and it goes viral?

What are the chances?

It just really sucks that instead of my brush with viral fame catapulting me to television-writing superstardom, it's what ended my career.

My phone dings with another text from my mom at the same moment the video hyperzooms in on my tearstained face. This is where it really gets good. And by *good*, of course, I mean downright horrifying.

I lift my finger to swipe away another one of her messages. I love my mom and her hopeless positivity, but after moving back into my childhood home a month ago—exactly thirty-one days after my life took a drastic turn toward the absolute worst—with no signs of getting out, I'm in the mood for self-pity.

"Collins Marie Carter!" My mom's thick midwestern lilt rings out from the other side of my much-too-thin door. "Don't you ignore that!"

I shoot out of bed and accidentally send my phone sailing through the room. "Holy shit, Mom!"

Just another perk of moving back home as a twenty-nine-year-old woman.

Privacy? Never heard of her.

"First of all, watch your language," she says, still right outside my door. "Second of all, that's the third text I've sent you this morning and you haven't responded to one."

I scramble around my room trying to find something to wear before giving up and grabbing an old T-shirt off the ground and pulling on the bike shorts busting at the seams. Because really, what's even the point of trying when your life is completely ruined?

"Mom." I throw open the door and try to harness every ounce of patience I have. "You know how much I love you, but I think with about forty percent fewer texts and fifty percent more space, we'll all be much happier."

"You need to stop watching that darn video; it's not good for you." She gives me a disapproving once-over and continues to speak as if I didn't. "Also, didn't you wear that yesterday? I know you're depressed, but you'll never feel better wearing the same dirty clothes and never brushing your hair."

If there were a chance brushing my hair and changing my clothes could turn back the cruel hands of time and convince me to never date Peter Hanson, I'd have a fresh updo and be wearing a fucking evening gown. Alas, formal wear is not the key to time travel and I'd rather be comfortable while I continue down this path of self-loathing.

"Just let me be miserable for one more week." *Or fifty-two.* "And I promise to try to rejoin society again. It's still too fresh. I still get recognized in the streets."

Being looked down on, on the bitter, hard streets of LA is

one thing, but getting the cold shoulder in the suburbs of Ohio? Absolutely not. A person can only handle so much.

"I'll give you thirty more minutes," she says, clearly not understanding the meaning of compromise. "I'm hosting Friday church group and I can't have you wandering around the house like a sad, godless puppy. Plus, I told the ladies you'd be joining us." She shoves the bedazzled Bible I didn't notice she was holding into my hands. I'm surprised I don't dissolve into a pile of ash. "Just in case you need to catch up."

"While sitting in the kitchen and gossiping under the ruse of good intentions does sound like a blast, I'm going to have to pass." I return her Bible, only slightly concerned that lying while holding it resulted in one more brick in my pathway to hell. "I promised Dad I'd help him get things for the yard today."

My dad, Anderson Carter, is perhaps the most precious human to ever human. A recently retired pharmacist, he's living his full gardener fantasy. Seeing this six foot, two inch, 320-pound Black man fiddling around the yard has been the only highlight of returning home. Unfortunately for me, once I told him that, he became relentless in his pursuit to recruit me into this vitamin D–filled hobby of his. I wasn't thrilled when I finally gave in, but now that it's saving me from an afternoon listening to the Karens—no shade, there are literally three different women named Karen in the group—drone on about how wonderful their boring kids are doing, I'm going to have to buy him lunch . . . if my bank account will allow it.

"Oh darn. Well, maybe next time." My mom pouts and the fine lines of aging pull on the corners of her delicate mouth, which has never muttered a single curse word. "At least Dad's going to get some quality time with you."

She may not curse, but those lips are well-versed in spewing passive-aggressive jabs.

"We watched an entire season of *House Hunters* last week; quality time doesn't get any better than that." I can almost see the wheels turning in her brain to come up with a retort, but she stays quiet because even she knows it's true. Nothing can bond two humans more than watching incompatible couples argue about a house they can't afford and screaming at a television about gray laminate floors.

"Fine, but if you're set on abandoning me and Jesus, can you at least make sure Dad doesn't forget to get the white oak tree while you're at the nursery?" She steps to the side as I squeeze past her.

She follows close behind as I try to keep my eyes trained on the carpet they replaced last year and ignore the barrage of inspirational quote art littering the walls. The collaged picture frames filled with every single one of my school pictures break up Bible verses, proof of days when I loved overly teased bangs and scrunchies working overtime to keep me humble.

As if I have any pride left.

"Sure, Mom." I pull open the cabinet and grab the "World's Best Dad" mug I gave my dad for Father's Day when I was in third grade. I pour in some of the hazelnut coffee my mom is still trying to convince me doesn't taste like sludge and hope that today will be the day I learn to love it. "Text me the name, though, because I definitely won't remember."

"The white oak." Dad's deep voice bounces off the white cabinets before he enters and drops a chaste kiss onto my mom's mouth. They celebrated their thirty-sixth wedding anniversary in February. He still kisses her every time he enters a room and my mom still blushes each time she lays eyes on him. It's sickeningly sweet. "That's what we're going to get; I had to order it. Noreen called me last night to tell me it finally came in."

"Really?" My mom's face lights up and I'm not sure if it's because she's married to a man who does thoughtful shit like special ordering her trees or because she loves landscaping that much. "You didn't tell me!"

They planted a tree in the front yard when our house was built thirty years ago. Unfortunately, two winters ago, it fell victim to a blizzard that knocked out power lines and roots alike. And while the Reserve at Horizon Creek may be a stifling hellhole put on Earth only to torture me in my lowest moments in life—let's not talk about being one of ten people of color in my middle school of more than a thousand—it's been around long enough that I can't say it's ugly. The trees planted at the inception of the neighborhood have grown into beautiful, mature trees many planned communities can't brag about.

If the opportunity presented itself, there's a 98 percent chance I'd sell my soul to be back in LA. But even so, no palm tree can compare to the droopy willow tree in the backyard where I spent countless summer days losing myself between the worn pages of my favorite books. Now with my dad dedicating all his spare time to the flourishing vegetable garden and rosebushes, it's almost possible for me to pretend we're not in the middle of Ohio when I step into our fenced-in backyard.

Almost.

"Well, since it seems as if you two need a little alone time"—I hand my dad the remaining coffee, which I don't think I'll ever adjust to—"I'm going to run and get some caffeine I can actually stomach. Do either of you want a bagel or something?"

My mom opens her mouth, probably to defend her choice of hazelnut, but my dad beats her to it.

"Two everything bagels, toasted, with cream cheese." He recites the order they've shared for years. "Just make sure to drink your coffee there and take the long way home after."

He wiggles his eyebrows and my mom giggles.

My stomach turns, but I can't blame the coffee this time.

"Filthy." I grimace and shake my head in their general direction, trying to avoid direct eye contact. "And before church group, Mom? What would the Karens say?"

"Oh, honey." She swipes a stray hair out of her face, and with one glance at her expression, I regret ever getting out of bed this morning. "Trust me. The Karens and every other woman in this neighborhood would love to experience anything like I do with your father."

"La la la!" I stick my fingers in my ears and pretend to be disgusted by their overt and never-ending PDA. "I didn't hear any of that!"

I hurry to my bathroom with my parents' laughter chasing after me and make quick work of brushing my teeth and wrestling my curls into a careless bun. In LA, I never left the house without putting ample effort into my appearance. Living in the land of opportunity, I was convinced I was always one outing away from meeting someone who'd change my life.

I needed to be prepared.

So of course the one time I was caught slipping in public happened to be the one time everyone witnessed. Life is rude like that.

I contemplate putting on a bra before heading to the chain coffee shop down the road before deciding against it.

Standards? Don't even know her!

This is Ohio. The only two people I actually liked from high school left this town as soon as the opportunity presented itself. I don't have anyone to impress anymore.

Not even myself.

It's just too bad my mom won't agree.

And sure, nearing thirty should mean I don't have to sneak out of the house anymore. However, according to the laws of Kimberly Carter, I'll never be too old to be told to change my outfit and put on lipstick. Which is why, at twenty-nine and three-quarters years old, I tiptoe down the hallway and run out the front door. I leap into the front seat of my mom's old minivan and peel out of the driveway without a backward glance.

Burning rubber out of my quiet suburban hometown may not be my finest moment, but it's not my worst either. My life right now is a total dumpster fire and while there aren't many bright sides about my current situation, at least I know I can't sink any lower.

Watch out, Ohio.

It's only up from here.

2

I DRIVE PAST a moving van as the white picket fences of the Reserve at Horizon Creek fade in the rearview mirror of the minivan I still don't understand my parents buying. I'm an only child; we would've been fine with a sedan.

I adjust the radio, turning off Dad's sports talk and finding the local station I used to listen to in high school. I'm a sucker for pop music, and the Top 100 song that blasts through the speakers soothes my soul. I've gotten lost in the mindless lyrics, tapping my fingers on the steering wheel, when my phone rings.

Ruby's name lights up the screen and I contemplate letting her go to voice mail. Today has already been a day, and as much as I appreciate the motivational speeches she's been giving me since the video hit the internet, I'm not sure I can handle any of her lawyerly logic right now.

However, I do know I can't deal with her wrath at being ignored.

"What it do?" I answer, lacking the usual enthusiasm I greet her with.

There's a long pause before her brash voice bursts through my phone. "Ew. What's wrong with you?"

"Besides the obvious?" I switch the phone to the speaker, securing it between my chest and seat belt so I can keep both hands on the wheel. Safety first and all. "Not much."

"Kim's still sending you inspirational memes and Bible verses, isn't she?" She throws out her accurate guess on the first go.

Ruby has been my best friend since middle school. When her parents divorced when we were fifteen, she practically lived at our house. That's to say that she, too, has been on the receiving end of Kimberly Carter's never-ending good-vibes-only routine.

"Kim's gonna Kim," I confirm what she already knew. "But today escalated to an invitation to join her church group."

"Oh god. The Karens?" I can hear her shudder through the phone. "Were you able to get out of it? Do you need to brainstorm excuses with me?"

The worry in her voice is the first thing to cheer me up all day. Only Ruby understands the abject torture of being trapped in a room with my mom and the Karens.

"I'm good," I reassure her. "I'm going to grab a coffee now and then I'm heading to a garden center with Dad to pick up a tree for my mom and probably more vegetable plants for him."

Our backyard has enough tomatoes to supply Olive Garden. I doubt even he knows how many he has.

"I love that for—" she starts, but then her tone changes and the sound is muffled. "Luke, are you serious? I've asked you to knock a hundred times. This is a law firm, not your buddy's place. You can't just barge in here." I hear poor Luke's faint apology in the background before Ruby cuts him off. "Not now. I'm on a very important phone call."

Before Ruby's parents divorced, she was a pageant girl to the max. Her mom was a doctor and, breaking the societal norms, her dad was the one who drove her over state lines to compete in whatever pageant she was in that weekend. She had the bright white teeth, so much hairspray it was a miracle her hair didn't fall out, and an entire room dedicated to housing her evening gowns. I would tag along sometimes, and even though she denies it now, she really loved competing. She was the reigning champ for a reason.

However, when news of her dad's infidelity came to light, something inside her snapped. She quit doing pageants and made it her mission to make every man who crosses her path pay for her father's sins. Now she's a divorce attorney who only represents women (and men or nonbinary people) divorcing their husbands. Countless therapists have told her she has displaced anger, but she still hasn't made any moves to address it.

"Sheesh." I hit the directional and turn right into the shopping center where Cool Beans is located. "You're always so hard on the poor guy."

"Oh please. I've given him ample opportunities to change his behavior." I don't even need to see her to know she's rolling her eyes. "If he did his job like I've asked, there'd be no problems. I mean, really, how hard is it to knock before entering a room?"

If this was the first time I heard her talk to an assistant like this, maybe I'd buy what she's selling. But we talk every day and I know that's a complete load of crap.

"Ruby, come on." I pull into a parking spot and put my phone back to my ear. "You've never liked a single one of your assistants. Is it possible that you're the problem?"

"First of all, how dare you? Second, fuck off. If we're talking about being our own problems, then are we going to talk about how you still haven't opened your computer since you let Peter run you out of LA? Did you at least email that Reggie guy back?"

I knew I should've let her go to voice mail.

"Hold up. How did you being mean to Luke somehow turn into an attack on me?"

"Because if you think that was mean, then I've clearly been treating you with kid gloves for way too long."

Ruby's sent me emails about remote writing opportunities and has let me vent about my broken, humiliated heart without judgment. I knew it wouldn't last forever, but I definitely wasn't prepared for her to rip into me in a strip mall parking lot.

Up until right now, she's danced around the subject of my ruined career and scumbag ex. I shouldn't have told her about Reggie emailing me. He's the only person from the industry who's reached out to me, but the cynic in me can't tell if he's reaching out from genuine concern or morbid curiosity. It's not fair to put that on him; he was the first showrunner I ever worked with and has never been anything but wonderful to me, but I'm still too nervous to email him and find out. It would be a hit I'm not sure I could handle to find out he's not the person I thought he was.

"Please." I turn off the car and grab my purse. "You don't have kid gloves and you know it."

Ruby has a strong left hook and a stronger right, and each punch is laced with an uncomfortable amount of truth.

"I do too." The lawyer in her can't help but argue. "If I didn't, I would've already told you that it doesn't matter that Peter screwed you over; you can't just wallow in fucking *Ohio* and watch Little Mix reaction videos on YouTube all day. We got out of there as soon as we could for a reason. If you don't get your crap together, who are you going to end up like?"

I'm about to launch a full-out defense of my Little Mix obsession—they should have hit it huge in America and I will never forgive the music industry—but it all disappears the moment my feet hit the sidewalk and I set eyes on the last person I ever thought I'd see today.

Scratch that.

The last person I *wanted* to see. Ever.

"Oh my god, Nate."

"Exactly!" Ruby yells into the phone, obviously not grasping the severity of this situation. "You could end up like Nate the Snake! I wonder what he's doing. Didn't he say he wanted to be an accountant? What kind of teenager dreams of being an accountant?"

"No, Ruby!" I hiss into the phone, spinning out of view and plastering my back to a brick wall. "I mean Nate, here. At the coffee shop."

"Oh shit." She whispers into the phone as if he could hear her. "What's he doing there?"

Admittedly, I don't have any friends left here. But just because I don't have friends doesn't mean I don't have archenemies.

I do.

And his name is Nathanial Adams.

I don't need to explain why he's the worst. The name says it all. Everything about him is stuck-up and overly serious.

"It's a coffee shop; he's getting coffee." Because of course he is. God forbid one thing in my life not turn into a total, utter disaster.

"Well? How's he look?" she whisper-shouts into the phone.

"Seriously, Ruby? That's what you're asking me right now?" The heat from the brick exterior is seeping through the thin cotton shirt I threw on before I left the house and people passing by are starting to stare.

"What? He was an arrogant jerk, but he was also super cute." She may hate men, but she still very much appreciates them—to look at, not to talk to, she always tells me. "He's not on social media and curious minds want to know how he's held up over the years."

"You're ridiculous, and curious minds are going to have to stay curious," I inform her. "I'm waiting out here until he leaves."

"Let me get this straight. You're hiding outside of a coffee shop to avoid a guy you didn't like in high school and I'm the ridiculous one?"

Well, when she says it like that . . .

"Fine, I'll go in." I push off the wall and the slight breeze in the air instantly relieves my burning back. "But only because I'm starting to get a migraine from my lack of caffeine."

"Tell yourself whatever you need."

For a split second, I consider driving back home and settling for hazelnut sludge, but then I remember my parents' need for alone time. *Gross.*

I shake away thoughts of what might be happening on the

kitchen counters and draw in a deep breath before breaching the corner.

And because the universe absolutely fucking despises me, I run right into Nate.

"I'm so sor—" His deep voice ignites a fire in my veins. My body remembers him even though my mind has fought to forget everything about him. "Collins?"

"Nate." The soles of my feet itch with the need to run, but I stand firm. Unfortunately for me, my stubbornness outweighs my desire for self-preservation. "Hi."

"Oh my fucking god," Ruby screams into the phone and nearly shatters my eardrum.

"Gotta go, bye." I hang up before she can scream some more and pray to all that is holy that he didn't hear her. But if the condescending smirk on Nate's face is indicative of anything, he heard more than enough.

Have I mentioned how much I hate Ohio?

"Ruby?" He nods his chin in the direction of my phone. "Sounds like not much has changed."

I tuck my phone into my purse even though I want to throw it at him.

You'd think after ten years apart from someone, they'd lose the ability to bring you to violence with a simple nod. But not Nathanial Adams. No, everything about his stupid, symmetrical face is utterly punchable.

I'm not sure if it's because he's wearing a cable-knit sweater in June or because he's aiming the same smug smile he tortured me with in high school at me, but all of a sudden my mind is empty save for every single wrong he's ever done me. And why, if I hate Peter with the fire of the sun, I hate Nate with the power of two.

I guess that's what happens when the guy you thought was your best friend goes away one summer and completely ghosts you when he gets back.

Time, in fact, does not heal all wounds.

"A lot has changed, actually." I try to present an air of confidence I most definitely do not feel. "But she's still Ruby."

"I bet." He steps to the side as an older man sidles by. "I can't imagine either one of you ever changing too much."

Poison laces the innocuous words. Nate thinks he's smarter than everyone around him and has somehow tricked the masses into going along with it. He's the type of person who can insult people with such ease, they end up thanking him. Whereas I struggled to make friends growing up, people naturally gravitated toward Nate.

The urge to tell him to fuck off is on the tip of my tongue, but my mom has eyes and ears everywhere. The last thing I need is one of the Karens bringing hot gossip about me causing a scene outside Cool Beans to Bible study.

"Yeah, unfortunately, we can't all experience such radical growth." I let my eyes travel the length of his body—which looks better than it has the right to, encapsulated in khakis and a pullover—before meeting his stare. "Accountant chic, living in the burbs? Who would've thought?"

Bullseye.

His hazel eyes narrow and the tips of his ears flame red. It's so much more fun to go head-to-head with a person when you're aware of their tells.

"And you? Are you finally visiting your parents? I know you couldn't be bothered to come to Mr. Carter's retirement party." He leans in, his voice dropping despite having nobody near us. "Or did you have to move back home because you couldn't hack it in LA?"

The wound is still too fresh. I flinch as his words slice straight through the oozing hole I've been trying to fill with tequila shooters and Netflix movies.

He knows he hit his mark, and much like my reaction, his sadistic grin widens.

The really messed-up part is that I'm not even mad about his jab; I'm angry I let him see that his words affected me. Pissed I reacted.

I've gotten soft.

I blame Mom's love of inspirational quotes.

But this is a wake-up call. If I'm going to be living in my own literal hell, I have to be prepared for the devil to strike at any moment. And by *the devil*, I mean Nate.

Obviously.

"Well." I push past him and pull open the glass door to Cool Beans. "As much as I'm enjoying standing around and pretending like it's good to see you, I'd rather be doing literally anything else."

"Real nice, Collins." He reaches into his pocket and pulls out a key fob. "Classy as ever."

He clicks a button on the fob and the lights on a midsized sedan blink.

"Really? A Buick?" I yell with one foot in the coffee shop. "Are you eighty?"

His steps don't even falter as he crosses the pothole-riddled parking lot and tosses his parting shot over his shoulder. "At least I have a car."

Quick and effective.

Just like he was when he changed his number and pretended like he didn't know me when I saw him at the movies with his new cool friends.

I forget all about my mom's church friends. I lift my middle finger straight into the air and hold it steady for him to see as he drives away.

I knew coming back home wasn't going to be fun, but not even being the internet's favorite tragedy could have prepared me for this. Nathanial Adams is the one person I didn't account for, and I'm now realizing what a grave mistake that was.

Photo by Kristie Chadwick

ALEXA MARTIN is a writer and stay-at-home mom. A Nashville transplant, she's intent on instilling a deep love and respect for the great Dolly Parton in her four children and husband. The Playbook series was inspired by the eight years she spent as an NFL wife and her love of all things pop culture, sparkles, leggings, and wine. When she's not repeating herself to her kids, you can find her catching up on whatever Real Housewives franchise is currently airing or filling up her Etsy cart with items she doesn't need.

VISIT ALEXA MARTIN ONLINE

AlexaMartin.com

🅕 AlexaMartinBooks

🅞 AlexaMBooks

Ready to find
your next great read?

Let us help.

Visit prh.com/nextread

Penguin
Random
House